THE
HUMAN
EXPERIENCE

THE
HUMAN
EXPERIENCE

.ↄ.

CONTEMPORARY
AMERICAN AND SOVIET FICTION
AND POETRY

Edited by the
Soviet/American Joint Editorial Board
of the Quaker US/USSR Committee

with forewords by
William Styron and Daniil Granin

JOSHUA ODELL EDITIONS

CAPRA PRESS ✂ SANTA BARBARA

Copyright © 1989 by the Quaker US/USSR Committee

Foreword © 1989 by William Styron
Foreword © 1989 Daniil Granin

All right reserved under International and Pan-American Copyright Conventions.

Published by arrangement with Alfred A. Knopf, Inc.

Joshua Odell Editions/Capra Press
Box 2158, Santa Barbara, CA 93120

Owing to limitations of space, all acknowledgments of permission to reprint previously
published material will be found at the end of the book, following "Biographies."

ISBN 1-877741-05-1

1. American literature–20th century.   2. Russian literature–20th
century–Translations into English.   I. Quaker US/USSR Committee.
Soviet/American Joint Editorial Board.

PS536.2.H86 1991
810.8'0054–dc20

91-31763
CIP

Printed in the United States of America
First Paperback Edition

CONTENTS

The names of Soviet writers are in italics.
*indicates poetry.

Contents

ACKNOWLEDGMENTS

The Quaker US/USSR Committee wishes to thank the following persons and organizations for their financial and spiritual support. We apologize for any omissions or errors:

Patrons: Bequests Committee of Philadelphia Yearly Meeting; Central Philadelphia Monthly Meeting; The Anna H. and Elizabeth M. Chace Fund Committee; Friends Institute of Philadelphia Yearly Meeting; The Allen Hilles Fund; Homewood Friends Meeting (MD); George Hughes; Viva and Ralph Lugbill; The John Pemberton Fund, Philadelphia Yearly Meeting; In gratitude for the life of Ross Quaintaince (R.E.Q.); Henry W. Ridgway, Sr.; The Soros Foundation—Soviet Union; Theodore H. and Angela Von Laue.

Sponsors and Donors: John Bernheim; Charles H. Bonner / Veterans for Peace (PA); Margaret Strawbridge Clews; Ann Duncan-Treviranus; John and Chara Haas; Gene Knudsen-Hoffman; Miles White Beneficial Society; Lucile B. Patrick; John N. Phillips; Plumsock Farm Trust (Willistown Friends Meeting, PA); Richmond Friends Meeting (VA); Winston Riley III; Davis Anthony Scott; Janet Shepherd; The Thomas H. and Mary Williams Shoemaker Fund; Magda E. and Robert J. Vitale.

Supporters: Kay Anderson; Robert E. Asher; Marion and Frederic L. Ballard, Jr.; Augusta Beadenkopf; Mark Bergner; J. Thomas Bertrand; Bethesda Friends Meeting (MD); Bluebird Appliances; Edwin S. Bond; Jane Cuyler Borgerhoff; Carol Bosworth; John and Helen Bross; Edwin and Isobel Cerney; Charlotte Friends Meeting (NC); Jessie Cocks; Community Friends Meeting (OH); Leni and Keith Covington; David R. Cundiff, M.D.; Lloyd and Mary Danzeisen; Davis Friends Meeting (CA); Steven L. Fisher; Robert C. Folwell III; Friends from Goose Creek Meeting; Philip & Alice Gilbert; Clifford and Mildred Gillam; Sidney Greenberger; Gerry N. Groupe; Wilma Gurney; Walter W. Haines; Nancy Arnot Harjan; George S. and Janet C. Harker; Ferne E. Hayes; Karen and Dieter Hessel; John J. Howell; Mary Smucker Hulburt; In memory of Dale W. Johnston; Mabel S. Kantor; Peter Kaspar; Lancaster Friends Meeting (PA); Langley Hill Friends Meeting (VA); Los Angeles Friends Meeting (CA);

Donna Dillon Manning; Orlando and Valerie Martino; Robert and Jonda McFarlane; Middletown Friends Meeting (PA); Cully and Carolyn Miller; John and Jeanne Newman; Elizabeth H. Noble; Norristown Friends Meeting (PA; Oakland Avenue Soviet-American Friendship Society (Columbus, OH); Rita and Richard Post; Princeton Monthly Meeting (NJ); Lilith Quinlan; Reno Friends Meeting (NV); Michael and Genevieve Ritzman; Ross Roby; Janice Stultz Roddenbery; Guinevere Feckler Scott; Laurel Scull; Robert K. Shaffer; Edward F. Snyder; Elfriede M. Sollomann; St. Petersburg Friends Meeting (FL); Gail Stallings; David and Jean Stoffregen; Ann Stokes; Erica and Virgil Swadley; Bajendra Tandon; Hubert and Dorothy Taylor; David and Barbara Tecosky; Edward and Mildred O. Teitelman; Harry Tischbein; Paul and Marie Turner; Sue and Tom Vargo; Galja B. Votaw; Robert and Rosalind Williams.

Contributors: Hermione Baker; Peter Barry; Mary Lou and James Beatman; Elizabeth F. Boardman; Dona M. Boyce-Manoukian; William S. Bradfield, Jr.; Gary Briggs; Edward S. Brinton; Jean Martindale Brown; Buckingham Friends School (PA); Camden Friends Meeting (DE); Barbara Longbotham Caplow; Stephen G. Cary; Charlottesville Friends Meeting (VA); Hugh Ashley Cole; Rose Cologne; F. H. Conroy Family; Robert and Sally Cory; Eliza Critchlow; J. Dudley Dawson; Orlin and Nancy Donaldson; Marilyn A. Dyer; Ray C. Ellis; Emma P. Engle; Barbara H. Finck; Frank and Sandy Fisher; Irene Garrow, M.D.; Dorothy Glanzer; Gray Panthers Peace Task Force of Greater Columbus (OH); Greg Haas; Harrisonburg Friends Meeting (VA); Haverford Friends Meeting (PA); J. Bernard and Sylvia Haviland; Priscilla and Michael Heim; Lea Heine; Mary Lane Hiatt; Barbara Marx Hubbard; Ellen and Gerhard Krebs; Evelyn Kressler; Margaret S. and Paul A. Lacey; Roselynd Golden Largman; Karen Lawrance; Lexington Friends Meeting (VA); Elizabeth Mansfield; Esther L. Martin; John McCarthy and Kathryn Barnhart; Stanley T. McGrail; Meriden Peace Trust; Mary H. Mikesell; Montclair Friends Meeting (NJ); Alex Morisey; Newtown Friends Meeting (PA); Clarence and Helen Parker; Philadelphia Yearly Meeting (PA); Peter Rabenold; Rancocas Friends Meeting (NJ); Matthew Roazen; Cornelia and George Ryan; John V. Saly; Sevenoaks Pathwork Center; Jane R. Smiley; Hannah Stapler; Kingdon W. Swayne; Elizabeth Leeds Tait; Susan Thesenga; J. Ann Tickner; Gretchen Tuthill; Winifred Walker-Jones; Wallis Printer Center, Philadelphia; Prudence Wayland-Smith;

George and Eleanor Webb; Westfield Friends Meeting (NJ); William and Antoinette Whaley; W. Janney Wilson; Winchester Centre Friends Meeting (VA); David Lorenz Winston; Sarah Winston; Woodstown Friends Meeting (NJ); Jay and Carolyn Worrall. *Special Thanks:* Barbara Benton; Oleg P. Benyukh; C. Baird Brown; Margaret Calabrese; Elizabeth Cattell; France Conroy; Dan Davidson; Christopher Davis, *A Friendly Letter*; *Friends Journal*; Friends Meeting of Washington Peace Committee; Agnes Gruliow; Leo Gruliow; Johanna Hardin; Michael Hays; Judith Hernstadt; George H. Honig; Holland Hunter; Vladimir Karpov; Roy Kim; Maya Klimova; Stanley Kunitz; Kent R. Larrabee; Masha Lechic; Anthony Manousos; Audrey Melkin; Joseph Meredith; Helen Oseneva; Alexei V. Pushkov; F. D. Reeve; Janet Riley; Matthew Roazen; Kathleen Ross; Irene Salnikova; Kathy Schinhofen; Oleg Severgin; Jack Shepherd; Lamont Steptoe; Teaching in a Nuclear Age, Margaret Lippincott; Sharlie Ushioda; David Lorenz Winston; Carolyn Worrall; Vladimir Zaretsky; Eugene Zykov.

The Quaker US/USSR Committee
France Conroy*
Hillary Conroy*
Ann Duncan-Treviranus*
Sylvia Greene
George Hughes*
Dale Keairns (Clerk)
Von Keairns
Sylvia Mangalam
Anthony Manousos (Editorial Director)*
Zandra Moberg*
Janet Riley
Winston Riley III
Janet Shepherd (Former Clerk)*
John Shuford
Nadya Spassenko
Gail Stallings*
Suellen Wilson*
Jay Worrall, Jr. (Former Clerk)*
Jay Worrall III

*indicates former Committee Member

*The Committee's offices are located at
1515 Cherry Street, Philadelphia, PA 19102.*

INTRODUCTION

In the midst of a bitterly cold Russian winter, with temperatures hovering around twenty below zero, two Quakers from Philadelphia arrived in Moscow with a dream. They wanted to produce an anthology of Soviet and American fiction and poetry that would be edited jointly and published in both countries. They hoped that such a collaborative effort would improve understanding and build trust between Americans and Soviets. Nothing quite like this had ever been done before, and many knowledgeable people were skeptical.

Somehow (whether by chance, or the agency of some higher power), this pair of Quakers were led to the office of a Soviet publisher with a similar dream. He responded warmly to the idea of a "literary bridge" between Americans and Soviets, and offered his support. When a leading Soviet translator of American fiction heard about the project, she eagerly joined in.

An editorial board comprising both Soviets and Americans was formed to select manuscripts, and the long, sometimes frustrating, often exhilarating process of collaboration was begun. Meetings were held in the United States and the Soviet Union; questions of literary taste and judgment, as well as the practicalities of publication, were discussed with frankness, openness and good humor. The editorial board made its decisions by consensus. Those involved in this fascinating and revealing process came to know and appreciate each other better as human beings.

The result was this book. *The Human Experience* represents what we feel is some of the best of current Soviet and American writing, but it also represents something more: the spirit that unites us in spite of cultural and political differences. Although the settings and characters of these stories and poems reflect specific cultural contexts and situations, their themes—growing up, working, relationships, old age, mortality—are universal. For the first time, American and Soviet readers will have a chance to compare and contrast some of their best writers within the covers of a single volume.

This project was inspired by a vision of "spiritual linkage" between Americans and Soviets. By "spiritual linkage" we mean the inner life and the connectedness we all share. In 1983, the Quaker US/USSR Committee was formed to explore this vision and discover ways in which Americans and Soviets could come together and learn to appreciate each other at a deeper human level. After a year of meetings and discussions the idea for this cooperative book emerged.

The writings in this book are about everyday life, and the infinite worth of each human being which transcends national, political, and social differences. In the seventeenth century, the Quaker William Penn founded Pennsylvania as a "holy experiment" where people of different nations and religions could live together in mutual respect and harmony. "Let us try then what love will do," Penn wrote, "for if people did once see we love, then we should soon find they would not harm us." Leo Tolstoy, a writer whose impact on world literature has been enormous and whose religious vision has much in common with Quakerism, expressed the spirit of our project over a century ago: "I know that my unity with all people cannot be destroyed by national boundaries and government orders" (*My Religion*, 1884). Perhaps no more compelling expression of this spiritual unity can be found than in the poems by Wendell Berry and Yevgeny Yevtushenko that open this book.

One last word about *The Human Experience*: It is not intended —nor could a work of such relatively limited size aspire in any case—to be a comprehensive anthology. It should be read instead as a series of "literary snapshots" reflecting the tastes of a highly diverse editorial group. We hope that this collection will inspire others to similar efforts. It is our conviction that such joint literary projects will enable American and Soviet readers to know each other better and experience the "deep and touching solidarity" that our writers have expressed so movingly.

The Joint Editorial Board

FOREWORD BY
WILLIAM STYRON

I have recently indulged myself in a genial fantasy. In order to be appreciated, the fantasy must be seen as the reflections of a Japanese historian, elderly perhaps and a bit jaded, who is writing in the middle of the next century and who is concerning himself with a period in the history of two once-great superpowers—the United States and the Soviet Union. In the year 2050 Japan, allied with China and Korea, shares global ascendancy with Brazil, and these four nations produce virtually all the world's manufactured goods. It is a time of relative peace marred only by the incendiary tribal wars that dot the planet and that are accepted at last as part of the inevitable status quo. The United States and the Soviet Union, disarmed of their nuclear potential like all the countries of the world, have descended into the good-natured sloth of second-rate agrarian powers—like Canada or Spain today—and have become each other's primary trading partner, engaged in such felicitous and humdrum commerce as the exchange of Texas grapefruit for Siberian furs. Culturally and economically, the two nations are as cheerfully interdependent as the present European Common Market: visas are unknown, there is much travel back and forth, cooperation and a gentle concord mark the relations between Moscow and Washington. Rueful and puzzled, the Japanese historian reminds his readers of how appallingly different conditions were during the first three-quarters of a century of the two nations' association with each other. One of the grimmest periods in history, it was an epoch containing such mysterious contradictions as to defy analysis.

What strikes the historian most forcibly is how similarly the two countries behaved as powers in the world arena and how, in ideals and ambitions, they so closely resembled each other—although any resemblance at all was something that both would strenuously (at times even hysterically) deny. For example, there was the matter of national identity. Each country believed that its political system was not only superior but the absolute salvation of humanity. So zealously did both nations hold to this belief that most of the vast energies expended by the communications apparatus in each land was dedicated to the horrors and deficiencies of the other system. Such blind bullheadedness caused universal fear and invincible mistrust; the rest of the world looked on with trepidation as each superpower, gaining mastery of propaganda, vied for human hearts and minds, accusing the other of ruthless exploitation, of injustices to its citizens, of monstrous inequities in such domains as civil liberties, distribution of wealth and the administration of justice.

The Japanese historian finds that, given the melancholy data, he cannot in good conscience absolve either country of these grave charges; some of his harshest criticism of both America and the Soviet Union is contained in the chapter entitled "Self-righteousness." He also reflects on the way this mutual enmity led to the buildup of war machines unprecedented not only in their size and scope but in their cost; money which might have been spent to promote the welfare of the people was squandered in each country on perennially outmoded armaments. This produced devastating debt and also murderous and futile subnuclear wars. In order to further their ideologies, both nations supplied client states and subversive forces throughout the world with weapons to help fight civil conflicts, and upon at least two major occasions each actively participated in civil wars on alien territory, losing tens of thousands of young men in prolonged bloodbaths that were all the more tragic for producing no victory or clearcut resolution.

"The greatest common sin of the U.S. and the USSR," writes the Japanese historian, "lay in not leaving other nations and other people alone, to work out their destinies on their own terms. This was the curse of being a superpower in the twentieth century. Their only even remotely friendly rivalry was in the exploration of space; all else was bitter, savage. In both countries, the lust for aggression and the impulse toward war were largely the creation of the power structure—the politicians who found an eager response only in the military and the mob of fanatics that always thrills to the promise of Armageddon. The overwhelming majority of Soviet and American people had an abhorrence of war. Their main concerns were the joys and difficulties of being human in great societies which demonstrated many virtues and strengths, but which still had a long way to go in ensuring happiness for all of their citizens. The people of the United States and the Soviet Union possessed many fascinating cultural differences, but what strikes one is not their differences but their common humanity—their quirks and amusements, their delights and their shadowy discontents, the longings and personal upheavals and moments of discovery that made a Californian and a citizen of Kiev brother and sister in spirit. Certainly, from the literature of the period, there is no serious evidence to suggest that either people did not cherish peace above all the attributes of life."

The stories and poems in the present volume tend to validate the opinion of my imaginary historian. If these selections are fairly representative of recent writing in the United States and the Soviet Union—and I think they are—at least one fact is made consistently clear: people do not concern themselves much about war. It may be that the idea of war is simply intolerable. War may exist in the past tense, as an echo or as a bad memory, but war as a possibility—the threat of nuclear conflict—does not really intrude much in people's lives. (Yury Kuznetsov's "An Atomic Fairy Tale" and C. K. Williams's stark poem "The Dream" would be among the few exceptions.) The rituals of Soviet and American people seem chiefly to involve the frustrating business of muddling through—of making accommodations, of seeking small pleasures amid the heaviness of the daily grind, of somehow getting a little bit ahead; of suffering humiliations, experiencing minuscule glints of delight; of being terrified (or bemused or enraged) by the enigma of existence; of engaging in that old, old quest for somebody to love. Because the past few decades have seen far more American literature translated into Russian than the other way around, it is quite likely that Soviet readers, while appreciating the American offerings, will not gain the sense of revelation, of newness, that an American reader will have upon encountering some of the Soviet writers. As an example I would cite Arnold Kashtanov's "Hypnosis," a grim tale which not only told me much about the treatment of alcoholism in the Soviet Union, but also contributed insights about the connivance, nepotism, and secret dealing that seem to be so much a part of Soviet institutional life. It is an honest, harrowing story with disturbing resonances.

But I don't mean to imply that the Soviet selections can—or should—be read for their novelty or with the idea in mind that we are at last going to be given an exposé of the seamier side of life in Moscow. There is plenty that is seamy in these stories, Soviet and American, but the poetry and prose from both countries are marked by a variety and an eclectic spirit that is appropriate to a collection entitled *The Human Experience*. In Central Asia a man attending a conference becomes gradually bewitched by a chatterbox female colleague and experiences a sharp pang of loss when she suddenly departs. A man in New England, sifting through the detritus of an attic, discovers in the old games he discards a poignant metaphor for his broken marriage. In different ways, Valentin Rasputin's "French Lessons" and Joyce Carol Oates' "Capital Punishment" reveal a piercing alienation. In America and the Soviet Union there are jagged, dramatic confrontations. A haunting counterpoint unites such stories as Anatoly Kim's "Road Stop in August"—a scenically evocative, troubling tale about a morally bedeviled soldier-prisoner and his superior officer—and John Sayles' "The Halfway Diner," which deals in another way with prisoners and their impact on the lives of others. Crime and its shattering conflicts are part of the fabric of life in both countries, as this volume reveals; but lest the reader be concerned that the vision of all our writers is unremittingly bleak, it should be pointed out that there are other perspectives, other moods: the flamboyant assertiveness of Yevtushenko in his "Fuku" verse, for example, or the zany rapture of Donald Barthelme's "The King of Jazz." This book does not pretend to give, even remotely, a "cross-section" of the present-day cultures of the United States and the Soviet Union; but within its relatively modest scope it presents a fair and colorful sampling of the way life here and there is lived, or endured, or nervously confronted, or enjoyed.

Alexis de Tocqueville, writing of America as the last century neared its midpoint, made a remarkable prediction: he foresaw a time when the chief adversary of the United States would be Russia. This was amazing prescience at a time when America was an extremely minor player on the world stage and Russia had withdrawn into its remote, wintry isolation. He was of course proved right, but his prophecy went only so far, foretelling the bitter discord of the early and mid-periods but hesitating to try to fathom what might happen as history unrolled into what we now perceive to be, so close at hand, the twenty-first century. Surely it is not inconceivable—especially in the light of recent events—that this further stage might be marked by amity, understanding, and peace. Writers and poets are almost never capable of changing political attitudes or diplomacy directly, or of affecting the ponderous and usually inexplicable forces that shape the destinies of nations. They do, however, possess the valuable ability to influence the minds of individuals, to make them see and feel in a different way: thus, while they may have little sway over politicians (who rarely are readers anyway), their voices are heard across boundaries by the people through whose collective consciousness societies remain civilized. There is pathos in the fact that for seventy years these voices have been making themselves heard, stirring hearts, touching souls, while the politics of the two great nations noisily clash and collide, ogrishly confronting each other with implacable ill will. The voices are from the present, but also speak to us from our great literary pasts: Tolstoy, Hawthorne, Dostoevsky, Mark Twain, Turgenev, Dreiser, Gogol, Hemingway, Akhmatova, Frost, Mandelstam.

When these writers wrote of politics (and some did), they rarely wrote their best. They wrote their best about love and betrayal, hilarity and desperation, the arrival of seasons and homely comforts; of the cruelty of war, of madness and drunkenness and friendship, of love's preposterous agues and chills. The watershed moment in the education of many a young American may have come when he was seized by a wild-eyed classmate who said, "You must read *Crime and Punishment*"—and he complied, with resulting gratitude. And of course, the gift is reciprocal: the impact of *Huckleberry Finn* on generations of Russian young people is legendary. These writers and poets have preserved the human dialogue during decades when the vernacular of the bureaucrat and the adman has corrupted common speech and the synthetic grammar of technocracy has supplanted the warm rhythms of everyday language. They have created, too, vivid and lasting identities. Commissars vanish, cabinet members are swallowed up in oblivion. Anna Karenina and Tom Sawyer, Gatsby and Raskolnikov—they endure.

It is exciting that the writers of a new generation are brought together in this volume, for the first time coexisting harmoniously, as it were, under the same roof. These are the heirs of Mark Twain and Akhmatova. After a long and frigid apartness, there could be nothing more propitious than this gathering of literary talents. Totally aside from the insight and pleasure they might provide, their communion here may be symbolic of an even greater and more lasting solidarity, as America and the Soviet Union choose friendship over the folly of perpetual strife. Since we have come to this admirable pass, the alternative—the reversion to old ways—does not bear thinking about.

William Styron

FOREWORD BY
DANIIL GRANIN

This is apparently the first joint anthology of works by Soviet and American writers. In 1988 a collection of articles by American and Soviet scholars titled *Breakthrough* came out, which discussed the development of the new thinking. The anthology *The Human Experience* discusses nothing. It brings together short stories and poems from the two literatures. The reason people read Mark Twain, Faulkner, or Oates is not to learn about Americans. They read them because they are good writers. The same can be said of Chekhov or Platonov. But in the process of reading them, you also find out something about people. How people live over there in the various states. They appear neither for the sake of making an impression nor for the sake of advertising American life. And our Soviet people, in our stories, talk, laugh, and berate one another without the slightest idea that foreigners, somewhere over the sea, are listening to them.

. Trust requires openness. The problem of trust has turned out to be the key problem today. Everyone is afraid to be the first to put down his gun. All you can see through the gunsight is an enemy, an adversary. It's hard to make out a human being through it. A play, a book, or a film can serve here. In them one can see the common human element in two different worlds. People on both shores, separated by an ocean, are alike in the ways they love, suffer from loneliness, act foolishly, fear death, and are vulgar, brave, or evil. Feeling the oneness of the earth and recognizing your own thoughts and feelings in other people is the best pathway to trust.

There is something significant about the way universal troubles and dangers have been burgeoning. Suddenly coastal waters turn up polluted in both the Soviet Union and the United States; lakes and rivers are poisoned; the air is poisoned; chemicals hold oppressive sway; animals die. Neither country knows what to do with radioactive waste, where to bury it, how to rid itself of those infernal rays, how to protect itself against acid rain, or against AIDS and the new viruses that lie in wait for us.

In the summer of 1988 it turned out that one couldn't swim

in the Baltic, or in the Black Sea, or at Sochi, or near Leningrad, or at Odessa, or in the Sea of Azov.

We must build treatment facilities, install scrubbers and filters, save the air, find cures for cancer, cures for AIDS. . . . No nation can cope with all this on its own.

Entry into the nuclear age forces states to change their attitudes; instead of just their own security, they must be concerned with the general security. Peoples and nations also have to moderate their customary self-importance. It is increasingly hard to justify a sense of superiority over one's neighbors, over other peoples, when you know a lot about one another. Sooner or later we all have to admit that our own social thought is not the only correct thought, that our own system is not better than others, that people may live in different ways and have different ideas about justice and happiness. It turns out that people may differ, ideals may differ, and other societies have the right to be different. Intolerance becomes dangerous in today's unstable world. In order to survive, we must recognize the basic law of a new way of life: Others may be different.

Literature asserts this right every day. It makes the world transparent; it sees the world whole but preserves the diversity of its nuances. The variety of the world and the diversity of the political map are not just sources of beauty, they also become sources of world stability.

The history of literature over thousands of years is the history of its struggle for independence. The literature that has triumphed is the literature that has known how to defend itself. But independence does not mean detachment.

The best books appear not at the authorities' behest but despite the authorities. That is what happened, for example, in Soviet literature with novels about the fate of the countryside and the life of the peasants. They were written out of pain and anger.

Perestroika has put a great deal in its proper place and restored to things their true value. For a long time writers were required to view the Great Patriotic War solely as the story of the Victory. The victory cult prevented many of us from telling about the agonies of war and the steadfastness and courage of the soldiers—and, for that matter, of everyone else. Now, as never before, among books about the war—and the war occupies a large place in our literature—the ones that live are those that cry out with the suffering of human beings, the great sacrifices made by the people, and the eternal questions of glory and infamy, love and fidelity, and the value of life and death.

I knew a woman who in the terrible months of the siege of Leningrad had to decide which of her two children would remain alive; she was unable to feed them both. She had to make that unthinkable choice. What did the problem of choice consist of in this case? I returned again and again to the story of that woman, to what happened to her afterwards, and what happened to the child she saved, until I understood one simple thing (but it's only now that it has become simple for me): Despite everything, she preserved her capacity to love; that is, she did not lose her humanity. She accepted full blame for the loss and death of the second child. In conditions beyond endurance, I was struck by how people remained human beings to the end, defending the humanity in themselves. That inmost urge, almost an instinct, unconscious, like a call from someone—where does it come from? Either the soul hears it, or it does not, and here you touch on something incomprehensible but infinitely important, if one thinks about the fate of humanity.

And think about it we must.

In our country *perestroika*, democracy and *glasnost* are rapidly freeing minds from fear, mental stupor, and other people's imposed truths. Crises in many spheres of life have been revealed to our society in all their severity. It is no wonder that readers' attention has been captured by essays, journalism, history, and economics. People want to understand what happened to them, what has to be changed, and how to do it. Probably the best way to change the world is to understand it. When people are unable to understand, they change their world through violence; that's how people behave who do not believe in the power of reason.

Things are not easy for literature today. To participate, but how? This anthology is an act of participation. An attempt. A first, still awkward contact, an appearance together before the reader, accompanied, perhaps, by a tinge of jealousy and cautious hesitation. How will the American reader and our Soviet reader perceive this book? Merely as a chance encounter? Or as a necessity, an unexpected conjunction to form an almost integral book?

Daniil Granin

TRANSLATED BY GORDON LIVERMORE

THE
HUMAN
EXPERIENCE

TO A SIBERIAN WOODSMAN

(after looking at some pictures in a magazine)

·❧·

Wendell Berry

1

You lean at ease in your warm house at night after supper,
listening to your daughter play the accordion. You smile
with the pleasure of a man confident in his hands, resting
after a day of long labor in the forest, the cry of the saw
in your head, and the vision of coming home to rest.
Your daughter's face is clear in the joy of hearing
her own music. Her fingers live on the keys
like people familiar with the land they were born in.

You sit at the dinner table late into the night with your son,
tying the bright flies that will lead you along the forest streams.
Over you, as your hands work, is the dream of the still pools.
　　Over you is the dream
of your silence while the east brightens, birds waking close by
　　you in the trees.

2

I have thought of you stepping out of your doorway at dawn,
　　your son in your tracks.
You go in under the overarching green branches of the forest
whose ways, strange to me, are well known to you as the sound
　　of your own voice
or the silence that lies around you now that you have ceased to
　　speak,
and soon the voice of the stream rises ahead of you, and you
　　take the path beside it.
I have thought of the sun breaking pale through the mists over
　　you
as you come to the pool where you will fish, and of the mist
　　drifting
over the water, and of the cast fly resting light on the face of the
　　pool.

3

And I am here in Kentucky in the place I have made myself
in the world. I sit on my porch above the river that flows muddy
and slow along the feet of the trees. I hear the voices of the wren
and the yellow-throated warbler whose songs pass near the
    windows
and over the roof. In my house my daughter learns the
    womanhood
of her mother. My son is at play, pretending to be
the man he believes I am. I am the outbreathing of this ground.
My words are its words as the wren's song is its song.

4

Who has invented our enmity? Who has prescribed us
hatred of each other? Who has armed us against each other
with the death of the world? Who has appointed me such anger
that I should desire the burning of your house or the
    destruction of your children?
Who has appointed such anger to you? Who has set loose the
    thought
that we should oppose each other with the ruin of forests and
    rivers, and the silence of birds?
Who has said to us that the voices of my land shall be strange
to you, and the voices of your land strange to me?

Who has imagined that I would destroy myself in order to
    destroy you,
or that I could improve myself by destroying you? Who has
    imagined
that your death could be negligible to me now that I have seen
    these pictures of your face?
Who has imagined that I would not speak familiarly with you,
or laugh with you, or visit in your house and go to work with
    you in the forest?
And now one of the ideas of my place will be that you would
    gladly talk and visit and work with me.

5

I sit in the shade of the trees of the land I was born in.
As they are native I am native, and I hold to this place as
    carefully as they hold to it.

I do not see the national flag flying from the staff of the
    sycamore,
or any decree of the government written on the leaves of the
    walnut,
nor has the elm bowed before monuments or sworn the oath of
    allegiance.
They have not declared to whom they stand in welcome.

6

In the thought of you I imagine myself free of the weapons and
    the official hates that I have borne on my back like a
    hump,
and in the thought of myself I imagine you free of weapons and
    official hates,
so that if we should meet we would not go by each other
    looking at the ground like slaves sullen under their
    burdens,
but would stand clear in the gaze of each other.

7

There is no government so worthy as your son who fishes with
    you in silence beside the forest pool.
There is no national glory so comely as your daughter whose
    hands have learned a music and go their own way on the
    keys.
There is no national glory so comely as my daughter who
    dances and sings and is the brightness of my house.
There is no government so worthy as my son who laughs, as he
    comes up the path from the river in the evening, for joy.

ON BORDERS

A Verse from "Fuku"

· ✌ ·

Yevgeny Yevtushenko

In every border post
                    there's something insecure.
Each one of them
                    is longing for leaves and for flowers.
They say
            the greatest punishment for a tree
is to become a border post.
The birds that pause to rest
                                on border posts
can't figure out
                    what kind of tree they've landed on.
I suppose
            that at first, it was people who invented borders,
and then borders
                    started to invent people.
It was borders who invented police,
                                    armies, and border guards.
It was borders who invented
customs-men, passports, and other shit.
Thank God,
            we have invisible threads and threadlets,
born of the threads of blood
                                from the nails in the palms of Christ.
These threads struggle through,
                                    tearing apart the barbed wire
leading love to join love
                            and anguish to unite with anguish.
And a tear,
            which evaporated somewhere in Paraguay,
will fall as a snowflake
                            onto the frozen cheek of an Eskimo.
And a hulking New York skyscraper
                                    with bruises of neon,

mourning the forgotten smell of plowlands,
dreams only of embracing a lonely Kremlin tower,
but sadly that is not allowed.
The Iron Curtain,
                    unhappily squeaking her rusty brains,
probably thinks:
            "Oh, if I were not a border,
if jolly hands would pull me apart
and build from my bloody remains
                    carousels, kindergartens, and schools."
In my darkest dreams I see
                    my prehistoric ancestor:
he collected skulls like trophies
                    in the somber vaults of his cave,
and with the bloodied point of a stone spearhead
he marked out the first-ever border
                    on the face of the earth.
That was a hill of skulls.
                    Now it is grown into an Everest.
The earth was transformed
                    and became a giant burial place.
While borders still stand
                    we are all in prehistory.
Real history will start
                    when all borders are gone.
The earth is still scarred,
                    mutilated with the scars of wars.
Now killing has become an art,
                    when once it was merely a trade:
From all those thousands of borders
                    we have lost only the human one—
the border between good and evil.
But while we still have invisible threads
joining each self
                    with millions of selves,
there are no real superpower states.
Any fragile soul on this earth
                    is the real superpower.
My government
            is the whole family of man, all at once.
Every beggar is my marshal,
                    giving me orders.

THE HUMAN EXPERIENCE

I am a racist,
               I recognize only one race—
the race of all races.
How foreign is the word *foreigner*!
I have four and a half billion leaders.
And I dance my Russian,
               my death-defying dance
on the invisible threads
               that connect the hearts of people.

TRANSLATED BY ANTONINA W. BOUIS AND
ALBERT C. TODD

FRENCH LESSONS

.♉.

Valentin Rasputin

To Anastasia Prokopevna Kopylova

*It is a strange thing: why is it
that, just as with our parents,
we always feel guilty towards our
teachers? And not at all because
of things in school, no, because of
what becomes of us afterwards.*

In 'forty-eight I entered the fifth form—or to be more exact, I traveled to it, because our village had only an elementary school; so to continue after the fourth I had to go fifty kilometers, to the small town which was the district center. My mother went there a week beforehand, arranged lodgings for me with someone she knew, and on the last day of August, Uncle Vanya, who drove the only truck the kolkhoz possessed, set me down on Podkamennaya Street where I was to live, helped me carry in my bundle and bedding, gave me an encouraging slap on the back and drove away. I was eleven years old, and I was on my own.

Those were still hungry years, and Mother had three of us to feed—I was the eldest. In the spring when things were especially difficult I swallowed and made my sister swallow the eyes of potatoes and grains of rye and oats, hoping they would grow inside us and we wouldn't be thinking about food all the time. All the summer we watered our seeds from the Angara, but for some reason there was no crop, or such a small one that we never felt it. Incidentally, I think our experiment wasn't completely useless and might come in handy for people someday; but we had had no experience and must have done something wrong.

It is difficult to say just how Mother made up her mind to send me to town. We had no father, life was a struggle, and I suppose she decided that whatever she did things couldn't be worse than they were. I had done well in the village school. I liked studying and had won quite a name for learning. I wrote and read letters for the old folk. I read all the books in our very modest library and in the evening told the other children tales from them, adding a good bit of my own. But my great prestige came from checking the winning numbers of state bonds. People had collected a great many during the war, the lists of winners were frequent, and when they arrived everyone brought their certificates to me. They said I had a lucky eye. And as a matter of fact, winning numbers did turn up; usually the winnings were small, but in those lean years collective farmers were glad of even a few coins, and here I would be, announcing some unexpected sum. Some of the joy spilled over to me; I was singled out among the other boys, and even treated to some extra food. One day Uncle Ilya, as a rule stingy, scooped up a whole bucketful of potatoes for me after winning four hundred rubles; and that spring, a bucket of potatoes was wealth.

It was because I could understand the lists and the numbers on the vouchers that people began to tell Mother, "That lad of yours has got a head on him. You ought to have him taught. Learning never comes amiss."

So in spite of all our troubles Mother got me ready and made the arrangements, although before that nobody else had gone to school in town. I was the first. Naturally, I had no clear idea of what lay before me, or the difficulties I would encounter in this new place.

There, too, I did well at school. After all, that was what I had come for, I had no other interests. At that time I always did my best at anything; it was the only way I knew. I would hardly have dared to approach school with a single lesson unprepared, and consequently I always got the top mark—five. Except in French.

My trouble with French was the pronunciation. I could easily remember words and grammar, I translated fast, I coped with all the spelling difficulties, but the pronunciation was blocked by all my Angara forebears back through the generations, none of whom had ever pronounced foreign words—even if they suspected their existence. I rattled out my French after the manner of our village tongue-twisters, swallowed half the sound as superfluous and rapped out the other half in short barking bursts. When the French teacher, Lydia Mikhailovna, listened to me, her face twisted painfully and she shut her eyes. She had never heard anything like it. Again and again she explained and showed me how to pronounce nasal sounds and vowel combinations, and asked me to repeat them after her, but I only floundered, wooden-tongued. It was just no use.

My bad time was when I came home from school. There, I was always occupied with something, doing something, the other boys carried me along with them; whether you want it or not you have to run about, join in games, and at lessons keep your mind on them. But once I was alone homesickness descended in a crushing weight; I ached for home, for the village. I had never been away from my family for even a day, and was quite unprepared for living among strangers. It was a hideous feeling, worse than any sickness. There was only one thing I wanted, one thing I dreamed of—to be at home. I got so thin that Mother was frightened when she came to visit me at the end of September. While she was here I kept a grip on myself, I never complained or let a tear show, but when she was actually leaving I gave way and chased after the truck, crying noisily. She waved to me from the back of the truck—stop, don't disgrace yourself and me!—but nothing of it reached me. Then she made up her mind and asked the driver to pull up.

"Get your things," she said briefly when I ran up to her. "You've got your learning, it seems, so now we'll go home."

I recovered myself and ran back.

It was not only homesickness that made me thin; I never had enough to eat. In the autumn, when Uncle Vanya came with grain for sale to the state at a center near the town, he brought me food fairly regularly, about once a week. But the trouble was, it was never enough. There was only bread and potatoes, and now and then a jar of curds for which Mother had bartered something, because we had no cow of our own. When he brought it it seemed a lot, but in a couple of days there was nothing. I soon found that a good half of my bread mysteriously vanished. I checked up and found that was correct. It had been there, now it was gone. The same thing happened to the potatoes. I never knew who had taken them—my landlady, a noisy busy woman fending alone for three children, one of her two older girls, or young Fedka; I shrank even from thinking of it, let alone trying to find out. But it was hard—there was Mother depriving the little ones of the last they had so as to feed me, and a good part of it I never got. However, I made myself accept this, too. It wouldn't make Mother feel any better if she knew the truth.

Being hungry here was quite different from being hungry in the village. There, especially in autumn, you could always find something to grab, pluck, dig up; there were fish in the Angara and birds in the forest. But here, there was only bare *nothing* all round—strange people, strange kitchen gardens, strange soil. The small river was strained through fishing nets, ten rows of them. One Sunday I sat all day with my rod and caught only three tiny gudgeon, no bigger than teaspoons. You won't get fat from that kind of fishing. I didn't go again, why waste time? In the evenings I hung about the teahouse and the market, noting the prices, swallowing saliva, and finally going back empty-handed. A kettle stood on the stove; I would drink some hot water to warm my belly and go to bed. In the morning—school again. So it went on until the happy moment when the truck drove up to the gate and Uncle Vanya knocked at the door. Ravenous as I was, and knowing full well that the food wouldn't last long, however sparing I was, I ate till I was full, till I writhed with pain, and then, after a day or two, went hungry again.

One day—it was still September—Fedka asked me, "Are you game to play 'fires'?"

"What's that?"

"It's for money. If you've got any, come on and we'll play."

"I haven't any."

"Me too. All right, let's go and watch. You'll see, it's grand."

Fedka led me behind the kitchen gardens, then we went past a long ridge thick with nettles, already black and tangled, dangling their bunches of poisonous seeds; we jumped from hummock to hummock across an old tip and went down into a hollow where we saw a cluster of boys on a small, level patch. We went closer while they eyed us. They were all about the same age as myself except for one, a tall, strong fellow with a long reddish cowlick on his forehead, who seemed to be the boss there. I remember that he was in the seventh form at school.

"What have you brought *him* for?" he asked Fedka.

"He's all right, Vadik, he lives with us," Fedka said ingratiatingly.

"Want to play?" Vadik asked me.

"I haven't any money."

"Mind you—if you try to sneak—!"

"I don't sneak!" I said indignantly.

Since nobody took any more notice of me, I moved closer and watched. They weren't all playing, only six or seven; the rest were like me, watching; they all seemed to be rooting for Vadik, who was obviously cock of the walk.

The game was easy enough to understand. Each player put in ten kopeks. Then the coins were arranged in a pile, "tails" upwards, on an area bounded by a thick line a couple of meters from the kitty, then at the other end by a sunken boulder which served as a footrest when a player threw a round flat stone. It had to be aimed so as to roll as close as possible to the line but without passing over it. The closest then had the right to break up the kitty. That was done by striking the coins with the same flat stone, trying to tip them so that they turned over "heads" up. The "heads" coin was yours, go on and try another, but the really winning shot was when the thrown stone hit the pile; then, if even one of them fell "heads" up, the whole kitty went into your pocket and the game began afresh.

Vadik was clever. He went to the boulder last, when the whole picture was clear and he could see where to throw in order to forge ahead. The money was won by the first, it seldom lasted up to final players. Probably everyone understood Vadik's cleverness but nobody dared say a word. It's true, he played with skill. At the boulder he would bend his knees slightly, eyes narrowed, aim the stone at the mark, rise with unhurried smoothness and the stone slid from his hand and went exactly where he had aimed. With a quick movement he tossed back the cowlick from his forehead, spat casually to one side and with deliberate slowness advanced to the money. If the coins were heaped up he struck a sharp ringing blow, but when they lay separately he gave them a light, careful touch so that the coin did not jump high or tumble over a number of times, but rose slightly and settled on its other side. Nobody else could do that. The boys hit wildly and then got out more coins, and those who had none joined the spectators.

If only I had had money, I felt I could have played. In the village we had played knucklebones, and that too needs a sure eye. In addition, I liked to set myself targets to hit. I would collect a handful of stones, find a difficult target and go on throwing until I had gained my objective—ten hits out of ten. I threw from above, round my shoulder and from below, bringing the stone down on my target. So skill I had. But I had no money.

Mother sent me bread because she had no money, otherwise I could have bought it where I was. Where would we get it on the kolkhoz? A couple of times, Mother had slipped a five-ruble note into a letter—fifty kopeks by the present coinage—to buy myself milk. It was no great sum, of course, but it would buy me five half-liter jars of milk at the market—a ruble a jar. I was supposed to drink milk because of anemia, I sometimes got dizzy spells for no apparent reason.

The third time I got a five-ruble note, however, I did not spend it on milk, I changed it into small coins and went to the tip. The place had certainly been well chosen—a level patch closed in by mounds, not overlooked from anywhere. At home in the village, where grownups could see what you did, you got into bad trouble for gambling, with threats of the headmaster and even the militia. But here there was nobody to disturb us. And it was nearby, you could get there in ten minutes.

The first time I lost ninety kopeks, the second time sixty. I hated seeing the money go, but I felt I was getting my hand in; my fingers were becoming accustomed to the stone, I was learning just how much strength to use so as to make it go where I wanted while my eye could predict where it would fall and how far it would roll. In the evenings, when the others had gone, I would go back, take out the stone which Vadik had hidden under the boulder, get my small change out of my pocket and go on throwing until darkness fell. In the end, out of ten throws the stone came right down on the money three or four times.

At last the day came when I could count my winnings.

It was a dry, warm autumn; although it was October one could go about in a shirt; rain fell rarely and seemed almost accidental, blown over by a breeze from some place of bad weather. The sky was summery-blue, but seemed lower, and the sun sank earlier. When it was clear the air seemed to shimmer over the low hills, filled with bitter, intoxicating scents of dry wormwood; distant voices came clearly and birds were gathering in circling flocks for their migration. The grass on our patch, although yellow and limp, was still soft and alive. The boys not playing—mostly those who had lost—fooled about on it.

Now I hurried off there every day after school. The boys changed, some fell out and new ones appeared, only Vadik never missed a game and indeed, without him it never started. He was followed like a shadow by a squat boy nicknamed Chicken with a big cropped head. I had never noticed Chicken at school, but —to anticipate—in the second term he descended on our form like snow on our heads. It appeared that he had been left for a second year in the fifth form, but on some pretext or other had managed to extend his holiday until January. Chicken too usually won—not so much as Vadik, but he always left better off than he came. One reason probably was that he was hand-in-glove with Vadik, who gave him a bit of sly assistance.

Another boy in our form, Tishkin, came sometimes. He was a blinking fidgety boy who liked to shoot his hand up during lessons. Whether he knew the answer or not, up went his hand; then when he was asked, he was silent.

"Why did you put your hand up?"

He blinked. "I remembered it, but when I got up I forgot."

I did not make friends with him. I had not made friends with any of the boys at that time—from tongue-tied shyness, village reserve, but mainly because my dreadful homesickness left me with no desire for it. They showed no desire for my company, either, so I remained alone, not realizing that I was lonely or trying to escape from it. I was alone because I was here and not at home, in the village where I had plenty of friends.

Tishkin seemed not to notice me on our playing patch. He lost quickly, vanished and did not return for some time.

I won. I had started winning steadily, every day. I had worked out my play: not to roll the stone over the ground, trying for the first blow. When there were many players this wasn't simple: the closer you came to the line, the greater the danger of rolling over it and being the last. The thing was to cover the kitty when you threw the stone. That was what I did. Of course, it was a risk, but with my skill the risk was worth it. I could lose three or four times running, but with the fifth, when I took the kitty, I regained what I had lost twofold. Then I would lose again and get it back again. I seldom struck the coins with the stone, but here too I had my own way. Vadik struck to turn the coin to him, but it meant that the stone supported the coin, prevented it from spinning and, falling back from it, made it flip.

Now I had money. But I did not let the game keep me there until evening; I needed a ruble, just one ruble every day. Once I had it I went off, bought a jar of milk at the market (the market women grumbled at my bent, misshapen coins but poured out the milk), then I had supper and sat down to my lessons. I still hadn't enough to eat, but knowledge that I was drinking milk gave me strength and eased my hunger. And those dizzy spells were much less frequent.

At first Vadik took my success calmly. It meant no loss to him, I doubt very much if anything from his pocket came my way.

Sometimes he even praised me: that's the way to throw, learn how to do it, you fumblers. But soon he noticed that I left far too quickly and one day he stopped me.

"Hi, you—grabbed the kitty and making off? Clever boy, aren't you? Come on, play."

"But I have to do my lessons, Vadik," I protested.

"If you want to do lessons, don't come here."

Chicken backed him up.

"Where'd you get the idea you can play for money like that? Look out or you'll win something you don't want! Get me?"

After that Vadik never let me have a go at the stone before himself. He threw well, and I often had to dive into my pocket for another coin without touching the stone. But I threw better, and if I got the chance the stone went straight to the money like iron to a magnet. I was surprised at my own skill; I should have had enough sense to hold it back, to play without attracting attention, but I was still too simple and continued to bombard the kitty. How could I know that nobody is ever forgiven for going too far ahead? Let him never hope for mercy or seek a defender, to the others he's an upstart and is hated most of all by the one just behind him. This was the knowledge which I learned that autumn the hard way.

I had thrown on the money again and was going to collect it when I saw Vadik had his foot on a coin which had fallen somewhat aside. All the rest were "tails" up. In such cases it is customary to shout "Warehouse!" before throwing, in order, if there was no "heads," to collect the money into a pile to strike, but as usual, relying on success, I hadn't shouted.

"No warehouse," Vadik announced.

I went up and tried to move his foot from the coin, but he pushed me away, quickly picked it up and showed me "tails." But I had had time to see it lie with "heads" up—otherwise he wouldn't have covered it.

"You turned it over," I said. "It was 'heads,' I saw it."

He pushed a fist under my nose.

"And this—you see it? Take a smell!"

I had to give up. It was no use insisting, if a fight started not one of them would take my part, not even Tishkin, who was there too. Vadik glared at me, eyes angrily narrowed. I stooped, struck the nearest coin, turned it and moved a second. "If not one way, then another," I decided. "I'll collect them all the same." Again I held the stone to strike but had no chance to complete the stroke:

somebody behind kneed me hard and I fell awkwardly, my face striking the ground. Sniggers. I turned. Chicken stood behind me, grinning. I was taken aback.

"What did you do that for?"

"Who said it was me? You're dreaming!"

"Give me that!" Vadik held out his hand for the stone but I held on to it. Anger had burned out fear, I wasn't afraid of anything. Why did they do that to me? What for? What had I done to them?

"Give it here!" Vadik ordered.

"You did turn the coin!" I yelled at him. "I saw it, I saw you do it! I saw it!"

"Say that again," he said, advancing ominously on me.

"You turned it," I said, more quietly now, knowing well what that would bring.

The first to hit me was Chicken, again from behind. I shot towards Vadik, who quickly, accurately, without taking aim, smashed his head into my face. I fell with blood spurting from my nose. I was barely up when Chicken went for me again. I could have broken away and run, but for some reason I never thought of it. I was tossed between Vadik and Chicken, hardly defending myself, my hand over my nose with the blood pouring from it; and desperately, furiously, stubbornly I kept on shouting, "You turned it! You did! You did!"

They hit me in turn, one and two, one and two, one and two. Some third boy, small and vicious, kicked my legs—afterwards I found they were black and blue. My one thought was not to fall, not to fall whatever happened, even in those moments I felt that would be a disgrace. But in the end they did get me down, and stopped.

"Get out before I kill you!" Vadik bawled. "Get!"

I rose, sobbing, sniffling through a numbed nose and climbed the hill.

"Just try to blab—I'll kill you!" Vadik shouted after me.

I didn't answer. I was a tight knot of humiliation and anger, I could not force out a word. It was only when I was at the top that something burst, and mad with fury, I shouted with all my lungs—loud enough for the whole place to hear, "You did turn it!"

Chicken started up after me but stopped at once—probably Vadik felt they'd done enough to me and called him back. For about five minutes I stood there looking at the patch where play had started again, then went down the other side of the hill into a hollow filled with blackened nettles, collapsed on the harsh dry grass and gave way to loud weeping.

In all the world that day there was no one more miserable than I.

In the morning I looked at myself in the mirror, appalled. My nose had swollen up like a potato, I had a black eye and below it, on my left cheek, was a blood-filled bruise. How could I go to school looking like that? But go I must, I couldn't miss whatever happened. Well, nature had given some people noses as big as mine, you would never have guessed it was a nose but for the place where it stood; but the bruise, and the black eye—there was no explaining those away, anyone could see it was no wish of mine that they were blazing there.

I slipped into the classroom, covering my eyes with my hand, sat down at my desk and dropped my head. Of course, the first lesson had to be French. Lydia Mikhailovna, our form mistress, was particularly alert and it was difficult to hide anything from her. She would come in and say "Good morning," but before she told us to sit down she would always look at each one of us, with remarks which, although couched in joking form, were meant to be heeded. Of course she noticed the indications on my face at once, however I tried to hide them; I saw that by the way the others began to turn and look at me.

"Well," said Lydia Mikhailovna, opening the register, "I see we've got a wounded here with us today."

The others laughed and Lydia Mikhailovna raised her eyes to me again. She had a slight cast and appeared to be looking past me, but by that time we had learned to know where she was really looking.

"What happened to you?" she asked.

"I fell down," I blurted out; I hadn't thought to prepare a plausible explanation.

"Dear me, how unfortunate. Was it yesterday or today?"

"Today. No, I mean yesterday, when it was dark."

"Tee-hee—fell down!" squealed Tishkin, choking with glee. "It was Vadik from the seventh gave it to him. They were gambling and he started to argue and got it. I saw it. And now he says he fell down!"

I was thunderstruck at such treachery. Was he just stupid, or was he doing it on purpose? You could be expelled for gambling.

I was in for it. My eyes darkened and there was roaring in my ears. I was lost. Tishkin! He'd done me a good turn! It was all out now.

"Tishkin, it was something else I wanted to ask you," Lydia Mikhailovna checked him, showing no surprise, speaking in the same quiet, ordinary voice. "Come up to the board, since you want to talk, and get ready to answer." She waited while Tishkin, confused and apprehensive, came forward and then told me briefly, "You'll stay behind after school."

My worst fear was that Lydia Mikhailovna would take me to the headmaster. This would mean that in addition to today's talk, I would have to come forward at assembly tomorrow and explain what had induced me to engage in such disgraceful conduct. That was what the headmaster, Vasily Andreyevich, always asked a culprit, whatever he had done—broken a window or smoked in the lavatory: "What induced you to engage in such disgraceful conduct?" He would pace up and down in front of the school, hands behind his back, jerking his shoulders forward in time to his pacing so that it looked as though his tightly buttoned, projecting trench coat moved independently, slightly out of synch with the headmaster; he would hurry the unhappy boy with "Answer, answer. We're waiting. Look, the whole school's waiting to hear what you have to say." The boy would try to stutter some excuse, but the headmaster cut him short: "Answer the question, the question. What was it?" "What induced me—" "Exactly. What induced you. Well, we're listening."

As a rule it ended in tears; only then was the headmaster satisfied and we went to our classrooms. It was more difficult with the big boys, who didn't want to cry but couldn't answer Vasily Andreyevich's question. Once the first lesson began ten minutes late; all that time the headmaster had questioned a ninth-former, but, getting nothing coherent out of him, went off to his office.

But what could I say? Better if they expelled me at once. As I thought of that, it flashed through my mind that then I could go home—but I took fright as though I'd burned myself: no, I couldn't go home in disgrace. It would be different if I dropped school myself. But then they might say I couldn't be depended on since I hadn't been able to do what I'd wanted, and everyone would look askance at me. No, not that, either. I could stick it out here, I'd get used to it, but to go home like that—NO!

After school I waited for Lydia Mikhailovna in the corridor, half dead with fear. She came out of the teachers' room and nodded to me to follow her into the classroom. As usual she sat down at the table; I wanted to go to the back row, farther away, but she indicated the front desk, directly before her.

"Is it true that you've been gambling?" she began at once.

She spoke too loudly, I had a feeling that here in school such things should only be whispered, and my fear grew. But it was no use trying to get out of it. Tishkin had given me away completely.

"It's true," I mumbled.

"Well—do you usually win or lose?"

I didn't know which was the best thing to say, so I said nothing.

"Come on, tell me the truth. You lose, I suppose?"

"N-no, I win."

"That's one good thing, anyway. So you've been winning. What do you do with the money?"

It had taken me a long time to get used to Lydia Mikhailovna's voice, it had always confused me. In our village people brought their voices up from somewhere deep inside them so that they boomed, but Lydia Mikhailovna's voice was small and light, one had to listen; it wasn't because it was weak, she could speak powerfully if she wanted, it seemed as though she were holding back her breath, a kind of unnecessary economy. I was ready to blame French; naturally, while she was studying, getting used to a strange language, her voice had been constrained and had got weak, like a bird in a cage, you had to wait for it to recover its volume and strength. Now, too, Lydia Mikhailovna questioned me as though she were busy with something else, something more important; but there was no evading her questions.

"Well? What do you do with the money you win? Buy sweets? Or books? Or are you saving up for something? You must have a lot by now."

"No, not much. I only win a ruble."

"And then you don't play any more?"

"No."

"And the ruble? Why just a ruble? What do you do with it?"

"I buy milk."

"Milk?"

She sat there before me, neat, wise, good to look at in her way of dressing and in her young womanliness which I vaguely felt; a faint perfume came to me. I thought it was her breath. And then, too, it wasn't just arithmetic she taught, or history, but that mysterious French language, and that, too, held something magical, not attainable by ordinary people—well, like me, for instance. I dared not raise my eyes to her, but I dared not deceive her. And after all, why should I tell lies?

She sat looking at me in silence, and I felt through all my skin that under the gaze of her eyes with that slight cast, all troubles and problems seemed to become enormous and swollen with a malignant power. Of course, there was something for her to look at: a thin awkward boy with a battered face, fidgeting in front of her, motherless, unkempt, lonely, in an old washed-out jacket with sagging shoulders, fitting over the chest but with sleeves far too short; in limp pale-greenish pants made over from his father's riding breeches tucked into the rough slippers called *chiriki* and bearing traces of yesterday's fight. I had already noticed Lydia Mikhailovna's interested glance at my *chiriki*; nobody else in our form wore them. It was only the following autumn, when I refused point blank to wear them to school any longer, that Mother sold the sewing machine, our only treasure, and bought me rough top-boots.

"All the same, you shouldn't play for money," said Lydia Mikhailovna thoughtfully. "You can manage without, somehow. Can't you?"

Hardly daring to believe that I was to be spared, I promised easily, "Yes—I can."

I was sincere, but what can you do if sincerity cannot be tied on with rope!

To be truthful, things were very bad for me those days. The autumn was a dry one, the kolkhoz had completed its grain deliveries early, and Uncle Vanya didn't come any more. I knew that Mother would be worried sick about me, but that didn't make things any easier. The sack of potatoes Uncle Vanya had brought on his last trip melted away as quickly as though it were being fed to cattle at the very least. It was a good thing I had had the idea of hiding some of them in an abandoned shed out in the yard; it was this secret store that kept me alive. After school I would sneak out like a thief, slip into the shed, push some potatoes into my pockets, and run off to the hills to make a fire in some cozy hidden place. I was constantly hungry, even in my sleep I could feel waves of dry cramps in my stomach.

Hoping to find other gamblers, I started investigating the neighboring streets, wandering about the wastelands, watching the boys who went to the hills. But it was all no good, the season was over, ended by the cold October winds. It was only in our old clearing that the boys still gathered. I hung about nearby, saw the stone gleaming in the sunshine, saw Vadik brandishing his arms as he ordered the others about and the familiar figures bending over the kitty.

In the end I couldn't hold out, and went down. I knew this was humiliation, but it was no less humiliation to reconcile myself once and for all to being beaten up and driven away. I was itching to see how Vadik and Chicken would react to my appearance, and how I myself would behave. But the main driving force was my hunger. I needed a ruble—not for milk, but for bread. And I knew no other way to earn it.

As I approached, the play stopped and all turned to stare at me. Chicken was wearing a cap with earflaps turned up, cocked at a bold, careless angle like everything he wore, and a checked short-sleeved shirt hanging outside his trousers; Vadik was smart in a fine thick tunic with zipper fastening. Jackets and coats were piled up nearby with a small boy, about five or six, sitting on them.

The first to speak was Chicken.

"What have you come for? Want some more of the same?"

"I've come to play," I said as calmly as I could, looking at Vadik.

"And who said we want you, you—" Chicken added a few choice epithets.

"Nobody."

"Hi, Vadik, shall we give it him now or wait a bit?"

"Let him alone, Chicken." Vadik looked at me, narrow-eyed. "Can't you see, here's a fellow come to play. Maybe he wants to win ten rubles off each of us."

"You haven't got ten," I said, just to show I wasn't afraid.

"We've got more'n you think. Put yours down and shut up, before Chicken gets real angry. He's a hot-headed sort of fellow."

"What if I give him one, Vadik?"

"No, let him play." Vadik winked at the others. "He plays real well, wipes his feet on all of us."

I had learned my lesson, however, and knew just how much Vadik's benevolence was worth. He was probably tired of dull, uninteresting play, and had decided to let me in so as to make it more exciting. Let me but touch his vanity, however, and I'd be in for it again. He'd soon find some pretext, and there was Chicken more than ready.

I decided to play cautiously and not make any big killing, I threw the stone fearing to hit the money by accident, then quietly struck the separate coins, with a glance to make sure Chicken wasn't behind me. Those first days I did not venture to think of a ruble, twenty or thirty kopeks for a piece of bread—that was better than nothing, that was what I wanted.

But, of course, the end was sure. On the fourth day, when I had won a ruble and wanted to go, I was beaten up again. True, this time the beating was less, but the traces showed in a badly swollen lip. I had to bite it all the time in school. But Lydia Mikhailovna saw it, whatever I did. She called me up to the blackboard and made me read a French text. Even with ten good lips I couldn't have got the pronunciation right, with one swollen there wasn't a chance.

"Stop, oh stop!" cried Lydia Mikhailovna, raising a hand as though to ward something off. "What's this meant to be? No, I'll have to give you extra tutoring. There's no other way."

That was the start of rackingly uncomfortable days. From morning on, I would apprehensively await the time when I should have to remain alone with Lydia Mikhailovna and break my tongue in the effort to repeat after her words invented to torment one. Now, why on earth must three vowels be jammed together into a thick long "o", except deliberately for torment?—as in the word *beaucoup*, which you could choke on? Why did you have to make groaning sounds through your nose when it had always served a quite different purpose? Common sense ought to set *some* limit. I sweated, turned crimson and choked, while Lydia Mikhailovna without pity or letup forced me to twist my poor tongue. And why only me? There were plenty of boys in the school who spoke French just as badly as I did, but they were out playing, doing whatever they wanted, while I, like a scapegoat, was punished for all of them.

But there was worse to come. Lydia Mikhailovna suddenly decided that there was too little time before the second shift at school, and told me to come to her home in the evening. She lived in one of the teachers' houses beside the school. She had half a house and the other part was the headmaster's.

I went there as if to a torture chamber. I was naturally shy and awkward, confused by trifles, and in that clean, neat apartment I was afraid to breathe. I had to be told to take my things off, to come in, to sit down, I had to be moved about like a piece of furniture, and it cost real effort to squeeze a word out of me. This hardly helped my French. But—strange!—we seemed to work for a shorter time here than at school, where the second shift was supposed to have come too quickly. Not only that, Lydia Mikhailovna, busy with her own domestic chores, asked me questions or talked about herself. I suspect that she invented for my benefit the story that she had deliberately chosen the French faculty because she had been unable to come to terms with the language at school and had wanted to prove to herself that she could manage it just as well as anyone else.

Huddled in a corner, I listened and longed for the moment when she would let me go. There were a great many books in the room, and on a stool by the window stood a big handsome radio-phonograph, a rare thing at the time and to me a marvel. Lydia Mikhailovna put on records, and again a man's well-modulated voice taught French. There was no getting away from it. Lydia Mikhailovna moved about the room in her plain house-frock and soft felt slippers, making me flinch every time she approached. I simply couldn't believe that I was sitting in her room, everything was too strange and startling for me, even the air, which seemed impregnated with the faint, unfamiliar scent of a life different from anything I knew. I had the feeling of peering into that life from outside, and in awkward shame shrank into my scanty jacket.

Lydia Mikhailovna must have been about twenty-five at that time; I well remember her face, regular-featured and consequently not very animated, her eyes slightly narrowed to hide that cast, her tight smile that rarely widened to the full and her short, quite black hair. There was nothing in her face of the hardness which, I later noticed, becomes with the years almost a professional badge of teachers, even those naturally gentle and kind, but there was a kind of cautious, amused dubiousness concerning herself, as though wondering: How did I land here and what am I supposed to be doing? I believe now that she had been married—there was assurance and experience in her voice, in her walk—supple, free and confident, in her whole style and manner. Besides, I have always thought that girls who study French or Spanish become women earlier than those who study, say, Russian or German.

I'm ashamed now to remember how alarmed and embarrassed I was when Lydia Mikhailovna, our lesson finished, called me to supper. Ravenous as I had been just before, that invitation drove all appetite out of me. No, no! To sit at the same table with Lydia Mikhailovna! Better to learn the whole French language by heart tomorrow, so as never to come here again! Even a piece of bread would have stuck in my throat. I don't believe I'd ever guessed before that Lydia Mikhailovna ate ordinary food like all of us and not some kind of heavenly manna—she seemed far too unique, too unlike everybody else.

I jumped up, mumbled something about having eaten, not wanting anything, while I tried to edge along the wall towards the door. Lydia Mikhailovna looked at me, surprised and hurt, but nothing could stop me. I turned and ran. This happened several times until Lydia Mikhailovna gave up and stopped inviting me to table. I breathed more freely.

Then one day I was told there was a parcel down in the cloakroom for me, a man had brought it. Uncle Vanya, of course, who else could it be! Probably the house was locked up, and Uncle Vanya couldn't wait till school was over, so he had left it there. I could hardly hold out until the end of lessons and then I rushed down. Our school cleaner pointed to a white plywood box, the kind used for parcel post, standing in a corner. That surprised me—why the box? Mother usually sent food in an ordinary sack. Perhaps it wasn't for me at all? No, there was my name and form written on top. Uncle Vanya must have written it there, so there wouldn't be any mixup. Where had Mother got the idea of nailing things up in a box? Look how townified she was getting!

I was so eager to find out what was inside that I couldn't wait till I got home. Not potatoes, of course. For bread it was too small, and inconvenient, too. Besides, she had sent bread only a while before and I still had some. What was it, then? I crawled under the stairs where I remembered an axe was kept, found it, and opened up the box. It was dark under the stairs so I crawled out again and, peering round, set the box up on the nearest windowsill.

I looked inside and stared, stupefied. There on top, covered by a neat sheet of paper, lay macaroni. That was something! The long yellowish tubes lying closely, evenly, were rare wealth to my dazzled eyes—better than anything I could imagine. Now it was clear why Mother had found a box—so that the macaroni wouldn't be broken and crushed, but come to me in all its perfection. I carefully lifted a tube, looked at it, blew through it and, unable to hold back, began crunching it greedily. Then I took a second and a third, wondering where I could hide the box to keep the macaroni safe from the far too greedy mice in my landlady's larder. It wasn't for them Mother had used her last money to buy it. No, I wasn't going to lose that macaroni. This wasn't potatoes.

I started. Macaroni. Yes, where *had* she got it? There had never been any in the village, you couldn't buy it for any money. What did it all mean, then? Hastily, in hope and despair, I pushed the macaroni to one side and beneath it found several big pieces of loaf sugar and two slabs of hematogen. That settled it. The parcel had not been sent by Mother. But who, then? I looked at the top again—yes, my form, my name. Queer, very queer.

I pushed the nails fastening the lid back into their holes and, leaving the box on the windowsill, went up the stairs and knocked at the door of the teachers' room. But Lydia Mikhailovna had gone. That didn't matter, I knew where she lived all right. So that was it: if you won't sit down to table, you get the food sent home. Nothing doing. It couldn't be anyone else. It wasn't Mother, she'd have put a note in, told me where all this wealth had come from, and how.

When I edged in sideways Lydia Mikhailovna put on a look of bewilderment as I set the box down in front of her.

"What's that? What have you brought? What for?" she said in a tone of surprise.

"It was you," I said in a shaking, breaking voice.

"What was me? What are you talking about?"

"You sent this to the school. I know it was you."

Lydia Mikhailovna blushed and looked embarrassed. That was probably the one and only time I was not afraid to look her straight in the eye. I didn't care if she was a teacher or my own aunt. I was asking the questions now, not she, and asking them not in French but in Russian, with none of those articles. And let her answer.

"Why do you think I sent it?"

"Because we never have macaroni at home. Or hematogen, either."

"What! Never?" Her surprise was so genuine that she gave herself away completely.

"No, we never have it. You ought to have known."

Lydia Mikhailovna burst out laughing and tried to hug me, but I evaded her.

"Yes, you're right, I ought to have found out. How could I neglect it?" She thought for a moment. "But it was difficult to guess—honestly! I've always lived in towns. So you never have it, you say? What do you have, then?"

"Peas. And winter radish."

"Peas. Winter radish. In the Kuban we have apples. Oh, how

many there must be now! I wanted to go to the Kuban this year, but somehow I came here instead." Lydia Mikhailovna sighed and glanced quickly at me. "Don't be angry with me. I meant it for the best. Who'd have guessed I could give myself away with macaroni? Never mind, I'll know better. But take the macaroni—"

"No!" I cut her short.

"Why are you like that? I know you don't get enough to eat. And I live alone and I've plenty of money. I can buy anything I want, but when I'm alone—and anyway I don't eat much, I'm afraid of putting on weight."

"I've got all I want to eat."

"Don't argue. I know. I've talked to your landlady. What's bad about it if you take that macaroni and make yourself a good supper? Why can't I help you—just once? I promise not to send any more parcels. But take this one—please. You must have enough to eat if you're going to study. We've got plenty of well-fed dunces here who don't take anything in and probably never will, but you're a boy with brains, it would be all wrong for you to leave school."

Her voice began to have a soporific effect; I was afraid she might convince me, I was angry with myself because I knew she was right, and because I wouldn't let myself accept it. Shaking my head and muttering something, I made a dash for the door.

Our lessons didn't stop, I continued to come to Lydia Mikhailovna, but now she really got down to business. It was as though she had decided: if it's to be only French, then French let it be. And something really began to come of it, I gradually learned to pronounce French words quite creditably; they no longer fell like heavy stones to my feet but rang and tried to fly.

"Good," Lydia Mikhailovna encouraged me. "You won't get a five this term, but you certainly will next."

We never mentioned the parcel, but I was on the alert—just in case. You never could tell what Lydia Mikhailovna might think up. I knew from myself: if something doesn't come off, you don't give up, you try some other way. I could feel that Lydia Mikhailovna kept looking at me expectantly, and then laughed to herself over my savagely shy independence; it made me angry, but strange as it might be, that anger gave me more confidence. I was no longer that meek, helpless boy afraid to move a step here, I gradually got used to Lydia Mikhailovna and to her room.

I was still shy and huddled into a corner, hiding my *chiriki* under my chair, but my former tongue-tied constraint had gone, I ventured to ask Lydia Mikhailovna questions and even to argue with her.

She tried once more to make me join her at table but there was nothing doing. I stood firm. I had obstinacy enough for ten.

We might well have stopped the extra lessons, I had already mastered the main difficulty, my tongue had become supple, I could manage the rest at the ordinary lessons. There were plenty of years ahead. What would I do later on if I learned it all from beginning to end now? But I didn't venture to say anything of this to Lydia Mikhailovna, and she evidently didn't consider that we had got through our program, so I continued grinding away at French. Incidentally, was it really a grind? Somehow or other, I myself hardly knew how, I had begun to acquire a taste for the language and in free moments without any urging hunted through the dictionary and looked at lessons we had not yet reached in the textbook. The grind had become a pleasure. Then, too, I was spurred on by pride: I hadn't been able to do it, but now I would, and as well as the best. Was I any worse than they? If only I hadn't had to go to Lydia Mikhailovna. I could have done it alone.

One day, about a fortnight after the parcel, Lydia Mikhailovna asked me, "Well, don't you play for money any more? Or do you all get together somewhere to play?"

"How could we play now?" I said, with a look outside the window where the snow already lay.

"What was the game? How did you play?"

"What d'you want to know for?" I was suspicious.

"Just for interest. When I was a child we used to play, too, I was wondering if it was the same game. Tell me, don't be afraid."

"What'd I be afraid of?"

I told her—saying nothing, of course, about Vadik, Chicken and the small tricks I used in playing.

"No." Lydia Mikhailovna shook her head. "I've never heard of 'fires' before. We used to play 'chika.' Do you know it?"

"No."

"Look here." She jumped up lightly from the table where she was sitting, found some coins in her handbag and moved a chair away from the wall. "Come here, look. I strike a coin against the wall." She struck a light blow and the coin, jingling, descended in a curve to the floor. "Now—" and she gave me a second coin—"you strike. But remember, you've got to make your coin fall as close to mine as you can. To measure, you must reach both with the fingers of one hand—sometimes we called it 'measures.' If you can reach both you've won. Here, try it." I struck, but my coin fell on its edge and rolled away into a corner.

"Now you begin. But another thing—if my coin touches yours, even with its edge, I win double. That's 'chika,' I suppose from 'chiknut,' 'to touch.' Understand?"

"Nothing hard there."

"Shall we play?"

I couldn't believe my ears.

"Me—play with you?"

"Why not?"

"But you're a teacher!"

"Well, and so what? You think a teacher isn't human? Sometimes I get sick of being nothing but a teacher all the time, teaching and teaching and no end to it. Always holding myself back, mustn't do this, mustn't do that." Lydia Mikhailovna's eyes narrowed more than usual as she looked thoughtfully, absently out of the window. "Sometimes it's good to forget you're a teacher —or you can turn into a walking 'must' and 'mustn't,' until it's boring for real-life people to be anywhere near you. I sometimes think the most important thing for a teacher is not to take oneself too seriously, to remember that it isn't so very much one can teach, after all." She gave a little start and gaiety returned. "When I was a child I was ready for anything, always in scrapes. My parents had plenty of trouble with me. And even now I often want to run and jump or go chasing off somewhere, or do something that isn't in the program or the timetable—just something I want. It isn't when you've lived a great many years that you get old, but when you forget about being a child. I'd like to jump every day, but Vasily Andreyevich lives next door. And he's a very serious man. He must never know we play 'chika.' "

"But we aren't playing. You only showed me."

"We can play not for money, just for fun. But all the same, don't give me away to Vasily Andreyevich."

Heavens, the things that can happen! It wasn't so long since I'd been terrified that Lydia Mikhailovna would take me to the headmaster for gambling, and now she was asking me not to give her away. A miracle, nothing else. I looked about me, scared, although I couldn't have said why, and blinked in confusion.

"Well, shall we try? We can stop if you don't like it."

"All right," I said hesitantly.

"You start."

We picked up our coins. I could see that Lydia Mikhailovna really had played, while I was just getting my eye in, it was not yet clear how to make the coin strike the wall—on its edge or flat, how high, and how much force I needed. My strokes were blind, if we'd been reckoning I'd have lost plenty in the first minutes, although actually there was nothing so very difficult about "chika." And of course, it was embarrassing to be playing with Lydia Mikhailovna, and that added to my awkwardness. I could never have dreamed of it, even in my wildest imaginings. It took time before I got myself in hand, and when I did and began to give my attention to the play, Lydia Mikhailovna stopped it.

"No, this isn't interesting," she said, straightening up and pushing back the hair from her eyes. "If we're going to play, then— real play; we're like three-year-olds!"

"But that'll be—gambling," I mumbled hesitantly.

"Of course. But what have we got in our hands? Nothing else takes the place of play for money. That's both good and bad. We can make the stakes quite tiny, but all the same there's interest, excitement, a thrill." I said nothing—I didn't know what to say.

"Are you really afraid?" Lydia Mikhailovna stung me.

"Not likely! I'm not afraid of anything."

I had some small change with me. I gave Lydia Mikhailovna her coin and got my own from my pocket. All right, Lydia Mikhailovna, we'll gamble if that's what you want. What do I care, I didn't start it. Vadik too thought nothing of me at first, but then he changed his mind and used his fists. I learned there. I can learn here. This isn't French! And in time I'll bridle that French too!

I had to agree to one condition: since Lydia Mikhailovna's hand was bigger and her fingers longer, she measured with thumb and middle finger, while I used thumb and little finger. That was fair and I agreed.

We began again. We moved from the room to the entry where there was more room, and struck against a smooth wooden partition. We struck, got down on our knees, crawled about the floor bumping into one another, stretching our fingers to measure, then getting up again, while Lydia Mikhailovna announced the reckoning. She played noisily, squealed, clapped her hands, teased me —in fact she was more like a schoolgirl than a teacher; I wanted to yell at her sometimes. But all the same she won and I lost.

Before I knew where I was, I had lost eighty kopeks; with great difficulty I reduced it to thirty, but then Lydia Mikhailovna's coin fell from a distance on mine, which brought my debt up to fifty again. I began to worry. We had agreed to settle up at the end of the play, but if it went on like this, I soon wouldn't have enough. I had only a little over a ruble. So I mustn't let it pass the ruble or I'd be disgraced, a lifelong disgrace.

Suddenly I saw that Lydia Mikhailovna wasn't trying to win. When she measured, her fingers were bent; where she said she couldn't reach the coin, I reached it without any difficulty. I rose, offended.

"No," I said, "I won't play like this. It isn't honest."

"But I really can't reach it," she protested. "My fingers are sort of wooden."

"You can."

"All right, all right, I'll try."

I don't know how it is in mathematics, but in life the clearest proof comes from opposites. When I saw the next day that Lydia Mikhailovna slyly moved a coin closer so as to touch it, I was thunderstruck. Somehow or other she didn't seem to notice when she looked at me that I had seen her obvious cheating, she went on moving the coin.

"What are you doing?" I said indignantly.

"Me? What do you mean?"

"Why did you move it?"

"But I didn't, it was right here." She denied it, Lydia Mikhailovna did, brazenly, almost gladly—just like Vadik or Chicken.

Of all things! And a teacher, too! I had seen for myself, from a twenty-centimeter distance, that she had touched the coin, and there she was insisting that she hadn't touched it, and laughing at me, too. Did she think I was blind? Or a small kid? A teacher of French! I forgot completely that only yesterday she had been trying to make me win and only watched to see that she didn't cheat. Lydia Mikhailovna, indeed!

That day we had spent only fifteen or twenty minutes on French, and after that it was even less. We had another interest. Lydia Mikhailovna would have me read a passage, correct me, hear me once more, and then we would start to play. After two small losses I started to win. I soon got the idea of "chika," probed all its secrets, knew how and where to strike.

So I had money again. I could go to the market and buy milk, now in frozen circles. I carefully cut the cream off the top of the disk, pushed the crumbling icy fragments into my mouth and felt its filling sweetness in my whole body. Then I turned the disk upside down and with my knife hacked off the greenish sweetish bottom. The rest I thawed and drank with a piece of black bread.

So that was all right, I could manage; and very soon, when the war damage was repaired, things would be better for everyone.

Of course, I felt uncomfortable, taking money from Lydia Mikhailovna, but I told myself it was honest winnings. I never asked to play, it was always her suggestion. I did not venture to refuse. I thought she enjoyed it, she was gay, she laughed and hurried me.

If we could have known beforehand how it was all going to end!

Kneeling in front of each other, we were arguing about the count. I believe we'd been arguing about something else before that, too.

"Get it into your fat head," she said, moving towards me, waving her hands, "why would I trick you? I'm doing the counting, not you. I know better. I lost three times running, and before that there was 'chika.' "

"I don't count that."

"Why not?"

"You'd 'chika' too."

We were shouting, interrupting each other, when all of a sudden we heard a surprised, if not appalled, but firm, ringing voice.

"Lydia Mikhailovna!"

We froze. Vasily Andreyevich was standing in the doorway.

"What's the matter with you? What's going on here?"

Slowly, very slowly, Lydia Mikhailovna rose from her knees, red and tousled, and smoothed back her hair.

"I would have expected you to knock before coming in, Vasily Andreyevich."

"I did knock. Nobody answered. What's going on here—will you please explain? I have the right to know, as headmaster."

"We're playing 'chika,' " she said quietly.

"You're playing for money—with him?" Vasily Andreyevich jerked a thumb at me, and I, terrified, crawled behind the partition to hide in the room. "Gambling—with a pupil? Have I understood you rightly?"

"Yes."

"You—" The headmaster choked, gasped for air. "I'm at a loss for words. Your conduct! It's a crime! Corruption! Perversion!

And—and—I've worked in schools for twenty years, I've seen many things in my time, but this—!" He flung up his hands.

Three days later Lydia Mikhailovna left. On her last evening she met me after school and walked home with me.

"I'm going back to the Kuban," she said as we parted. "You go on with your studies and don't worry, nothing'll happen to you for this foolish business. I'm the one to blame. So study and do well." She rumpled my hair and went.

I never saw her again.

In the middle of winter, just after the January holidays, I received a parcel by post. When I opened the box—with that same axe from under the stairs—I saw macaroni lying in neat rows. Under them, in a wrapping of cotton wool, were three red apples.

TRANSLATED BY EVE MANNING

THE CHILDREN'S WING

·2·

Joyce Johnson

The summer Nicky was so sick, I would leave work a little early and go to the Chinese takeout place on Forty-ninth Street. After a while it was my regular routine. Nicky would call me at the office and place his order. "An egg roll, of course," he'd say. "And sweet and sour shrimp. And Mom, would you bring me a Coke?" I didn't like him to have soft drinks, but he'd say, "Please, please," trying to sound pitiful, and I'd always get one for him in the end. It was hard to refuse him anything that summer. When I'd get to the hospital the other mothers would be there already with their shopping bags. Soon whole families would be gathered around the bedsides of the children, everyone eating out of foil containers or off paper plates, like an odd kind of picnic or a birthday party that had been displaced.

The children's wing was in the oldest part of the hospital, one of those gloomy gray stone buildings put up at the turn of the century. There was a marble rotunda on the ground floor. When you took the elevator up, there was no more marble, just dim green corridors and unending linoleum and muffled fake laughter from all the television sets.

I was never in the ward when the television wasn't on. The kids must have pressed the switches the moment they woke up. If you came in the afternoon, it would be soap operas or game shows; in the evening it would be reruns of *M*A*S*H* or *The Odd Couple*. There was a volunteer who called herself The Teacher and came around with little workbooks. She told me once she was going to bring Nicky some literature to explain what a biopsy was. In a stern voice I said, "I'd much rather you didn't."

I kept thinking Nicky's time in the children's ward would irrevocably change him. A shadow was falling across his vision of life and there was nothing I could do. Once I went to talk to a psychiatrist. He said, "What can I tell you? Either this will do damage to your son, or he will rise to the occasion and be a hero."

This immediately comforted me, though it's hard to say why. Somehow I could accept the logic of that answer. Nicky had seniority in Room K by August. New little boys kept coming and going, accident cases mostly. They lay beached on those high white beds, bewildered to find themselves in arrested motion. Each had been felled by some miscalculation—running out too fast in front of a car, jumping off a fence the wrong way. They'd go home with an arm or leg in a cast and sit out the summer, listening for the bell of the ice-cream truck, driving their mothers crazy. "Hey man, what you break?" they'd ask Nicky, looking at the plaster around his torso with respect. "You break your back or something?"

He could explain his condition as if he were a junior scientist laying out an interesting problem, using the language he'd picked up from the doctors—"left lumbar vertebra . . . unknown organism." He'd say, "You see, in the X-ray there's a white swelling on the left lumbar vertebra." There were men in a laboratory hunting the unknown organism. He made it sound like a movie —you could imagine the men in their white coats bent over their test tubes. All they had to do was find it, he'd say in a confident voice, and then they could cure him.

Sometimes I'd look around the room and stare at all those simple broken limbs in envy. I wondered if Nicky did that, too. Why had it been necessary for him to learn the awful possibilities, how your own body could suddenly turn against you, become the enemy?

He was the little scientist and he was the birthday boy. When the pain would come, he'd hold on to my hand the way he had at home on those nights I'd sat up with him. "Do you see that?" he'd say, pointing to the decal of a yellow duckling on the wall near his bed. "Isn't that ridiculous to have that here, that stupid duck?"

I agreed with him about the duck and Room K's other decorations—brown Disneyesque bunnies in various poses, a fat-cheeked Mary and her little lamb, all of them scratched and violently scribbled over. I could see how they threatened the dignity of a ten-year-old. The hospital would turn you into a baby if you didn't watch out.

I kept buying Nicky things; so did his father. With a sick child, you're always trying to bring different pieces of the outside in, as if to say, *That's* the reality, not this. There was a game called

Boggle that he was interested in for a week, and his own tape recorder, which fell off the bed one day and broke, and incredibly intricate miniature robots from Japan. All this stuff piled up around him. The fruit my mother brought him turned brown in unopened plastic bags.

Nicky liked only one thing, really; he could have done without all the rest. A fantasy war game called D&D that was all the rage among the fifth graders. I never even tried to understand it. I just kept buying the strange-looking dice he asked for and the small lead figures that he'd have to paint himself—dragons and wizards and goblins—and new strategy books with ever more complicated rules. "I want to live in a fantasy world," he told me. I remember it shocked me a little that he knew so explicitly what he was doing.

He refused to come back from that world very much. There were nights he'd hardly stop playing to talk to me. He'd look up only when I was leaving to tell me the colors he needed. When I'd encourage Nicky to get to know the other kids, he'd look at me wearily. "They don't have the same interests," he'd say.

"Maybe you could interest them in what you're doing."

"Mom . . . I can't. I'd have to start them from the beginning."

Still, I was grateful to the makers of D&D, grateful he had a way to lose himself. There were things happening in the children's wing I didn't want him to find out about, things I didn't want to know. If you walked those corridors you passed certain quiet, darkened rooms where there were children who weren't ever going to get well; there were parents on the elevator with swollen faces who'd never look you in the eye. A little girl in Room G died during visiting hours. I could hear her as soon as I got off on the fifth floor, a terrible high-pitched, rattling moan that I'll never forget. It went on and on and there were doctors running down the hall with machinery.

I walked into Nicky's room with my shopping bag from the Chinese takeout place. He was staring at all his figures lined up in battle formation; he didn't say hello. The other kids weren't saying much either. Their parents hadn't come yet. One little boy, looking scared, asked me, "What's that noise out there?" "Oh, someone's very sick tonight," I said, and I closed the door. I just shut the sound out. I suppose any other parent would have done the same. The strange thing was, I felt I'd done something wrong, that we all should have acknowledged it somehow, wept for the child who was dying.

I used to try to get Nicky out of bed for some exercise. We'd walk up and down outside his room very slowly, the IV apparatus trailing along on its clumsy, spindly stand like a dog on a leash. Some nights we'd sit on the brown plastic couch in the visitors' lounge, and Nicky would drink his Coke and go over his strategy books.

A mentally disturbed boy appeared there one night. He was tall and had a man's build already, muscled arms and shoulders, though I later found out he was only fifteen. He had a face that could have been beautiful, but you didn't want to see his eyes. They were red and inflamed, emptier than a statue's. I thought of the word *baleful* when I saw them. The boy with the baleful eyes. He was wearing dirty jeans and an old gray T-shirt. I thought he might have come in off the street.

Nicky and I were alone. This boy walked right over and stared down at us. I spoke to him softly, trying to sound calm. "Are you looking for someone?" I said.

He shook his head, grinning. "Who? Looking for Mr. Who. Have you seen Who?"

I said I hadn't seen him.

"Are you a nurse? You're not a nurse."

"The nurses are outside," I said. "Just down the hall."

He sat down next to Nicky. He rapped on Nicky's cast with his knuckles. "Hello, Mr. Who. Want a cigarette?"

Nicky was sitting very still. "No thanks. I don't smoke," he said in a small voice.

The boy laughed and stood up. He took out a pack of cigarettes and some matches. He lit a match and held it up close to Nicky's face for a moment. Then he lit his cigarette with it and stared down at us a while longer. "My name is Joseph," he said. "Do you like me?"

"I like you very much," I said.

He studied me a long time, almost as if I were someone he remembered. Then he threw the cigarette on the floor and drifted out.

Earlier that day, a boy from Nicky's room had gone home. When we got back there, we saw that the empty bed had been taken. A small suitcase stood beside it and a nurse was tucking in the blanket, making hospital corners. A little while later an intern led Joseph in, dressed in pajamas. "Mom," Nicky whispered. "They're putting him in *here*."

"Don't worry about it, honey," I told him.

I went out to the nurse on duty at the desk and made a complaint. They had no right to put a boy like that in with sick children. The children would be frightened, they had enough to contend with.

"It's the only bed available," the nurse said. "There's no private room for him now. Try to understand—he's sick, too, he needs care. We're going to watch the situation very carefully." I told her about the cigarettes and the matches. She said, "My God. We'll take care of that."

"Where does he come from, anyway?" I asked, and she told me the name of some institution upstate.

My telephone rang in the middle of the night. A nurse said, "Hold on. Your son insists on speaking to you."

Nicky got on the phone, all keyed up and out of breath. "Mom, you have to give me some advice. You know that guy Joseph?"

"What's the matter, Nick?" I said.

"Well, guess who he's picked to be his friend? He keeps getting off his bed and coming over to talk to me. It's too weird. I don't know what to say to him, so I just listen."

I wanted to go straight to the hospital and bring Nicky home. I said, "I guess you're doing the right thing, honey." I asked him if he was scared.

"Not so much. But it's hard, Mom."

"The next time he bothers you, just pretend you're asleep. Maybe he'll go to sleep, too."

"O.K.," Nicky said. "Can I call you again if I have to?"

I turned on the lights and sat up and read so I'd be sure to hear the phone. I called him back early in the morning. Joseph was sleeping, Nicky told me. The nurse had finally given him some kind of pill.

I went to the office as usual but I couldn't get much accomplished. Around three I gave up and went to the hospital. They were mopping the corridors and a game show was on in Room K. A housewife from Baltimore had just won a walk-in refrigerator and a trip for two to Bermuda. "Yay! It's the fat lady! I knew it!" a kid was yelling. I found Nicky propped up in bed painting a dragon, making each scale of its wing a different color. I looked around for Joseph, but I didn't see him.

"I'm concentrating, Mom," Nicky said.

"Is everything O.K.?" I whispered.

With a sigh he put down his brush. "Joseph is taking a walk. That's what Joseph does. But don't worry—he'll be back." Then he said, "Mom, sometimes Joseph seems almost all right. I ask him questions and he tells me very sad things."

"What kinds of things?"

"Stuff about his life. He doesn't go to school, you know. He lives in a hospital with grown-ups. He thinks he's going to live there a long time—maybe always."

When Nicky was little, I used to take him to nursery school on the way to work. It wasn't convenient, but I never minded. The place, as I recall it, was always yellow with sunlight. Green sweet-potato vines climbed up the windows and there were hamsters dozing in a cage. In the morning the teacher would put up the paintings the children had done the day before. You could smell crayons, soap, chalk dust. And all the little perfect children pulling off their coats had a shine about them, a newness. I was getting my divorce then. Sometimes the thought of that bright place would get me through the day, the idea that it was there and that Nicky was in it—as if I'd been allowed a small vision of harmony.

I thought of it again that afternoon at the hospital. I couldn't get back to it; it was lost, out of reach.

In the institution Joseph came from, they must have kept him very confined. In the children's wing he roamed the corridors. One day a nurse found him standing in a room he shouldn't have been in and had to bring him back to Room K. "Joseph, you stay in here," she admonished him. He walked up and down, banging his fists against the beds. He poked at little kids and chanted at the top of his voice, "Hey! Hey! What do you say today!"— which might have been a form of greeting.

He stopped by Nicky's bed and watched him paint the dragon. He pressed down on it with his thumb. "Hey, the mad monster game!"

"Wet paint, Joseph," warned Nicky.

Joseph took the dragon right off the night table. "Joseph, you creep!" Nicky yelled, his eyes filling with tears.

I went over to him and held out my hand. "I'm sorry. Nicky needs his dragon." It was odd how Joseph inspired politeness.

He stared down at my open palm as if puzzling over its significance. "That wasn't Nick's," he said.

Joseph stood by the door in the evening when the families came, when the bags of food were opened and the paper plates passed around. I went out to get Nicky a hamburger and a chocolate milkshake. When I came back, the room smelled of fried chicken and everyone was watching *The Odd Couple*. Joseph lay on his bed. He had put his arm over those red eyes, as if the light were hurting him.

Nicky tapped my arm. "Do you see that, Mom? No one came for him."

I said, "Maybe there's no one to come, Nicky."

"Someone should."

I handed him his milkshake. He peeled the paper off the straw and stuck it through the hole in the lid of the container. For a while he twirled it around. "Mom, I think you should get him something. Can you?"

I went down to the machines in the basement and got Joseph an ice-cream sandwich. I put it on his dinner tray. I said, "Joseph, this is for you." His arm stayed where it was. I touched his shoulder. "Do you like ice cream?" I said loudly.

Mrs. Rodriguez, who was sitting beside the next bed, talking to her son Emilio, whispered to me fiercely. "*Loco. Muy loco.* You understand? No good here. No good."

She wasn't wrong. I couldn't argue. The ice-cream sandwich was melting, oozing through its paper wrapping. I went back to Nicky and took him for his walk.

Later, out in the corridor, we saw Joseph. He took a swipe at Nicky's cast as we passed him and yelled after us, "Dragon Man and the Mom!" There was chocolate smeared all over his mouth.

The next day I bought an extra egg roll at the takeout place. It seemed I'd have to keep on with what I'd started, though I had no idea how much Joseph would remember. I kept thinking of him during visiting hours, lying there alone. What I really wanted was to walk into Room K and find him gone, some other arrangement made, so I could remove him from the list of everything that troubled me.

When I got to the hospital, some of the other parents were there, earlier than usual. They were standing in the corridor near the head nurse's desk. One of the mothers had her arm around Mrs. Rodriguez, who was wiping her eyes with some Kleenex.

They gestured to me to join them. "The supervisor is coming to talk to us about our problem," someone said.

"What happened?" I asked Mrs. Rodriguez.

She blew her nose; it seemed hard for her to speak. "Joseph! Joseph! Who do you think?"

Joseph had somehow gotten hold of some cigarettes and matches. He had held a lighted match near Emilio's eyes. "To burn my son!" cried Mrs. Rodriguez. Emilio was only eight, a frail little boy with a broken collarbone.

I put down my shopping bag and waited with the others. When the supervisor came, I spoke up, too. Irresponsibility, negligence, lack of consideration—the words came so fluently, as if from the mouth of the kind of person I'd always distrusted, some person with very sure opinions about rightness and wrongness and what was good for society.

The supervisor already had his computer working on the situation. "Just give us an hour," he said.

In Room K an orderly had been posted to keep an eye on Joseph. He'd made Joseph lie down on his bed. The children were subdued; they talked in murmurs. Even the television was on low, until a parent turned up the volume. There was an effort to create the atmosphere of the usual picnic.

Nicky looked wide-eyed, pale. "Did you hear what Joseph did to Emilio?"

I leaned over him and pushed the wet hair off his forehead. "Nicky, don't worry about Joseph anymore. They're going to move him in a little while to a room by himself."

I started opening containers from the Chinese takeout place, and there was the egg roll I'd meant to give Joseph. I angled my chair so that I wouldn't have to see him. It was as though life were full of nothing but intolerable choices.

"Eat something," I said to Nicky.

In a loud, dazed voice, a kid in the room was talking on the phone. "Hey, Grandma, guess who this is? I'm gonna see you soon, you bet. I'm gonna get on a plane and fly. Yeah, I'll bring my little bathing suit. Gonna see you, Grandma. Gonna see you."

"Mom," Nicky whispered. "Can you hear him?"

We were there when he left, everyone was there. Two nurses came in and walked over to him. "Joseph, it's time to get moving now," one of them said. "Let's get your personal things together."

They got him out of bed very quickly. One took his suitcase;

the other had him by the arm. The orderly positioned himself in front of them. Nicky turned his face into the pillow when they started walking between the rows of beds. I was holding his hand and he kept squeezing my fingers, not letting go.

As he passed by us, Joseph broke away from the nurse. For a moment he loomed over Nicky and me. He kissed me on the top of the head. Then they took him out into the long, dim corridors.

When Nicky was thirteen, he said he couldn't remember much about his childhood. He wanted to, but he couldn't. The whole subject made him very angry. "What I remember," he said, "is Joseph."

Nicky got well but he got old.

LOVES ME,
LOVES ME NOT

·2·

Tatyana Tolstaya

"The other kids get to go out by themselves, but we have to go with Maryvanna!"

"When you get to be seven, you'll get to go out alone. And you don't say 'disgusting' about an elderly person. You should be grateful to Maria Ivanovna that she spends time with you."

"She doesn't watch us, on purpose! And we're going to get hit by a car, I'm sure! And in the park she talks to all the old women and complains about us. And she says: 'spirit of contradiction.' "

"But you really do do everything to spite her."

"And I will! I'm going to tell all those stupid old women 'how *don't* you do' and '*bad*-bye.' "

"Shame on you! You must respect the old! Don't be rude, listen to what they say: they're older and know more than you."

"I do listen! All Maryvanna talks about is her uncle."

"And what does she say about him?"

"That he hanged himself because he had a bad bladder. And that before that he was run over by the wheel of fortune. Because he was in debt and had crossed the street improperly."

. . . Small, heavyset, and short of breath, Maryvanna hates us and we hate her. We hate the hat with a veil, the holey glove, the dried pieces of "sand cookies" she feeds to the pigeons, and we stamp our feet at those pigeons to scare them off. Maryvanna takes us out every day for four hours, reads books to us, and tries to converse in French—basically, that's what she is hired for. Because our own dear beloved Nanny Grusha, who lives with us, doesn't know any foreign languages, and doesn't go outside anymore, and has trouble getting around. Pushkin loved her very much, too, and wrote about her and called her "My ancient dove." And he didn't write anything about Maryvanna. And if he had, he'd have written "My fat piggy."

But what's amazing—absolutely impossible to imagine—is that Maryvanna was the beloved nanny of a now grownup girl. And Maryvanna brings up that girl, Katya, every day. She didn't stick out her tongue, didn't pick her nose, ate everything on her plate, and hugged and kissed Maryvanna—she was crazy.

At night, in bed, my sister and I make up conversations between Maryvanna and the obedient Katya.

"Finish up the worms, dear Katya."

"With pleasure, sweet Maryvanna."

"Eat a marinated frog, child."

"I already have. Please give me some more mashed mice."

In the park that Maryvanna calls "the boulevard," pale Leningrad girls dig in the darkened autumn sand, listening to adults talk. Maryvanna, quickly making the acquaintance of some old lady in a hat, takes out her stiff old photographs: herself and Uncle leaning against a grand piano and behind them a waterfall. Could that white airy creature in lace gloves be buried somewhere in the bowels of that gasping fat? "He was father and mother to me and wanted me to call him simply George. He educated me, he brought me out into society. Those pearls—you can't see them well here—were a gift from him. He loved me madly, madly. See how handsome he is here? And here we're in Piatigorsk. That's my friend Yulya. And here we're having tea in the garden."

"Marvelous pictures. Is that Yulya too?"

"No, that's Zinaida. George's girlfriend. She's the one who bankrupted him. He was a gambler."

"Oh, so that's it."

"Yes. I should throw away this picture, but I can't. It's all I have left of him. And his poems—he was a poet."

"You don't say."

"Yes, yes, a wonderful poet. There aren't any like him nowadays. So romantic, a bit of a mystic. . . ."

The old lady, silly twit, listens with her mouth open and smiles dreamily, looking at me. She shouldn't stare at me. I stick out my tongue. Maryvanna, shutting her eyes in shame, whispers hatefully, "Hideous creature!"

That night she'll read her uncle's poetry to me again:

Nanny, who screamed so loudly outside,
Flashing past the window,
Creaking the porch door,
Sighing under the bed?

Sleep, don't worry,
God will watch over you,

Those were ravens calling,
Flying to the cemetery.

Nanny, who touched the candle,
Who's scratching in the corner,
Who's stretched in a black shadow
On the floor from the door?

Sleep, child, don't worry,
The door is strong, the fence is high,
The thief won't escape the block
The axe will thud in the night.

Nanny, who's breathing down my back,
Who's invisible and climbing
Ever closer up my
Crumpled bed sheet?

Oh child, don't frown
Wipe your tears and don't cry.
The ropes are pulled tight,
The executioner knows his job.

Well, after a poem like that, who could find the courage to lower her feet from the bed to, say, use the chamber pot? Everybody knows that under the bed, near the wall, is the Snake: in lace-up shoes, cap, gloves, motorcycle goggles, and holding a crook in his hand. The Snake isn't there during the day, but he coagulates by night from twilight stuff and waits very quietly: who will dare lower a leg? And out comes the crook! He's unlikely to eat you, but he'll pull you in and shove you under the plinth, and you'll fall endlessly, under the floor, between the dusty partitions. The room is guarded by other species of nocturnal creatures: the fragile and translucent Dry One, weak but terrible, who stands all night in the closet and in the morning goes into the cracks. Behind the ungluing wallpaper are Indrik and Hindrik: one is greenish and the other gray, and they both run fast and have many feet. And in the corner on the floor is a rectangle of copper grating, and under that a black abyss: "ventilation." It's dangerous to approach even in the daytime; the Eyes stare out, without blinking. Yes, the most horrible is the nameless one who is always behind me, almost touching my hair (the uncle is witness). Many times he plans to reach out, but he keeps missing his chance and slowly, sadly, lowers his incorporeal hands. I wrap myself tight in the blanket, only my nose sticking out—they don't attack from the front.

Having frightened me with her uncle's poems, Maryvanna goes back to her place in a communal apartment, where, besides her, live Iraida Anatolyevna with her diabetes, and dusty Sonya, and the Badylovs, who were deprived of parental rights, and the hanged uncle. . . . And she'll be back tomorrow if we don't get sick. We often get sick.

Many times, 104-degree flus would scream and bang at my ears, banging on red drums, surrounding me from eight sides and, swirling wildly, show a film of delirium, always the same: a wooden honeycomb filling up with three-digit numbers; more numbers, louder noise, more urgent drums—all the cells will be filled now, just a little time left. My heart can't take anymore, it'll burst—but it's been postponed, I've been released, forgiven, the honeycomb taken away, a round loaf of bread with a nasty smile runs along an airfield on spindly legs—and it grows quiet . . . except for tiny planes like dots of bugs which scurry along the pink sky, carrying away the black cloak of fever in their claws. It's passed.

Shake the crumbs from my sheet, cool my pillow, smooth my blanket so that there isn't a single wrinkle, otherwise the planes with claws will be back. Without thoughts, without desires, I lie on my back, in the coolness, in semidarkness—a half-hour's breather between two attacks of the drummers. A fan of light crosses the ceiling from corner to corner, then another fan, and another. The cars have their headlights on, the evening has descended, a rug of light has been pushed under the door into the next room: they're having tea there, the orange lampshade is glowing, and one of the adults is making forbidden braids in its fringe, "ruining it." Before the planes come back, I can leave my corporeal shell pounding with fever among the cast-iron sheets and mentally slip beyond the door—long nightgown, cold slippers—sit invisibly at the table (I'd forgotten this cup over the week) and, squinting, travel by gaze along the orange humps of the shade. The lampshade is young and skittish, it isn't used to me yet—Papa and I got it only recently at the flea market.

Oh, there were so many people there, so many owners of quilted cotton and plush jackets, of brown Orenburg scarves. And they all gabbled and bustled and shook blue diagonal remnants before

Papa's face and shoved sturdy black felt boots in his nose. Such treasures there! And Papa: he blew it, missed out, he didn't bring back anything but the lampshade. He should have bought up everything: vases and saucers and flowered scarves, stuffed owls and porcelain pigs and rag rugs. We could have used the pussycat banks, and whistles and paper flowers—poppies with inked cotton in their centers—and paper fans, red and green trembling jabots on two sticks: you turn the sticks out and the fringed, impermanent lace shakes, turn them some more and it folds back up and disappears. Marvelous oilcloth paintings flickered: Lermontov on a gray wolf snatching up a swooning beauty; or him again wearing a caftan and aiming from bushes at swans with gold crowns; or doing something on a horse . . . but Papa dragged me on, farther, farther, past invalids with lollipops, to the lampshade row.

A man grabbed Papa's leather sleeve. "Master, sell me your coat!"

Don't bother us with nonsense, we need a lampshade, we have to get over there; I turn my head, I glimpse brooms, baskets, painted wooden eggs, a piglet—watch it, that's it, let's go back. Where is it? Oh, there. We push our way back through the crowd, Papa has the lampshade, still dark and silent, but already a member of the family: it's ours now, one of us, we'll come to love it. And it waited quietly: where was it being taken? It didn't know that time would pass and it, once the favorite, would be mocked, cast down, discarded, exiled, and a new favorite would take its place: a fashionable white five-petaled "shorty." And then, insulted, mutilated, betrayed, it would go through the last mortification: it would serve as a crinoline in a children's play and then plunge forever into wastebin oblivion. *Sic transit gloria mundi.*

"Papa, buy me that, please."

"What is it?"

A merry, bundled-up peasant woman, glad to see a customer, is spinning in the cold, hopping up and down, stamping her felt boots, shaking the chopped-off golden braid as thick as a hawser.

"Buy it!"

"Papa, buy it!"

"Have you lost your mind? A stranger's hair! Don't even touch it—there are lice."

Phooey, how horrible! I freeze: and really, there they are, enormous lice, each the size of a sparrow, with attentive eyes and shaggy legs and claws clutch the sheet, climb on the blanket, clap hands, louder and louder. . . . The delirium hums again, the fever screams, the fiery wheels spin: *flu!*

. . . A dark urban winter, a cold stream of air from the corridor: one of the adults is hauling in a huge striped sack of firewood to heat up the round brown water heater in the bathroom. Scat, you're underfoot, get out of the way! Hurrah, we're going to have baths today! A wooden railing is placed across the tub: heavy chipped basins, pitchers of hot water, the sharp scent of pitch soap, soaked wrinkled skin on the hands, the steamy mirror, stuffiness, the clean, ironed underwear, and *whizzz*, run down the cold corridor, and *plop!* into fresh sheets: heaven!

"Nanny, sing a song."

Nanny Grusha is terribly old. She was born in a village and then was brought up by a kindly countess. Her gray head holds thousands of stories about talking bears, and blue snakes that cure people with tuberculosis by climbing in through the chimney during the night, about Pushkin and Lermontov. And she knows for a fact that if you eat raw dough you'll fly away. And when she was five—like me—the tsar sent her with a secret package to Lenin at Smolny Institute. There was a note in the package: "Surrender!" And Lenin replied: "Never!" And shot off a cannon.

Nanny sings:

> *The Terek flows over rocks,*
> *Splashing with a stagger . . .*
> *An evil Chechen crawls ashore,*
> *Sharpening his dagger . . .*

The curtain trembles on the window, a threateningly shining moon appears from behind a winter cloud; from the murky Karpovka Canal a black Chechen climbs onto the icy shore, shaggy, baring his teeth. . . .

"Sleep, my darling, sleep tight."

. . . Yes, things aren't going too well with Maryvanna. Should I be sent to a French group? They go out for walks, and get a snack, and play Lotto. Of course, send me. Hurrah! But that evening, the Frenchwoman returns the black sheep to Mother.

"Madame, your child is completely unprepared. She stuck her tongue out at the other children, tore up pictures, and threw up her farina. Come back next year. Good-bye. *Au revoir.*"

"*Bad*-bye!" I shout, dragged away by my disappointed mother. "Eat your own crummy farina! No *revoir!*"

("Is that so? Well, just get out of here! Take your lousy kid!"—"Who needs it! Don't think you're so hot, madame.")

"Forgive us, please, she's really quite difficult."

"It's all right, I understand."

What a burden you are!

. . . Let's take colored pencils. If you lick the red, it gives a specially smooth, satiny color. Of course, not for long. Well, enough for Maryvanna's face. Put a huge wart here. Fine. Now the blue: a balloon and another balloon. And two columns. A black pancake on her head. In her hands, a purse; but I don't know how to draw one. There. Maryvanna's done. She's sitting on a peeling vernal bench, her galoshes spread and planted firmly, eyes shut, singing:

> *I was going ho-o-ome . . .*
> *My heart was fu-ull . . .*

Why don't you go home? Why don't you go to your precious Katya?

"Georges always bought halvah for me at Abrikosov's—remember?"

"Yes, yes, of course. . . ."

"Everything was dainty, delicate. . . ."

"Don't I know it. . . ."

"And now. Take these: I thought they were intellectuals! But they cut their bread in huge chunks."

"Yes, yes, yes . . . and I . . ."

"I always used the formal 'you' with my mother. I showed respect. But these ones, well, all right, I'm a stranger to them, but their parents, at least their parents, but no . . . nothing. . . . And they grab at the table. Like this! With their hands, their hands."

Lord! How long must we bear each other?

And then they shut the little park to let it dry out. And we simply walk the streets. And one day suddenly a tall thin girl— a white mosquito—throws herself screeching on Maryvanna's neck, weeping, and caressing her shaking red face!

"My nanny! My dearest nanny!"

And look: that lump, weeping and gasping, also grabs the girl, and they—strangers—right here before my eyes, are both shouting and weeping over their stupid love.

"My dearest nanny!"

Hey, girl, what's the matter with you? Rub your eyes! It's

Maryvanna. Look, look, she has a wart. It's our Maryvanna, our laughingstock: stupid, old, fat, silly.

But does love know that?

. . . Get out of here, girl! Don't hang around here . . . with all that goopy stuff. . . . I push on, angry and tired. I'm much better than that girl. But Maryvanna doesn't love me like her. The world is unfair. The world is upside down. I don't understand anything. I want to go home! But Maryvanna has this radiant look, holds me tight by the hand, and puffs along ahead.

"My feet hurt!"

"We'll make a circle and head back . . . soon, soon. . . ."

Unfamiliar parts. Twilight. The light air rose and is suspended over the houses; the dark air came out and is standing in the doorways and arches, in the holes of the street. An hour of depression for adults, of depression and fear for children. I'm all alone in the world, Mama has lost me, we're going to get lost any second now. I'm in a panic and I clutch Maryvanna's cold hand.

"That's where I live. There's my window—second from the corner."

Disembodied heads frown and open their mouths—they'll eat me—under every window. The heads are horrible, and the damp darkness of the archway is creepy, and Maryvanna is not family. High up, in the window, nose pressed against the dark glass, the hanged uncle waits, running his hands over the glass, peering. Bug off, uncle! You'll climb out of the Karpovka at night, disguised as an evil Chechen, grin under the moonlight—eyes rolled back into your head—and you'll run real fast on all fours over the cobblestone street, across the courtyard to the front door, into the heavy, dense dark, with bare hands up the icy steps, along the square staircase spiral, higher, higher, to our door. . . .

Hurry, hurry home! To Nanny! O Nanny Grusha! Darling! Hurry to you! I've forgotten your face. I'll huddle against your dark skirts, and your warm old hands will warm my frozen, lost, bewildered heart.

Nanny will unwind my scarf, unfasten the button digging into my flesh, and take me into the cave warmth of the nursery, where there's a red night-light, where there are soft mountains of beds, and my bitter childish tears will drip into the light blue plate of self-important kasha that praises itself. And seeing that, Nanny will also cry, and sit close, and hug me, and won't ask but understand with her heart, the way an animal understands an animal, an old person a child, and a wordless creature its fellow.

Lord, the world is so frightening and hostile, the poor homeless, inexperienced soul huddling in the square in the night wind. Who was so cruel, who filled me with love and hate, fear and depression, pity and shame, but didn't give me words: stole speech, sealed my mouth, put on iron padlocks, and threw away the keys.

Maryvanna, having had her fill of tea and feeling cheerier, drops by the nursery to say good night. Why is this child crying? Come on, come on. What happened? Cut yourself? Stomachache? Punished?

(No, no, that's not it. Shut up, you don't understand! It's just that in the light blue plate, on the bottom the geese and swans are going to catch the running children, and the girl's hands are chipped off and she can't cover her head or hold her brother.)

"Come on, wipe those tears, shame on you, you're a big girl now! Finish up your plate. And I'll read you a poem."

Elbowing Maryvanna aside, lifting his top hat and squinting, Uncle George comes forward:

> *Not white tulips*
> *In bridal lace—*
> *It's the foam of the ocean*
> *On distant shores.*
>
> *The ship creaks*
> *Its ancient wood.*
> *Unheard-of pleasures*
> *Beyond the foam.*
>
> *Not black tulips—*
> *It's women in the night.*
> *Noon passions*
> *Are hot at midnight too.*
>
> *Roll out the barrel!*
> *The native women are fine!*
> *We've waited for this night—*
> *Let's find our pleasure!*
>
> *Not crimson tulips*
> *Floating on his chest—*
> *The captain's camisole*
> *Has three holes in front;*

The merry sailors
Grin on the ocean floor . . .
The women in that country
Had beautiful hair.

"What horrors at bedtime for the child," grumbles Nanny.
The uncle bows and leaves. Maryvanna shuts the door behind
herself: until tomorrow.

Go away all of you, leave me alone, you don't understand
anything.

A prickly ball spins in my chest, and unspoken words bubble
on my lips, smeared by tears. The red night-light nods. Why, she
has a fever, someone far far away cries, but he can't shout over
the noise of wings, geese and swans attacking from the noisy sky.

. . . The kitchen door is shut. The sun breaks through the frosted
glass. Noon spills gold onto the parquet floor. Silence. Beyond
the door Maryvanna weeps, and complains about us.

"I can't take anymore! What is this—day after day, it gets worse
. . . contrary, spiteful. . . . I've lived a hard life, always among
strangers, and I've been treated in many ways, of course. . . . No,
the terms—I'm not complaining, the terms are fine, but at my age
. . . and with my health. . . . Where does that spirit of contradiction, that hostility, come from. . . . I wanted a little poetry, lof-
tiness. . . . Useless . . . I can't take anymore. . . ."

She's leaving us.

Maryvanna is leaving us. Maryvanna blows her nose into a
tiny handkerchief. She powders her red nose, stares deeply into
the mirror, hesitates, seems to be seeking something in its inaccessible, sealed universe. And really, deep in its twilight forgotten
curtains stir, candle flames flicker, and the pale uncle comes out
with a black piece of paper in his hands.

Princess Rose grew weary of life
And ended it at sunset.
She wet her lips sadly
With poisoned wine.

And the prince froze like a statue
In the grim power of sorrow,
And the retinue whispers condolences
That she was innocent.

The porphyry parents
Had their heralds announce
That the grieving populace
Lower flags in the towers.

I enter the funeral procession
As a funereal violin,
I place narcissus on the princess's
Grave with a melancholy smile.

And pretending sorrow,
I lower my eyes, so that they cannot see:
What a wedding awaits me!
You've never seen its like.

The chandeliers are covered with deathly white netting, and the mirrors with black. Maryvanna pulls down her heavy veil, gathers the ruins of her purse with trembling hands, turns and leaves, her worn shoes scuffing over the doorsill, beyond the limit, forever out of our lives.

Spring is still weak, but the snow is gone, and the remaining black crusts lie only in stone corners. It's warm in the sunshine.

Farewell, Maryvanna!

We're ready for summer.

TRANSLATED BY ANTONINA W. BOUIS

GRYPHON

·❧·

Charles Baxter

On Wednesday afternoon, between the geography lesson on ancient Egypt's hand-operated irrigation system and an art project that involved drawing a model city next to a mountain, our fourth-grade teacher, Mr. Hibler, developed a cough. This cough began with a series of muffled throat-clearings and progressed to propulsive noises contained within Mr. Hibler's closed mouth. "Listen to him," Carol Peterson whispered to me. "He's gonna blow up." Mr. Hibler's laughter—dazed and infrequent—sounded a bit like his cough, but as we worked on our model cities we would look up, thinking he was enjoying a joke, and see Mr. Hibler's face turning red, his cheeks puffed out. This was not laughter. Twice he bent over, and his loose tie, like a plumb line, hung down straight from his neck as he exploded himself into a Kleenex. He would excuse himself, then go on coughing. "I'll bet you a dime," Carol Peterson whispered, "we get a substitute tomorrow."

Carol sat at the desk in front of mine and was a bad person—when she thought no one was looking she would blow her nose on notebook paper, then crumple it up and throw it into the wastebasket—but at times of crisis she spoke the truth. I knew I'd lose the dime.

"No deal," I said.

When Mr. Hibler stood us in formation at the door just prior to the final bell, he was almost incapable of speech. "I'm sorry, boys and girls," he said. "I seem to be coming down with something."

"I hope you feel better tomorrow, Mr. Hibler," Bobby Kryzanowicz, the faultless brown-noser, said, and I heard Carol Peterson's evil giggle. Then Mr. Hibler opened the door and we walked out to the buses, a clique of us starting noisily to hawk and raugh as soon as we thought we were a few feet beyond Mr. Hibler's earshot.

Since Five Oaks was a rural community, and in Michigan, the supply of substitute teachers was limited to the town's unemployed community college graduates, a pool of about four mothers. These ladies fluttered, provided easeful class days, and nervously covered material we had mastered weeks earlier. Therefore it was a surprise when a woman we had never seen came into the class the next day, carrying a purple purse, a checkerboard lunchbox, and a few books. She put the books on one side of Mr. Hibler's desk and the lunchbox on the other, next to the Voice of Music phonograph. Three of us in the back of the room were playing with Heever, the chameleon that lived in a terrarium and on one of the plastic drapes, when she walked in.

She clapped her hands at us. "Little boys," she said, "why are you bent over together like that?" She didn't wait for us to answer. "Are you tormenting an animal? Put it back. Please sit down at your desks. I want no cabals this time of the day." We just stared at her. "Boys," she repeated, "I asked you to sit down."

I put the chameleon in his terrarium and felt my way to my desk, never taking my eyes off the woman. With white and green chalk, she had started to draw a tree on the left side of the blackboard. She didn't look usual. Furthermore, her tree was outsized, disproportionate, for some reason.

"This room needs a tree," she said, with one line drawing the suggestion of a leaf. "A large, leafy, shady, deciduous . . . oak."

Her fine, light hair had been done up in what I would learn years later was called a chignon, and she wore gold-rimmed glasses whose lenses seemed to have the faintest blue tint. Harold Knardahl, who sat across from me, whispered, "Mars," and I nodded slowly, savoring the imminent weirdness of the day. The substitute drew another branch with an extravagant arm gesture, then turned around and said, "Good morning. I don't believe I said good morning to all of you yet."

Facing us, she was no special age—an adult is an adult—but her face had two prominent lines, descending vertically from the sides of her mouth to her chin. I knew where I had seen those lines before: *Pinocchio*. They were marionette lines. "You may stare at me," she said to us, as a few more kids from the last bus came into the room, their eyes fixed on her, "for a few more seconds, until the bell rings. Then I will permit no more staring. Looking I will permit. Staring, no. It is impolite to stare, and a sign of bad breeding. You cannot make a social effort while staring."

Harold Knardahl did not glance at me, or nudge, but I heard him whisper "Mars" again, trying to get more mileage out of his single joke with the kids who had just come in.

When everyone was seated, the substitute teacher finished her tree, put down her chalk fastidiously on the phonograph, brushed her hands, and faced us. "Good morning," she said. "I am Miss Ferenczi, your teacher for the day. I am fairly new to your community, and I don't believe any of you know me. I will therefore start by telling you a story about myself."

While we settled back, she launched into her tale. She said her grandfather had been a Hungarian prince; her mother had been born in some place called Flanders, had been a pianist, and had played concerts for people Miss Ferenczi referred to as "crowned heads." She gave us a knowing look. "Grieg," she said, "the Norwegian master, wrote a concerto for piano that was . . ."— she paused—"my mother's triumph at her debut concert in London." Her eyes searched the ceiling. Our eyes followed. Nothing up there but ceiling tile. "For reasons that I shall not go into, my family's fortunes took us to Detroit, then north to dreadful Saginaw, and now here I am in Five Oaks, as your substitute teacher, for today, Thursday, October the eleventh. I believe it will be a good day: all the forecasts coincide. We shall start with your reading lesson. Take out your reading book. I believe it is called *Broad Horizons*, or something along those lines."

Jeannie Vermeesch raised her hand. Miss Ferenczi nodded at her. "Mr. Hibler always starts the day with the Pledge of Allegiance," Jeannie whined.

"Oh, does he? In that case," Miss Ferenczi said, "you must know it *very* well by now, and we certainly need not spend our time on it. No, no allegiance-pledging on the premises today, by my reckoning. Not with so much sunlight coming into the room. A pledge does not suit my mood." She glanced at her watch. "Time *is* flying. Take out *Broad Horizons*."

She disappointed us by giving us an ordinary lesson, complete with vocabulary and drills, comprehension questions, and recitation. She didn't seem to care for the material, however. She sighed every few minutes and rubbed her glasses with a frilly handkerchief that she withdrew, magician-style, from her left sleeve.

After reading we moved on to arithmetic. It was my favorite time of the morning, when the lazy autumn sunlight dazzled its way through ribbons of clouds past the windows on the east side of the classroom and crept across the linoleum floor. On the playground the first group of children, the kindergartners, were running on the quack grass just beyond the monkey bars. We were doing multiplication tables. Miss Ferenczi had made John Wazny stand up at his desk in the front row. He was supposed to go through the tables of six. From where I was sitting, I could smell the Vitalis soaked into John's plastered hair. He was doing fine until he came to six times eleven and six times twelve. "Six times eleven," he said, "is sixty-eight. Six times twelve is . . ." He put his fingers to his head, quickly and secretly sniffed his fingertips, and said, ". . . seventy-two." Then he sat down.

"Fine," Miss Ferenczi said. "Well, now. That was very good."

"Miss Ferenczi!" One of the Eddy twins was waving her hand desperately in the air. "Miss Ferenczi! Miss Ferenczi!"

"Yes?"

"John said that six times eleven is sixty-eight and you said he was right!"

"*Did* I?" She gazed at the class with a jolly look breaking across her marionette's face. "Did I say that? Well, what *is* six times eleven?"

"It's sixty-six!"

She nodded. "Yes. So it is. But, and I know some people will not entirely agree with me, at some times it is sixty-eight."

"When? When is it sixty-eight?"

We were all waiting.

"In higher mathematics, which you children do not yet understand, six times eleven can be considered to be sixty-eight." She laughed through her nose. "In higher mathematics numbers are . . . more fluid. The only thing a number does is contain a certain amount of something. Think of water. A cup is not the only way to measure a certain amount of water, is it?" We were staring, shaking our heads. "You could use saucepans or thimbles. In either case, the water *would be the same.* Perhaps," she started again, "it would be better for you to think that six times eleven is sixty-eight only when I am in the room."

"Why is it sixty-eight," Mark Poole asked, "when you're in the room?"

"Because it's more interesting that way," she said, smiling very rapidly behind her blue-tinted glasses. "Besides, I'm your substitute teacher, am I not?" We all nodded. "Well, then, think of six times eleven equals sixty-eight as a substitute fact."

"A substitute fact?"

"Yes." Then she looked at us carefully. "Do you think," she asked, "that anyone is going to be hurt by a substitute fact?"

We looked back at her.

"Will the plants on the windowsill be hurt?" We glanced at them. There were sensitive plants thriving in a green plastic tray, and several wilted ferns in small clay pots. "Your dogs and cats, or your moms and dads?" She waited. "So," she concluded, "what's the problem?"

"But it's wrong," Janice Weber said, "isn't it?"

"What's your name, young lady?"

"Janice Weber."

"And you think it's wrong, Janice?"

"I was just asking."

"Well, all right. You were just asking. I think we've spent enough time on this matter by now, don't you, class? You are free to think what you like. When your teacher, Mr. Hibler, returns, six times eleven will be sixty-six again, you can rest assured. And it will be that for the rest of your lives in Five Oaks. Too bad, eh?" She raised her eyebrows and glinted herself at us. "But for now, it wasn't. So much for that. Let us go on to your assigned problems for today, as painstakingly outlined, I see, in Mr. Hibler's lesson plan. Take out a sheet of paper and write your names on the upper left-hand corner."

For the next half hour we did the rest of our arithmetic problems. We handed them in and then went on to spelling, my worst subject. Spelling always came before lunch. We were taking spelling dictation and looking at the clock. "Thorough," Miss Ferenczi said. "Boundary." She walked in the aisles between the desks, holding the spelling book open and looking down at our papers. "Balcony." I clutched my pencil. Somehow, the way she said those words, they seemed foreign, mis-voweled and mis-consonanted. I stared down at what I had spelled. *Balconie.* I turned the pencil upside down and erased my mistake. *Balconey.* That looked better, but still incorrect. I cursed the world of spelling and tried erasing it again and saw the paper beginning to wear away. *Balkony.* Suddenly I felt a hand on my shoulder.

"I don't like that word either," Miss Ferenczi whispered, bent over, her mouth near my ear. "It's ugly. My feeling is, if you don't like a word, you don't have to use it." She straightened up, leaving behind a slight odor of Clorets.

At lunchtime we went out to get our trays of sloppy joes,

peaches in heavy syrup, coconut cookies, and milk, and brought them back to the classroom, where Miss Ferenczi was sitting at the desk, eating a brown sticky thing she had unwrapped from tightly rubber-banded waxed paper. "Miss Ferenczi," I said, raising my hand. "You don't have to eat with us. You can eat with the other teachers. There's a teachers' lounge," I ended up, "next to the principal's office."

"No, thank you," she said. "I prefer it here."

"We've got a room monitor," I said. "Mrs. Eddy." I pointed to where Mrs. Eddy, Joyce and Judy's mother, sat silently at the back of the room, doing her knitting.

"That's fine," Miss Ferenczi said. "But I shall continue to eat here, with you children. I prefer it," she repeated.

"How come?" Wayne Razmer asked without raising his hand.

"I talked to the other teachers before class this morning," Miss Ferenczi said, biting into her brown food. "There was a great rattling of the words for the fewness of the ideas. I didn't care for their brand of hilarity. I don't like ditto-machine jokes."

"Oh," Wayne said.

"What's that you're eating?" Maxine Sylvester asked, twitching her nose. "Is it food?"

"It most certainly *is* food. It's a stuffed fig. I had to drive almost down to Detroit to get it. I also brought some smoked sturgeon. And this," she said, lifting some green leaves out of her lunchbox, "is raw spinach, cleaned this morning."

"Why're you eating raw spinach?" Maxine asked.

"It's good for you," Miss Ferenczi said. "More stimulating than soda pop or smelling salts." I bit into my sloppy joe and stared blankly out the window. An almost invisible moon was faintly silvered in the daytime autumn sky. "As far as food is concerned," Miss Ferenczi was saying, "you have to shuffle the pack. Mix it up. Too many people eat . . . well, never mind."

"Miss Ferenczi," Carol Peterson said, "what are we going to do this afternoon?"

"Well," she said, looking down at Mr. Hibler's lesson plan, "I see that your teacher, Mr. Hibler, has you scheduled for a unit on the Egyptians." Carol groaned. "Yesssss," Miss Ferenczi continued, "that is what we will do: the Egyptians. A remarkable people. Almost as remarkable as the Americans. But not quite." She lowered her head, did her quick smile, and went back to eating her spinach.

After noon recess we came back into the classroom and saw that Miss Ferenczi had drawn a pyramid on the blackboard close to her oak tree. Some of us who had been playing baseball were messing around in the back of the room, dropping the bats and gloves into the playground box, and Ray Schontzeler had just slugged me when I heard Miss Ferenczi's high-pitched voice, quavering with emotion. "Boys," she said, "come to order right this minute and take your seats. I do not wish to waste a minute of class time. Take out your geography books." We trudged to our desks and, still sweating, pulled out *Distant Lands and Their People.* "Turn to page forty-two." She waited for thirty seconds, then looked over at Kelly Munger. "Young man," she said, "why are you still fossicking in your desk?"

Kelly looked as if his foot had been stepped on. "Why am I what?"

"Why are you . . . burrowing in your desk like that?"

"I'm lookin' for the book, Miss Ferenczi."

Bobby Kryzanowicz, the faultless brown-noser who sat in the first row by choice, softly said, "His name is Kelly Munger. He can't ever find his stuff. He always does that."

"I don't care what his name is, especially after lunch," Miss Ferenczi said. *"Where is your book?"*

"I just found it." Kelly was peering into his desk and with both hands pulled at the book, shoveling along in front of it several pencils and crayons, which fell into his lap and then to the floor.

"I hate a mess," Miss Ferenczi said. "I hate a mess in a desk or a mind. It's . . . unsanitary. You wouldn't want your house at home to look like your desk at school, now, would you?" She didn't wait for an answer. "I should think not. A house at home should be as neat as human hands can make it. What were we talking about? Egypt. Page forty-two. I note from Mr. Hibler's lesson plan that you have been discussing the modes of Egyptian irrigation. Interesting, in my view, but not so interesting as what we are about to cover. The pyramids, and Egyptian slave labor. A plus on one side, a minus on the other." We had our books open to page forty-two, where there was a picture of a pyramid, but Miss Ferenczi wasn't looking at the book. Instead, she was staring at some object just outside the window.

"Pyramids," Miss Ferenczi said, still looking past the window. "I want you to think about pyramids. And what was inside. The bodies of the pharaohs, of course, and their attendant treasures. Scrolls. Perhaps," Miss Ferenczi said, her face gleeful but unsmiling, "these scrolls were novels for the pharaohs, helping them to pass the time in their long voyage through the centuries. But then, I am joking." I was looking at the lines on Miss Ferenczi's skin. "Pyramids," Miss Ferenczi went on, "were the repositories of special cosmic powers. The nature of a pyramid is to guide cosmic energy forces into a concentrated point. The Egyptians knew that; we have generally forgotten it. Did you know," she asked, walking to the side of the room so that she was standing by the coat closet, "that George Washington had Egyptian blood, from his grandmother? Certain features of the Constitution of the United States are notable for their Egyptian ideas."

Without glancing down at the book, she began to talk about the movement of souls in Egyptian religion. She said that when people die, their souls return to Earth in the form of carpenter ants or walnut trees, depending on how they behaved—"well or ill"—in life. She said that the Egyptians believed that people act the way they do because of magnetism produced by tidal forces in the solar system, forces produced by the sun and by its "planetary ally," Jupiter. Jupiter, she said, was a planet, as we had been told, but had "certain properties of stars." She was speaking very fast. She said that the Egyptians were great explorers and conquerors. She said that the greatest of all the conquerors, Genghis Khan, had had forty horses and forty young women killed on the site of his grave. We listened. No one tried to stop her. "I myself have been in Egypt," she said, "and have witnessed much dust and many brutalities." She said that an old man in Egypt who worked for a circus had personally shown her an animal in a cage, a monster, half bird and half lion. She said that this monster was called a gryphon and that she had heard about them but never seen them until she traveled to the outskirts of Cairo. She wrote the word out on the blackboard in large capital letters: GRYPHON. She said that Egyptian astronomers had discovered the planet Saturn but had not seen its rings. She said that the Egyptians were the first to discover that dogs, when they are ill, will not drink from rivers, but wait for rain, and hold their jaws open to catch it.

"She lies."

We were on the school bus home. I was sitting next to Carl Whiteside, who had bad breath and a huge collection of marbles. We were arguing. Carl thought she was lying. I said she wasn't, probably.

"I didn't believe that stuff about the bird," Carl said, "and what she told us about the pyramids? I didn't believe that, either. She didn't know what she was talking about."

"Oh yeah?" I had liked her. She was strange. I thought I could nail him. "If she was lying," I said, "what'd she say that was a lie?"

"Six times eleven isn't sixty-eight. It isn't ever. It's sixty-six, I know for a fact."

"She said so. She admitted it. What else did she lie about?"

"I don't know," he said. "Stuff."

"What stuff?"

"Well." He swung his legs back and forth. "You ever see an animal that was half lion and half bird?" He crossed his arms. "It sounded real fakey to me."

"It could happen," I said. I had to improvise, to outrage him. "I read in this newspaper my mom bought in the IGA about this scientist, this mad scientist in the Swiss Alps, and he's been putting genes and chromosomes and stuff together in test tubes, and he combined a human being and a hamster." I waited, for effect. "It's called a humster."

"You never." Carl was staring at me, his mouth open, his terrible bad breath making its way toward me. "What newspaper was it?"

"*The National Enquirer*," I said, "that they sell next to the cash registers." When I saw his look of recognition, I knew I had him. "And this mad scientist," I said, "his name was, um, Dr. Frankenbush." I realized belatedly that this name was a mistake and waited for Carl to notice its resemblance to the name of the other famous mad master of permutations, but he only sat there.

"A man and a hamster?" He was staring at me, squinting, his mouth opening in distaste. "Jeez. What'd it look like?"

When the bus reached my stop, I took off down our dirt road and ran up through the backyard, kicking the tire swing for good luck. I dropped my books on the back steps so I could hug and kiss our dog, Mr. Selby. Then I hurried inside. I could smell brussels sprouts cooking, my unfavorite vegetable. My mother was washing other vegetables in the kitchen sink, and my baby brother was hollering in his yellow playpen on the kitchen floor.

"Hi, Mom," I said, hopping around the playpen to kiss her. "Guess what?"

"I have no idea."

"We had this substitute today, Miss Ferenczi, and I'd never seen her before, and she had all these stories and ideas and stuff."

"Well. That's good." My mother looked out the window in front of the sink, her eyes on the pine woods west of our house. That time of the afternoon her skin always looked so white to me. Strangers always said my mother looked like Betty Crocker, framed by the giant spoon on the side of the Bisquick box. "Listen, Tommy," she said. "Would you please go upstairs and pick your clothes off the floor in the bathroom, and then go outside to the shed and put the shovel and ax away that your father left outside this morning?"

"She said that six times eleven was sometimes sixty-eight!" I said. "And she said she once saw a monster that was half lion and half bird." I waited. "In Egypt."

"Did you hear me?" my mother asked, raising her arm to wipe her forehead with the back of her hand. "You have chores to do."

"I know," I said. "I was just telling you about the substitute."

"It's very interesting," my mother said, quickly glancing down at me, "and we can talk about it later when your father gets home. But right now you have some work to do."

"Okay, Mom." I took a cookie out of the jar on the counter and was about to go outside when I had a thought. I ran into the living room, pulled out a dictionary next to the TV stand, and opened it to the Gs. After five minutes I found it. *Gryphon:* variant of griffin. *Griffin:* "a fabulous beast with the head and wings of an eagle and the body of a lion." Fabulous was right. I shouted with triumph and ran outside to put my father's tools in their proper places.

Miss Ferenczi was back the next day, slightly altered. She had pulled her hair down and twisted it into pigtails, with red rubber bands holding them tight one inch from the ends. She was wearing a green blouse and pink scarf, making her difficult to look at for a full class day. This time there was no pretense of doing a reading lesson or moving on to arithmetic. As soon as the bell rang, she simply began to talk.

She talked for forty minutes straight. There seemed to be less connection between her ideas, but the ideas themselves were, as the dictionary would say, fabulous. She said she had heard of a huge jewel, in what she called the antipodes, that was so brilliant that when light shone into it at a certain angle it would blind whoever was looking at its center. She said the biggest diamond in the world was cursed and had killed everyone who owned it, and that by a trick of fate it was called the Hope Diamond. Diamonds are magic, she said, and this is why women wear them on their fingers, as a sign of the magic of womanhood. Men have strength, Miss Ferenczi said, but no true magic. That is why men fall in love with women but women do not fall in love with men: they just love being loved. George Washington had died because of a mistake he made about a diamond. Washington was not the first *true* President, but she didn't say who was. In some places in the world, she said, men and women still live in the trees and eat monkeys for breakfast. Their doctors are magicians. At the bottom of the sea are creatures thin as pancakes who have never been studied by scientists because when you take them up to air, the fish explode.

There was not a sound in the classroom, except for Miss Ferenczi's voice, and Donna DeShano's coughing. No one even went to the bathroom.

Beethoven, she said, had not been deaf; it was a trick to make himself famous, and it worked. As she talked, Miss Ferenczi's pigtails swung back and forth. There are trees in the world, she said, that eat meat: their leaves are sticky and close up on bugs like hands. She lifted her hands and brought them together, palm to palm. Venus, which most people think is the next closest planet to the sun, is not always closer, and, besides, it is the planet of greatest mystery because of its thick cloud cover. "I know what lies underneath those clouds," Miss Ferenczi said, and waited. After the silence, she said, "Angels. Angels live under those clouds." She said that angels were not invisible to everyone and were in fact smarter than most people. They did not dress in robes as was often claimed but instead wore formal evening clothes, as if they were about to attend a concert. Often angels *do* attend concerts and sit in the aisles, where, she said, most people pay no attention to them. She said the most terrible angel had the shape of the Sphinx. "There is no running away from that one," she said. She said that unquenchable fires burn just under the surface of the earth in Ohio, and that the baby Mozart fainted dead away in his cradle when he first heard the sound of a trumpet.

She said that someone named Narzim al Harrardim was the greatest writer who ever lived. She said that planets control behavior, and anyone conceived during a solar eclipse would be born with webbed feet.

"I know you children like to hear these things," she said, "these secrets, and that is why I am telling you all this." We nodded. It was better than doing comprehension questions for the readings in *Broad Horizons*.

"I will tell you one more story," she said, "and then we will have to do arithmetic." She leaned over, and her voice grew soft. "There is no death," she said. "You must never be afraid. Never. That which is, cannot die. It will change into different earthly and unearthly elements, but I know this as sure as I stand here in front of you, and I swear it: you must not be afraid. I have seen this truth with these eyes. I know it because in a dream God kissed me. Here." And she pointed with her right index finger to the side of her head, below the mouth where the vertical lines were carved into her skin.

Absentmindedly we all did our arithmetic problems. At recess the class was out on the playground, but no one was playing. We were all standing in small groups, talking about Miss Ferenczi. We didn't know if she was crazy, or what. I looked out beyond the playground, at the rusted cars piled in a small heap behind a clump of sumac, and I wanted to see shapes there, approaching me.

On the way home, Carl sat next to me again. He didn't say much, and I didn't either. At last he turned to me. "You know what she said about the leaves that close up on bugs?"

"Huh?"

"The leaves," Carl insisted. "The meat-eating plants. I know it's true. I saw it on television. The leaves have this icky glue that the plants have got smeared all over them and the insects can't get off 'cause they're stuck. I saw it." He seemed demoralized. "She's tellin' the truth."

"Yeah."

"You think she's seen all those angels?"

I shrugged.

"I don't think she has," Carl informed me. "I think she made that part up."

"There's a tree," I suddenly said. I was looking out the window at the farms along County Road H. I knew every barn, every broken windmill, every fence, every anhydrous ammonia tank, by heart. "There's a tree that's . . . that I've seen . . ."

"Don't you try to do it," Carl said. "You'll just sound like a jerk."

I kissed my mother. She was standing in front of the stove. "How was your day?" she asked.

"Fine."

"Did you have Miss Ferenczi again?"

"Yeah."

"Well?"

"She was fine. Mom," I asked, "can I go to my room?"

"No," she said, "not until you've gone out to the vegetable garden and picked me a few tomatoes." She glanced at the sky. "I think it's going to rain. Skedaddle and do it now. Then you come back inside and watch your brother for a few minutes while I go upstairs. I need to clean up before dinner." She looked down at me. "You're looking a little pale, Tommy." She touched the back of her hand to my forehead and I felt her diamond ring against my skin. "Do you feel all right?"

"I'm fine," I said, and went out to pick the tomatoes.

Coughing mutedly, Mr. Hibler was back the next day, slipping lozenges into his mouth when his back was turned at forty-five-minute intervals and asking us how much of his prepared lesson plan Miss Ferenczi had followed. Edith Atwater took the responsibility for the class of explaining to Mr. Hibler that the substitute hadn't always done exactly what he, Mr. Hibler, would have done, but we had worked hard even though she talked a lot. About what? he asked. All kinds of things, Edith said. I sort of forgot. To our relief, Mr. Hibler seemed not at all interested in what Miss Ferenczi had said to fill the day. He probably thought it was woman's talk: unserious and not suited for school. It was enough that he had a pile of arithmetic problems from us to correct.

For the next month, the sumac turned a distracting red in the field, and the sun traveled toward the southern sky, so that its rays reached Mr. Hibler's Halloween display on the bulletin board in the back of the room, fading the pumpkin head scarecrow from orange to tan. Every three days I measured how much farther the sun had moved toward the southern horizon by making small marks with my black Crayola on the north wall, ant-sized marks only I knew were there.

And then in early December, four days after the first permanent snowfall, she appeared again in our classroom. The minute she came in the door, I felt my heart begin to pound. Once again, she was different: this time, her hair hung straight down and seemed hardly to have been combed. She hadn't brought her lunchbox with her, but she was carrying what seemed to be a small box. She greeted all of us and talked about the weather. Donna DeShano had to remind her to take her overcoat off.

When the bell to start the day finally rang, Miss Ferenczi looked out at all of us and said, "Children, I have enjoyed your company in the past, and today I am going to reward you." She held up the small box. "Do you know what this is?" She waited. "Of course you don't. It is a Tarot pack."

Edith Atwater raised her hand. "What's a Tarot pack, Miss Ferenczi?"

"It is used to tell fortunes," she said. "And that is what I shall do this morning. I shall tell your fortunes, as I have been taught to do."

"What's fortune?" Bobby Kryzanowicz asked.

"The future, young man. I shall tell you what your future will be. I can't do your whole future, of course. I shall have to limit myself to the five-card system, the wands, cups, swords, pentacles, and the higher arcanes. Now who wants to be first?"

There was a long silence. Then Carol Peterson raised her hand.

"All right," Miss Ferenczi said. She divided the pack into five smaller packs and walked back to Carol's desk, in front of mine. "Pick one card from each one of these packs," she said. I saw that Carol had a four of cups and a six of swords, but I couldn't see the other cards. Miss Ferenczi studied the cards on Carol's desk for a minute. "Not bad," she said. "I do not see much higher education. Probably an early marriage. Many children. There's something bleak and dreary here, but I can't tell what. Perhaps just the tasks of a housewife life. I think you'll do very well, for the most part." She smiled at Carol, a smile with a certain lack of interest. "Who wants to be next?"

Carl Whiteside raised his hand slowly.

"Yes," Miss Ferenczi said, "let's do a boy." She walked over to where Carl sat. After he picked his five cards, she gazed at them for a long time. "Travel," she said. "Much distant travel.

You might go into the army. Not too much romantic interest here. A late marriage, if at all. But the Sun in your major arcana, that's a very good card." She giggled. "You'll have a happy life."

Next I raised my hand. She told me my future. She did the same with Bobby Kryzanowicz, Kelly Munger, Edith Atwater, and Kim Foor. Then she came to Wayne Razmer. He picked his five cards, and I could see that the Death card was one of them.

"What's your name?" Miss Ferenczi asked.

"Wayne."

"Well, Wayne," she said, "you will undergo a great metamorphosis, a change, before you become an adult. Your earthly element will no doubt leap higher, because you seem to be a sweet boy. This card, this nine of swords, tells me of suffering and desolation. And this ten of wands, well, that's a heavy load."

"What about this one?" Wayne pointed at the Death card.

"It means, my sweet, that you will die soon." She gathered up the cards. We were all looking at Wayne. "But do not fear," she said. "It is not really death. Just change. Out of your earthly shape." She put the cards on Mr. Hibler's desk. "And now, let's do some arithmetic."

At lunchtime Wayne went to Mr. Faegre, the principal, and informed him of what Miss Ferenczi had done. During the noon recess, we saw Miss Ferenczi drive out of the parking lot in her rusting green Rambler American. I stood under the slide, listening to the other kids coasting down and landing in the little depressive bowls at the bottom. I was kicking stones and tugging at my hair right up to the moment when I saw Wayne come out to the playground. He smiled, the dead fool, and with the fingers of his right hand he was showing everyone how he had told on Miss Ferenczi.

I made my way toward Wayne, pushing myself past two girls from another class. He was watching me with his little pinhead eyes.

"You told," I shouted at him. "She was just kidding."

"She shouldn't have," he shouted back. "We were supposed to be doing arithmetic."

"She just scared you," I said. "You're a chicken. You're a chicken, Wayne. You are. Scared of a little card," I singsonged.

Wayne fell at me, his two fists hammering down on my nose. I gave him a good one in the stomach and then I tried for his head. Aiming my fist, I saw that he was crying. I slugged him.

"She was right," I yelled. "She was always right! She told the truth!" Other kids were whooping. "You were just scared, that's all!"

And then large hands pulled at us, and it was my turn to speak to Mr. Faegre.

In the afternoon Miss Ferenczi was gone, and my nose was stuffed with cotton clotted with blood, and my lip had swelled, and our class had been combined with Mrs. Mantei's sixth-grade class for a crowded afternoon science unit on insect life in ditches and swamps. I knew where Mrs. Mantei lived: she had a new house trailer just down the road from us, at the Clearwater Park. She was no mystery. Somehow she and Mr. Bodine, the other fourth-grade teacher, had managed to fit forty-five desks into the room. Kelly Munger asked if Miss Ferenczi had been arrested, and Mrs. Mantei said no, of course not. All that afternoon, until the buses came to pick us up, we learned about field crickets and two-striped grasshoppers, water bugs, cicadas, mosquitoes, flies, and moths. We learned about insects' hard outer shell, the exoskeleton, and the usual parts of the mouth, including the labrum, mandible, maxilla, and glossa. We learned about compound eyes, and the four-stage metamorphosis from egg to larva to pupa to adult. We learned something, but not much, about mating. Mrs. Mantei drew, very skillfully, the internal anatomy of the grasshopper on the blackboard. We learned about the dance of the honeybee, directing other bees in the hive to pollen. We found out about which insects were pests to man, and which were not. On lined white pieces of paper we made lists of insects we might actually see, then a list of insects too small to be clearly visible, such as fleas; Mrs. Mantei said that our assignment would be to memorize these lists for the next day, when Mr. Hibler would certainly return and test us on our knowledge.

APHRODITE THE
FIREWOMAN
·❧·
Ruslan Kireyev

I don't like Tuesdays. I haven't since childhood, when the Svetopol
Circus was dark and depressing on Tuesday. That was the day it
was closed. But the rest of the week I hung around there practically
every night. I didn't have a ticket, but that didn't matter. I would
wait and watch until the latecomers started to throng in, then I
would quietly slip in among them. Looking prim and proper, and
wearing a somber expression, like a good little boy whose intellectual parents were taking him to introduce him to art.

Sometimes it worked, and sometimes it didn't. "Your ticket?"
a voice would suddenly ring out. And no matter how you tried
to look like a little professor who had absentmindedly gotten lost
from his parents, no matter how you raised your brows and cast
your eyes about with a distressed look on your face—why, they
were just here!—the game was lost. They'd throw you out. Shouting at you! Right in front of everyone.

But I kept coming back. I was drawn there like a moth to the
light. It was instinct. Something inside me must have remembered
other festivals and other shows. It was the slapstick shows at
marketplaces, performed to the accompaniment of hucksters'
shouts, the din and the laughter of the crowd, and the pungent
aromas of foods. My love for the circus came to me from afar—
from far afar. It was something primitive and primordial, whereas
interest in other arts is the work of later times.

The circus is disinterested. It doesn't teach; it entertains. But
let's be careful before removing it from the pedestal of art for this
reason. We would do better to remember that Homer, too, entertained. And Shakespeare, the storyteller of theater. And Cer-
vantes, impetuously dashing off his parodic novel. First and
foremost, they entertained; and all the rest came after that.

Of course, back then I wasn't thinking anything of the sort.
What concerned me was something else: to sneak inside, and once
I was inside, under the two-headed canvas dome flapping in the
wind, to hold out until the spotlights came up, and the band up

above, springing forth from the darkness, played the overture. To hell with them! Now I feared no one. Not even Aphrodite. She knew me inside out—we lived on the same courtyard. She could have shown kindness toward me, as a neighbor; instead of keeping a careful eye out for me, she might at least have let me get through once without a ticket. But no such luck! She kept a menacing lookout from above over the crowded rows that receded downward from where she stood. Only the aisles remained vacant; and what a wonderful seat we could have had on the steps if it hadn't been for that witch! You see, we were breaking the fire safety rules, and she had been put there to enforce them. Aphrodite was (and remains to this day) the only woman fireman I have ever known.

Actually, she was called Annushka, but because of her Greek origin some juvenile scholar had stuck her with the name of the goddess of love. It was a cruel joke. Swarthy, mustachioed Aphrodite could hardly have gladdened anyone's eye. Now, if only her hair . . .

When she stood at attention at her fireman's post, her hair was gathered into a bun, and her uniform hat with its cockade barely stayed on it; but at home she would let it hang free, and it would fall in a black cascade practically to her ankles. That's how she would walk around the courtyard—her hair down, the whites of her eyes shining, and her throaty, harsh voice sounding like a crow's.

She had a husband, a little red-headed *muzhik* called Uncle Petya, an inveterate domino player; even in winter, in the snow, he would be out playing dominoes. And she had a son, but he lived on a collective farm—somewhere near Dzhigansk, I think. He worked as a driver and from time to time would pay a call on Svetopol in his truck with presents from the countryside. Sometimes he would bring melons, sometimes corn. Aphrodite would boil the corn on her primus stove in a huge kettle. Seating herself on her porch, her hair down over her chest, she would plunge her metal teeth into a glistening ear.

From there, on her high porch, she had a perfect view of everything. God forbid we should start playing with matches! She would stand up at once, letting her hair fall down, throw up her hands, and shout in her crowlike voice for the whole courtyard to hear: "Okay, stop it! Fooling around with fire. . . ."

She did that, I realize now, not out of zeal for her job but from a sense of duty.

We would tease her. If you wrap a tightly rolled film in newspaper, set it on fire and then quickly put it out, you get a magnificent "smoke bomb." Vadka Kon was the unsurpassed master at such things. Black smoke would pour out, and Aphrodite, panting, would fly as fast as she could to extinguish the fire. By herself! But by the time she got to the homemade missile, which would be spinning like a top, it would already have burned out and died down. We would be triumphant. From afar, from a safe distance, although our safety was illusory. Aphrodite couldn't get us, but we would have forgotten about Uncle Petya, that quiet little *muzhik* who seemingly saw nothing but his dominoes.

But he did see! Putting down his dominoes, putting down his cigarette, he sneaked up behind us and immediately grabbed two of us, me and Vadka Kon, by the ears. We practically lost our footing, and our mouths, which had just been laughing, turned down at the corners.

His little blue eyes stared at us with interest—first one of us, then the other—and his fingers kept twisting our unfortunate, our horribly crunching ears; we kept twisting and turning, and it was all we could do to keep from howling at the top of our lungs.

Aphrodite came quickly. Barefoot, with a half-gnawed ear of corn in her hand. Her black eyes wide open, she was saying something at a rapid-fire rate, but, half-crazy with pain, we didn't understand a word, which is probably why we later decided she had been speaking Greek.

Uncle Petya didn't make a sound. He held us until his wife, that swarthy fire extinguisher, had spent herself completely; then he released his fingers, calmly returned to his table, and stuck a cigarette in his mouth.

But what were our childish games compared to the festival of fire that was staged—perfectly legally—at the circus! And yet there were victims. Yes, real victims! Before the eyes of hundreds of spectators a frail girl would burn to ashes, bestowing an enchanting farewell smile on the audience. How did Aphrodite react to that? I don't know. At those moments I forgot about her.

Magic tricks were my favorite genre. But "magic tricks" is too general a term: that's what dilettantes call them; while I already had figured out perfectly well what was illusion, what was sleight of hand, and what was, say, mnemonic technique.

There was a lot, a whole lot, that I figured out right away, and there were some tricks that I could even duplicate—in simplified versions—but there were also some that I could not decipher for a long time. For example, the feature act of the illusionist, Mikhail Vakhto.

The posters portrayed an imposing man sitting in an armchair. He had arms, legs and a paunch, but no head. As though it had been sliced off with a razor. How I would stare at that fantastic picture! How avidly I counted the days that remained until his premiere performance!

It was the last engagement of the season. It was fall. The first fall in which girls had appeared in our hitherto all-male school. Segregated classrooms were a thing of the past.

This is where the lyrical part of my story begins, a part that is bound up in the closest way possible—for me personally—with the circus. Bound up, in particular, with the illusionist act of Mikhail Vakhto, and with his sensational trick that stirred the entire city.

I realize now that "stirred" and "entire city" are too strong, but at the time I was convinced that, like me, everyone around could think of nothing but the headless gentleman.

"And afterwards," Tolya Skat, who had recently taken to hanging around with our class, asked ironically, "afterwards who sews his head back on?"

I knew who he was showing off for, and for whose sake he had started hanging around with us. It was for Valya Burtovskaya.

She would stand there and listen, biting her lip with her white teeth. Her gray eyes weren't laughing. How straight she held her head! How she walked! Her legs moved silently and rapidly in her soft shoes, her arms barely stirring in the process. Not a month had passed since she crossed the threshold of our school, and our whole class had gone crazy over her. And not just our class. Tolya Skat shunned his own classmates and hung around with us. He was a ranked gymnast, and for Valya, an athletic girl—what couldn't she do in her sky-blue tights on the parallel bars and balance beam!—that meant something. True, he was a little shorter than she was; but that didn't bother him.

The reader has probably already realized that Valya's secret admirers included me, apologist for the circus. I spoke of it with such ardor, defended its omnipotence so passionately, that I aroused Valya's curiosity, and once, while we were erasing the blackboard during a break, she suddenly asked what I was getting so carried away about, anyway.

We were alone together in the classroom. I think we were

alone. . . . Her eyes were smiling, and I didn't know what to answer. But if she wanted . . . I fell silent.

"What?" she asked, without lowering her hands.

Two little ribbons were woven into her braids, which were crossed over and attached together.

"We could go, if you want," I managed to say. My heart was going boom, boom, boom.

"I do."

I didn't believe it.

"Really? I'll . . . I'll buy the tickets. We'll get in with tickets."

The little ribbons started bouncing up and down. With laughter.

"Of course, with tickets."

I stood there in front of her, blushing, completely crimson, realizing with horror that I had given myself away.

But the invitation had taken place. Now I had to get the tickets. I had a bit of luck. A neighbor, Zinaida Borisovna, had had some new chairs delivered, and she called to me to carry the old ones to the basement, for which she rewarded me royally with ten rubles. I borrowed the rest from Vadka Kon. And so I had the money, but . . .

For days there had been a "Sold Out" sign hanging on the ticket office. With what pleasure I would read it—for me it was a guarantee, in the first place, that the engagement would not be canceled and, in the second place, that the show really would be remarkable, since so many adults, serious people, were eager to see it.

But what was I going to do now?

I went to see Aphrodite.

She was sitting on her porch in her invariable pose of guardian of order, shelling sunflower seeds with her teeth and eating them. Her hand stopped when I appeared in front of her.

"Hello, Aunt Anya."

She remained silent, peering at me anxiously. Never in her life had she been called that—Aunt Anya. Grownups called her Annushka, and we called her Aphrodite—behind her back, that is; to her face we called her nothing.

"Could you help me out?" I said clearly and distinctly, following my well-rehearsed text. "I need two tickets. Please."

A cat was sitting in her lap. Black as his mistress, he looked at me, as she did, uneasily? They weren't used to company.

"What do you want?" Aphrodite muttered. A sunflower husk was stuck to her fat lip.

I repeated that I needed two tickets, but once again I did not say for what. I thought that went without saying, but she couldn't figure out what sort of tickets I was pestering her about. For a train, or something?

"To the circus," I said. "Two tickets to the circus. Please."

"But where would I get them for you? They're at the ticket office."

"The ticket office doesn't have any."

"What do you mean, doesn't have any? The ticket office . . ." And she brushed away the husk. "The ticket office has tickets."

"The ticket office doesn't have any, Aunt Anya," I explained to her politely. "But if you ask . . . Please! You work there."

"Where?" she asked suspiciously.

"There. At the circus."

"Yes," she affirmed with pride. "But the tickets are at the ticket office."

I had to explain the whole thing all over again. She frowned. Her loosened hair, with gray strands, framed her swarthy face, which no longer seemed frightening to me at all. On the contrary.

"Please, Aunt Anya," I begged. "I really need them. Here's the money." And, putting down two folded five-ruble notes and a ruble beside the plate of hot sunflower seeds—they were still giving off heat—I sidled down the stairs.

The next day I had barely gone out in the courtyard when her throaty cry rang out: "Hey! Listen here!"

We all turned around, surprised. She was standing on her porch at full height, with her hair down, waving her hand and beckoning to someone.

To me, who else? I rushed headlong to her.

Aphrodite was smiling. I think it was the first time I had seen her smile. She was smiling and holding out two strips of the pink paper that I had seen so many times in other people's hands but had never once held in my own.

Need I say with what reverence I accepted them?

"Thank you very much."

"My pleasure," she replied with a look of satisfaction, and immediately withdrew the tickets.

"Here's the place," she said, pointing with her finger, "where you sit."

"Yes, yes," I nodded. "I know. Thank you very much."

"My pleasure." But she didn't let go of the tickets. "Right side. Sixth row."

She spoke rapidly, without looking. (Later I learned that she couldn't read at all.)

I met Valya at the circus. She wasn't wearing her school uniform, but a dress, a pink dress; and she wasn't wearing her braids, but some sort of grownup hairdo. She seemed taller. Or did she have on heels?

The long yellow benches were empty. The seat numbers looked like June bugs on them, getting closer together as they got farther away. The empty arena looked unimpressive and small. The bandstand was empty. But then one musician came out, bent over in the half-darkness and put his foot up on a chair. Was he lacing his shoe? I stole a sideways glance at my lady: would she see? But no, thank God, she wasn't looking that way. She was looking in the other direction. I followed her glance and saw Aphrodite. She was standing in her fire hat with the cockade, swarthy, big-nosed and looking right at us, flashing her metal teeth in a smile. She was admiring her handiwork. Flattered by her attention—not just anyone, but a circus employee!—I bowed courteously.

Valya was sitting with lowered eyes.

"Who's that?" she whispered.

"Aphrodite. Our neighbor. She's a fireman."

But neither the exotic name nor what was a strange occupation for a woman surprised Valya Burtovskaya. I suddenly noticed what a long chin she had, and I liked that (I liked everything about her). Parting her lips slightly, she asked: "But why is she looking like that?"

I carefully turned my head. Aphrodite seemed to have been waiting for that, and she started smiling even more joyfully and nodding. I was on tenterhooks, feeling her contented gaze on the back of my head.

But then the third bell rang, and the usherettes started to bustle around, seating the latecomers. The musical instruments started squeaking and squealing in a loud cacophony. They started up, then fell silent, and the spotlights came on; however, they illuminated not the arena but the band, which the slender director stood facing with raised baton. And the music burst forth. At this point I forgot not only Aphrodite but my beautiful companion. My spirit soared to the dome—if you'll forgive the high-flown expression. The smartly dressed circus performers poured out and in an instant noiselessly formed two rows. The show had begun.

Not all the varieties of circus acts delighted me equally. For example, I was indifferent to the trained animals (Filatov's bears later dispelled that prejudice), especially to the various sorts of animal tamers. I adored the clowns. And besides that, I loved the so-called "original" acts, which excited and intrigued you precisely because they were undefined. You always knew in advance what to expect from acrobats, jugglers, tightrope walkers, aerial gymnasts, comic musicians; but the "originals" promised surprises. And what surprises!

I'll never forget the Georgian performer Sandro Da-Desh (he later appeared under his real name, Dadeshkiliani). A tall, handsome man wearing a black cape and hat would come rushing out into the arena, throw off his cape into the hands of his female assistant with a shrug of his shoulder, and rapidly remove his hat. He would do it so quickly that you didn't immediately realize that he had taken it off with his foot rather than his hand. And his hands? His hands hung motionless in snowy white gloves.

He would quickly sit down to a little low table and pick up a pen (with his feet, everything with his feet! He had special polished boots with openings for his toes) and rapidly, evenly and handsomely write: Da-Desh, Da-Desh, Da-Desh. His assistant would pass these pieces of paper out to the audience.

Moving to another little table, which was elegantly set for a meal, he would begin eating. He would open a bottle, pour some water into a tall wineglass, wipe his mouth with a napkin and use a fork and knife more artfully than some people manage with their hands. An easel would be set up, and with a few strokes he would sketch a caricature of a clown, and when the clown got angry, he would grab him by the ear (with his foot!). Then he would load a rifle, lie on his back, and shoot at little rubber balls—without a miss!

People said that he had been born without hands. Perhaps so. In any case, it was a unique act. I saw it some ten times. But that wasn't during the season I'm talking about now—it was later.

Indisputably, Mikhail Vakhto's magic act was considered the high point of the current program. It was the finale, but in the meantime the regular program was going on. To me, it was familiar, but Valya Burtovskaya didn't take her eyes off the arena. She especially liked the gymnasts. I felt the invisible presence of our ranked athlete, Tolya Skat. The applause with which they were rewarded was a knife in my heart. I fidgeted and rustled my program. No matter, I thought, no matter, my time will come. I had faith in Mikhail Vakhto.

During the intermission wooden, colorfully painted planking —an invariable prop for all illusionist acts—was laid out in the arena. The barrier was spread with a brightly colored runner. I scrutinized it professionally to see whether there wasn't some sort of secret, while I enthusiastically recounted the tricks of the famous Kio. Valya's eyes remained fixed on me—now she was looking at me and not at her gymnasts.

Someone touched me on the shoulder. I shuddered as though I had been caught red-handed. As though I had no tickets in my pocket. I turned . . .

Before me stood Aphrodite. She was smiling and nodding, and to all appearances she had no intention of throwing me out. I caught my breath.

"Hello," I muttered.

She didn't answer. She backed away, smiling and bowing contentedly, rising higher and higher up the aisle.

The second part began with an aerial flight, then a tightrope-walker came out on the free wire ("They're sparing the arena," I thought, with a rush of emotion), and then . . .

After every trick Valya would turn to look at me as if to say, "Is it possible?" I would give her a reserved nod of confirmation.

After putting together a little box before the eyes of the audience, Mikhail Vakhto stuck a fluttering chicken in it, covered it with a handkerchief, removed the handkerchief and nimbly spread open the box. The chicken was gone. Valya gave me a knowing look: "It's in the table."

I smiled and gestured with my eyes toward the arena: Look! Mikhail Vakhto didn't let me down. He pulled off the tablecloth and in a twinkling dismantled the table. Nothing.

With what trustful wonder my friend looked at me! With a regal glance, I directed her back to the arena. Just see what else was in store!

Mikhail Vakhto was brought out in a tall armchair, not to the middle of the arena, however, but only to the entrance, and there he was left, right beside the tightly drawn door curtain itself. He had a telephone and some papers. He was playing a bureaucrat. Loudly, through a speaker, he said he was not receiving visitors, that he was busy, etc. Then he got absorbed reading a magazine, completely covering his face with it, and when he took away the magazine, his head was gone. His hands were moving—live hands, with no gloves; his legs were moving, and his voice continued to be heard, but his head was gone. In its place was a dark, smooth, even surface surrounded by a white collar.

Valya Burtovskaya turned to me, stunned.

"An illusionist act," I pronounced, and the words sounded weighty and enigmatic.

In the meantime, the headless bureaucrat was waving his hands demanding something (apparently, that his head be returned), and then suddenly—something even I did not expect. Suddenly Mikhail Vakhto, in person, appeared in the arena. From the central, spectators' entrance. The chair with the torso was pulled back through the door curtain, the band played a flourish, and the great artiste threw up his plump little hands.

There was little applause—magicians always get little applause, since you need some time to gather your wits, but the master of ceremonies, clever woman, did not let him go, and I clapped my hands for all I was worth. And then, turning, I saw a look that I will never forget.

A tender rapture shone in her eyes. To my gallant question, "Well, how did you like it?" she replied almost inaudibly: "A lot."

"After you!"

With a smile of gratitude, she shyly slipped by me, very close, almost brushing against me, but not touching me even with her dress. I noticed that her face was flushed and that her lowered eyelashes, which were very long, were trembling.

A new life began. It didn't matter that the others noticed nothing, that even the self-assured athlete Tolya Skat continued to ignore us, convinced I was no rival for him; I knew that there was something special between Valya and me. What can I say about it? There were no declarations of love, no notes, not even any desperate brushing of hands—none of that. Just a look, just a smile, just a tone of voice.

Could I have been mistaken? Maybe I took ordinary politeness for God knows what? No. She didn't smile at others that way, or didn't smile at all, or, upon smiling, immediately turned away and forgot about that person. But her gaze rested on me. It was soft and slightly questioning, that look, as though she was searching out something in me. As though she was expecting something from me.

She waited but didn't hurry me. And she never reminded me

either of the circus or of the wonders that she had seen there. Except, perhaps, just once.

It happened in the physics lab. We were doing an experiment together, in a group of five or six people (and the fact that we ended up in the same group was also no coincidence). When the dyed water, contrary to common sense, moved upward through the glass tube and everyone clapped for joy, Valya said softly: "Like Vakhto."

Her eyes, fixed on me above the heads bowed over the table, were laughing. She didn't lower them when I raised my eyes, but kept looking, and biting her lip.

Isn't that proof for you? But there was something even more consequential than that.

Once she got hold of my assignment book. But just *how* she got hold of it is worth noting. She took it off my desk without asking permission—simply reached out her hand. I didn't protest. I merely sighed: my assignment book and her assignment book! The point wasn't the grades, which in my case varied from A's to E's, while she had nothing lower than a B, but the assignment books themselves. It was their appearance. Hers was neat and tidy, covered in pink paper and carefully filled out. But mine!

How much time does it take to write out a schedule of lessons for the week? Five to seven minutes. At the most ten, if you write everything out in a perfect hand.

I never had those five minutes. On blank pages, I would have scattered around: "Russ.," "Engl.," "Hist.," and beside them, scribbles indicating topics or problem numbers. That was at best. At worst, there would be nothing.

I still have that assignment book. It is all marked up with red notations, while one of them, with variations, runs all the way through from cover to cover: "Untidy assignment book," "Very untidy assignment book," "Keeping assignment book—D."

But what is this? Six pages in a row filled out from top to bottom in a large, even, amazing hand. There is no "Hist." or "Engl.," but full subject names respectfully written out. I don't remember which adventure novel it is where the captain orders a half-dozen barrels of oil to be poured overboard onto the raging sea, which is immediately calmed, as though someone had waved a magic wand. That's what my assignment book looks like.

In this case there was no magic wand. Just an ordinary pen that Valya Burtovskaya, that proud girl, had taken in her slim fingers and, biting her lip, used to fill out, without stopping, six whole pages. For three weeks in advance. Then, after carefully blotting it, she had closed the assignment book and, without a word, put it back on top of my desk.

And so? At that point not just my spirit but I myself soared to the ceiling.

That same day I was waiting for her at the school gate carrying my bookbag. A shiny brown chestnut with a black patch in the center hit the sidewalk with a resonant thud, bounced up, rolled toward the fence and disappeared into a pile of leaves as though it had fallen into some animal's hole. I carefully poked through the leaves with my stocking foot. No chestnut. I poked around a little more and then bent over and spread the leaves with my hand. It wasn't there. I even started laughing in astonishment—though at the time I would laugh at anything—and when I raised my head, standing there, two steps away in an unbuttoned coat, was my Valya. Biting her lip.

"Did you lose something?"

"Uh-huh," I mumbled, "a chestnut."

She looked at me with merry eyes. Then she stuck her hand in the diagonal opening of her pocket and held out in her palm— the chestnut. Exactly like the one that had hidden in the leaves. Maybe even the very same one.

I shook my head: "No, no, I don't need it."

The chestnut shone in the sun. I saw that without looking at it. And I also saw the pale freckles on her face.

Almost three decades have passed since that time. More than a quarter of a century, but I can see that scene as though it were right before my eyes. A scrawny little boy in a worn jacket with the sleeves a little short—I was growing fast, and my grandmother couldn't keep up with me—and an erect young girl with ribbons in her hair. A whitewashed school fence and, above it, a huge tree still thick with reddish-green leaves and hanging with bright, prickly little spheres. The sun is shining. The center of the chestnut shines polished in the palm of her hand. . . . From what terrible height am I seeing this? It is warm down below, and leaves are rustling on the sidewalk. She looks askance at the chestnut, as though she herself is surprised and can't figure out where she got it, then sticks it back in her pocket, turns slowly and walks away. I come up alongside her. Or not exactly alongside her, but a little behind her, but I still see that she is thinking intently about something, lowering her long eyelashes and smiling quietly about something.

I know what about. About the fact that I still hadn't figured out the trick. She is waiting. And maybe starting to doubt whether I can. I felt such an impostor. Almost an impostor.

But I hadn't been sitting idle. The headless man was simply haunting me, and I thought about him constantly, even dreamed about him, but I couldn't figure out his secret. Almost every evening I went, if not to the circus, then near it, and I would slip in for the second part for sure. But now it was harder for me. The problem was that I was always in panic for fear that Aphrodite would catch sight of me. Whereas it hadn't mattered to me much before what the vigilant firewoman thought of me, now that she had beheld me sitting in the reserved seats "like proper folks" with tickets that she herself had obtained, and with a young lady, I simply couldn't fall in her eyes again!

She would single me out among the boys in the yard. She would nod and smile when I walked near her high porch, and once she even beckoned to me with her finger, and I climbed up the stairs to her.

Beside her, like that other time, lay a plate of roasted sunflower seeds, but she did not offer me any; instead, she brought out a whole sunflower from the house—huge, dry and ripe even in the center. I got embarrassed and was about to refuse it, but she stuck it in my hand.

"Eat it. It's very good. Eat!"

I think it was on that very day that the idea dawned on me of questioning this employee of the circus who was so well disposed toward me. On duty there every night and having the opportunity (or, possibly, even required by her job?) to be behind the scenes, she couldn't help but know how that trick was done. They were probably forbidden to tell, but if I asked her . . . If I really begged her . . .

Now I would quite deliberately hang around near her porch. Once Aphrodite was frying something—a sweet, buttery aroma spread over the courtyard. Seeing me, she opened her metallic mouth and called. Trying not to betray myself with excessive haste, I approached gradually.

She was frying quince. I couldn't believe my eyes. Quince? Yes, quince. I don't know where she got that dish—maybe from her native Greece—but it was very tasty. Hot, golden slices that were tart and sweet, with a paper-thin, tender skin.

But as you know, what had me agitated was not gastronomical wonders, but wonders of a different sort.

I launched a direct assault on my target. I started talking about the circus, but Aphrodite didn't keep up the discussion. She was far more concerned with the quince. She was tending it carefully to keep the slices from burning while making sure they were thoroughly cooked. Lifting them up with a knife, she would slip butter in under them.

"And Vakhto!" I tried to outshout the noise of the primus stove. "He's something, isn't he?"

She raised her Greek eyes and looked at me.

"What?"

"Vakhto. Mikhail Vakhto. The illusionist. The magician. The headless man."

She understood. "O-oh," she said without interest and sprinkled sugar on the quince.

Finally everything was fried, the stove was put out, and my hostess, sitting on a stool with her hair thrown over her shoulders (the ends touched the cleanly washed, still-damp cement), started in on the delicacy.

I realized I wouldn't find a better moment. I took the bull by the horns.

"How does he do it?"

She brought her hand to a stop, just before putting a fiery slice in her mouth. She didn't understand.

"Why, that . . ." And I made a devil-may-care gesture that signified: I take a head (my own, for example), twist it off like an ear of corn, and throw it off the porch—let it roll and bounce!

Aphrodite followed that rolling head with concern.

"How does he do it?" I repeated. "How, Aunt Anya? You must know. How? Don't be afraid, I won't tell anyone."

She looked at me in perplexity.

"What won't you tell?" The quince slice that she had forgotten outside her mouth was darkening before my eyes.

I explained everything once again. Only this time I did not use a gesture to depict it—I explained it in words.

She smiled with relief.

"Why, he's an artiste!" She was amused by my naïveté. "An artiste." And, satisfied, she put the quince in her mouth.

I tried in vain to argue that it was beyond the ability of even the absolutely greatest artiste to cut off his own head and then put it back on. What's more, to do it day after day. Year after year.

She listened to my prattle with affectionate condescension.

What a child this was before her! And so I left her empty-handed, unless you count the fact that I had tried a dish that I had never heard of before.

I was left to rely on my own resources. I applied myself with diligence. On Tuesdays I would be bored, loitering about restlessly and aimlessly (I don't like Tuesdays!), but every other night I would spend at the circus. I would aim to get a spot as close as possible to the performers' entrance, in the seats that are considered bad because you have to turn around and look backwards, but they afford the opportunity to peek behind the scenes—or, more precisely, behind the curtain that the mysterious armchair stood up against.

Why there, and not in the center of the arena? After all, usually everything takes place in the center.

My perseverance paid off. Once the curtain failed to be drawn tightly, and my avid eye penetrated to the inner sanctum.

What did I see? Ordinary little lights were burning, like those on a stairwell. They illuminated a man who was standing bent over the armchair, on the other side of its tall back, with his head sticking through to the arena. It was Mikhail Vakhto.

And who was in the armchair? In the armchair sat another, unknown man with his head hidden in a suit outwardly identical to the one worn by Mikhail Vakhto.

How poorly I slept that night! How long it lasted, and how I burned with impatience to tell everything as soon as possible to Valya Burtovskaya.

I could see her eyes. Eyes that had the same expression with which she had looked at me that time at the circus.

I didn't wait for school to be over. During the first break between classes I gave her a conspiratorial look and called her aside to the window, where I told her everything.

She listened without interrupting me. She didn't ask about anything. As though she understood everything at once, yet there were so many subtleties involved! I had worked them all out, tossing and turning from side to side the night before. But how could she know them?

My eyes were ablaze. I could feel them burning, while hers, I saw, went out. There was none of the ecstasy in them that I had anticipated with such relish. There wasn't even any particular interest. She drawled, "Uh-huh," and gave me a flat look. Not inquiring, as before, and no longer searching anything out in me. Flat.

That was the end. No, she did not declare that she was disenchanted with me or that I, say, had bored her. I didn't hear a single hurtful word. Moreover, she tried to be particularly nice to me. Once, when I got up the courage to ask her to go with me to a documentary film about the famous Kio—I had already seen it twice—she answered regretfully: "I can't. I've got practice."

Her practice was at the sports school. The same one where the small and persistent Tolya Skat, the ranked gymnast, shone.

He had achieved his goal: Valya, tactfully turning away all of her classmates, would walk with him. Holding hands. I didn't see them, but others in the class said so.

On the other hand, Aphrodite was filled with more and more feeling for me. Calling me up to her porch, she would treat me either to walnuts—I would stuff my pockets with them, but that wasn't enough for her, and she would fashion a sack out of newspaper—or to carnelian cherries—big, fleshy and moist with crimson juice, or to caramelized sugar that had not yet cooled. In order to at least thank her in some way, I let her in on the secret of Mikhail Vakhto's feature act.

It was on the last day of his engagement—the season was ending. She listened to me, like Valya Burtovskaya, without interrupting, but, in contrast to Valya, she didn't believe me. She even grew indignant.

"But he's an artiste! An artiste, you understand."

He was an artiste, and I was slandering him with God knows what. I was practically accusing him of fraud.

"You can look, if you don't believe me," I advised her, offended. "It's not too late."

She angrily rejected my shameless suggestion. But then she immediately calmed down and said that I was still young and understood nothing. And since I was still young, she went in the house and brought out a yellow pear that must have weighed more than a pound.

"Eat! Eat it now. Right here."

And she watched with pleasure with her big black eyes as I obediently bit into the juicy flesh.

TRANSLATED BY GORDON LIVERMORE

LITTLE GIRL
WAKES EARLY

·♃·

Robert Penn Warren

Remember when you were the first one awake, the first
To stir in the dawn-curdled house, with little bare feet
Cold on boards, every door shut and accurst,
And behind shut doors no breath perhaps drew, no heart beat.

You held your breath and thought how all over town
Houses had doors shut, and no whisper of breath sleeping,
And that meant no swinging, nobody to pump up and down,
No hide-and-go-seek, no serious play at housekeeping.

So you ran outdoors, bare feet from the dew wet,
And climbed the fence to the house of your dearest friend,
And opened your lips and twisted your tongue, all set
To call her name—but the sound wouldn't come in the end,

For you thought how awful, if there was no breath there
For answer. Tears start, you run home, where now mother,
Over the stove, is humming some favorite air.
You seize her around the legs, but tears aren't over,

And won't get over, not even when she shakes you—
And shakes you hard—and more when you can't explain.
Your mother's long dead. And you've learned that when
    loneliness takes you
There's nobody ever to explain to—though you try again and again.

SUNDAY
IN THE PARK

·✌·

Bel Kaufman

It was still warm in the late-afternoon sun, and the city noises came muffled through the trees in the park. She put her book down on the bench, removed her sunglasses, and sighed contentedly. Morton was reading the *Times Magazine* section, one arm flung around her shoulder; their three-year-old son, Larry, was playing in the sandbox: a faint breeze fanned her hair softly against her cheek. It was five-thirty of a Sunday afternoon, and the small playground, tucked away in a corner of the park, was all but deserted. The swings and seesaws stood motionless and abandoned, the slides were empty, and only in the sandbox two little boys squatted diligently side by side. *How good this is*, she thought, and almost smiled at her sense of well-being. They must go out in the sun more often; Morton was so city-pale, cooped up all week inside the gray factorylike university. She squeezed his arm affectionately and glanced at Larry, delighting in the pointed little face frowning in concentration over the tunnel he was digging. The other boy suddenly stood up and with a quick, deliberate swing of his chubby arm threw a spadeful of sand at Larry. It just missed his head. Larry continued digging; the boy remained standing, shovel raised, stolid and impassive.

"No, no, little boy." She shook her finger at him, her eyes searching for the child's mother or nurse. "We mustn't throw sand. It may get in someone's eyes and hurt. We must play nicely in the nice sandbox." The boy looked at her in unblinking expectancy. He was about Larry's age but perhaps ten pounds heavier, a husky little boy with none of Larry's quickness and sensitivity in his face. Where was his mother? The only other people left in the playground were two women and a little girl on roller skates leaving now through the gate, and a man on a bench a few feet away. He was a big man, and he seemed to be taking up the whole bench as he held the Sunday comics close to his face. She supposed he was the child's father. He did not look up from his comics, but spat once deftly out of the corner of his mouth. She turned her eyes away.

At that moment, as swiftly as before, the fat little boy threw another spadeful of sand at Larry. This time some of it landed on his hair and forehead. Larry looked up at his mother, his mouth tentative; her expression would tell him whether to cry or not.

Her first instinct was to rush to her son, brush the sand out of his hair, and punish the other child, but she controlled it. She always said that she wanted Larry to learn to fight his own battles.

"Don't *do* that, little boy," she said sharply, leaning forward on the bench. "You mustn't throw sand!"

The man on the bench moved his mouth as if to spit again, but instead he spoke. He did not look at her, but at the boy only.

"You go right ahead, Joe," he said loudly. "Throw all you want. This here is a *public* sandbox."

She felt a sudden weakness in her knees as she glanced at Morton. He had become aware of what was happening. He put his *Times* down carefully on his lap and turned his fine, lean face toward the man, smiling the shy, apologetic smile he might have offered a student in pointing out an error in his thinking. When he spoke to the man, it was with his usual reasonableness.

"You're quite right," he said pleasantly, "but just because this is a public place . . ."

The man lowered his funnies and looked at Morton. He looked at him from head to foot, slowly and deliberately. "Yeah?" His insolent voice was edged with menace. "My kid's got just as good right here as yours, and if he feels like throwing sand, he'll throw it, and if you don't like it, you can take your kid the hell out of here."

The children were listening, their eyes and mouths wide open, their spades forgotten in small fists. She noticed the muscle in Morton's jaw tighten. He was rarely angry; he seldom lost his temper. She was suffused with a tenderness for her husband and an impotent rage against the man for involving him in a situation so alien and so distasteful to him.

"Now, just a minute," Morton said courteously, "you must realize . . ."

"Aw, shut up," said the man.

Her heart began to pound. Morton half rose; the *Times* slid to the ground. Slowly the other man stood up. He took a couple of steps toward Morton, then stopped. He flexed his great arms, waiting. She pressed her trembling knees together. Would there be violence, fighting? How dreadful, how incredible. . . . She must do something, stop them, call for help. She wanted to put her hand on her husband's sleeve, to pull him down, but for some reason she didn't.

Morton adjusted his glasses. He was very pale. "This is ridiculous," he said unevenly. "I must ask you . . ."

"Oh, yeah?" said the man. He stood with his legs spread apart, rocking a little, looking at Morton with utter scorn. "You and who else?"

For a moment the two men looked at each other nakedly. Then Morton turned his back on the man and said quietly, "Come on, let's get out of here." He walked awkwardly, almost limping with self-consciousness, to the sandbox. He stooped and lifted Larry and his shovel out.

At once Larry came to life; his face lost its rapt expression and he began to kick and cry. "I don't *want* to go home, I want to play better, I don't *want* any supper, I don't *like* supper. . . ." It became a chant as they walked, pulling their child between them, his feet dragging on the ground. In order to get to the exit gate they had to pass the bench where the man sat sprawling again. She was careful not to look at him. With all the dignity she could summon, she pulled Larry's sandy, perspiring little hand, while Morton pulled the other. Slowly and with head high she walked with her husband and child out of the playground.

Her first feeling was one of relief that a fight had been avoided, that no one was hurt. Yet beneath it there was a layer of something else, something heavy and inescapable. She sensed that it was more than just an unpleasant incident, more than defeat of reason by force. She felt dimly it had something to do with her and Morton, something acutely personal, familiar, and important.

Suddenly Morton spoke. "It wouldn't have proved anything."

"What?" she asked.

"A fight. It wouldn't have proved anything beyond the fact that he's bigger than I am."

"Of course," she said.

"The only possible outcome," he continued reasonably, "would have been—what? My glasses broken, perhaps a tooth or two replaced, a couple of days' work missed—and for what? For justice? For truth?"

"Of course," she repeated. She quickened her step. She wanted only to get home and to busy herself with her familiar tasks; perhaps then the feeling, glued like heavy plaster on her heart, would be gone. *Of all the stupid, despicable bullies,* she thought, pulling harder on Larry's hand. The child was still crying. Always before she had felt a tender pity for his defenseless little body, the frail arms, the narrow shoulders with sharp, winglike shoulder blades, the thin and unsure legs, but now her mouth tightened in resentment.

"Stop crying," she said sharply. "I'm ashamed of you!" She felt as if all three of them were tracking mud along the street. The child cried louder.

If there had been an issue involved, she thought, *if there had been something to fight for.... But what else could he possibly have done? Allow himself to be beaten? Attempt to educate the man? Call a policeman? "Officer, there's a man in the park who won't stop his child from throwing sand on mine...."* The whole thing was as silly as that, and not worth thinking about.

"Can't you keep him quiet, for Pete's sake?" Morton asked irritably.

"What do you suppose I've been trying to do?" she said.

Larry pulled back, dragging his feet.

"If you can't discipline this child, I will," Morton snapped, making a move toward the boy.

But her voice stopped him. She was shocked to hear it, thin and cold and penetrating with contempt. "Indeed?" she heard herself say. "You and who else?"

Bulat Okudzhava

I remember how I was reunited with Mama in 1947. We had been separated for ten years. When she was taken away I was a twelve-year-old boy, and here I was, a university student of twenty-two who had seen and experienced much—who had fought and survived wounds in the Second World War—although, as I recall myself now, I was probably pretty shallow and undiscerning.

Ten years of forced separation: Well, everyone knows what went on in those years, how those bitter losses and long separations happened. We understand it all full well, we explain it, we look back on it as a fact of history, but sometimes we forget how we ourselves stewed in all that, were ourselves caught up in it, and were ourselves hurt.

Ten years seemed a lifetime to me then; not like now, when the years flit by so that you look back one evening and realize they have passed. In those days a decade seemed endless. If I had grown up and lived through so much in those years, I thought, Mama must have become a white-haired old lady. A frightening thought.

After I returned from the war I entered Tbilisi University. I lived in a room in a communal flat, on the ground floor of an apartment building. My aunt had left the room to me when she moved to another town. I was enrolled in the language and literature department, wrote imitative verse, and lived like any bachelor student in those postwar years, without money, without despair, without trying to look ahead to the future. I fell in love and burned with passion; it helped me forget hunger. And I thought, I'm alive, I'm healthy, what more can I want? But I kept a dark secret in my heart, remembering Mama—the bitter secret of our separation.

I had several photos of her as a young woman with big, dark brown eyes. She wore a dark dress with a white collar. Her hair was combed flat and gathered into a bun at the back. Her face was austere, but her lips seemed about to break into a smile. I remembered her voice, her laugh, tender words, all kinds of trifles. I loved that fading image, but it was no more than a symbolic image, dear, faint, lofty and remote.

My neighbor, Meladze, a Georgian, occupied the room next to mine. He was elderly, corpulent, and slovenly, with ears that stuck out and showed tufts of gray hair around them. He was frowning and taciturn, especially with me, as if he were afraid I might ask for a loan. No one ever saw him enter the building when he returned from work each evening. I don't remember what his work was. Maybe I never knew. I think he flew out the window in the morning with his worn brown briefcase and flew in through it in the evening. He hardly ever emerged from his room. We were both of us without family; what did he do alone in there all evening?

I guess it was hard for him to live in the room next to mine. Sometimes groups of my fellow students, lively, noisy, and hungry, came with their girlfriends, and we made flat cakes of cornmeal and opened bottles of cheap wine. Through the thin partition Meladze heard our shouts, our laughter, and the sounds of glasses clinking; whispers, kisses. He seemed to put up with our noise with displeasure, and I thought he probably despised me. At that time I could not appreciate his tolerant and noble spirit. Never once did he complain. He simply ignored me, and if I sometimes asked him, as a neighbor, to let me have a pinch of salt or a match or a needle and thread, he never refused, but gave them to me silently, without looking me in the eye.

I came home late that evening. I don't remember where I had been. He met me in the kitchen, which was our common room, and handed me the envelope.

"A telegram," he said in a whisper.

The telegram from Karaganda burned in my fingers. "Meet train 501. Love. Mama."

Meladze shifted from foot to foot, sniffled and watched me. I put the tea kettle on the unlit kerosene burner. I started to brush the crumbs from the kitchen table. I lit the burner but did not put the kettle back on the flame. I began to wipe the oilcloth but dropped the dust cloth.

So the incredible had happened! What I had dreamed of hopelessly and wept over secretly at night had become almost tangible now.

"Karaganda?" Meladze said softly. It was a desert region of

camps and exiles. "That's far away." He clicked his tongue and sighed loudly.

"Train No. 501," I said. "Probably a mistake. Do trains have three-digit numbers?"

"No, it's not a mistake," he said, still softly. "Five-oh-one, a happy train."

"Why happy?" I asked, mystified.

"A slow freight, my friend, takes a long time on the way. Doesn't that make it a happy journey?"

I couldn't fall asleep that night. I heard Meladze coughing behind the wall. In the morning I set off for the railroad station.

The fear that I would not recognize Mama pursued me all the way down the hill and all along Jaures Street to the station. I imagined myself in a throng on the railroad platform, envisioned a white-haired old lady appearing in its midst, and the two of us rushing into each other's arms. I conjured up scenes of us riding to my room on streetcar No. 10 and then having dinner in the room. I pictured her delight at the pleasures of tranquillity and civilization, at new times, new surroundings, and everything I would tell and show her, things she had managed to forget or had grown unaccustomed to as she wept over my rare letters in Karaganda.

The train with the unusual number did indeed exist, although it was not listed in any timetable and followed no schedule. The time of its arrival was a mystery even to the dispatcher. Nevertheless, he expected it, and even hoped it would reach Tbilisi by evening.

I went home. I scrubbed the floor and washed the only tablecloth and my one towel, all the time trying to imagine the moment when I would meet Mama and how hard it would be to recognize her.

Long before evening, I was back at the station, but the happy 501 was lost somewhere in space. Now it was expected by nightfall. I went home again. It was May. I don't remember how I kept my fever in check. I moved about senselessly. I fussed with this and that, did something or other, but the fever did not abate, and I rushed back to the station.

I knew that when that improbable train drew up at the platform, I would have to run from car to car to find my mama in a crowd of thousands. I would recognize and embrace her, clasp her to me, a small, frail, gray, exhausted woman. We would dine at home, the two of us. She would tell me about her life, I would tell her about mine. We wouldn't try to figure out why it had happened or who was to blame. Well, so it had happened; it was over, the important thing was that we were together again.

Then I would take her to the movies to get her mind off everything. I had already chosen the film. Come to think of it, I didn't have to choose. There was only one motion picture that counted. It was the talk of all Tbilisi. It was *Girl of My Dreams*, a film the troops had brought back from Eastern Europe. It starred the stunning, irresistible Marika Reik. All of the city's normal life came to a stop, and people spoke of nothing else. They rushed off to see it every spare minute. Melodies from the movie besieged the ears of all Tbilisi. The melodies were whistled on the street and spilled from pianos at every open window. It was a color film, with songs, dancing, a love story and comic interludes, a loud, bright musical, staggering the imagination of viewers in those grim postwar years. I had myself seen the movie fifteen times, and though I knew it by heart it was fresh and new each time. I lived through all the experiences of the characters, and I was secretly in love with the luscious Marika and her blinding smile. No wonder I was certain the film would revive Mama's spirit after those ten years of suffering and hopelessness in the desert. She had only to watch Marika, young and exuding happiness. What an actress! Nature had endowed her with a supple figure, golden skin, an enchanting bosom and long, faultless legs. When she opened wide her laughing blue eyes, the emotional Tbilisi people drowned in them. She showed perfect lips and teeth as she smiled, and she danced with a bevy of equally ardent and carefree beauties. She accompanied me everywhere I went and even sat on my worn old trestle bed, crossing her legs and transfixing me with her blue eyes, her strange perfume and her glowing Austrian health. Of course I didn't dream of bringing her down to the level of my rude existence or troubling her with postwar sorrows or hints of Karaganda deserts crisscrossed with barbed wire. She was oblivious to the existence of those overpopulated deserts, so far removed from her beautiful blue Danube, where she danced in happy ignorance of such things. Injustice and grief did not touch her. Us, but not her. I treasured her like a precious gem that I could admire from time to time for the brightness with which it glittered from a screen smelling of carbolic disinfectant.

When I reached the square in front of the railroad station, a crowd was milling about. Suitcases and packs were heaped on the pavement. There was a deafening hubbub. Some people were shouting, calling to one another or speaking sharply, others laughing, crying and embracing. I thought I had missed the arrival of 501, but it turned out that a train had come in from Batumi. The news lifted a weight from my heart. I elbowed my way through the crowd to the information booth and called out my question about No. 501, but the woman in the booth, deafened and tugged every which way by many questions at once, did not understand, tried to answer several at the same time, until, when she understood, she shouted back desperately that the damned 501 had come in an hour ago, that crazy train was gone long since, everyone had left, it was no use looking, its platform was empty.

A bent old woman sat amid a pile of suitcases in front of the station, as if at a Sunday bazaar, and looked about helplessly. I went toward her, thinking for a moment that I detected something familiar in her features. My legs moved woodenly. She saw me, looked at me suspiciously and placed her small hand protectively on the nearest suitcase.

I set out for home on foot in hope of overtaking Mama, but arrived without meeting her. My room was silent and empty. Meladze was coughing behind the wall. I had to return to the station. I left, chilled by the thought of my helplessness. And there, on the next corner, I saw her! She was walking slowly toward the house, carrying a plywood suitcase. She was just as I remembered her, tall and handsome. She wore an ill-fitting, wrinkled gray cotton dress, but she was young and deeply sunburned, not old or bent.

It was dusk. She hugged me, cheek to cheek. Her suitcase sat on the sidewalk. Passersby paid no attention. In Tbilisi, where everyone embraces and kisses when they meet, there was nothing out of the ordinary in our hugs.

"How you've grown!" she exclaimed. "My boy, my little one!" And it was just as it used to be long ago.

We walked slowly toward the house. I put my arm around her shoulder and wanted to ask, as one asks of someone who has just arrived from a journey, "How are you? How was it there?" but caught myself and held my tongue.

We entered the building. The room. I gave her a chair. Behind the wall Meladze coughed. I looked into her eyes. Those large brown almond-shaped eyes were so close. Preparing to meet her, I had expected tears and lamentations, and I had stored up words of comfort: "See, Mama, I have my health, everything is fine, you're healthy and just as lovely as before, and everything will

be all right, now that you've returned and we're together again."
I had repeated the words to myself over and over as I prepared
for the first embraces and the first tears and everything that one
expects after ten years apart. Now I looked into her eyes. They
were dry and vacant. She was looking at me but didn't see me.
Her face was frozen, impassive, the lips slightly parted, her strong,
sunburned hands motionless on her knees. She said nothing, only
nodded from time to time at my comforting babble as I chatted
on emptily about anything except what was written in her face.
It would have been better if she had sobbed, I thought. She lit a
cheap cigarette, stroked my cheek, put out the cigarette and folded
her hands again on her knees like a guilty schoolgirl.

"We'll eat soon," I said cheerily. "Are you hungry?"

"What?" she asked.

"Do you want to eat?"

"I?" She didn't understand.

"You." I laughed. "Of course you."

"Yes," she said obediently, "and you?" and it seemed to me
she even smiled, but went on sitting in the same position, hands
on her knees.

I rushed off to the kitchen, lit the kerosene burner, mixed a
batter of the remaining cornmeal, and sliced a wedge of cheese
that was miraculously among the leftovers in my insignificant
larder. I laid the cheese before Mama, to please her—as if to say:
See the kind of son I am, see the household I have. Everything
is working out. We are stronger than circumstances, we have
overcome them with our courage and love. I fussed around
her, but she remained impassive and just smoked one cigarette
after another. Then the tea kettle came to a boil and I set it
on the table. Never before had I dealt so adroitly, so quietly and
so neatly with dishes, the kerosene burner and food. I wanted
her to see that she could depend on me. Life went on. Life
went on.

As I lifted the first cornmeal cake from the frying pan in the
kitchen, the door creaked and I heard Meladze sniffle. I turned.
He was holding out a bowl of lobio, a spicy bean dish.

"Oh!" I said, "you didn't have to go to all that trouble. We
have everything, thank you."

"Take it, friend," he said gloomily. "I know, I know."

I took the bowl but he did not leave.

"Come," I said, "I'll introduce you to my mama," and I threw
open the door of my room.

Mama was still seated as I had left her, hands on her knees. At sight of a guest I expected her to rise and smile, as is customary—"Pleased to meet you," and all that. But she merely held out her hand silently and then put it back on her knee.

"Have a seat," I said, and offered him a chair.

He sat facing us and, just imagine, he also put his hands on his knees. It was growing dark. Framed against the window like stooped statues, they were both of them frozen in identical poses, and in profile they bore a resemblance.

I don't know what they spoke about, or whether they spoke at all, while I hurried back to the kitchen. Not a sound came from my room. When I returned, their foreheads were almost touching, but their hands remained on their knees.

"Batyk," Meladze said in the silence. It was the name of a Karaganda village.

"Oh, Batyk," Mama said. "No, Zharyk." Then she glanced at me and smiled in embarrassment.

I left and returned. They were still exchanging incomprehensible words and brief phrases, and all this almost in whispers, moving only their lips. Meladze clicked his tongue and shook his head. I remembered that Zharyk was the station where Mama had been. It was the postmark on her infrequent letters, informing me that she was well, that she was in good spirits, that everything was fine, just study, son, study hard; and it was to Zharyk that I sent the news that I was alive and well and everything was going well and I was working on an essay about Pushkin, everyone praised me, don't worry about me, I'm sure everything will work out in the end and we'll meet.

Now we had met, and soon she would ask about the essay and other irresponsible fibs.

When I brought in the tea Meladze excused himself and vanished. For the first time, Mama looked at me with awareness.

"What about him?" I asked in a whisper. "Was he there, too?"

"Who?" she asked.

"Who, who? Meladze."

"Meladze?" she wondered, and stared out the window. "Was he?"

"Who is Meladze?"

"What do you mean, who?" I let fly angrily. "Mama, do you hear me? Meladze is my neighbor whom I have just now introduced. Was he there, too?"

"Ssh, ssh." She frowned. "Let's not talk about it, son."

O Meladze, sniffling, shuffling, lonely Meladze! After all, you too were once slim and straight as a dogwood branch, and your youthful features, with their hot lips and trim moustache, had lit up with a million wishes. Now the lips had paled, the moustache drooped, the once inspired cheeks were sunken. I used to ridicule you and point you out to my friends on the sly and say, "See, fellows, if you don't behave you'll come to resemble this old duck." We, still full-lipped and bright-eyed, went into peals of suppressed laughter as you waddled clumsily about and moved warily through the kitchen door. What were you afraid of, Meladze?

We drank our tea. I wanted to ask her what it had been like there, but I refrained. Instead, I began to lie hastily about my own situation. She seemed to listen, nodded, made a show of interest, and even appeared to smile as she ate slowly. She patted the side of the kettle and looked at her smudged palm.

"Never mind," I reassured her. "I'll wash the kettle. It's nothing. The kerosene burner smokes."

"My poor son," she said vacantly and suddenly burst into tears. I soothed and comforted her. She wiped the tears, pushed aside her empty cup and broke into a smile of embarrassment.

"That's all, that's all. Just ignore it." She lit a cigarette.

Meladze coughed behind the wall.

Never mind, I thought, it will be all right. We'll finish the tea and I'll take her to the movies. She doesn't know what awaits her. What a pleasure it will be—the blue Danube, music, sunlight and Marika Reik—after all that she's been through. My eyes narrowed in anticipation. It will be the best gift I can give her, I thought. I came out with it then and there.

"You know, I have a surprise for you. We'll have to go out and walk to it."

She frowned. "Leave the house?"

"Never fear." I laughed. "Nothing will happen. There's nothing to be afraid of now. You're going to see something marvelous, honest! Do you hear me? Let's go."

She rose obediently.

We walked through the twilit streets. Once more I wanted to ask her about her life there, but again I held back. I didn't want to cast a pall over our evening. Everything was going so well, it was so soft and calm roundabout, and I was so happy to be walking with her, arm in arm. She was handsome and lovely, my

mama, even in that wrinkled gray cotton dress, so un-Tbilisi-like;
even in shapeless, patched sandals. Straight from there, I thought,
into this gentle warmth, into this light that pours through the
plane trees, into our gay streets. I also thought I ought to make
her spruce up somehow, change into different clothing. It was a
shame to be wearing the same dress that she had worn there. She
ought to put all that behind her.

We walked down Rustaveli Avenue. She didn't ask questions.
While I bought the tickets she stood motionless against the wall
of the movie theater. I nodded to her from the cashier's booth,
and I think she smiled.

When we were seated in the stuffy auditorium I told her:
"You're going to see something marvelous. I can't describe it."
Then: "Did they show movies there?"

"Movies?" she asked.

"Yes. Films." I realized how foolish my question was. "At least
once in a while," I added lamely.

"Us?" she said, and chuckled softly.

"Mama, what's wrong?" I whispered in annoyance. "So I
asked! Just say they didn't show movies."

"They showed them, they showed them," she said vacantly.

I looked now at the screen, now at Mama. I was giving her the
best gift I could. The audience laughed, sighed, groaned, applauded, and hummed along with the tunes. Mama hung her head,
her hands on her knees.

"Look, look," I whispered. "The best part is coming now. Isn't
it wonderful? Look."

No, I thought to myself, God knows, this sparkling Austrian
carnival clashed with everything she had come from; but I couldn't
tear myself from the screen or keep from exclamations of delight.

"Look, look!"

Mama heard my cry, raised her head, saw nothing, and lowered
her head again. The beautiful Marika sat nude in a barrel filled
with soap bubbles. She was washing as if nothing had happened.
The hall buzzed in worshipful rapture. I guffawed and glanced
at Mama. She tried to smile in response but suddenly whispered:
"Let's go."

"How can we?" I was horrified. "The most interesting part is
coming."

"Please let's go."

We walked home slowly. Silently. After Marika's dazzling,

luxurious wardrobe, Mama's dress seemed even more drab and depressing.

"You're so sunburned and handsome," I said. "I expected to meet an old woman, but you're young and attractive."

She pressed my arm.

We entered the room. She took the same chair as before and sat staring before her, palms on her knees, while I feverishly made up the beds, the folding cot for myself and my only bed for her. She tried to object and to insist that I take the bed; she preferred the cot, yes, yes, and: no, please, you're my son, you must obey me (she tried to speak with playful severity), I'm your Mama and you have to accept my wishes—I'm Mama—and then, speaking to no one, to the air: Ma-ma . . . Ma-ma. . . .

I went to the kitchen to give her time to undress for bed. In violation of all his habits, Meladze was seated on the kitchen stool. He looked at me inquiringly.

"I took her to a movie," I complained in a whisper, "and she left in the middle, she didn't like it."

"To a movie? Which movie? She needs to rest."

"She's changed," I said. "Maybe there's something I don't understand. When I ask a question she repeats it as if she hadn't heard."

He clicked his tongue.

"When a person doesn't want to say too much," he said, still in a whisper, "he talks slowly. He stalls for time. He's thinking, do you understand? Think-ing. He needs time. She has acquired the habit."

"She's afraid to say too much *to me?*" I asked.

He grew angry.

"Not to you, not to you, my friend." He raised an index finger. "You weren't there. Others questioned her there—who, why, what for. Do you understand now?"

"I understand," I said.

I put my hope in tomorrow. After a while everything would be different. She had to shake off the heavy yoke of the past. It will all be forgotten, yes, Mama? We'll go back to the blue Danube, we'll mingle in the happy throng, we'll be just like everybody else. Yes, Mama?

"Buy fruit for her," Meladze said.

"What kind of fruit?"

"Cherries. Buy cherries."

Meanwhile, Mama had curled up on the cot in her gray dress,

without a blanket. She looked up at me when I entered, and she smiled weakly, simply a good-night smile.

"Mama," I said reproachfully, "I'll sleep on the cot."

"No, no," she said with childlike stubbornness, and laughed.

"Do you like cherries?" I asked.

"What?" She didn't understand.

"Cherries. Do you like cherries?"

"I?" she asked.

TRANSLATED BY LEO GRULIOW

CAPITAL PUNISHMENT

·2·

Joyce Carol Oates

It will be over Evander Jones that the trouble begins between Hope Brunty and her father but even if Hope guesses this, at the time, she doesn't care. At the time, she is fifteen years old and a sophomore in high school.

Hope's parents have been divorced for six years. She hasn't seen her mother in nearly five years: Mr. Brunty was "awarded custody" of her.

Hope's mother's name is Harriet but it is a name never spoken at home. Hope never hears her father speak it. She knows that her mother has remarried, that she has moved away, to California. She has three small children—twin boys, and another daughter. Is this girl Hope's half-sister? She has no interest in her, keeps forgetting her name. She has no idea how old the child is. The woman she remembers as her mother is thin, nervous, pretty, with pale heated skin, plucked eyebrows, a red lipsticked mouth, hennaed hair. She smells perfumy, but also of cigarettes; her breath smells sometimes of sweet red wine. When she cries Hope runs away to hide. When she and Mr. Brunty speak in quick raised voices to each other she runs away to hide. Why is the slick flirty image of Chiquita the Banana mixed up with Hope's mother in Hope's mind . . . ? She is two or three years old, staring from the picture of the red-mouthed smiling woman with the high-piled black hair to her mother who stands above her—her mother who is saying something to her she can't understand. One of the women is tiny and flat, only a drawing. The other is "real."

Hope's mother lives with her new family in Redwood City, California, which is thousands of miles away. Too far to visit if she is ever invited. Hope dreams sometimes of a city that is a redwood forest, tall straight trees stretching out in all directions and the shade so dark it is always night. In this city, no houses or inhabitants are visible.

Since Mrs. Brunty moved away from the one-story asphalt-sided shingle-roofed house on Lewiston Street where Hope and

her father live, Hope has grown into a big healthy strapping girl,
as the relatives say. How she's grown! they are always saying,
looking to Mr. Brunty as if he were to be congratulated, or
blamed. Mr. Brunty is a big man himself, accustomed to being
the biggest man wherever he goes. People naturally make way for
him, the way smaller dogs defer to larger. Hope has seen him
edge into the front of a line, push out of a doorway ahead of
others; she has been with him numberless times in the car when
he bullies his way forward and others drop back intimidated. She
does not know whether Mr. Brunty is aware of these habits, or
whether they are unconscious—"just his way." She overhears the
relatives tell Mr. Brunty that Hope takes after *him* and she feels
a thrill of pride nonetheless.

Once Hope overheard Mr. Brunty telling a friend of his, a man,
that all the things women pretend to like in you—a sense of humor
for instance, teasing and kidding around, standing up for your
own rights and not letting other people run over you, that sort
of thing—they'll twist around one day when they want to, until
they're the exact same things they hate in you. Say your hair is
brown, Mr. Brunty said. Say your eyes are blue. Say you tell
certain jokes they always laughed at only now they can't stand.
Most of all it's you being the man you are and not some other
man they'll twist around when it suits them, when they're ready.
    His heart had been broken, he said, but it could only be broken
once. The women he knew now he could take them or leave them
and he hoped they understood that.
    "I hope they feel the same way about me," he said.

Evander Jones, the Death Row prisoner who went insane while
awaiting execution, is related in some mysterious way to one of
Hope's classmates at Locktown High School: a boy named Delano
Holland who had been elected vice-president of their class in
eighth grade. He was the first Negro elected to any class office in
the history of the school district, which was part of the excitement
of electing him. Hope Brunty helped in his campaign and has
considered herself a friend of his ever since.
    The rumor is that Evander Jones is Delano's half-brother even
though he's so much older than Delano: thirty-seven, it said in
the paper. Nobody wants to ask Delano about Jones and in the
past week or two Delano hasn't been coming to school regularly
but once, when he does, Hope Brunty approaches him in the

cafeteria line in that way of hers that's shy but pushy too and she asks how he is how things are going she says she hasn't seen him around much she hopes they are still friends and Delano goes stiff smiling his twitchy smile and looking over her head. Since eighth grade he has grown into a lanky curve-shouldered boy who speaks to whites in monosyllables or doesn't speak at all.

Hope loses her courage and doesn't ask whatever it was she'd wanted to ask. She *is* pushy, but there are limits.

She has grown into the kind of girl who doesn't have *boy friends* but who does have *boy-pals*, *boy-buddies*. Sometimes they get rowdy joking around in the halls, shouting with laughter. Hope is a big-boned girl who isn't afraid to punch back when she's rabbit-punched but it's all just teasing; it's all just fun. The boys seem willing to forgive her for being an A student and Hope knows that being rowdy among them is better than nothing at all.

But Delano Holland doesn't like her anymore. The other black boys don't like her anymore. And the black girls: she'd never had any friends among them, anyway. She'd tried, but she never had a one.

Mr. Nicholson their tenth-grade civics teacher brings up the subject of Evander Jones in his class, invites discussion: should a person who has been sentenced to death be executed if he has been declared by doctors *non compos mentis?* (Mr. Nicholson writes *non compos mentis* on the blackboard.) When the debate club debates the "moral, ethical, and/or legal" issues involved Hope Brunty, though only a sophomore, stands out among the debaters—she is so passionate, so serious, remarkably mature for a girl her age except for her habit of now and then interrupting others, saying hurtful sarcastic things.

Still, Hope's side wins. Which thrills her so much that for a brief while she almost thinks that things in the real, adult world have been altered.

"Now Daddy please pay *attention*," Hope says excitedly. She has hurried him into the living room to see the six o'clock news, which features, tonight, four nights before the scheduled electrocution, an interview with the doomed man up at the Mecklenburg Prison. "You sure are damned bossy these days," Mr. Brunty says. Hope says, "Daddy don't *talk*."

There is Jones in his dull gray prison uniform smiling and blinking and craning his neck, fixing his wide-open stare at the television camera. His eyes are disconcertingly big—pop eyes. He is a much smaller man than Hope expects, with a very dark skin that looks oiled. His hair is trimmed short, a tight little cap of wool going unevenly gray.

He is flanked by two white men—one of them a regular newscaster, the other a lawyer from the State Bureau of Public Advocacy. As they introduce him Jones squirms and twitches and continues to stare at the camera as if he's unaware of what is being said about him, or uninterested. It is immediately obvious, Hope thinks, frightened, that the man is "not right."

Mr. Brunty too seems shaken. He says they shouldn't show such things on television: a poor bastard off his rocker like that.

Hope pokes him in the arm. "Daddy *hush*."

Evander Jones is a war veteran, was awarded a Purple Heart, honorably discharged at the end of the war. Nine years ago he was convicted of first-degree murder in a drugstore holdup and sentenced to die in the electric chair but his case had been reopened and the date of execution postponed several times and finally it was discovered that the man had gone insane on Death Row and did not understand that he was going to die. He seemed not to know where he was, or why he was there.

Jones is not faking! His is an authentic case. He has been examined by officials and psychiatrists many times since the situation came to light and not even those in the employ of the state are willing to testify that he is sane. He suffers from acute paranoid schizophrenia—auditory hallucinations, obsessive thoughts, fixed delusions. Nine years of incarceration on Death Row are responsible, the lawyer says. In a truly humane society capital punishment would be abolished; it is a barbaric custom—an eye for an eye, a tooth for a tooth. (Indeed, the fact that Evander Jones has gone insane came to light only after another inmate on Death Row was discovered hanging in his cell a few weeks ago. The man's method was said to be "ingenious" but authorities would not give details.)

At first Jones sits smiling and mute as the white men in their suits and ties discuss him. It is revealed that the governor will make an announcement about his case sometime before 11 p.m. on Friday—the time of his scheduled execution. It is mentioned that public opinion is "sharply divided": most of the telephone calls and telegrams the governor has received are in favor of his execution being postponed (or the sentence commuted altogether) but some are in favor of no interference. Jones, asked how he feels, sits mute for a long awkward moment as if he has not heard the question, or has not understood it. "What is your feeling about your situation, Mr. Jones?" the newscaster asks in his earnest, compassionate voice, and Jones begins to squirm with what appears to be pleasure. His pop eyes widen, his purplish-black skin exudes moisture. His voice leaps from him like a small frenzied animal and at first neither Hope nor Mr. Brunty can understand a word.

He has had, Jones says excitedly, "a Visitation from the Lord." He has seen "the Way, the Truth, and the Light." How long ago he doesn't know—it could have been yesterday, it could have been the hour of his birth. An angel appeared to him. Jesus Christ appeared to him. He is ready, he says, for "the Rapture." He is ready for "the Trumpet Call."

The lawyer tries to interrupt Jones to ask him about the circumstances of his trial—an all-white jury, a white judge, his common-law wife's testimony discredited—but Jones keeps on talking, more and more rapidly. Mr. Brunty says it isn't right for them to listen to this, the man is crazy as a loon and it's obvious, he's going to turn the television off—but Hope gives a little scream and holds him back. "Daddy what do you mean! Daddy don't you *dare*!"

Jones is saying that he listens every instant for the Trumpet Call. There is a Rapture that is hard to bear but it must be borne. He is hopeful to be embraced in the Bosom of the Lord. "Praise the Lord! Praise the Lord! The Lord giveth and the Lord taketh away! Blessed be the name of the Lord!" he cries. "I am ready. I am hopeful. Goin to meet the Lord. The Rapture is hard to bear but the Rapture is upon us. O yes Lord. O yes Lord. I bein the first to go pavin the Way for the rest of em sinners. O yes Lord—!" A warm light seems to break from his face and ray outward . . . but the interview is over; Jones is rudely interrupted in mid-syllable.

The news anchorwoman concludes by saying that the controversy has attracted national and international attention. Is Evander Jones's imminent execution a miscarriage of justice, as some argue, or a grim necessity, as others insist. Viewers are invited to call WWCT–TV immediately following the show, or write postcards, voicing their opinions. But they must hurry!

Bright and sassy, a commercial for new Buicks comes on the screen and Hope and Mr. Brunty sit there staring at it. Hope's face is streaked with tears; she waits—she is waiting—for her father to glance at her, to notice. But he doesn't. He heaves himself from his chair with no comment and goes out into the kitchen. Opening the refrigerator, Hope hears, getting another beer.

Hope tests certain words, phrases. She is consciously improving her vocabulary in what might be called an exalted direction but she experiments with other words too, murmuring them under her breath, gauging their weight. She thinks of Mr. Brunty, whom she loves, as a "big lug." A "big dumb lug." A "big dumb ox." She will leave him soon though he doesn't know it. She will leave Locktown altogether!—a place of "mediocre sensibility" (as her civics teacher Mr. Nicholson has said), "to all intents and purposes, soulless."

Hope sees that Mr. Brunty's eyes, though they are a pale washed-out blue, resemble Evander Jones's eyes: protuberant, heavy-lidded. The man is fattish and graying and his nose is getting red-veined but he's still considered a handsome man. Women are attracted to him—that's for sure. (Hope has never cared in the slightest what her father does with his string of girlfriends so long as he doesn't do it anywhere near her, and doesn't talk about it. She's satisfied not even knowing any names.) Both Mr. Brunty and Hope have big broad faces and squarish jaws and noses that are disproportionately small—snubbed—as if they'd been pushed in as a prank, like clay noses. Genetic determinism, Hope thinks. They'd studied all that grim stuff in biology class.

Once when Mr. and Mrs. Brunty were quarreling in the kitchen very late at night Hope appeared in her pajamas in the doorway and saw that they weren't people she knew, exactly—there was this shiny-faced woman in a nightgown slapping at this big joking-angry man and the woman wasn't covered the way she was supposed to be, the top of her nightgown had been yanked down over one shoulder, one of her breasts was exposed, and the man, when he turned to see Hope, when his wild eyes fastened on her—she saw a thin trickle of blood running down from his nose and splashing onto the bronze-fuzzy hairs that covered his chest. Hope began to scream.

A long time ago.

In secret they are making their plans: telephoning one another and speaking in lowered voices or in whispers—none of their parents is to know. Who initially made the suggestion about cutting classes, taking the Greyhound bus to the capital, joining what newspapers have called the "coalition" of diverse groups protesting Evander Jones's execution—whose sense of justice sparked the adventure, the trespass into adult territory—no one will want to say afterward. It wasn't Hope Brunty, the only sophomore in the group, but as soon as Hope learned of their plans she insisted upon being included.

Originally there are quite a few students from Locktown involved—twelve members of the debate team, among them four girls. By Wednesday evening two or three have backed out, by Thursday morning all but six have backed out. Hope Brunty is the youngest, and the only girl.

*   *   *

The first Miles Brunty knows of his daughter Hope's involvement in the demonstration for Evander Jones is when the call comes for him from the juvenile detention facility where Hope is being held. Five to twelve of a Thursday morning and he's told to take a telephone call up front and his heart stops for a moment then starts in again with a deadly little kick. You aren't called out of the machine shop to be told good news: that's the kind that can wait.

It takes Mr. Brunty several minutes to understand what he hears. He must make an effort to comprehend the fact that Hope isn't in Locktown as he'd assumed, she isn't in school as he'd assumed, she is 115 miles away at the state capital in a juvenile detention facility. She was brought in with a number of other minors after an unauthorized gathering on the steps of the capitol building got out of hand and she is being held pending release in his custody. The word "minor" strikes Mr. Brunty's ear oddly—he isn't accustomed to hearing his daughter so designated.

"Is she all right? Is my daughter all right?" he asks excitedly. And the police matron, who knows what he means by "all right," assures him that, yes, she is.

Maybe a bit shaken. Like many of the younger demonstrators.

Mr. Brunty, who is very agitated, is carefully told that none of the minors involved has been formally arrested; none will be charged with any crime or misdemeanor. But should he wish to engage legal counsel he has the opportunity now to do so.

And when he comes to get his daughter he should bring identification for both himself and her, and Hope's birth certificate.

Does he understand? The police matron speaks slowly and patiently, repeating her information several times. She is accustomed to dealing with parents in various states of shock and incomprehension.

Afterward it will come out that Hope and five other students from Locktown High School took a bus to the state capital that morning, instead of going to school, so that they could participate in a demonstration in support of Evander Jones (in support of the postponement of his execution, that is) planned by a number of liberal and pacifist organizations in the state. In all, approximately 150 people turned out, among them a sprinkling of high school students; unfortunately a number of angry and in some cases violent demonstrators turned out against *them*—which the organizers seemed not to have foreseen.

"She isn't hurt? You're sure?" Mr. Brunty asks. And the police matron assures him she is not. And puts Hope, who is crying, on the line.

It takes him an hour and forty-five minutes to get to the detention facility—which looks, and smells, more like a clinic than a jail—and once he's there they make him wait. The place is busy, crowded, understaffed, other parents have come to get their children, there is a constant milling in the lobby and in the lounge where Mr. Brunty paces, telling himself repeatedly that the main thing is his little girl is all right.

That's the main thing, the rest will come later.

He finds himself thinking past Hope to Hope's mother. How, one night, a long time ago, after he and Harriet had made love, one of their not-great times, he'd said something he maybe shouldn't have said; and after a moment Harriet said, "Then you won't mind me leaving you, will you . . . you won't mind it a lot, will you," and he knew the woman wasn't joking. And she wasn't asking it as a question either.

He's called into a windowless room, he's asked questions, told to fill out forms, sweating inside his clothes (he'd gone home to change into a suit, clean white shirt, tie) like a guilty man. Several times he tells the juvenile officers that he'd had no idea what Hope was up to: no idea at all! Misunderstanding him they assure him he isn't to blame.

He and Hope are brought together in another windowless room, walls painted a pale sickly green and fluorescent lighting that throws queer dented shadows downward on their faces and here is Hope stumbling into his arms sobbing as he hasn't heard her sob in years: Daddy thank God you're here, oh Daddy I'm so sorry, I'm so scared, I'm so *scared*.... What strikes him is how tall she's grown, how solid and ample and heated her flesh. He embraces her, deeply moved, embarrassed, not really knowing what to do. He lookes over her head at the juvenile officers as if hoping for support or solace. He has never seen Hope quite so agitated in any public place, before witnesses.

He calls her sweetheart; comforts her; tells her not to cry, she's coming home now. It's all over now, he says. Or whatever he says: it's as if another man, another father, were standing in his place, clumsy and flush-faced in his suit and tie, saying words not his but appropriate to the occasion.

It's a long drive, Mr. Brunty thinks, back home. He hopes they get there.

Of course Mr. Brunty is aware of the fact that Hope isn't like other girls her age. His sisters and aunts are always taking him aside to ask shouldn't Hope lose a little weight? Does Hope have any boyfriends? Why is Hope so unfriendly? (Meaning, why does Hope think she's so superior to us?) Mr. Brunty tells them he's damned grateful his daughter is as different from her mother as night and day. Or he tells them it isn't any of their business, which it isn't.

These teenaged girls Mr. Brunty sees downtown or in the neighborhood, strolling along the sidewalk as if they owned it, breathless and giggling and quick to notice if they're being watched . . . he *is* grateful his own daughter bears so little resemblance to them. The other day he'd happened to be watching this girl no older than Hope with her hair peroxided and falling down her back and her face all gummed up like a grown woman's wearing jeans and a skimpy red halter top and this was in a Rexall's where she was leaning against a counter—arms straight out, chewing gum studying things for sale on the counter but at the same time pushing in with her arms against her breasts to make the cleavage more noticeable and she wasn't unaware of Mr. Brunty close by, not by a long shot. Hot little bitch, Mr. Brunty thought. Did they know what they were inviting, watching a man old enough to be their father slantwise like that . . . ? Damp pink tongue wetting her lower lip as if, sure, she *was* just contemplating the top of the counter.

Most summers Hope wears jeans too but they're loose-fitting, and her shirts and pullovers are likely to be loose too; she wears soiled white sneakers that make her feet look enormous; and, sometimes, an old sweat-stained visored cap backwards on her head, as if for a joke—the way Mr. Brunty wears his. You wouldn't know, seeing her loping along the street, or sprawled in the living room reading one of her library books, that she was an honors student at the high school; would hardly be able to tell if she was a boy or a girl.

And she's increasingly critical of him: nagging him about his table manners, his taste in television programs, his lack of a "political conscience." Since the Evander Jones publicity hit the newspapers and TV she'd picked at him saying some people (like him?) are born morally "apathetic" and the way the word "apathetic" rolled off her tongue allowed Mr. Brunty to know she was using it to mock him. Not just that she was saying *he* was apathetic but she chose to use a word no one had ever used in Mr. Brunty's presence, that he knew of. A word she probably thought he didn't understand, being a seventh-grade dropout from a country school, and not a hot-shit honor student like herself.

They were in the kitchen just before supper. Mr. Brunty stopped what he'd been doing and looked at her and after an uneasy moment she glanced around and saw him. And her eyes pinched a little and he could see that she knew: she knew how close she was to trouble. Her mouth opened just slightly and the peeved-looking expression on her face faded and though Mr. Brunty had not taken a step in her direction she stumbled back, clumsy, banging her hip against the edge of a counter.

Mr. Brunty said quietly, "You want to say all that again? Explain what it is you been saying? Spell it all out for me? Do you?" And Hope, to give her credit, laughed a little and shook her head no, no, no, no she didn't.

On the interstate he questions her but doesn't push her, doesn't want to get her crying again. That scared him—the way she'd broken down and pushed herself, big as she is, into his arms. As one of the officers told him, young people are naturally idealistic and what his daughter did, what most of the demonstrators did, was generous and civic-spirited; a little imprudent, as it turned out, but they couldn't have known that beforehand.

"I understand that," Mr. Brunty said curtly. Though he was thinking, What about her deceiving *me*?

So he asks Hope a few questions, mainly why she got involved with something that had so little to do with her. And how could she and her friends have thought that the governor would be influenced by *them* . . . ? That isn't the way politicians operate, Mr. Brunty says.

Hope says quietly that there were a lot of people involved, not just kids. He'd see on the television news. "And it isn't over yet," she adds.

"What isn't over yet?"

"The governor still has to make his decision."

There is a queer dazed sleepwalker's look to Hope that Mr. Brunty doesn't like. She is sitting unnaturally straight beside him (she usually slouches in the car) as if she's afraid to relax. He can feel the tension in her body.

Hope fumbles for a tissue in her purse and blows her nose noisily. She seems to be breathing hard, almost panting; she runs her fingers repeatedly through her snarled hair. It's like her, Mr. Brunty thinks, not to have a comb. The only fifteen-year-old girl in the state without a comb.

Suddenly he asks, "You're sure nobody laid a hand on you?— no cop, or—"

"No."

"You were all piled into a police van, weren't you?"

"It was all right."

"Were you handcuffed?"

"*No* Daddy."

"And you're sure nobody at school put you up to this? This Mr. Nicholson you're always talking about?"

"Yes Daddy. I'm sure."

"You're sure?"

"Daddy *please*," She laughs in a harsh melancholy way—no mirth, just a hissing expulsion of air.

Mr. Brunty lets it go for the time being. He's thinking all along that this is the girl who deceived him. Not lying exactly because he hadn't asked her point-blank that morning was she going to go to school that day, or did she have other plans. So it wasn't exactly lying but could he ever believe her again?

He's thinking it has been years since he has laid a hand on his daughter and he can't start in again now. Not now. One blow and she'd try to defend herself, she'd fight back, and God knows what would happen then, if she provoked him. So he can't start.

He's that angry, isn't he? But he can't, won't, start.

Though it's too early for supper they stop at a restaurant on the interstate: Mr. Brunty missed lunch and is ravenously hungry.

Hope says wanly that she hasn't much appetite. The way human beings behaved that day, pushing and jostling one another, so much anger and so much hatred, all that that says about human nature—she doubts she'll ever have much appetite for food ever again.

"You'll eat," says Mr. Brunty. "If you know what's good for you."

The restaurant is surprisingly crowded for this hour of the afternoon but they are waited on quickly and their food is brought to them with startling swiftness, on gray lightweight plastic plates. Thin slices of fatty roast beef, scoops of lukewarm mashed potatoes; canned peas and tiny diced carrots. Two small bowls of applesauce. . . . During the course of the meal Mr. Brunty thickly butters five or six pieces of white bread and wipes his plate as he eats. An old habit Hope has criticized in the past but now she keeps very still. Mr. Brunty says of the food, "It isn't bad, is it? Not as bad as it looks."

Meaning to be friendly he adds, "This will save you cooking supper, at least."

Hope sighs and picks at her food as if to please him. Very likely she was fed at the detention facility; and Mr. Brunty had noticed a wall of vending machines in one of the corridors. Candy bars, potato chips, peanuts. When Hope feels sorry for herself she stuffs herself with things like that, hidden away in her room with the door shut against him.

He sees that she went off that morning, all that distance, in ordinary school clothes—plaid blouse, cotton skirt, white ribbed cotton socks. In her over-the-shoulder bag is a wallet containing $2.35 and the return Greyhound ticket; a small notepad and a ballpoint pen. (Hope had intended to write up the demonstration for the school newspaper.) Her blouse is sweat-stained under the arms and her skirt is, as usual, badly rumpled, as if she has been sleeping in it. There is a strange flush to her face like sunburn.

Mr. Brunty feels sorry for Hope, picking at her food like that. He is about to ask if she wants to order something else from the menu when her eyes suddenly snap up at him. "I will never forget this day," she says. "This is a day of ignominy."

"A day of *what?*"

"Shame and disgrace."

Mr. Brunty stares at her. He says, "Yes it is. It certainly is. I buy that—it certainly is."

"I suppose you're happy with the way things turned out."

"*Happy?* Driving across the state to bail you out? Are you serious?" Mr. Brunty laughs angrily. "When we get home—"

Hope's mouth is trembling. Her eyes brim again with tears and Mr. Brunty is panicked she will start crying again, here in the restaurant. Those half-dozen times Harriet lost control—went into hysterics—laughing, crying, gasping for breath, clawing at her own face with her nails—had scared him shitless.

Mr. Brunty changes the subject, asks Hope if she would like to order something else from the menu: a tuna fish sandwich, maybe. He will eat what's left of her roast beef and order another beer.

Hope says politely, "No thank you."

"You sure?"

"*Yes* Daddy."

"You don't need to be sarcastic."

"I wasn't being sarcastic."

"Everything you say is sarcastic."

"Then what can I do about it!" Hope gives a sudden scream, bringing both fists down hard on the tabletop. "If everything I say is sarcastic what can I say that isn't!"

Mr. Brunty is appalled; other customers have turned to look at them. "Take it easy, for Christ's sake," he says.

They sit trembling, not looking at each other. After a moment Mr. Brunty says cautiously, "You're all right now, you're safe now, and you know it."

"What do I know! I don't know anything!" she says. Then, in a quieter voice, "I feel sick, Daddy. I'm going to the restroom." But she doesn't budge from her side of the booth; remains sitting with her elbows on the table, fists pressed against her face. Big sad homely girl, *his* girl. Mr. Brunty feels a pang of helpless love for her, and dislike.

He finishes his food, and most of Hope's. Orders another beer. And asks, as if casually, why Hope and her classmates got involved with Evander Jones in the first place: she never did explain. Some poor black bastard none of them had ever heard of a few days ago.

Hope sighs and shrugs.

Mr. Brunty says, eyeing her with derision, "Did you kids think he'd give a damn about you? You think he even *knows* about *you*? He doesn't."

Hope rubs her hands briskly over her eyes. "That isn't the point, Daddy," she says.

"Why isn't it the point? What point? People like that don't care for us so why should we care for them? You tell me, you got all the answers."

"If you have to ask a question like that, Daddy, you can't understand any answer I can give you."

"What's that supposed to mean?" Mr. Brunty asks belligerently. "I'm just asking, in plain English. A man like that—a Negro, or whoever—a complete stranger—in prison because he shot and killed another man—"

"Maybe he *didn't*, maybe he was *innocent*," Hope interrupts. "He didn't get a fair trial."

"You think he cares about *you*? Even knows about *you*? He'd slit your throat if he could."

"Daddy that isn't the *point*," Hope says weakly. "You just don't get the *point*."

"I'm sitting here waiting for you to tell me," Mr. Brunty says, trying to keep his voice low. "Aren't I listening? So tell me."

"Tell you what?"

"Why I should care about somebody who doesn't care about me. Tell me."

"Because—"

"Yes?"

"Because—it's why we're here."

"Here? Where?"

"Here on earth."

"*Where?*"

"Oh Daddy never mind," Hope says. "I don't know."

Mr. Brunty leans forward, staring at his daughter. He is thinking she's somebody he doesn't know and wouldn't be talking with, sitting in this booth with, if it weren't for the accident of —their connection. If it weren't for a chain of things he can't quite remember now except to know that they happened and that, when they began happening, it was without his full knowledge or consent.

You could say that in a way they hadn't anything to do with him.

"Why we're here, right here, right now—that's the question,"

Mr. Brunty says loudly. "I mean right here in this booth in this God-damned joint in the middle of nowhere."

When Hope doesn't reply he says, as if he can't resist prodding her, pushing, "This poor asshole Jones! You might as well kiss him goodbye, you and your friends. He's good as dead this minute. Want to bet? He's good as dead this minute."

Hope looks up at him, her eyes pinching. "That isn't so," she says. "You're just saying that."

"Good as dead," Brunty repeats, lighting up a cigarette.

"The governor—"

"The governor! Come off it! If he lets one of these guys live he'll have to let them all live. Open the prisons and turn them all out."

Hope fixes him with a look of loathing. She says, "I don't believe anything you say. I don't even listen to anything you say! You're such a hypocrite—telling people my mother left us when you know you made her leave."

"I what?"

"You *made* her leave."

"You don't know what the hell you're talking about."

"You forced her out and then you told everybody she left you. You said she left *us*. That's what hypocrisy is!"

"I never forced anybody to leave," Mr. Brunty says angrily. He is aware of a couple in the adjoining booth listening to their conversation, which only makes him all the angrier. "What the hell do you know about it?—you were only a little girl at the time."

Hope has shifted into her old self: mocking, derisive, tough as nails. Mr. Brunty could reach out and slap her smug face.

"Hypocrite," she says. "You know what you are."

"I never made anybody leave me! Your mother—"

Hope stretches her mouth and sings "I never made anybody leave . . . me . . ." to the tune of "You'll Never Know Just How Much I Love You."

"Yeah," says Mr. Brunty, "—you don't know *shit*."

Hope giggles and falls silent. Just in time, her father is thinking. She snatches up her purse and announces she's going to the women's room.

Mr. Brunty finishes his beer and lights up another cigarette and goes to pay the cashier. Hope is taking her time about coming back; by now it's early evening and the restaurant is getting crowded. Many families with young children. Squalling babies. Mr. Brunty is thinking that one-third of a man's life is a hell of a long time to be on Death Row but that's how things work out: an eye for an eye, a tooth for a tooth.

The women's restroom has double doors which are continually swinging in and out. Each time a figure appears Mr. Brunty thinks it's his daughter and each time it's a stranger. Where is she? Keeping him waiting on purpose? She wouldn't have gone directly to the car he's sure but where the hell is she?—five minutes, ten minutes, Mr. Brunty tosses his cigarette onto the dirty tile floor and grinds it out with the heel of his foot though there's an ashtray a few feet away.

The woman cashier, Mr. Brunty's age, perky and heavily made up and not bad looking except for the pinkish synthetic wig she's wearing, calls over, "You look like you're waiting for somebody!" as if it were a witty remark.

Mr. Brunty says coldly, "That's right." And gives the bitch a look that shuts her up fast.

Fifteen minutes. He begins to understand that something is wrong. Half consciously he has drawn closer to the doors as if, at a slant, he might see inside—might catch a glimpse of Hope. Women going in and coming out begin to eye him suspiciously. When the next woman comes out—a hefty girl carrying a baby —Mr. Brunty stops her apologetically to ask if she has seen a girl who resembles Hope. He refers to Hope as "my daughter, fifteen years old, sort of big for her age," and tries to remember what she is wearing.

The girl is sympathetic but says she doesn't know if she noticed anyone like that inside; would Mr. Brunty like her to go back and check? "No, that's all right, sorry to bother you," Mr. Brunty says. A moment later he could kick himself.

He is thinking such weird thoughts like things scuttling in the dirt when you overturn a rock: what if Hope has hanged herself in one of the toilet stalls? (That would be just like her.) She might also have slashed her wrists in a place he couldn't enter and that would be just like her too. . . . Hadn't he read that women are more likely to slash their wrists than to hang themselves. Or take an overdose of pills.

He has been waiting for Hope so long that women leaving the restroom are all women he has seen going in. And no Hope! In desperation he stops a friendly-looking woman of about his age and asks her did she happen to see a girl resembling Hope but the woman seems not to have heard his question, or not to wish to answer it. In a vehement voice she tells him that there is a pack of women inside—some mothers changing their babies' diapers too and it isn't a very pleasant place. "You wouldn't get that in the men's room," she says with an air of reproach. Mr. Brunty sees that the woman is slightly off—that look in the eye, that eager smile—and he tries to edge away. "You have to wait a long time in there to use the toilet," the woman says. "You know why?" "Why?" Mr. Brunty asks reluctantly. "Because some of the toilets don't work," the woman says. "They don't flush. It's a disgrace—it's disgusting." "Yes," Mr. Brunty says, edging away.

Two teenaged girls leave the restroom, laughing loudly together; both smoking cigarettes. Mr. Brunty wonders if, on the sly, Hope smokes cigarettes like so many teenagers. He decides he will forgive her if he learns that she does.

The cashier in the pink wig is watching him. Mr. Brunty regrets having snubbed her because now he might enlist her help.

Then it occurs to him that Hope has climbed out a rear window to escape from him!—what could be simpler, more obvious. As he'd seen a tricky woman do in a TV movie the other night. This beautiful model desperate to escape some nut who'd threatened to kill her and in a restaurant in New Orleans the woman pushed open a window and forced herself—this took time, this was tense and dramatic—through an excruciatingly small narrow space. "Sweet fucking Jesus," Mr. Brunty says, wiping his hands on his trousers. He wonders if he is losing his mind.

He leaves the restaurant to see if Hope is hitch-hiking on the highway: that would be the way her mind worked. But no one is there. Trucks roar past, semi-detached rigs, thunderous vehicles, strangers' cars—nothing.

He goes to his car and unlocks the door, his hands shaking. His heart is beating hard and his senses are keenly but pointlessly alert, as if he is about to fight another man. No one inside the car but of course he knew that: the doors were all locked.

Then he hears someone speak, drawling, and of course it's Hope—sauntering toward him from a grove of picnic tables close by. Her hair is flying in the wind, still snarled, but her face looks washed, scrubbed. She regards her daddy with an expression of wide-eyed innocence.

"Where were you?" Mr. Brunty says angrily. He's embarrassed that he must look so worried.

Hope opens her eyes still wider. "Where were you?" she says. "—I've been waiting out here for ages."

"I was waiting for you inside," Mr. Brunty says. He feels clumsy, exposed. His heart is still beating uncomfortably hard and he looks at his daughter with a peculiar eagerness, as if he is waiting for her to say something further, to explain herself, or him.

But she doesn't, of course. She is playing dumb. She repeats that she was waiting for him out here and as she settles into the passenger's seat she stretches and yawns and adds with a small mock-smile, "Didn't think you'd lost me, did you?"

* * *

Years later when Hope Brunty is living in New York City her father, from whom she has been amicably estranged for a very long time, sends her a clipping from the Locktown newspaper. For a moment Hope has no idea what it is, what it can possibly have to do with her.

A woman named Evita Swann—a black woman, judging from her photograph—was arrested by Locktown police on charges of passing bad checks and while under questioning suddenly volunteered the information that, twenty-nine years before, she had lied to police; she'd lied on the witness stand in a murder trial. She had sworn that her common-law husband Evander Jones— one of the last prisoners in the state to be executed before the repeal of capital punishment—had been with her on the night of the murder but in fact he had not been with her. Where he'd been, she never knew. "He never told me and I never asked," she said. The article is headed WOMAN CONFESSES PERJURY AFTER 29 YEARS.

Hope reads the clipping several times, feeling a rush of hurt, indignation. Isn't it like her father to send her something like this torn from the newspaper, with no accompanying note!—when they correspond so rarely.

Isn't it like him, not to forget.

She has not thought of Evander Jones in many years and does not want to think of him—of that incident—now. She crumples the clipping and throws it away. She tells herself it's amusing, really—an old man, Miles Brunty, with nothing better to do with his time.

By degrees—by default it sometimes seems—Hope has become one of the adults of the world though she has never married, has had no child. She finds herself, in young middle age, waiting with apprehension for news of her relatives' deaths though she is not close to her relatives; she waits with a particular dread for news of her father's death knowing that, when he dies, she will grieve terribly for him—her life will be wrenched in two. Yet, mysteriously, she seems powerless to forestall the guilt while he is alive. She loves Mr. Brunty yet cannot get along with him just as he loves her (she believes) and cannot get along with her.

Hope left home, left him, when she was seventeen years old and had yet to complete her senior year at the high school. She boarded with a family who lived near the school and worked part-time at a dairy to support herself: she'd wanted, stubbornly, even defiantly, to support herself that final year in Locktown.

A few months after Hope moved out, Mr. Brunty remarried. A woman he'd been seeing off and on for years and Hope felt no animosity toward her, only a cheery forced uneasiness; some disappointment perhaps that the woman wasn't glamorous—a solid, likeable person, in fact.

Why leave home? Did you and your father quarrel?—so Hope was asked repeatedly and she evaded answering because she didn't really know why she'd left home. Because it was time: she was quite mature for her age. Because Mr. Brunty had not tried to stop her. "Do what you want to do," he'd said ironically. "It's what you're going to do anyway."

And then of course Hope had gone away to the state university and after that to a distinguished eastern university and she never came back to Locktown to live; rarely came back to visit. Her life is busy, crowded, stimulating, rewarding, she has many friends and she believes passionately in her work and she isn't lonely, though living alone. Though it sometimes surprises her to be referred to as a "success." She thinks of her life as constant striving, constant pressure—is this what "success" is?

Mr. Brunty, she has heard, is proud of her, in her absence.

Mr. Brunty, she has heard, *does* love her—though he never writes and their telephone conversations are strained and Hope feels more comfortable with his wife whom she scarcely knows.

In recent years she has come to think of him often, far oftener than he might guess. He is a riddle to her; or, rather, *she* is a riddle to herself, in relationship to him. A knot she can't untie. This evening, alone, Hope will prepare a solitary meal, will read a book while she eats, or try to read, thinking all the while about Mr. Brunty who'd ripped that news item out of the paper to send to her—wondering what thoughts had gone through his mind; what feelings of vindictiveness, satisfaction, irony. Or had he wanted her simply to know—to know how one strand of one story turned out, after so many years. All stories come to an end eventually but do we know their endings?

She recalls with shame that sly mean-spirited trick of hers, that inexplicable child's trick she'd played on her father that day— slipping out of the women's room in the restaurant, hurrying outside to hide around the corner of the building, heart beating hard in excitement. Why had she done it? Had it been deliberate? Or had it just happened?—one of those numberless things that take place between people who live together for a long time, who are bound together by ties of blood, feeling, fate? Hope recalls laughing to herself, Hope recalls the sheer childish impulsiveness of what she'd done. Hiding from Daddy and would he know where to find her and would he worry, would he be frightened, when he couldn't find her?

Capital punishment, she'd thought. Now you know.

Of course it was a senseless thing to have done on that day of all days. Seeing the fatigue and worry in her father's face, the deepening lines, the pale eyes so like her own. And that look of helplessness as he'd turned to her, car keys in hand. He hadn't caught on that it was a prank. That she'd meant it to wound.

"Did you think you'd lost me?" Hope dared to ask. Brazening it out, stretching and yawning. And the way he'd looked at her, blinking, squinting as if to get her into focus, told her no, probably not, he hadn't caught on and never would.

I KNOW LIFE WELL

·2·

Yevgeny Vinokurov

I know life well. I studied it a lot,
tightly gritting my teeth. What a bitter pleasure
to get acquainted! The basic principle
is harsh experience. There's no greater treasure
than an understanding of life. So I made an effort
to read what it had stored, knocked myself senseless
puzzling it out. But now I'll offer a course—
would you like a series of lectures? I know my business.
I know life well. But then there's my young son—
he'll have nothing to do with what his father learned.
To him what I did is water over the dam.
Gritting his teeth,
            he's going to dig it all up
                        again.

TRANSLATED BY F. D. REEVE

STILL OF SOME USE
·2·

John Updike

When Foster helped his ex-wife clean out the attic of the house where they had once lived and which she was now selling, they came across dozens of forgotten, broken games. Parcheesi, Monopoly, Lotto; games aping the strategies of the stock market, of crime detection, of real-estate speculation, of international diplomacy and war; games with spinners, dice, lettered tiles, cardboard spacemen, and plastic battleships; games bought in five-and-tens and department stores feverish and musical with Christmas expectations; games enjoyed on the afternoon of a birthday and for a few afternoons thereafter and then allowed, shy of one or two pieces, to drift into closets and toward the attic. Yet, discovered in their bright flat boxes between trunks of outgrown clothes and defunct appliances, the games presented a forceful semblance of value: the springs of their miniature launchers still reacted, the logic of their instructions would still generate suspense, given a chance. "What shall we do with all these games?" Foster shouted, in a kind of agony, to his scattered family as they moved up and down the attic stairs.

"Trash 'em," his younger son, a strapping nineteen, urged.

"Would the Goodwill want them?" asked his ex-wife, still wife enough to think that all of his questions deserved answers. "You used to be able to give things like that to orphanages. But they don't call them orphanages anymore, do they?"

"They call them normal American homes," Foster said.

His older son, now twenty-two, with a cinnamon-colored beard, offered, "They wouldn't work anyhow; they all have something missing. That's how they got to the attic."

"Well, why didn't we throw them away at the time?" Foster asked, and had to answer himself. Cowardice, the answer was. Inertia. Clinging to the past.

His sons, with a shadow of old obedience, came and looked over his shoulder at the sad wealth of abandoned playthings, silently groping with him for the particular happy day connected to this and that pattern of colored squares and arrows. Their lives had touched these tokens and counters once; excitement had flowed along the paths of these stylized landscapes. But the day was gone, and scarcely a memory remained.

"Toss 'em," the younger decreed, in his manly voice. For these days of cleaning out, the boy had borrowed a pickup truck from a friend and parked it on the lawn beneath the attic window, so the smaller items of discard could be tossed directly into it. The bigger items were lugged down the stairs and through the front hall; already the truck was loaded with old mattresses, broken clock-radios, obsolete skis and boots. It was a game of sorts to hit the truck bed with objects dropped from the height of the house. Foster flipped game after game at the target two stories below. When the boxes hit, they exploded, throwing a spray of dice, tokens, counters, and cards into the air and across the lawn. A box called Mousetrap, its lid showing laughing children gathered around a Rube Goldberg device, drifted sideways, struck one side wall of the truck, and spilled its plastic components into a flower bed. A set of something called Drag Race! floated gently as a snowflake before coming to rest, much diminished, on a stained mattress. Foster saw in the depth of downward space the cause of his melancholy: he had not played enough with these games. Now no one wanted to play.

Had he and his wife avoided divorce, of course, these boxes would have continued to gather dust in an undisturbed attic, their sorrow unexposed. The toys of his own childhood still rested in his mother's attic. At his last visit, he had crept up there and wound the spring of a tin Donald Duck; it had responded with an angry clack of its bill and a few stiff strokes on its drum. A tilted board with concentric grooves for marbles still waited in a bushel basket with his alphabet blocks and lead airplanes—waited for his childhood to return.

His ex-wife paused where he squatted at the attic window and asked him, "What's the matter?"

"Nothing. These games weren't used much."

"I know. It happens fast. You better stop now; it's making you too sad."

Behind him, his family had cleaned out the attic; the slant-ceilinged rooms stood empty, with drooping insulation. "How can you bear it?" he asked, of the emptiness.

"Oh, it's fun," she said, "once you get into it. Off with the old, on with the new. The new people seem nice. They have *little* children."

He looked at her and wondered whether she was being brave or truly hardhearted. The attic trembled slightly. "That's Ted," she said.

She had acquired a boyfriend, a big athletic accountant fleeing from domestic embarrassments in a neighboring town. When Ted slammed the kitchen door two stories below, the glass shade of a kerosene lamp that, though long unused, Foster hadn't had the heart to throw out of the window vibrated in its copper clips, emitting a thin note like a trapped wasp's song. Time for Foster to go. His dusty knees creaked when he stood. His ex-wife's eager steps raced ahead of him down through the emptied house. He followed, carrying the lamp, and set it finally on the bare top of a bookcase he had once built, on the first-floor landing. He remembered screwing the top board, a prize piece of knot-free pine, into place from underneath, so not a nailhead marred its smoothness.

After all the vacant rooms and halls, the kitchen seemed indecently full of heat and life. "Dad, want a beer?" the bearded son asked. "Ted brought some." The back of the boy's hand, holding forth the dewy can, blazed with fine ginger hairs. His girlfriend, wearing gypsy earrings and a NO NUKES sweatshirt, leaned against the disconnected stove, her hair in a bandanna and a black smirch becomingly placed on one temple. From the kind way she smiled at Foster, he felt this party was making room for him.

"No, I better go."

Ted shook Foster's hand, as he always did. He had a thin pink skin and silver hair whose fluffy waves seemed mechanically induced. Foster could look him in the eye no longer than he could gaze at the sun. He wondered how such a radiant brute had got into such a tame line of work. Ted had not helped with the attic today because he had been off in his old town, visiting his teen-aged twins. "I hear you did a splendid job today," he announced.

"They did," Foster said. "I wasn't much use. I just sat there stunned. All these things I had forgotten buying."

"Some were presents," his son reminded him. He passed the can his father had snubbed to his mother, who took it and tore up the tab with that defiant-sounding *pssff*. She had never liked beer, yet tipped the can to her mouth.

"Give me one sip," Foster begged, and took the can from her

and drank a long swallow. When he opened his eyes, Ted's big hand was cupped under Mrs. Foster's chin while his thumb rubbed away a smudge of dirt along her jaw which Foster had not noticed. This protective gesture made her face look small, pouty, and frail. Ted, Foster noticed now, was dressed with a certain comical perfection in a banker's Saturday outfit—softened blue jeans, crisp tennis sneakers, lumberjack shirt with cuffs folded back. The youthful outfit accented his age, his hypertensive flush. Foster saw them suddenly as a touching, aging couple, and this perception seemed permission to go.

He handed back the can.

"Thanks for your help," his former wife said.

"Yes, we do thank you," Ted said.

"Talk to Tommy," she unexpectedly added, in a lowered voice. She was still sending out trip wires to slow Foster's departures. "This is harder on him than he shows."

Ted looked at his watch, a fat, black-faced thing he could swim under water with. "I said to him coming in, 'Don't dawdle till the dump closes.' "

"He loafed all day," his brother complained, "mooning over old stuff, and now he's going to screw up getting to the dump."

"He's very sensi-tive," the visiting gypsy said, with a strange chiming brightness, as if repeating something she had heard.

Outside, the boy was picking up litter that had fallen wide of the truck. Foster helped him. In the grass there were dozens of tokens and dice. Some were engraved with curious little faces—Olive Oyl, Snuffy Smith, Dagwood—and others with hieroglyphs— numbers, diamonds, spades, hexagons—whose code was lost. He held out a handful for Tommy to see. "Can you remember what these were for?"

"Comic-Strip Lotto," the boy said without hesitation. "And a game called Gambling Fools there was a kind of slot machine for." The light of old payoffs flickered in his eyes as he gazed down at the rubble in his father's hand. Though Foster was taller, the boy was broader in the shoulders, and growing. "Want to ride with me to the dump?" Tommy asked.

"I would, but I better go." He, too, had a new life to lead. By being on this forsaken property at all, Foster was in a sense on the wrong square, if not *en prise.* He remembered how once he had begun to teach this boy chess, but in the sadness of watching him lose—the little furry bowed head frowning above his trapped king—the lessons had stopped.

Foster tossed the tokens into the truck; they rattled to rest on the metal. "This depresses you?" he asked his son.

"Naa." The boy amended, "Kind of."

"You'll feel great," Foster promised him, "coming back with a clean truck. I used to love it at the dump, all that old happiness heaped up, and the seagulls."

"It's changed since you left. They have all these new rules. The lady there yelled at me last time, for putting stuff in the wrong place."

"She did?"

"Yeah. It was scary." Seeing his father waver, he added, "It'll only take twenty minutes." Though broad of build, Tommy had beardless cheeks and, between thickening eyebrows, a trace of that rounded, faintly baffled blankness babies have, that wrinkles before they cry.

"O.K.," Foster said. "You win. I'll come along. I'll protect you."

HYPNOSIS

·2·

Arnold Kashtanov

Psychotherapist Vladimir Mikhailovich Kumanchin took up jogging. He had nursed the intention for a long time. He felt flabby, depressed and irritable, and he thought jogging might help. At the beginning of summer, he finally forced himself to rise earlier than usual, donned his blue track suit and his running shoes and jogged around the block, slightly embarrassed when neighbors caught sight of him. He saw himself in their eyes, short, stout and forty, with eyeglasses and a bald spot and breathing hard as he jogged. Panting, he slowed to a walk as he neared his apartment building. A neighbor, leaving for work, greeted him with a smile: "Worried about the condition you're in, Volodya?"

Goggle-eyed, openmouthed and gasping for breath, he could not explain that he wasn't really worried, he simply felt he ought to keep in shape. He climbed the stairs to his apartment, showered and thought: It works.

Dr. Kumanchin treated alcoholics. His office at the hospital was in a wing with a separate entrance. Narrow windows in the thick stone walls gave little light, and heavy blinds made it darker. In May, when they turned off the central heating, the room felt like a cellar. After the last patient of the day left, Kumanchin stepped out on the porch to warm himself in the sun.

Whether because the morning jog helped or this first real summer day cheered him, he felt good. Woods began just beyond the white brick wall of the hospital compound.

Sweetbrier and jasmine bloomed at the very porch. Their scent mingled with the odor of warm conifer needles and made him dizzy. Squinting, Kumanchin played with crazy thoughts and desires.

He was waiting for a visitor. Chief Doctor Yaroshevich had taken him aside after the morning staff meeting and told him that a woman, Tushkina, would call on him at the close of the working day. She was rather high-and-mighty; Kumanchin was to be as

nice to her as he could. To win him over, Yaroshevich tried
flattery: "You know, Volodya, you have a big name, patients seek
you out." It sounded as though he was fobbing one off on Kumanchin, as Yaroshevich had done more than once when friends
appealed to him for professional help which he could not give,
yet could not refuse. Whom else could he pass them on to but
Kumanchin?

That morning Kumanchin had been unable to present his own
request for help. His daughter Alenka had failed in the competition for admission to medical school last year. She wanted to
take the exams again this year. The competition was fierce—eight
applicants for each vacancy.

At one time, Chief Doctor Yaroshevich had more or less promised to help, through his influence in the psychiatry department
of the medical school. It was time to remind him of his promise.
An opportunity to mention it had seemed to afford itself when
Kumanchin and Yaroshevich found themselves together on the
previous evening. Yaroshevich had just returned from an out-of-
town trip. He had served with a commission that had toured the
province for a week to study fulfillment of the decree on com-
bating drunkenness. He returned tired and depressed by what he
had seen: In the old days, Volodya, drunkards had the fear of
going hungry, they had the fear of God in them, but now they
don't fear anything and devil knows what we can do about them.
Kumanchin, guiltily preoccupied with his own concern as he listened, tried to turn the conversation to the subject of Alenka:
Yes, we doctors are helpless to do anything and society treats us
accordingly, we're paid like unskilled labor, yet for some reason
young people compete like mad to get into medical school more
than any other; the competition for admission is incredible, which
says something about our profession . . . "Fools," Yaroshevich
said. "My own nephew is trying to enter medical school this year
and my sister has her heart set on getting him in. God forbid, I'll
have my hands full helping to get him admitted." After that Kumanchin could not bring himself to mention Alenka.

He was tempted to bring up the subject again in the morning,
but after Yaroshevich asked him to see Tushkina as a personal
favor he felt it would be crude and impudent then and there to
request a favor in return.

Waiting for this Tushkina now, he stood on the porch, face
held up to the sun and breathing the aromatic air, when a woman
approached along the flagstone path that crossed the lawn. She

proved to be not Tushkina, however, but the wife of one of his patients. She was surprised that he did not remember her.

"We're your neighbors," she said. "You live at No. 5, we're the Shirin couple in No. 7, right next door. My husband is in your care again, Vladimir Mikhailovich."

Kumanchin had been seeing her husband every day—a middle-aged, heavyset fellow, taking the cure for the third or fourth time—but Kumanchin could not remember the wife. After all, how many such wives had come to him in his seventeen years of practice? Thousands. They came, they telephoned, they complained of their alcoholic husbands, they pleaded with him to appeal to some employer unwilling to hire anyone with "a record"; they begged him to change their spouses' behavior, to threaten the husbands, to shame them, to intervene, to do this or that.

Shirina did not come up on the porch, but stood below, looking guilty, as if to say she was burdening him with her troubles but again needed help. Her thin hand twisted a button at the top of her dark dress. Kumanchin hoped she would not keep him long. Another woman, young and attractive, probably Tushkina herself, was coming along the path. It would be awkward to be talking with Shirina here, looking down at her as she stood below him, blocking the entrance; and it would be humiliating to have to bow and scrape before Tushkina in front of this one. Moving aside, he made way for Shirina to enter his office, bade her be seated, and switched on the "busy" light outside the office door to signal Tushkina.

"Well, tell me . . . hmm, hmm."

Alenka once aptly remarked that he worked with his ears. That was his fate—to listen. For seventeen years he had been listening to essentially one and the same story. He had learned to pretend to be paying attention without actually listening. People came anxiously and tried to make him share their anxiety. For the first few minutes everything within him resisted. An instinctive defense mechanism came into play. He had to overcome it each time by an effort of will. In the end he forced himself to enter into the strangers' lives, caught their anxiety himself, but he first had to break down his inner resistance, hanging back until he made up his mind. Nodding now to Shirina, he did not hasten to attune himself to her concern but took in her face, her scrawny neck, her flat breast. The woman was frail.

"There's nothing good to report, Vladimir Mikhailovich, nothing but trouble. He went back to drinking, as you know. You've been treating him again for a month now. I'm tied down at home with our child and I don't know which is worse—when he's at liberty I worry about what he might do in some drunken rage, and when he's in treatment here he's out of a job, and how can we afford to live? There is no solution. I don't work. I can't leave our son. Today I was able to get away because a neighbor offered to look in on the boy while he naps."

"How old is the boy?"

"Ten."

"Ten months?"

"Ten years," she said quietly. She showed no emotion.

Kumanchin's attention was engaged. He noted her calm, pleasant face, big gray eyes, the soft, melodious, controlled voice and the slow speech that cardiac patients develop in order to avoid becoming agitated. He was defenseless before just such helpless women. Cautiously he probed:

"What is the boy's problem?"

She twirled an index finger at her temple without losing her serious look.

"Born that way."

"And can't speak?"

"No way!"

Kumanchin averted his gaze. He could imagine what she had gone through. The doctors probably had proposed immediately that she surrender the child to an asylum. Most women in such circumstances did so. She could not make up her mind, hesitated, wavered and waited until it was too late. By that time she had become attached to the child; she could not give him up. Shirina had ruined her life. He had learned never to put himself in the patient's place, never to ask himself what he would have done— that was beyond the call of duty and could only hinder his work. It didn't matter whether she had chosen rightly ten years ago. Each person lives as best each can, fashioning his or her own destiny. Kumanchin did not try to pass judgment, but rather he sympathized out of his softhearted compassion. If she had given up the baby she would not have created a burden for the doctors treating her husband, she would not be sitting here, and there would be no need for him to plumb her misery.

"So your husband beats the child when he's drunk, is that it?"

"Beats Genka?"

Kumanchin again looked away from her unbearably gentle face.

Of course, he guessed, she herself has taken beatings at the hands of her drunken husband.

"No." But she blushed; she did not know how to lie. "As for beating Genka, no; well, maybe sometimes. Mostly he weeps over the child. You can't imagine how happy he was when Genka was born—*just as you said he would be*. But he didn't give up drinking. Maybe I was partly to blame."

She fell silent. It had all happened long ago, but she was afraid it would sound like a reproach, that "just as you said he would be." At those words Kumanchin realized that it was he who had persuaded her not to have an abortion, though at that time she, of course, had wanted it, not because of the hereditary damage that would be passed on from the father's line but out of ordinary practical considerations that he, Dr. Kumanchin, had dismissed as secondary, petty and unworthy of regard.

Kumanchin blocked the thought that he might have been to blame. He always told himself that he did not answer for the results, only for his work, which he did well. Otherwise it would be impossible to do anything. If he focused on the failures he'd have a nervous breakdown, and what good would he be then?

"Your husband has signed up for individual hypnosis. That's in addition to group sessions. I have already had several sessions with him."

Nevertheless, it was strange that he did not remember her. No doubt, he thought, she had been beautiful when she was twenty years old, but she had faded. That was probably why he did not recognize her now.

"Vladimir Mikhailovich, he has already been here for a month. How can we live without his earnings? I can't keep asking Mama to help—she has to count every kopek to make ends meet. If he hasn't been cured in a month of treatment, what sense is there in keeping him longer? You can't change his brain for a new one, can you, Vladimir Mikhailovich? I talked with him today and he swore he'd never go back to drinking, he said he has given it up for good, maybe somehow you might try him—couldn't you now?"

To release Shirin before he completed the cure would be a violation of the rules. Kumanchin tried to persuade her to wait. He realized how hard it was for her, he said, but she had suffered so much already, if only she could hold out for three or four more weeks and . . . She did not listen but just repeated: Vladimir

Mikhailovich, please, it's so hard, please. Kumanchin began to feel irritated and raised his voice: Stop and think, you've experienced enough grief; if I were to discharge him now he'd be drinking again next week. Have you forgotten what it is like to live with that? He gave vent to anger. If family members infected him with their sense of desperation he gave it back to them in double measure. How could he control himself when he was tired after a day's work and someone else's wife or daughter waited outside his door?

Shirina began to cry silently. She sat motionless, and were it not for the tears that coursed down her cheeks she would have seemed placid, so fixed and expressionless was her face.

"During the November holidays he kept himself in check, but I saw . . ." By frightening her Kumanchin himself had invited this further confession. He had to hear it out. Listening tired him more than advising. Most of his working life had been spent in an endless flood of others' agitated words. They held nothing back in their mysterious, overwhelming need to unburden themselves, to tell it all, a need that overcame reason, shame, will, upbringing, and instinct. Tipsy men who babbled unintelligible nonsense, lonely old women who were accustomed to talking to their cats or dogs—sometimes with each word the speaker's tension abated, but sometimes, on the contrary, the pitch rose, and then it was especially painful to listen; the rush of words acquired almost physical pressure.

Shirina froze. She hugged herself, quivering with the violence of her emotions.

Then she resumed. ". . . all right, I said, you're good and I'm bad, there's nothing I can do about it, I said, accept me as I am, teach me. . . ."

Tushkina knocked and glanced in. "Come in," Kumanchin said, "have a seat. I'll soon be finished."

Shirina, embarrassed, froze again.

"Oh, what have I done? You should have stopped me, Vladimir Mikhailovich. But please advise me."

"Try to hold out as long as you can," he said. "Do anything to hold out, borrow wherever you can, but let your husband complete the cure. Apply to the trade union committee at his last place of work. They're supposed to help."

It had no effect on her. Again she pleaded, again the tears came. She spoke of some brother-in-law of hers who organized a team of carpenters to build barns in the summer and was willing to hire Shirin—they didn't drink out there in the country all summer long. Wearily, Kumanchin gave a wave of his hand.

"All right, I'll think it over."

She concluded that she had won his consent.

"Oh, thank you, Vladimir Mikhailovich, thank you so much. Please excuse me. But what could I do? I've turned this way and that. Thanks so much!"

"I'll think it over, but . . ."

He could not bring himself to disillusion her. He said good-bye and invited Tushkina, who had been sitting in a chair by the window, to take the seat at his desk. "Please excuse us," he said.

"I apologize for taking up your time, Vladimir Mikhailovich, but Dr. Yaroshevich recommended that I talk with you. He spoke so highly of you that . . ."

Tushkina was blonde. She wore eyeglasses and was dressed modestly in an unusual mannish blouse and slacks, but he noticed that all the persons whom his superiors sent to him had something in common about their facial appearance. It was pleasant to rest his eyes on her and hear her lively voice. He tried to guess her age. Over thirty, he decided.

"I don't know how to say this. He has begun to drink. Actually it began long ago, even before our marriage, but somehow it was, well, moderate, shall we say? I wouldn't say that Igor is far gone, but . . . then he began going out with friends from his research institute and I noticed that he came home tipsy. And there were other indications."

"What kind?"

"It's not important."

"Nevertheless?"

"Intimate things."

"You mean impotence?"

She looked down.

"Yes, sort of. We learned"— recovering from her embarrassment, she went on—"that is, I was told, and some people hinted to his father, too, that Igor was drinking heavily. His father had a talk with him, we kept trying to stop him, and then suddenly there was a scandal at his institute, several people were dismissed, in short it continued undercover and grew worse. Before, at least he was careful about when he drank and with whom. But this week he missed work three days in a row. Honestly, it frightens me. I got really frightened and decided to consult Fyodor Nikitich—Dr. Yaroshevich. He said it would be better to talk with you. So there it is."

She fell silent, waiting for what he would say.

"Excuse me . . . er . . ."

"Yekaterina Andreyevna."

"Yekaterina Andreyevna, I can't diagnose the problem without seeing the patient," Kumanchin said, "but I am afraid I have distressing news for you. From what you tell me I have the impression that he's in a bad way. It sounds as if your husband will require hospitalization."

He did not like his own tedious, falsely sympathetic professional tone, but he could not avoid it. He realized all too well that something had happened to place her husband's job in jeopardy, she was alarmed for his career, but the husband would refuse to be hospitalized and would reject treatment. In a moment she would beg him to accept her husband as an outpatient. The hospital did not accept outpatients, and when he turned her down she would complain to Yaroshevich that he had refused to help her. He would survive her complaint, of course. But it was all so futile. He still hoped to talk to Yaroshevich about Alenka before the chief doctor left for the day.

"Do you think it is so serious?" Tushkina said with mounting anxiety.

"Yes," Kumanchin replied. "I'm almost certain."

"But he is director of a laboratory, he copes with such important work. . . ."

Kumanchin shrugged. "We see all kinds in our practice."

"If he accepts hospitalization, it will brand him for life."

"Well, in the first place, that isn't so."

"What if he wasn't registered as a hospital patient but simply came to you privately, so to speak? You understand. Not as head of a department of the hospital but . . ."

He understood what she meant.

"We don't accept outpatients," he said in the same professional tone. "You could try the borough narcotic clinic, but I don't advise it. He needs hospitalization. On the outside, on his own, he won't dry out. However, as I already told you, we can't make a diagnosis without seeing the patient. It would be best if your husband came himself and we could interview him."

"Yes, of course."

Probably he was going about it badly, he thought; he ought to try a different tack with her. She was dissatisfied with him and would complain. But what else could he say?

She did not rise to go, but stayed and made small talk. Was she trying to gain his favor and win his friendship, to be on the safe side? She even wanted to wait for him when he told her he had to stop in at his department ward in the hospital.

The patients were lounging in the corridor and wards, awaiting dinner. Kumanchin noticed Shirin, stocky, in tight-fitting pajamas, seated on a bench at the end of the corridor and holding forth seriously before a group of patients. His black eyes were bright and lively. Roosevelt, he was saying, was the wisest politician in the capitalist camp, but Churchill . . . He broke off to exchange greetings with Kumanchin.

"How long have you been in the hospital?" Kumanchin asked.

"Thirty-two days, Vladimir Mikhailovich."

"I'll discharge you tomorrow," said Kumanchin, thinking he was probably making a mistake.

In the office the intern Sklyansky was taking down the case history of a young, new patient who squirmed in his chair as he answered the unpleasant questions.

"I'm leaving," Kumanchin said.

"Everything's under control, Vladimir Mikhailovich." Sklyansky nodded. "Go ahead."

Tushkina was waiting on the porch. A very thin, elderly patient in hospital pajamas, walking along the wall of the compound, bent a jasmine branch toward his face and peered at the heart of the flower. For some reason his head was shaved and Tushkina, watching him apprehensively, remarked: "They look so—so scruffy."

They walked out on the flagstone path and down the poplar-lined lane. Tushkina looked about at everything as if trying to imagine her husband in this setting. They passed the boiler room, the garage, the kitchen and several five-story hospital buildings. Surprised at the size of the hospital grounds, a whole town enclosed by monastery-like walls, Tushkina asked:

"Do you like your work?"

Kumanchin shrugged. A pointless question. One might like or dislike spring because it could be compared with summer, autumn, and winter, but he had only one occupation and probably would never have another. That was life.

"I can give you a ride," Tushkina said. "I have my car."

Kumanchin said he had to remain to talk with the chief doctor. At the parking lot in front of the main building, Tushkina opened the door of a maroon Zhiguli auto. Here they parted, Kumanchin reminding her that he would expect her to bring her husband. As she slid behind the wheel and shut the door Kumanchin regretted that none of this would ever be his—neither a Zhiguli nor such an elegant woman.

The bookkeeper was with Yaroshevich. Kumanchin took a chair by the window and waited while they went on with their work.

"I had to disappoint this Tushkina," he said finally. "But there's no way we can take an outpatient."

Turning the pages of financial reports, Yaroshevich gave a wave of his hand: "Never mind."

"Fedya," Kumanchin plunged ahead, "do you have five minutes?"

Yaroshevich begged off. "Is it very urgent? Let's make it tomorrow, eh? I don't have a minute to spare, Volodya. I'm waiting for a call from the construction trust right now."

"All right." Kumanchin went to the door.

"Be sure to remind me tomorrow!" Yaroshevich called after him.

Three hours later Yaroshevich himself telephoned Kumanchin at home. "I just spoke with Tushkina. Hell, there must be some way to mollify her. You know how to handle these situations, Volodya, I don't have to tell you. Maybe it would make sense to meet with the husband."

"Let her bring him in. I suggested it myself. Did she complain about me?" Kumanchin asked. Yaroshevich had taken him away from the television set, on which he was watching the soccer match with the sound turned off so as not to disturb Alenka, studying in the adjoining room in preparation for taking the exams again.

"No, in fact she praised you highly," Yaroshevich lied in an uninspired tone. He too was watching the game on television. The sports commentator's voice could be heard in the background.

"She should bring him in. I'm free tomorrow morning."

"She said day after tomorrow at five."

It was his hour for consultation with patients. She *would* pick the wrong time.

"Give her an hour, Volodya," Yaroshevich entreated in his friendliest manner. "She's an important woman. Incidentally, did you know that she teaches at the medical school?"

Kumanchin did not know it. "You shouldn't miss such chances," Yaroshevich remarked.

Hanging up the receiver, Kumanchin could not understand why he felt uneasy. Ira had overheard the conversation from the kitchen.

"What does he want?" she asked.

"Nothing special," Kumanchin replied. "By the way, he's getting his nephew into medical school this year."

He had not meant to tell her this, but now he blurted it out for no reason at all. Ira pricked up her ears.

"Did he tell you that himself? What about Alenka? He promised, didn't he?"

They lowered their voices. They didn't want Alenka to hear.

"Well, not exactly. You can't say he promised."

"What do you mean, not exactly?"

"Well, Ira," said Kumanchin, cursing himself, "not in so many words."

"Have you spoken with him?"

"In general," Kumanchin said.

"What's this 'in general'?"

Kumanchin tried to divert the conversation into another channel. "Just what can Yaroshevich do for Alenka?"

"Exactly what he'll do for his nephew." Ira cut him off: "You didn't talk to him at all."

Kumanchin went back to the television, troubled by his own indiscretion. He had forgotten how to hold his tongue, a bad sign, he thought. He had to sharpen his mind and put his body in better condition. He would jog every day, in any weather, jog and shower. Seated before the television set, he suddenly realized what had made him uneasy about the telephone conversation. If Yaroshevich remembered to mention Tushkina's connection with the medical school, he was hinting at Alenka's need. That meant it was no accident that he had spoken of his nephew the other day; it was deliberate—his way of saying he couldn't do anything for Alenka this year. He had already done a good deal for her, getting her a job in the polyclinic not far from the Kumanchin apartment. Kumanchin could hardly complain.

He and Ira dined alone. Alenka did not emerge from her room, but kept at her studies. She had set herself a daily study assignment and she stuck to it. Like her father, she prided herself on self-discipline. Ira went on nagging. Yaroshevich would surely get his nephew into medical school, she said, even if the nephew didn't have a brain in his head. And the nephew would turn out to be the same kind of doctor as Yaroshevich himself. That's why there weren't any good doctors any longer. They neglected the patients, they reckoned they'd heal regardless of treatment. If the patients survived, they were lucky. But Alenka was cooped up, wearing herself out with study, she looked awful, and yet she'd still not gain admission. How could you win admission nowadays without pull? You had as much chance as to win the lottery. The neighbors' Natasha, who didn't have a thought in her head, got into medical school even though she'd never read a book in her life, used to copy the answers from Alenka, and couldn't pass up a single discotheque, but now her mother claims they didn't use influence. Let her try telling that to others! Ira knew better.

Kumanchin nodded, thinking she would soon be talked out.

"Absolutely nothing matters to you," Ira said and suddenly stopped.

"Why?"

"You're just indifferent to everything. Talking to you is like talking to a stone wall. I always knew it, I just keep forgetting what you're like."

Embarrassed, he drank his tea in silence. Indeed, he always guarded his feelings. But what would he do with feelings? Would he hate patients who beat their wives? A lot of healing he'd accomplish then! For years he had carefully weaned himself from indignation and other emotional reactions. What could he do about it now?

"It's probably professional," he said finally. "A doctor shouldn't sit in judgment, but understand and explain."

"I'm not thinking about your patients!" Ira cried. "I'm thinking about your daughter! Sure, you can explain anything under the sun. The more you explain, the less you understand what you yourself feel. You don't have any feelings at all! 'Beyond good and evil,' hah! Superman!"

Kumanchin smiled, so inappropriate did it sound applied to him: Superman.

"To understand isn't bad," he began.

"I don't want to hear about it!" Ira said furiously. "You're a father! Don't you have any human feelings?"

"Of course I do."

"You don't show it!"

"But what can I do?" he said. "I'm trying my best for Alenka."

"You just sit in front of the television," Ira said unjustly and irrelevantly. "Television, soccer, nothing else interests you."

"That's not true, Ira. I'm simply tired," he answered in a conciliatory tone. She was wrong, but nevertheless he felt a twinge of guilt.

At eleven he turned off the television and made up their folding bed. Ira read in bed, a pile of books on the stool beside her. They were all on one subject. She had been asked to write an introduction to *Studies in the History of Russian Psychiatry* and, being conscientious, she was preparing thoroughly. For his bedtime reading Kumanchin chose a book about Viktor Kandinsky. Ira fell asleep and he put aside his book and turned off the light. He couldn't sleep. He had developed his own method of relaxing when sleep would not come. Usually it helped. First he had to relax the muscles of the eyes . . . It didn't work. He remembered Shirina, quivering with the violence of her emotions and hugging herself with thin hands. He was familiar with the condition. Alenka's emotions also ran high, and he himself—

There they are, my feelings, Kumanchin thought.

Ira always needed a show of feelings. As if feelings signified something genuine, whereas reason was unreliable and suspect. Yet she herself knew that feelings were by no means spontaneous, as they seem to us, but are based on stereotypes, while we, without being aware of it, constantly adapt them to preconceived forms: old women weep in cemeteries but wipe away the tears the moment they pass beyond the cemetery gates, and Ira herself, encountering a baby, feels she has to melt and coo and launch into baby talk even if she is suffering from a terrible headache.

Feelings are energy—that is, life—he thought, that's the whole point, but reasoning is constraint, control. It is normal to be attracted to life and resist constraint. Feelings are infectious and that was why he himself was plugged into the television set during a soccer game as if it were a storage battery from which he got a charge.

In childhood he had dreamed of becoming manly and cold-blooded. Sensitive and impressionable, he found the pressure of feelings more than he could bear; he envied every cool and thick-skinned blockhead, and, like Kandinsky, lived with the temptation of suicide. It was Kandinsky who once helped him. Kumanchin recognized himself when he read *Pseudo-Hallucinations*. Kandinsky described a familiar condition. At age twelve he, Kumanchin, also had pseudo-hallucinations. He was in love with a classmate and when he wandered the streets alone of an evening, thinking of her, he saw her in his imagination as vividly as if the image were real. He saw her studying at home, turning to answer a question from her mother, reaching out to pick up a textbook. Reality and the image in his imagination existed simultaneously and affected him equally. It was all well and good for Ira to accuse him of having no feelings, but where would he be now if he had not learned self-control?

Two days later Yaroshevich reminded him in the morning that Tushkina would bring her husband at five o'clock. Surprised by the chief doctor's preoccupation with Tushkina, Kumanchin asked: "What kind of bird is she?"

"That kind," Yaroshevich said. "A bird."

She came alone at six. No husband. She sat before him in green blouse and green slacks, quite at ease as if they were old friends, and did not mention her husband, as if she had come only to pay a social visit. It's very pleasant here, she said, raising her eyeglasses toward the ceiling and examining the stucco molding. The jasmine, the quiet. . . . The medical school, she said, was in the hottest part of town, the windows didn't open, it was suffocating. She hated to go there and she had turned down the appointment, but they persuaded her to accept it. She liked the work itself, she liked the students. The boys were only so-so, but nowadays the girls were angels, slim, beautifully dressed, serious.

Clearly, she wanted to please him and it came easily to her. It wasn't often that people who came to his office talked so blithely. She did indeed enjoy being here. Kumanchin opened the window, and the shutter swung back and forth, casting patches of sunlight into the room. Flowering branches peeped in at the window. Kumanchin knew he had a way with people that inclined them to open up, and it was taking effect upon her. He felt that right away. She wanted to talk about herself, and if her purpose was to please him, the manner and the purpose coincided. Obviously she had been unable to prevail on her husband to come and so she had come alone to win over Kumanchin, which was why she deftly led the conversation around to the impressive fact that they had to persuade her to accept appointment to the medical school faculty when other doctors couldn't dream of being offered such a post. Kumanchin wondered whether Yaroshevich had told her about Alenka and whether that was why she brought up the subject of her connection with the school. Tushkina was self-assured. She showed no embarrassment at taking up his time. Laughing at her own talkativeness, she said Kumanchin was to blame for it—he must have hypnotized her to start the flow of words; she was very suggestible in general. She smiled: Seriously, Vladimir Mikhailovich, you'll discover that I really am suggestible.

Like the last time, she offered him a ride. She drove confidently. Seated beside her, Kumanchin watched her out of the corner of his eye as they overtook a bus, took advantage of every opening in the heavy traffic in the center of town, swung smoothly from lane to lane, and ran through a yellow light. She concentrated on the driving, mouth half-open in her concentration and smiling with satisfaction as they passed the crossing just before the light turned red, then began the next complicated maneuver. Admiring her adroitness, Kumanchin thought he could never drive like that, his reactions weren't fast enough and he lacked her mettle. She had spirit. A fantastic woman, to be able to cope with a hard-drinking husband, deal with the world and retain her buoyancy. He knew very well how hard it was to live with a second-degree alcoholic.

When they got through the center of town, she stopped at a shop to run in for a momentary purchase, and then drove out onto a broad and almost empty boulevard.

"I love to drive," Tushkina commented. "I could drive and drive. But there's nowhere to drive to. We live right near my place of work."

She said something more about her work, something about endocrinology and home consultations. She pocketed fifty rubles for a single private consultation. Kumanchin guessed what she was leading up to and he remained silent. Finally she came out with it:

"You say you don't have outpatient care at the hospital. But you could—well, as an exception in a special case. . . . Honestly, I was sure you did that kind of thing all the time. With your experience in hypnosis and your ability to win the patient's trust you could help so many people. I know many persons who would never enter a hospital for matters that concern their private lives. They find ways to get unofficial, private treatment, whatever the

price. Of course, moonlighting is illegal, but it takes only a hint
to arrange matters with a willing doctor. I know that in Moscow
many narcologists treat patients privately in the home. It's very,
very lucrative."

Kumanchin felt himself to blame because she was trying so
hard. He shrugged. He had never gone into illicit private practice
on the side. To make ends meet he worked one-and-a-half shifts.
Where would he have the time for outside earnings? He didn't
know about Moscow, but it just wasn't done at his hospital.

"Your daughter wants to enter our medical school, doesn't
she?" Tushkina suddenly asked. "I could arrange for a tutor in
physics from the school."

It took a few seconds for the thought to register that this was
a serious proposal—to introduce him to a tutor who would be
the same instructor who gave the exam and graded it. Kumanchin
reddened.

"Er, if you could, er, Yekaterina Andreyevna . . ."

"I'll try," she said.

Then he showed her where to turn off the boulevard and she
drove him right to the entrance just as Alenka and Ira approached.
Tushkina turned the car, waved and drove off. Alenka took in
the scene and said: "Oho! Not bad, not bad-looking!"

Following his wife and daughter up the stairs, Kumanchin
thought Ira had let herself grow indecently stout. She couldn't
resist a second helping at table and he was no better. It was all
very well to jog, but was that the answer? Tushkina was right:
indeed, he could earn a lot from private practice. He would buy
a car, for every minute would be precious. You had to live to the
full and get some things in life. The getting was what kept you
in shape, bodily and in spirit. Otherwise you soured and didn't
know why you felt dispirited. That feeling of emptiness, the sense
of frustration, was like stomach juices that require food, only it
was food of a different kind. One needed action and a goal,
otherwise everything appeared futile and the emptiness gnawed
away at one, as stomach juices without food ate away the lining
and left an ulcer.

In the apartment he waited until Alenka went off to her room
before telling Ira about the tutor. Ira opened her eyes wide.

"But that's bribery!" she said.

To ask Yaroshevich's help was different. They had every confidence in Alenka's ability. Hadn't she won a school medal?
Wasn't she talented and conscientious? Hadn't she won the school

quiz show? They knew they were merely asking for justice, assurance that she wouldn't be "bumped," and even so they hesitated to ask it as a favor. But this—!

Angry at Ira for her reaction, Kumanchin said:

"Sure it's bribery."

He thought she would explode. Instead, she asked in confusion:

"How much would it cost?"

He didn't have the slightest notion. Whatever it cost, they'd
find the money.

"What bastards!" Ira said, angry with him as much as with
them.

Again, he thought, his impressionable nature was at fault. When
he was with Tushkina it all seemed simple and easy, but with Ira
it seemed different. It was all beyond him.

Barely two hours later the phone rang. Tushkina. She hadn't
settled matters, but it looked as if it would all work out. No, she
didn't yet know what it would cost. Last year, she heard, the
instructor got four hundred rubles a pupil. He tutored in July.
She would find out, come to an understanding, and telephone
him. She was already calling Kumanchin familiarly by his nick-
name, Volodya.

Replacing the receiver, he marveled: "She even had our telephone number."

"What's so unusual about finding a telephone number?" Ira
said.

"Nothing, of course. But she's pretty sharp."

"I don't understand."

She was troubled. The price of four hundred rubles dismayed
her. On the one hand, she had heard that it cost incredible, un-
heard-of sums, thousands, to buy one's way into medical school
nowadays. On the other hand, four hundred was no small sum
either. No one charged such amounts merely for tutoring. So the
tutor did something more to earn it than simply coaching the
pupil. A pity they hadn't looked into the possibility last year.
They could have saved Alenka the pain of defeat then. This, of
course, was a rebuke to Kumanchin.

"Who stopped you?" he said.

Continuing to ponder the news, Ira sighed.

"Until we know how Alenka responds to the idea, let's not tell
her. Principles," she said.

"All right," Kumanchin agreed. "It's too soon to worry until
we have a definite proposal."

Nevertheless, he could not hold back when Alenka bounced from her room to get a glass of yogurt: "We've heard of a physics instructor who prepares students for the exams."

Alenka stared, wide-eyed: "Have we got money to throw around?"

She took the glass and went off to her room. But she was shaken. The closer the exams came, the less confident she felt. When they were preparing for bed that evening, she came out in pajamas and resumed the conversation. Who was this physics instructor? Kumanchin mumbled something about devil knows, someone at the hospital mentioned him. Ira took her cue from him and played along: "You should have written down his telephone, you never get things straight."

"Maybe, after all . . ." Alenka speculated. "I'd blow my month's vacation pay if he could help me bone up for the questions."

She had the illusion that her sixty rubles would cover the cost. Kumanchin, overjoyed that she agreed to the plan, said:

"Money is of no consequence in this situation."

For some reason this seemed funny to Alenka and Ira. Alenka grew lighthearted. It was a long time since she had been so gay. She began to romp about and play-act, mimicking the postures patients assumed when they stood before the X-ray screen to be fluoroscoped. She had the gift of mimicry. It was amusing. Then she put on an imitation of her father, pushing out her belly and pretending to hold up imaginary trousers without a belt. Ira was weak with laughter. Trying to think of another object to ridicule, Alenka remembered Tushkina. She winked at her father.

"She's pretty snazzy, isn't she, Papa?"

Now he was in for it, he thought, and remarked:

"Well, she wears an attractive blouse."

Alenka and Ira exchanged glances. Ira inquired cautiously: "Attractive how?"

"In a modest way."

The women exchanged glances again.

"Buy me one of those modest blouses someday," Ira said.

"Money is of no consequence in this situation," Alenka added.

Her expansive mood spilled over happily into humor. At one time Kumanchin had concluded that humor served as a safety valve for an overload of aggression, and accordingly he encouraged humor in Alenka. He guessed right.

Tushkina did not appear. Kumanchin and Ira avoided the subject.
A few days later, Ira could no longer contain herself.

"Your Tushkina seems to have disappeared. Perhaps we ought
to take the initiative ourselves."

"How?" he asked.

Ira didn't know how, but she thought he ought to know.

"Like—like everybody," she said.

Tushkina phoned that evening to ask whether she could come
to his office the next day. She would try to bring her husband.

"Come," Kumanchin told her.

Again she came alone. One of Kumanchin's former patients
was with him, a thirty-year-old plumber who had been discharged
a year ago, had broken down and now wanted to return, knowing
that if Kumanchin did not take him back the police would consign
him to a curative labor clinic. Kumanchin couldn't stand the sight
of him. These backsliders ruined their own lives and used up his
life; he was no machine, how much vain effort could he invest in
them when they didn't give a damn? Unburdening his heart, he
tried to arouse at least some fear in those innocent young eyes.

"How can I take you back? I have a two-month waiting list.
Do you think I don't know why you came to me?"

"Vladimir Mikhailovich, I swear this will be the last time."

Seeing him off, Kumanchin grumbled:

"Devil take you, come in tomorrow."

Rain rattled on the windowpanes, the room grew dark and he
turned on the overhead light. Tushkina wore a youthful windbreaker. Raindrops ran down its shiny waterproof cloth as if on
glass. Seated, she pressed her knees with her palms.

"I'm so sorry. Again he broke his promise to come with me. I
can't stand the sight of him any more. You can't imagine what
my life is like!"

There were drops of rain on her eyeglasses and they must have
blurred her vision, but she ignored them. They irritated Kumanchin. He wished she would wipe the lenses. She had to talk herself
out and she had no one to share her story with except this doctor.
He had to tune in to her wavelength and tune out all the extra-
neous thoughts he harbored. He was ashamed to be thinking
about his own concern: Had she arranged for the tutor? She
should have begun with that.

"I can't take it any longer. I've tried so hard to help him!
Everyone envied me for marrying into such a prominent family.

They ought to go through what I've suffered! What did the family do for me? I did it all myself! I bought the country cottage, I got my appointment in the medical school on my own, and if Igor became head of a research laboratory that was my doing, too, just between us. His father never lifted a finger. He just likes to talk. 'Katyusha, don't let him get out of hand, keep a tight rein on him!' All they care about is keeping up appearances. If I have to ask the father to exert some influence over his own son, he gets red in the face and slams the door. Off he goes to his room and they rush to bring him his medicine and look on you as if you were killing him. Sometimes I wonder whether it's worth going on. Let them fire Igor from his wonderful job, let him end up in a psychiatric ward, what do I care? I'll show them!"

Kumanchin nodded, fighting off a creeping numbness. He had caught a chill jogging in the rain that morning, and his bones ached, but that was not the trouble. It seemed to him that he had heard all this before from Tushkina. Or so he imagined.

". . . and they'll say it's all my fault. They'll just blame me! Oh, Vladimir Mikhailovich, I'm sick and tired of it all. He's such a nothing!"

She stopped. Her outburst had passed. She watched him silently and irresolutely.

"You're tired today," she said.

"No, it's nothing."

"I can see you're tired. It was so easy to talk with you last time, now it's so hard."

"I'm listening."

She wanted him to pity her. Where was he to find enough pity for them all? Tushkina was not the first today to complain to him of life's injustices. Moreover, there was a touch of flirtation in her reproach that it was hard for her to talk with him. He waited for the request that he knew she was leading up to. She hadn't come merely to unburden herself.

Tushkina sighed.

"I'll be frank, Vladimir Mikhailovich. The situation at Igor's research institute is very complicated. There's a careerist there who is just riffraff. He wants to get rid of Igor. People quickly forget to whom they're obligated! I want Igor to take a vacation and get treatment. Not here, of course. If he is registered at the hospital, everyone will know about it immediately. They'll promptly take advantage. It's out of the question, Vladimir Mikhailovich! You are our only hope. I'll do everything I can to dry him out. I'll strain every nerve, you don't know me, I can do anything."

"Yekaterina Andreyevna," he said, "I haven't even seen your husband and I can't imagine . . ."

"Volodya, please!" Tushkina pleaded. "What can I do with that idiot? I can't drag him here at the end of a rope. He won't come here. Come to our apartment. At least diagnose his case!"

Although he knew he would consent, he tried nevertheless to explain that in such circumstances there was almost no hope of succeeding. Tushkina would hear none of it. She insisted, and finally they agreed that he would come to their home on Sunday.

Having achieved her aim, she grew cheerful. They left together. The sky had cleared, the wind died down, the rain was letting up. It dripped silently on the jasmine and sweetbrier bushes. Their branches, bent by the downpour, began to lift as the water ran off. While Kumanchin locked the door Tushkina opened her umbrella and looked about.

"Lord, how lovely! It would be so good to be at the country cottage now, broiling shashlik on a spit. . . . I don't know why I bother with him. I wish he burned in hell! . . . I ought to invite you to the cottage. I make wonderful shashlik. You'd fall in love with me at the first taste!"

She was back in character as he had pictured her previously. Kumanchin responded to her tone, said something in jest, and she laughed and teased. She drove him home and as he left the car (yes, of course he would definitely come on Sunday, it was agreed) and climbed the stairs he felt young and thought how wonderful it was to feel strong, bold, and energetic, how good to be alive and to experience these infectious sensations; he must transmit this joy of living, this sense of vitality, to patients.

Ira noticed his liveliness and observed him thoughtfully. He told her about Tushkina and—what had not aroused pity in his office—that she was touching in her singlehanded struggle for happiness, slight and elegant and overburdened by the weight she bore. Ira was not enraptured.

"Yes, that's interesting, naturally, but what about Alenka?"

"We didn't discuss it," Kumanchin said, hesitating, and secretly and hastily trying to recall whether he had forgotten Alenka. No, he hadn't, he had borne her in mind. "It just didn't come up," he added.

"How could you not have asked?"

"Ira, how could I?"

"What's so difficult? She proposed it herself."

"But you can't bring it up when a person comes to you in misfortune."

He was not sure he was right. No doubt he should have asked. He simply hadn't been able to.

"Your daughter's future is at stake, but all that matters to you is your own overcompensation."

"What has overcompensating to do with it?"

"What, indeed! You're so pure! A healer! Chasing an attractive female. You're rationalizing!"

"How smart we are," he said sadly, rising from the table. "We know everything."

He wanted to wash the dishes. Ira wouldn't let him. She was angry. Like any woman, she was jealous. Jealous of Tushkina, and all her talk of overcompensation and rationalizing did not change the fact. He didn't want to search his soul and consider whether her jealousy was justified. Meantime, he felt ill, he ached and was feverish. Hoping that Ira would not notice—she had warned him not to go jogging in the rain that morning—he curled up on the couch with his book. He was sneezing. Ira remarked on it immediately.

"Have you caught a cold?"

"Just a chill."

"I told you. It's all these fads you follow. First it's yoga, then something else, now this silly jogging."

She knew he believed in the fads, had to try them, but she couldn't refrain from ruining his mood. And he, though he was aware that she had to let off steam, also could not remain silent.

"The fads may be bad, but I suppose it's better to indulge yourself and grow fat!"

"A lot I indulge myself!"

He had offended Ira. He shouldn't have said that about growing fat, of course. Smart as they were and knowing all about the psyche, there they were, quarreling.

The trouble was that Ira did not trust Tushkina and, turning the pages of the Kandinsky book, Kumanchin was annoyed at this mistrust, which now infected him too. His annoyance spread to everything else. Why did Alenka have to enter medical school? What did she know about medicine? Here he was, a doctor—so what? If she just kept on at her job for another year she would be granted preference as a worker, automatically upgrading her exam score enough to ensure admission. Her work was light, her job easy. Anyone else in her place would be happy to have it.

He shouldn't be reasoning this way about Alenka. Yes, another person might be pleased to have her position, but its mechanical routine stifled Alenka. She hated rote work. That was her nature. Take Kandinsky: though he suffered a mental disorder and overcame it only by a miracle, he could not stand the work of weaving baskets. He believed that only using his mind to the full would cure him. Hardly had his madness passed than he took to translating from French and German, and went on to conduct his own research. Few healthy minds managed to accomplish as much as he in a short period. His wife complained to the doctors that he was exhausting himself. She was wrong; he was saving himself. In the same way, Alenka could not live without a challenge to her mind.

Kumanchin read the memoirs that described Kandinsky's final moments. "He resumed work at the hospital too soon after beginning to recover from a bout of the illness. Driven by the urge to suicide that usually marked the stage of transition to recovery, he took a phial of opium from the medicine chest at the hospital. When he reached home he took an unquestionably lethal dose. His scientific self-possession did not desert him in those last minutes. He reached for a sheet of paper and wrote: 'I have drunk so-and-so many grams of opium. I am reading Tolstoy's "Cossacks." ' Then, in a weaker hand: 'It is becoming difficult to read.' He was found without any sign of life."

After his death his wife tried to raise funds to publish his manuscripts. She failed and used probably her last savings to publish his major works at her own expense, editing the manuscripts herself. Who else was there to see to it but she, who had been his companion from the start of his illness to the end? For eleven years she fought his constant suicide wish. The sacrifice made by a woman to give a man the will to live, thought Kumanchin.

The book contained photos of this woman, Liza Kandinskaya, and the house in which she lived. Kumanchin imagined the cold, dark, empty St. Petersburg apartment. When the work of publishing Kandinsky's writings was completed, her loneliness probably became unbearable. After seeing his books to press, Kandinskaya herself committed suicide.

Did he envy such people? Was that it? Private correspondence of that time used words such as "luminary" and "devotee of science." From the Fortress of Peter and Paul, where he was incarcerated, Pisarev, the leader of the radical intelligentsia of the late nineteenth century, wrote that in science alone lay the salvation of society. That was the happy age of the natural sciences. If only he, Kumanchin, had such faith in his work! Whether he was to blame or Fedya Yaroshevich or the patients who did not try to regain their health, he did not believe he was living properly. That was the whole trouble. The flickering of the black-and-white television screen resembled flickering underwater light, as if he had descended to the depths and was looking up at the surface. He had to push upward, swim to the surface, act!

All he had to do, it seemed, was to start. Tushkina had appeared just in time. With her help he would propel himself upward. Alenka would enter medical school, he would begin to receive patients at home, they would exchange their apartment for a larger one so that he would have an office in the home, he'd buy an automobile, he would always be in a hurry. It was not a matter of the auto or the apartment, what mattered was movement. It was like morning jogging!

After dinner on Sunday Ira took Kumanchin's brown suit out of the closet. He wore it on festive occasions, so rarely that it had gone out of fashion instead of wearing out. The trousers were too wide. So were the lapels.

"You never have proper clothes," Ira remarked.

He telephoned Tushkina to say he was ready to set out. She mumbled something about rain. He thought he detected some uneasiness in her voice and he was surprised that she did not offer to call for him in the car, as she had promised when he agreed to come. His cold lingered. He was taking sulfa and it left him weak. Waiting for the bus in the rain, he got soaked, then barely squeezed into the crowded vehicle and barely forced his way out at the Tushkins' stop, only to step right into a puddle.

A man in pajamas opened the door. He had a soft, puffy face. Staring awkwardly at Kumanchin, the man screwed up his eyes and ran all five fingers through his soft blond hair. He made a show of welcoming Kumanchin, gesturing unnecessarily as he invited him in.

This was Tushkin. Kumanchin heard Tushkina talking on the telephone somewhere deep in the large apartment.

The table was laid and two men, seated at it, waited for Kumanchin to remove his raincoat. He realized that he had come at the wrong time. Kumanchin shook hands. The conversation, interrupted by his arrival, resumed. The tall, wiry one in striped shirt and jeans introduced himself as Rashev. Seated sideways in his chair, he told Tushkin:

"I can't understand how you could stand to work for that outfit so long."

Tushkin laughed and sank into a seat on the soft couch.

"Well, you know how it is."

Listening to them, Kumanchin soon grasped the fact that Tushkin was leaving or already had left his research institute, not of his own free will; and, being timid, was frightened by this turn in his affairs. Rashev, fortyish and with a sporty air, was a friend, now trying to reassure Tushkin. The latter was obedient as a child, and Rashev knew exactly how to restore his self-confidence. Rashev treated Tushkin condescendingly, yet at the same time appeared to be somehow dependent on him. He seemed to be suppressing a sense of distaste or irritation. The tall, bony Rashev was not extending sympathy but trying to buck up the weakling, Tushkin. Beneath his reassurances he was more aggressive and harsh than he wanted to appear now.

Tushkin agreed with everything Rashev said: "Right, Vitek, right."

Consoled and warmed by the reassurances, Tushkin squinted at Kumanchin. In the company of his friends Tushkin found comfort and pleasure, whereas Kumanchin was an outsider, a stranger who had violated his airtight surroundings and brought a breath of alarm into the room.

The second of the guests, long silent, was powerfully built, had black hair and a ruddy face. He wore a black leather jacket. Leaning back in his chair, he teased Tushkin:

"I always told you, but you're a patsy."

"Yes, I'm a patsy," Tushkin agreed easily.

"Until they stuck it to you in the ass."

"That's right."

"Everyone knew they'd take you by the neck and pitch you out."

The ruddy-faced one enjoyed scolding Tushkin. His thick fingers picked up an imaginary Tushkin and tossed him out the door with obvious pleasure. Rashev gave Kumanchin a quick glance and laughed. He too was aware of the heavyset guest's enjoyment and shared it. But Tushkin saw only sympathy, nodded in gratitude and agreed:

"Right, Andrei, that's exactly the way it was."

There was something appealing in his slightly swollen face.

Tushkina made her appearance, wearing an apron over her dress, and apologized to Kumanchin for having been occupied on the telephone and because her hand smelled of onion. She waved away a double entendre by the ruddy-faced Andrei, who drummed on the table upon her appearance. She brushed aside his remark lightly enough, as the double entendre demanded:

"What can you expect of these fellows, Vladimir Mikhailovich? Come with me. At least it will be good to talk with a civilized person."

In the kitchen she explained hurriedly what Kumanchin had already guessed: everything had changed suddenly, her husband had had to leave the research institute. But Rashev was taking him on in the Product Standards Commission and now she didn't know what to do, it would be utterly inopportune for Tushkin to undertake the cure now, so perhaps they had better wait.

Somewhere close by he heard a woman's voice engaged in a telephone conversation.

"Please excuse us, Vladimir Mikhailovich. It's just that it has worked out this way," Tushkina said. "And oh, incidentally, as far as all these people are concerned, you're one of my colleagues. You understand."

Kumanchin agreed to the deception. Of course he understood and, by the way, he was expected at home. He had to leave.

"I won't hear of your leaving, Vladimir Mikhailovich. Not at all!"

He saw he ought to depart, that Tushkina herself wanted him out of the way. But the time to go had passed. Bottles were arrayed on the table now and Tushkin, in happy expectation, calmer, propitiated, bared his soul to his friends, already including Kumanchin among them, for at that moment he loved the whole world.

". . . and I was easy on people. If they had to take time off from work or begged off some duty . . ."

They were tiring of him. Rashev continued to sit sideways, polished the tablecloth with his palm, and repeated:

"To hell with it. You should have left long ago."

Andrei went on teasing. "When you gave women time off, they could always make it up by a little night work," he hooted.

Tushkin smiled as if he were being flattered. Rashev hemmed and hawed and launched into a serious description of how many factories Tushkin would inspect for the Product Standards Commission, how much the factories would be dependent upon him, how he would travel on business wherever he wished, and if he didn't want to he could send his subordinates.

Tushkin tried to focus his attention on Rashev's words, but his mind wasn't registering. His eyes flitted from Rashev's face to the bottles, to Rashev's wristwatch, to the door. He became alarmed as Rashev spoke of unfamiliar technology, and he sought reassurance.

"Listen, but I don't know . . . in general . . ."

"Don't worry, Igor, the fellows there know it all, they take care of everything, you don't have to tell them what to do."

"I . . . them!"

"Look, do you think I know anything about computers or multichannel communications? I know how to handle people, that's what counts. Relax. I vouch for you."

The women entered and took places at the table. Tushkina apologized for burning the meat, but the second woman, Rashev's wife, said it was fine. They drank to the friendship between Tushkin and Rashev, who apparently were not very well acquainted or had resumed a friendship after many years apart; the past was all very vague, with circumstances about which Rashev, after several drinks, talked obscurely and stubbornly, shaking his head: "It was all a lot of nonsense, Natasha, I always knew Tushkin was my friend."

By this time Tushkin was in his cups and was also making no sense. It didn't take much to get him drunk. He smiled softly, sometimes mumbled something indistinctly, but no one paid any attention. Kumanchin made a mental note: second-degree alcoholism. As Yaroshevich would say, he's one of ours. Rashev's wife, with a pale, narrow face, hardly drank at all and did not eat, but talked to Kumanchin about horoscopes, evidently under the illusion that his work had something to do with horoscopes. She pretended not to notice what was going on between Tushkina and Andrei, who was becoming more and more aggressive and put his arm around Tushkina as if in jest: "I'm going to steal your wife, Igor!"

Tushkina tried to remove his hand but saw it would only excite him further. She yielded. She too was becoming drunk. With his free hand Andrei refilled the glasses and said to Rashev:

"Vitya, drink up. I don't recognize any excuses."

Rashev shook his head.

"I've had enough."

"No excuses! Can't accept them. Bottoms up!"

Kumanchin realized he ought to leave, but he remained rooted to his chair. Then they all pushed their chairs back. Andrei tried to do a Cossack dance in the hallway and the smell of coffee wafted from the kitchen. Tushkin was asleep in a corner of the couch. Kumanchin reached the coat hanger in the hall, but Tushkina stopped him.

"Don't think of leaving, Volodya."

His head swam. He saw that Tushkina was in some confusion, but it wasn't because of him. Suddenly she decided to drive him home. He donned his raincoat and she was putting on her familiar shiny windbreaker. Rashev's wife tried to pull it off her and called to her husband to help. He pulled Tushkina back from the door and admonished her:

"Katya, you're drunk. You're drunk. Forget it. Where's the coffee? You went for coffee. Bring the coffee."

She tore free of him. They were all tipsy. She was still in control of herself, but she no longer wanted to remain sober. She wanted to be drunk.

Walking out of the building into the dark street, Kumanchin found himself in a chilly, fine drizzle. People waited under umbrellas at the bus stop, backs to the cold wind. The bus was long in coming. Kumanchin froze. He knew Ira would grumble, he knew it was his fault, he shouldn't have stayed, nothing prevented him from leaving right away except some incomprehensible weakness of will. He felt sick, he was dissatisfied with himself and he couldn't understand why he had to waste himself by constant self-constraint. The ones he left in the apartment were enjoying themselves, while here he was, feeling bad. They knew what was good for them and what was bad, and Tushkin's liver would outlast Kumanchin's nervous system, they all knew that.

Then the bus came and took him down the empty boulevard. When it was one block before his stop an ambulance moved out of his side street, turned swiftly and silently onto the boulevard and sped past toward the center of town. Occupied with his own thoughts, Kumanchin paid no attention. He entered his courtyard through the archway between buildings and at the far end saw people moving about in the light cast by automobile headlights at the adjoining building, No. 7. He felt a sudden alarm. A second ambulance drove into the courtyard and slipped past Kumanchin toward No. 7. A police car, lights flashing, faced the oncoming ambulance. A second police car's headlights played upon the grass, the fence and the figures of several policemen. A young intern and a nurse in white gowns stepped out of the newly arrived ambulance, and the driver, opening his door, looked toward the gathering and asked someone: "What happened here?"

"You're too late," came the answer. "They took her away already. Go back."

"Took whom away?" The driver, curious, stepped out onto the courtyard pavement.

The young intern and the nurse stood with a police captain who was saying: "She was still breathing. I don't know, maybe she jumped or maybe her husband pushed her."

No. 7 was a nine-story building with balconies on each floor above the first. People stood on the balconies, bending over to peer down or look up. A third ambulance arrived.

Kumanchin's heart beat faster and he felt a buzzing in his ears. He remembered Shirina saying: "We're your neighbors, you live at No. 5, we live in No. 7." A nimble old fellow in a padded jacket and a felt hat was telling something to a cluster of people and pointing up at a balcony. Kumanchin pushed into the center of the crowd, trying to make out what he was saying, but only fragmentary, indistinct words reached him. Some people interjected objections and the old fellow answered heatedly. A dispute sprang up; no one seemed to know anything. He thought he heard someone mention the name Shirin.

Kumanchin entered the poorly lit lobby, passed the row of mailboxes and went to the elevator. The elevator light showed red. Two women were waiting. One was telling the other something about a drunken husband pursuing a wife who, to escape him, fled onto the balcony, hoping to climb across to the balcony of the adjoining apartment, at which point the husband shoved her. It took a moment for Kumanchin to realize that she was speaking of an incident that had occurred somewhere else, he didn't know where or when. The elevator door opened, two young women in windbreakers and jeans emerged, and Kumanchin entered with the others. The elevator smelled of cigarette smoke. One of the women sniffed in disgust and said:

"Now they've taken to smoking even in the elevator. Next they'll set fire to the building."

The women got out at the fourth floor. Kumanchin pressed the button for the eighth without knowing why. When he left the elevator it started down immediately. It was dark and silent on the landing but he heard voices below. He ran down a flight of stairs. On the seventh-floor landing stood half-dressed people.

Corridors stretched in both directions. The people were clustered in the corridor on the right. Someone was leading an elderly woman by the arm from door to door. Women sobbed and hushed their children. Men cast sidelong glances at Kumanchin. Someone was telling a neighbor, "If you didn't see it, you didn't see it and you shouldn't talk about what you didn't see, that's what I think."

A young policeman walked swiftly toward the elevator, frowning and looking straight ahead. He waited, watching the red light. The men fell silent. Kumanchin quietly asked the policeman:

"Was it the Shirins' apartment?"

The policeman, failing to comprehend, frowned and shook his head. He glanced impatiently at the red light, then ran down the stairs.

One of the men in the corridor asked Kumanchin:

"Were you looking for somebody?"

"The Shirins."

"Is that the family with the boy who . . . ? That one? On the third floor, I believe."

"Thanks." Kumanchin started down to the ground floor. A weight had lifted from him and in his relief he almost ran. The ambulances were gone. Policemen were still interviewing the neighbors, about ten of whom remained in the courtyard. Kumanchin stood among them, listening, but learned nothing further. A drunken husband. The wife fell. Maybe she fell, maybe he pushed. An accident, or, as we call it in Russian, an unfortunate occurrence. What else could it be called?

Kumanchin's sense of relief began to recede. At first he swore to himself that never again would he give in to a woman's tears and discharge a patient prematurely. But what right did he have to decide people's lives and compel them to remain in the hospital? They could decide for themselves whether to accept treatment, and what could he do? He felt guilty, because he might have persuaded Shirina to hold out. Might have but hadn't. He hadn't wanted to make the effort. He couldn't bear tears, he had yielded. Tushkina had diverted him. There was no reason to reproach him, Kumanchin told himself. No one could expect more of him. He was a doctor, not a saint. Perhaps only a saint could prevail upon these people, but the time of the saints was long past, and what had he to do with it?

Ira and Alenka awaited him. Alenka was amused at his appearance, late, wet and with the smell of liquor on his breath.

"Great!" she said. "You're beginning to find out what life is all about!"

It was a joke but it struck a sore spot. When they had gone to bed and turned out the light Kumanchin told Ira:

"Nothing is going to happen. He won't take the cure. And since they don't need me she won't do anything."

As always when she was upset, Ira hastened to accuse him:

"Of course. You don't know how to go about these things."

They lay silent but did not sleep. Ira went on:

"I think she may yet phone."

"No," Kumanchin said.

"Try to call her yourself."

"How can I?" he asked. "And why should I try?"

"Because you're a doctor."

"What of it?"

"A doctor should be, well, compassionate."

Ashamed for himself and for Ira, Kumanchin observed:

"Her husband, if you please, headed a laboratory in a research institute. I don't know how well he did his job, but they paid him more than they pay you and Alenka and me put together. And now he'll run a department in the Standards Commission! Whether Alenka gets into medical school depends on the likes of him!"

"Shh," she whispered.

He lowered his voice. "You have to be without a sense of humor to talk of compassion. You memorize phrases out of old books but everything changed long ago. Compassion is a feeling of the powerful toward the weak, but who's powerful, they or we, if we depend on them and not they on us?"

Ira did not reply but after a while, dropping off to sleep, she said soothingly:

"Nevertheless, I think she'll phone."

Tushkina did not phone. Yaroshevich once asked whether she had come back. When he was told she hadn't, he shrugged. Then Kumanchin switched to another department of the hospital. Other people and other destinies filled his life, and he heard no more of the Tushkins.

Alenka got a grade of four on the physics exam. Then she took her composition and chemistry exams and got fives, and on the last one, biology, another four. Docent Melnikov graded her exams. They said he was pretty good-natured. Alenka, certain that she had answered all the questions correctly, was surprised: Why four? A woman sat alongside Melnikov, whispering to him, and he answered Alenka with a good-natured smile: "Four is a good grade, too." Her total score of eighteen out of twenty meant that Alenka was rejected.

She came home downcast—what use was it to study if they graded her like that?—but she bore up well. They sat in the kitchen, drinking tea. Kumanchin, comforting himself, said: "You can understand Melnikov, after all. With eight applicants for each vacancy it's impossible to grade carefully."

His habit of seeking to justify everything was at work. The last thing Alenka needed at that moment was his attempt to justify Melnikov. This objectivity on her father's part was to her a betrayal. She suddenly turned her head away, hid her face and fled the kitchen. She locked herself in the bathroom. Ira, sharing her daughter's feelings, looked at him reproachfully.

"The bastards," she said.

After Alenka had cried herself out she reappeared. She drank tea and said softly:

"Papa, maybe I shouldn't try to enter medical school."

"Why not?" he said guardedly, with a presentiment of some fresh turn or, as he and Ira put it, a kick-up.

"You were always against it. It's difficult to get in, the work is hard, it pays poorly. And I don't have the character to make a good doctor. I'll never love the patients, I know that for sure."

"Why love them?" he said. "You have to heal them, not love them."

"No, Papa, there you're wrong."

She looked at him suspiciously and waited. She was testing him. If he began to dissuade her from medicine, it meant he did not believe she would make the grade next year, either.

"I don't know," he said, "honestly, I just don't know what else one can work at nowadays."

She brightened, glad that he hadn't tried to dissuade her. After the exams last year she'd lain in bed for a week, head turned to the wall. Alenka had changed in this past year.

She wanted to look in the textbook to check the answers she had given in the exam. Perhaps she had overlooked something and deserved the grades of four. She overcame the urge. Enough of thinking about it. Next year she'd have two-year worker status and the preferential upgrading that went with it, and she'd surely make the grade.

They had the rest of the evening before them and they wondered whether to go to the movies, but Ira, as always when she encountered some unpleasantness, was overcome by irresistible drowsiness. She stretched out on the ottoman and immediately her eyes closed.

Alenka went to her room. Later, Kumanchin glanced in on her. She was lying on her back, eyes open. It frightened him. Were her strong will and self-discipline too much for her? Wouldn't she pay too high a price in the form of spasms of the intestine and heart, those ailments of the strong-willed? People had to react vigorously, not be shock absorbers accepting battering without resistance. They broke down if they didn't respond by venting their feelings. Taking the chair alongside her bed, Kumanchin said:

"You were unlucky to be graded by scum like Melnikov."

"Oh, Papa," she said, overjoyed. "He's such a rat, such a rat!"

"You should have told him so to his face. In front of everybody."

Alenka laughed. She felt better. She turned on her side, reached for his hand and placed it under her cheek, as she used to in childhood.

"Oh, Papa, you're wonderful. It would have been so good to say it!"

She still trusted him and he began to trust her and thought that she'd make something of herself yet.

TRANSLATED BY LEO GRULIOW

Henry Taylor

The plastic safety card
hangs from my hand unread as flight attendants
launch
   their deadpan puppet show; like a motel room,
   this familiar strangeness soothes me into ease
   at being nowhere in particular, relief
      that it is too late now to make sure
      I am on the right plane.

Out in the afternoon
at the taxiway's edge, men in hard hats are standing
around a backhoe. The purpose of their ditch
   is invisible from here, but as it lengthens,
   I see myself standing as they do, watching
   hydraulic feet swing down and dig in
      to steady the machine,

or the bucket pulling it forward,
as a man inches across a comic-strip desert.
   Like something alive, it changes the ground
   from which I will soon lift away; in the cab,
   a man with knowledge I have coveted
      sits touching controls and watching
      what hands can make happen.

An old story comes back,
from wartime, when steel was scarce, and broken parts
of farm machines had to be put back together;
   on such an errand, once, my father stood around
   for half a day, waiting his turn with a welder.
      To kill time, he wondered aloud
      how hard welding was,

and the shop foreman said,
"That dumb son of a bitch out there learned to do it."
 So, out of necessity, he mastered it,
 and I watched him for years; now greed gnaws at
 me
 whenever I watch some close work well done
 and remember the shop foreman's line,
 or mysteries I absorbed

 from my life among horses,
who taught me, in their way, most of what I know
 now.
 With less faith, I have acted in plays, taken up
 trim carpentry, writing computer programs,
 tuning Volkswagens . . . these sidelines and others
 have drawn me toward mastery
 approached, or barely imagined.

 For the sake of odd skills
I have shirked the labors I live by, and pursued
 one more curiosity for my collection, or puttered
 awhile with an old one, thereby evading
 the higher, more difficult arts, such as knowing
 at sight the life-changing moment
 when the right touch or word

 might turn aside the rage
that careens through the house like electrical wind,
 or when a hand, lightly placed on a child,
 might wean him without force from the TV set
 where, as long as the light of the world's last days
 washes over us, we can believe
 we will always be here.

 What more will I try
before turning again toward making what peace I can
 with the consequences of ignorant choices?
 What can I know now, but ice clicking in plastic
 at thirty thousand feet? So I daydream
 of earth-moving competence, held in air
 by the skilled hands of strangers.

SONG OF THE YEARS

·2·

Robert Rozhdestvensky

What if my hair has now turned gray—
winters can't frighten me like witches.
My years aren't just a heavy weight;
my years, my years—
                    they are my riches.

Often I tried to make time fly,
like a draft horse got used to being hitched,
never put a penny by.
My years, my years—
                    they are my riches.

"Thanks," I whisper to time gone
and swallow its bitter pill—years which
I'll never give up to anyone.
My years, my years—
                    they are my riches.

And if the ages turn to me
and say, "Alas, your star's extinguished,"
a child will lift for all to see
my years, my years—
                    all my riches.

TRANSLATED BY F. D. REEVE

THE CURE

·⚘·

Mary Ward Brown

When Ella Hogue continued to grow worse, her daughters all came home. Bee came first from nearby Vilula, then Andretta from Fort Wayne, and Lucindy from Miami. For two days and two nights they took turns sitting by the bed, waiting for the end. On the third day Ella began to improve. Consciousness came back first, then gradually alertness. Unbelieving, her daughters gathered around her.

Ella looked at them and sighed. "I ain't dead yet?" she said.

"Cose you ain't dead!" Lucindy scolded. "You 'live as anybody. You done got better."

"I don't want to be no better," Ella said, "if I can't get up and do, like everybody else."

She lay beneath a quilt she had pieced and quilted years ago, in a bed given to her by Doll's grandmother. The bed was of solid dark wood, with a high, carved headboard and a cracked foot. White women hunting antiques had wanted to buy it, or swap her something for it, for years. When her daughters arrived, the bedclothes had been dingy, and stale as the inside of the trunk where she kept them. Now the sheets on her bed were aggressively clean. The quilt had been aired in the sun. Ella's old head, tied up in a snowy rag, made the only dent in her pillow.

"You soon *be* up, Mama," Lucindy said positively. "You coming back thisaway!"

"How long you been here, Cindy?" she asked. She was too weak to move.

"I come Tuesday," Lucindy said. "Soon as Bee called up, I told my boss-lady, 'My mama sick in Alabama and I got to *go*.' Then I got on that bus!"

Lucindy was Ella's oldest, born the first year after puberty when Ella was barely fourteen. Her large frame, heavily fleshed through the hips and bust, was bony elsewhere. Zipped and buttoned into a polyester pantsuit, she was like a Christmas stocking half-filled with fruit. Her hair was a vigorous iron-gray, and her aging face was pleasant.

"I'm here too, Mama," said Andretta, who had been in Fort Wayne so long she talked like a Yankee. A copper-colored replica of Ella at the same age, Andretta leaned down to touch her mother's still, unresponsive hand.

"I see you, Retta," she said, and smiled.

Bee's presence was taken for granted. She was a mixture of her two half sisters, smaller and lighter in color than Lucindy, larger and darker than Andretta. Lucindy and Andretta were both "outside" children, but Bee had been born and raised in wedlock. After Bee there were no more, girls or boys, because Ella's husband had mumps that went down on him.

"What got the matter with me?" she wanted to know.

"You had a little sinking spell, is all," Andretta said. "You over it now."

"I don't know nothing about it . . ."

She turned her face toward the open door. She did not even know what month it was. Clusters of yellow berries were on the chinaberry tree, so it had to be fall. Across the road, mock oranges were green and a few lay on the ground.

A small fire burned in the fireplace. Bee began rattling lids on the stove in the kitchen and soon there were smells of cooking and smoke, but Ella felt no hunger. She felt nothing at all, except the faint presence of life itself.

"Has Doll been here?" she asked.

"Every day," Lucindy said proudly. "She be back after while. She don't know you done come to."

Bee pulled up a chair and sat down by the bed with a cup of hot soup.

"Take a sip of this, Mama," she said, holding out a spoon half-full.

Ella waited, then took a small taste. The soup was chicken with soft rice. When Bee held out the spoon again, she let herself be fed and kept on sipping until the spoon scraped bottom.

Afterward she closed her eyes and rested, listening to the girls tiptoeing around, whispering so as not to disturb her. She felt like dozing off, but first she had to attend to something.

"What time she coming?" she asked.

"Who, Doll?" Bee said. They had sat down around the fire to eat. "Why? You want her?"

"I wants her to get Dr. Dobbs to come work on me," she said, "and get me up from here."

All three women turned to look at her. Bee swallowed the food in her mouth, field peas, sprinkled with hot-pepper sauce, and cornbread.

"Dr. Dobbs *been* retired, Mama," she said carefully. "He ain't doctored on nobody in three-four years. I think he even kinda mindless now."

"Thas all right," Ella said. "I ruther have him mindless than them others. Dr. Dobbs know how to move my bowels and flush out my kidneys, and get me back on my feets."

"He could years ago, Mama, but he can't do nothing now . . . Your bowels can't move, noway, until you eat—and you ain't et till just now."

"Who made that soup?" she asked.

"I did, Mama," said Andretta. "Was it good?"

"It needed mo' salt," she said.

They looked at each other and smiled.

"One of y'all go tell Doll I wants to see her," she said in a clear, strong voice, and all the smiles vanished.

Each time someone knocked on the door, Sally Webb thought it was bad news about Netta (her childhood name for Aunt Ella), who had lived on the farm and worked for Sally's family most of her life. Though she dreaded Ella's passing with all her conscious mind, Sally was dimly aware of a subterranean impatience to get it over and behind her, for things to get back to normal, whatever the cost.

Both Sally's parents and all the other old people, black and white, who had lived on the place were now dead and gone. Ella had hung on, puttering around her house and yard, last not only of her generation but of a whole era.

She never asked for anything. On the contrary, she was always coming up with a jar of jelly, bunch of greens, or sack of something. Still, Sally felt responsible for her, down there alone. When she hadn't seen her out for several days last week, she stopped to find her in bed, slightly disoriented. She had called Bee, who came in a dented old car and took Ella to the doctor. Dr. Cox reserved a bed in the hospital, but once out of his office Ella refused to go. Bee brought her home and came to get Sally.

Ella lay on top of the covers in her old-fashioned Sunday clothes and lace-up, size five shoes.

"Dr. Cox wants you in the hospital, Netta," Sally explained, "where they can get you well. Bee and I don't know what to do for you, like they do."

"Yes'm." She looked off to one side. "I be all right here."

"But Bee needs to get back to work," Sally insisted. "There's nobody to look after you here."

"I don't need nobody," she said. "The Lord be with me."

Sally looked at Bee who looked helplessly back.

"Well, you have to go, Netta," Sally said firmly. "You need medical attention. . . . Now I'm going back to call the hospital while Bee packs your things. Bee and I will go with you, and stay as long as you need us."

Ella's face was a mask, stoical and lonely. When tears suddenly stood in her eyes, it was as though a woodcarving started to weep. She turned her head and a tear dropped off on the pillow.

"I wants to die at home, Doll," she said.

So Sally called the cafeteria where Bee worked and told them Bee would have to be out for a while. She talked to Dr. Cox on the phone and went to town for medicine. When Ella continued to grow weaker, Bee came up and called the others. Ella would not know now whether they took her to the hospital or not, but no one suggested it. Sally reported to Dr. Cox each day. Ella's daughters turned her frequently from one side to the other as he instructed, and kept her clean. It seemed a matter of time to the end.

Now it was Lucindy who knocked on the door, but Lucindy was smiling.

"Mama done woke up and et," she said. On the underside of the announcement, like an insect behind a sheer curtain, was a hint of disappointment.

"Well, thank the Lord," Sally said.

"Yes'm, but . . ." Lucindy would not come in the door Sally held open. "Now she want you. She want you to get Dr. Dobbs to come see her."

"Dr. Dobbs! Why, he's senile and alcoholic too, they say."

"That's who she want, though."

"Wait a second . . ." Sally went back for her keys and a sweater.

The moment she saw Ella alive and conscious after days beyond reach, her heart seemed to crowd the walls of her chest. Standing by the bed, she looked down at the slight figure beneath a quilt in which were sewn scraps from her own school dresses.

"You go'n get Dr. Dobbs fuh me?" Ella asked.

"I'll do my best," she said.

Dr. Dobbs sat bolt upright in the front seat of the car, beside his black driver, Elmo. A beard of fat hung down around his face, which was mapped with forking red and purple veins. Pale blue eyes stared out as from the raw white of an egg, in a look of fixed displeasure. He wore a dark suit of lightweight wool, a white shirt, and a striped silk tie. A large stomach pushed out against the buttons of his coat.

Sally was waiting on the porch when they drove up, and she hurried out to the long, black sedan.

"I'm Sally Webb, Dr. Dobbs," she said, when Elmo let down the window, "William and Mary Ann Webb's daughter. I'll ride down to Aunt Ella's with you."

"Get in, young lady," he said. "I wish I could assist you . . ."

"Aunt Ella must be nearly ninety now," Sally said, speaking up from the back seat. "But she thinks you can help her."

He seemed not to hear. Instead he turned his head from one side to the other, looking at a dilapidated cotton gin on the left and a leaning seed house on the right.

"This place looks run-down," he said. Each time he spoke an essence of alcohol filled the car as though sprayed from a bottle.

"Well, things have changed since my father's time, Dr. Dobbs," Sally said. "The cattle business is off, and there's nobody to clean up and patch up the way there used to be."

"Where's all the niggers?" he asked.

"Everything is done with machinery now," she said quickly. "Most of the black people have gone."

"Good riddance," he said. "I wish they'd all leave—go back to Africa. Except Bojangles, here . . . Wasn't for him, I'd be up the creek without a paddle."

Sally said nothing.

"What's the name of the old nigger woman?"

"It's Ella Hogue, Dr. Dobbs. Aunt Ella. She cooked for us and was your patient for years. You used to like her pecan pies."

"I don't recall," he said.

At Ella's house, a two-room cabin by the side of the road, Elmo helped the doctor from the car as though midwifing a birth. Once on his feet he was handed a cane, but his balance was yet to come by degrees. Glaring about him, he waited.

"Somebody get my bag," he said at last, then fixed his attention on walking.

At the porch steps he turned himself over to Elmo again, and a new struggle began.

Lucindy, Andretta, and Bee, freshly washed and dressed, stood in the open doorway. For the trip home, Lucindy and Andretta had each brought black outfits for a funeral, and not much else. Now they wore the same clothes, rinsed out and dried overnight, in which they arrived.

"Good morning," the old man said formally. "I'm Dr. Dobbs, and this is my companion, Elmo Green."

There was a ripple of greetings, all ending in "Doctor."

"Where have you got the patient?" he asked.

"Right here, Doctor."

The women backed into a room which had been thoroughly straightened, dusted, and swept. An empty cane-bottomed chair had been placed by the bed. In the middle of the room a hanging light bulb was turned on, and a kerosene lamp on the dresser had been lit. Clean, starched cloths, made of bleached feed sacks edged in coarse lace, covered the tops of the dresser, trunk, and one small table. A low fire burned in the fireplace, its hearth freshly brushed with Ella's sedge broom.

Dr. Dobbs made his way to the bed and propped his cane against the wall.

"Well, my old friend." Holding on to the head of the bed, he leaned down and shook Ella's hand. "How are you?"

"Pretty low, Doctor," Ella said. "Pretty low."

He turned to the onlookers. "If you will step outside now," he said, "I'll examine the patient."

First he moved the chair nearer the bed, so close it touched the mattress sideways, and sat down carefully. Then he picked up Ella's wrist, found her pulse, and took out a heavy gold watch on a chain. Counting with his lips, he watched the second hand jerk around its tiny course. Light played along the watch chain as his stomach rose and fell.

Ella's eyes followed with profound interest as he opened the bag on the floor, took out a stethoscope, and adjusted it in his ears.

"Open your gown, please," he said.

Ella did not recognize the gown they had on her. She could not find the opening.

"Pull it up from the bottom," he said. "You remember how to do that, don't you, Auntie?"

"Doctor!" she said, and laughed in spite of everything.

He placed the metal disk on the left side of her chest and looked away as he listened. He moved the disk and listened several times. He had Ella turn on her side and listened from the back.

He took her blood pressure, squeezing the bulb and waiting, squeezing and waiting. With a light, he looked into her eyes, ears, and nose. He felt the glands in her neck.

Finally he leaned back in the chair and called out, "Elmo!"

Elmo appeared in the doorway. "Sir?"

"I need to stand up," the doctor said.

Elmo came forward to pull him up by the arms like a monstrous baby.

"Now stay there and help me," he said.

Elmo reached beneath the old man's coat and gripped his belt firmly. As though holding a large fish on a line, he stood looking the other way while the doctor palpated Ella's stomach, then pulled down the covers to press her ankles for swelling. He examined her feet, one at a time, flexing them up and down and from side to side.

"Do your corns bother you much?" he asked.

"No sir. Not much," she said. "Just when it rains."

Ella helped him pull the covers up. Elmo let him back into the chair and went out, closing the door behind him.

He rested for a moment.

"What you've got, Auntie," he said, "is the same thing I've got—old age. There ain't but one cure for it."

"Sir?"

He spoke a little louder. "I said I can't cure you—but I can get you back up for a while."

"I knowed you could, Doctor. That's why I sent for you. I don't want to be a burden on nobody."

"That's what we all say. . . ." He began putting instruments back in the bag. Leaning over squeezed off his breath and he said no more, though Ella listened and waited. When he took out a prescription pad and began to write, she raised her head from the pillow.

"Doctor, I hope you put down that tonic used to hep me so much," she said.

"Tonic?" He stopped to think. "That was Vinatone, probably. In a sherry base." Suddenly he looked at her with fresh interest. "Hold on. Wait a minute. Now I recall! Ain't you the one used to make that good muscadine wine?"

Ella's eyes gleamed in the lamplight. "Scuppernong too," she said.

"Well, bless my time! It was the best in the country. . . ." His eyes opened wider. "Have you got any left?"

"Just call one of my girls, Doctor," she said.

"Hey, girl!" he called out, making his stomach heave. "One of you . . . ladies!"

Bee hurried in, plump and womanly. Her face was serious.

"Bring one of them jugs out the kitchen, Beatrice," Ella said. "And a clean glass."

"Bring two glasses, if you don't mind, Beatrice," the doctor said.

They stood in the yard and waited, until Sally began to feel awkward.

"I'll go on home, Elmo," she said. "Stop and blow at the house when you start back. I'll come talk to Dr. Dobbs and get the prescriptions."

When she had gone, the others sat down on the edge of the porch, two on each side of the steps, their feet on the ground. Elmo took a seat beside Andretta.

"Doll sho favors her mother, don't she?" Lucindy said.

"But she got ways more like her daddy." Andretta's speech had lapsed. It was now almost as southern as the rest.

Bee yawned. A sleepy midday pall had settled over them like a spell in a fairy tale. The air was pure and still. Even the birds were quiet. There was no sound except insects saying their mantras, out of sight in the trees and grass.

"He takes his time, don't he?" Lucindy said, at last.

Andretta looked at her wristwatch. "He been in there forty minutes now," she said.

Bee got up, eased to the door, and peeped through the crack. When she turned away, she was grinning.

"They in there sleep, both of 'em," she said, and sat back down. "He bout to fall out the chair . . ."

"Lawd . . ." said Lucindy.

"Jesus!" said Andretta.

Lucindy turned to Elmo. "What us go'n do, just wait till he wake up?"

"It won't be long," Elmo said. "He soon have to make water, drinkin all that wine."

Bee and Andretta chuckled. Smiles lingered on their faces, but Lucindy was frowning.

"Reckon will he do her any good?" she asked.

"If anybody kin, he will," Elmo said. "He a good doctor, and he ain't forgot his learning. He still reads them books we gets in the mail."

"How long you been with him, Mr. Green?" Andretta asked.

"Three years, last month. I started off just drivin him. Then his wife died and my wife left me, so now I stays with him twenty-four hours a day."

"Is that right?" said Bee, from the other side of the porch.

"He old and fractious," he said, "but he don't mean nothin by it. He ain't even woke, 'cept in the mornin-time. And we got a cook to wait on us, and all. He got plenty money . . ."

"Not changing the subject," Lucindy said, "but what us go'n do now, y'all? She can't stay by herself no longer."

"One of us just have to stay with her," Andretta said. "Or take her home with us."

"And that would kill her in a hurry," Bee said. "She done already cried and told Doll she want to die at home."

"Y'all could hire somebody to stay with her, like me," Elmo teased.

"Chile, we ain't no rich doctors," Lucindy said, and they laughed as though harmonizing, their voices weaving in and out of each other before fading into silence.

Andretta sighed. "I'd never find a job down here, good as the one I've got up there," she said.

"Old as I is, I couldn't find no other job a'tall," Lucindy said. "But if anybody stay, it ought to be me. I'm the oldest. I'm old enough to be y'all's mama, myself."

"I'm the closest, though," said Bee.

Elmo turned to Andretta. "Maybe you ought to relocate your-self, Miss Andretta, and come on back home."

She gave him a sidelong smile. "Why? You go'n still be round?"

"One thing we *ain't* go'n do," Bee said, "is put her in no nursing home like white folks."

There was instant agreement. "Naw!"

"I tell y'all something . . ." Lucindy looked off through bare trees to the wide, impersonal sky. "Old age is *bad*."

"You ain't wrong," Andretta said slowly.

They sat in silence until Lucindy's stomach began to growl, so loud that everyone smiled. "You hush!" she said, and hit it lightly with her hand.

The sun had reached high noon, and though the porch shaded

their bodies, it shone hot on their feet and legs. A house fly buzzed around first one and then the other, to be brushed absently aside. Now and then a leaf wandered down. Faced with changes as yet undefined, the thoughts of the women turned more and more inward. All three were grateful their mother had not died, but her living would be costly from now on. If one stayed, the other two would have to pay for it.

Elmo kept politely quiet, his eyes fixed on the road. Like actors on a stage, they waited for the old man to call out and let the ending begin.

·2·

Boris Yekimov

1

Bread wasn't delivered to the village every day. So people stocked up on it: extra for themselves, and for their privately owned cattle when they were short of grain in their storage bins. On delivery days, people came early to avoid being last in line at the store and having to plead for leftovers. They sat around the entrance, the women with their knitting, discussing the village news and everything else.

Now they were talking about Manya Kharitonova. Her sons had come for Manya and her husband the previous autumn, and taken them to live in the central settlement of the large collective farm, which included several scattered villages.

"I look around the bus station, and there's Manya. 'Hello, how are you!' And we chatted about this and that," recounted Arkhip, a lively, garrulous old man. Practically every week he was at the bus station, going off somewhere, on business or not, to Uryupinsk, sometimes even to the city, to visit relatives. "I say to her, 'I'm hurrying home to my old lady. The gardens are all in bloom now in the village. It's really beautiful!' And she, would you believe it, started to cry. 'I'll never see my village again,' she says. 'They've taken me off to some kind of barren steppe: not a garden, not a bush,' tears running right down here." Arkhip pointed with his nicotine-stained fingernail.

Someone sighed: "Sure, you'd cry, too. After all, she lived here all her life."

From the knoll where the store stood, the Kharitonov house, with its red tin roof, was clearly visible. It overlooked the river, like all the houses belonging to the old village families: the Inyakins, Fetisovs, Kleimenovs, Tarasovs. The houses, inhabited for centuries past, were near the water, stood on good plots, and had spacious vegetable and flower gardens. When houses and barns fell apart, they built new ones. The old folks died off: Mitron, Kolyaka, the legendary Fetis, whose bones were already dust but whom the whole village remembered, Nadyurka Kleimenova, Nadyozha—they were gone, but young people took their place, tended the old graves, and covered them with flowers on Parents' Saturday. So it was perfectly natural for Manya Kharitonova to weep, living on alien soil. They all understood her.

For a minute or two everyone waiting at the store was silent. A radio played loudly at the edge of the village, in the yard of the good-for-nothing Yurka Sapov. It brayed day and night in his yard.

Arkhip broke the silence. Sighing and rolling a cigarette, he said: "Well, why are we grieving for her? Like at a wake. They live with their own children, they don't go hungry. Don't have to think about anything. While here," he said, waving his hand, "just looking after our livestock is enough to wear us down."

"You're absolutely right," others chimed in. "It's good to live with your children. They do the washing, supply the food. What's so bad about that?"

They chatted about getting old, about illness, about everything under the sun. Knitting needles clicked in the women's hands, the old men smoked, and children played nearby, around the club, while they all waited for the bread.

Makhora Alifanova, nicknamed Kaznacheyeva, "Paymistress," dozed, sitting on a crate a little apart from the others near the wall of the store, with some knitting in her hands. In the old days, her grandfather had served as paymaster in the village administration. The old woman dozed peacefully in the hot spring sunshine, her gray head slumped on her chest. The kerchief slid off her shoulders, her knitting fell from her hands, and a thread of saliva ran from the corner of her mouth. She was having a good dream.

"Our Makhora was courting last night on the hill. Now she's sleeping it off," Arkhip said loudly. "I wondered who was singing in the middle of the night. Turns out to be her."

Hearing her name, Makhora woke and straightened her kerchief.

"You're raving, you old geezer." She laughed. "Bees alight on a beautiful flower, but not even the devil looks at an old woman. Maybe it was your Mashka singing there when you weren't keeping an eye on her."

"My Masha's on a leash, she doesn't run around."

Makhora picked up her knitting, but the hot spring sun made

her tired and sleepy. She'd gotten up before dawn. The day before, toward evening, a mischievous wind had blown through the village. It played havoc, whistling and sending dust flying, and did some damage—it scattered all the hay in her yard. Her hayrick had stood like a shaky mushroom, and that night the wind finally knocked it down. In the morning, Makhora set about raking it together after driving the animals from the yard to pasture. It was awkward to do it alone: she had to gather the hay, stack it, and tamp it down. She leaned a ladder against the haystack and climbed up on it. Her years didn't allow her to climb back and forth—sixty years old, five years already on pension. It took all her strength to sweep the hay together, cover it with roofing paper and brace it with planks so it would stay put until winter. The haystack was up, but its owner could barely totter to the store. And now she was resting and dozing in the sunlight.

They delivered a lot of bread that day, both white and dark. Makhora took six loaves. The weekend was approaching and her son and daughter might show up. She put the bread in a string bag, slung it over her shoulder like a sack, and started home.

Her neighbor Raisa caught up with her. Although they were the same age, Raisa was taller and heavier and walked with a soldier's stride, her voice a trumpet.

"Are you sleepwalking?" Raisa asked. "Did you really spend the night on the hill?"

There was a hill in the middle of the village where, as long as people could remember, children played during the day and the young folk courted at night.

"That's all I need," answered Makhora. "I'd have to be carried there hand and foot. That wind yesterday caused the trouble. It knocked over the haystack, and this morning I had to gather it. I'm exhausted, don't even feel my arms and legs."

"You should have called me."

"Can't call on good people for help all the time. You need help yourself—I noticed the other day you were digging potatoes all alone again."

"Who's going to help me? Mama can barely get around. Taisa's at the collective farm barns from morning till night. It's those wages, damn it. People envy those milkmaids, raking in three hundred rubles a month. All the same, you just try to do it! They get up at five in the morning for the first milking and work till nine. Lunchtime, they have to go back again. And in the evening, until the stars come out. By that time you don't even want the money."

"Has Valechka left?"

Valechka, Raisa's granddaughter, had finished elementary school the previous year and went almost as far as Moscow to learn to be a weaver. She had come back during the winter and now was off again, though not so far, to Uryupinsk.

"We saw her off," Raisa answered. "It makes your heart ache."

"Last summer," Makhora reminisced, "we were standing in the store waiting for the bread to come, and Valechka showed up. The women asked her, 'Valechka, what do you want to do?' And she said right away: 'I'm going to work with Mama on the livestock section of the collective farm, as a milkmaid.' Now she's changed her mind."

"She said she'd work alongside her mother, she was up to it. But she's just a simple girl," said Raisa, pressing her big hand to her breast. "Maybe God will help her find her own way, working in the textile mill. But there's no place like home. You're always safe from harm there. Still, she'll always be able to come back to tending livestock if she has to."

Raisa's deep voice trembled, and tears came to her eyes. Makhora hurriedly reassured her neighbor.

"She's a quick, hard-working girl, everyone says so. She's clever with her hands. She'll apply herself, learn a trade, find a good husband and have a happy family life. You'll be there to help her."

"We'll help." Raisa cheered up and her voice boomed out over half the village. "Of course we'll help our child!"

A calf dozing behind a fence started in fright and, tail erect, ran down the street. Raisa's voice was a bellow:

"It's not as if we were strangers. It's our own child! Thanks, Makhora. You've made me feel better. Now my soul is at peace. God bless you."

But that day it was evidently not God but the devil that was deciding Makhora's lot.

She ate some of the fresh bread with her cabbage soup and while eating decided that she'd sort the potatoes in her cellar. It would be a good idea to separate out the good ones and exchange them for grain at the collective farm. The bad ones would do to feed the pig.

She finished eating, crawled down into the cellar and found a disaster. At first, coming in from the daylight, she didn't realize what had happened: everything just looked dark. But when she looked closer, shock swept over her. The entire back wall of the cellar had collapsed, burying the potatoes and the canning jars. Only a barrel with leftover sauerkraut was sticking out of the heap of earth.

Just yesterday she'd come down for potatoes and seen nothing. And now . . .

Makhora fell on her knees, fingering the earth in disbelief, then burst out crying, burying her face in her soiled hands.

A chill thought flashed through her mind: The whole cellar might collapse and bury her; she had to climb out. But she was so bitterly dismayed, the fear merely flickered and died. "Let it," she thought. "Let it collapse and bury me."

It had been so hard to dig this new cellar! She had asked others for assistance, her sons had helped, she herself had worked at the digging. After all, how can anyone manage without a cellar?

The old one was no good. How much home brew the work had cost, how much money! And she'd felt in her heart that the cellar should be in a different location, because she'd had a dream: once there was a well here. But her son-in-law had dissuaded her, and so they dug it here.

Her tears flowed, and her thoughts were a muddle. She cursed her son-in-law, herself, her sons. She thought darkly of her late husband: he'd left her all alone, he was lying peacefully in the earth, while she . . .

It was quiet in the cellar. Daylight made its way through the opening and faded. Only a glimmer penetrated from above. And it was quiet, so quiet and peaceful, like the grave. One could lie here forever without thinking of anything.

Makhora finished crying and climbed out. She sat down on the stoop, folded her arms and seemed to doze off. She felt somehow cold and indifferent about everything. About the cellar—let it collapse; about her own life: to hell with it; and for some reason she remembered Manya Kharitonova. What was Manya crying about? About leaving the village? About her house, which would fall apart? About her cellar, which had probably collapsed too? She was living the good life. Imagine crying over that! Her sons had taken her in, they hadn't abandoned her. Well, live and let live. . . .

The sun was already high in the sky. It was time to milk the cow. Suddenly her tears and despair vanished. Makhora washed up and ran into the yard. She found the old saw and hacksaw, grabbed the axe, poured two bottles of home brew and hurried off with them to the metal-working shop.

The men were standing around in the low, dark shop, getting ready to go home to the midday meal.

"Listen, boys," said Makhora. "I'm in trouble. I need your help. I need to use the saw and the axe, but they're both dull. Sharpen them for me, please, for the love of Christ, and I'll make it up to you."

"Do you have them with you?" asked Petro Alifashkin, the foreman. "That will be a liter, for the two of them."

"I brought them, Petro, naturally. I'll go milk the cow and stop by afterward. Will you have them ready?"

"They'll be ready, Makhora."

The men were true to their word. On the way back Makhora picked up the sharpened saw and axe. While pouring the milk into crocks, she thought: "Maybe I should hire Arkhip," but immediately dismissed the idea. Arkhip wouldn't carry out the earth and sort the potatoes. Or even fix the wall. . . .

The year before, Raisa had hired him to build a storeroom. The old man took sixty rubles and fiddled about for the entire summer. He exercised his tongue more than his muscles and it seemed as if he would never finish. And there was no one else available in the village. She'd have to do it herself.

Makhora changed into old clothes, lit the lantern, and crawled down into the cellar. She cleared out the earth, first hauling it up in full buckets, then in half buckets, until night fell, without going to fetching her livestock. She worked without pause, like the ants. A pile of soft earth rose near the cellar.

Underground, the lantern smoked and the air reeked of burning kerosene. But aboveground the sun shone and the sky was a clear blue. Each time she emerged from the cellar's darkness, Makhora rejoiced in the bright light and the warmth.

By evening she'd cleared out the earth and carried out the potatoes. She was overdue to fetch the animals. Fortunately, Raisa had chased the goats home, and the cow and calf had made their way home by themselves, as if they sensed their owner didn't have time for them.

She busied herself with the cattle and chickens. She milked the cow by touch, in the dark. Zorka gave only a little milk—either she was offended, since she was high-strung, or more likely she hadn't had enough to eat. This spring had been dry, and the grass in the meadow was like stubble. The cows' noses were streaked with the soil. They should be fed, but that would have to wait. First Makhora decided to work a little longer to finish the job in the cellar. Otherwise it might collapse again.

In the dusk, the cottage and kitchen gleamed white. A band of greenish light and a dark island of blue cloud lingered above Vikhlyaev Hill, where the sun was setting. The stars in their multitudes gleamed overhead. No human voices were audible, but crickets chirped in the gardens and two or three nightingales trilled to one another in the thickets.

Makhora closed the house, walked over to the shed and went through the piles of wood there, looking for suitable pieces, then sawing them to size. She found soft willow wood, two varieties of elm, and iron-hard young oak, which rang under the saw.

Soon it grew cold. The nightingales were silent—it was too early for their song. A continuous chorus of bullfrogs hung over the river and lake. The woods grew dark, but Makhora could still see in the yard, or perhaps her eyes had adjusted to the darkness.

She began thinking of those far-off years after the war, when there were many people about in the evenings, planting and watering their gardens, and you heard their voices in the dark. The daytime was for collective farm work, but at night you were free to work in your own garden. No question, those were hard times, but somehow good to recall.

It seemed only yesterday that Makhora had left her father and mother and had come to this village, this very house, as a bride. The change was hard for her. Her parents' home was more prosperous—you were never hungry. While here—sometimes you couldn't swallow the acorn-flour biscuits. His was a big family; you'd sit at the table with a lump in your throat, wanting to cry. It seemed as if everyone was looking at you, judging you. After a while she got used to it. They felt sorry for her. Sister-in-law Ksenia indulged her and put hard-boiled eggs in Makhora's lunch bag. She'd sit down to eat in the field and find an egg. So sweet. Or a piece of suet. And Grandma Dunya and Mother Natasha were sorry for her. It would be a sin to complain. When Vanya was born, the men were really proud: She's given us a Cossack! Grandpa Ilyusha curled his mustaches contentedly. And Father Matvei was so pleased!

God in heaven, how many people there were! Evenings the house was full. A whole bucket of potatoes was peeled to make soup. So many people, and all relatives. She became one of them, they became very dear. But now the house was empty.

At the thought, Makhora put down the saw, and it was as if she saw them all in the darkness. A silent procession moved past: Grandpa Ilyusha and Grandma Dunya, Ksenia with her Volodya, Vasily, Olga, her father-in-law and Mother Natasha, and last of all her husband. . . . All passed by and were gone. Makhora remained alone in the whole world. Her children lived far away now and it was hard to count on them.

Night fell over the village. The stars shone overhead from horizon to horizon. A glow to the east promised the moon. Her arms were so heavy they seemed to be under water, but her head was clear. It was good to think, and she remembered the past as if it were yesterday.

At home, Makhora couldn't fall asleep right away. She lay and thought about the past. Photographs of relatives hung on the wall opposite. She couldn't see them in the dark; the glass alone shone in a stray beam of light. But Makhora saw them all as if they were alive, only she couldn't speak with them. And then she was asleep.

In the morning, in the real world, Nikolai appeared—a living relative. Makhora arose before dawn. The nightingales' counterpoint was just subsiding. A sliver of white moon gleamed, and the last stars were burning out. A cold yellow dawn rose over the fields.

She had just finished looking after the livestock and sawing the lumber for the cellar when Nikolai showed up. He was her late husband's youngest brother. He lived here in the village, but had somehow been alienated from the rest of the family since youth. Maybe it was his wife's fault, or perhaps his fondness for liquor. Since Makhora was left alone, Nikolai occasionally dropped by to ask for a morning-after drink. Today he walked into her yard and said immediately:

"Give me a drink, Makhora. I have a headache."

"At least say hello," she scolded.

"I have such a hangover, I forgot. Did you sleep well?"

"Not very well. The cellar caved in."

"When was it dug?"

"This past summer."

"It must be in a bad place. Let's take a look."

Nikolai groaned and sighed, rubbing the stubble on his cheeks while listening to Makhora.

"I remember that there was a well here once, near Grandma Natashka's kitchen. I warned Vasily not to dig here. But he was stubborn. Now it's fallen down and buried everything."

"Maybe I can help you," Nikolai said.

"Good. There's no one else. You're not herding the animals today?"

"No, I'm not."

"Then help me. Nursing a hangover is one thing, but let's get going. I'll pour you a few drops, but only a little."

"Pour it, Makhora. Yesterday we drank Churikhina's home brew."

Mama Churikhina's liquor was notorious throughout the village for its reek and devastating effect. The old woman added chicken droppings to her herbs.

"And who ordered you to drink it? Did they force you?"

"Kleimenov invited us. That's what happened."

Nikolai's life was not an enviable one: a big family, a wife none too affable, sickness, liquor. He was terribly thin, had a swarthy face, and was hoarse from constant smoking. Makhora felt sorry for him and helped him during his hangovers, giving him a bit to drink and something to eat, since she knew he was not indulged at home. She set out cabbage soup and a piece of salt pork.

They mended the wall quickly, now that there were four hands and male know-how. Nikolai noticed a serpentine crack in the other wall in that corner. Here too the earth could subside and cave in. They braced this wall as well, with old gates from the shed. The cellar, half of it shored up with boards, began to look safe and sound.

"Just like at the Tarasovs'," said Nikolai. "It'll last for a hundred years."

Tarasov was one of the village's first settlers. Makhora smiled: "Spin your tales, storyteller. There's only a tiny bit left of my life."

They crawled out of the cellar into the light of God's day. Nikolai was in a fine mood, anticipating his reward. He lit a cigarette and laughed.

"At your place, Makhora, everything's done properly. Your home brew is the best in the village. And your geese! I tell my family: Let's raise geese like Makhora's. We'll have noodle soup all winter. But they say—we're too sick."

"They're not that sick," Makhora said scornfully. "It's true, my geese really aren't doing badly. I put three to roost and now there are thirty-two goslings. Not one has died."

Makhora poured out the home brew and heated the cabbage soup. She cut a good-sized piece of lard and rolled it up in newspaper, saying:

"Take this, Nikolai. You don't have any at home."

"It's all gone," he admitted.

"You should have at least two or three geese for your family."

"They don't want any." Nikolai spread his hands.

Talking about it was a waste of time. Nikolai's wife didn't like collective farm work and liked working at home even less. She refused to keep pigs and geese, complaining that she was too sick. But even as a young woman she'd been as broad as she was tall.

After rewarding her helper, Makhora saw him off, saying:

"Now don't stop off anywhere. If you get drunk they'll blame me."

She accompanied him to the gate and watched as he went off. Seeing their mistress, the geese began honking and tried to get into the yard.

"You dimwitted devils," said Makhora, chasing them away. "And you, stupid, why don't you lead them?" she told the gander. "You should take them to the lake, you idiot. I'll have to chase you with the stick again."

Last year she'd had to replace the aged gander. The young one looked like an admiral, with a broad chest and large wings, but he turned out to be an utter fool. The goslings were already big and strong enough to be led to the lake, but their young admiral honked the whole day long in the yard, and nothing more.

Besides which, a pair of swans had settled on Lake Ilmen this spring. The male swan was the testy sort: he wouldn't tolerate the geese and chased them from the water.

Lake Ilmen was right by the village. The village street came down to its pockmarked, sandy shore. Stick in hand, Makhora chased the geese down to the lake. They waddled along in leisurely fashion. The yellow, short-winged goslings hurried behind, cheeping. The stupid gander didn't lead the gaggle, as nature intended, but lagged behind, honking discontentedly, as if he were swearing at Makhora.

"You're a stupid one," Makhora scolded. "Why do you like the yard so much? You're not a cock, to sit on the fence and crow. Go to the lake, swim, set an example to the goslings. Why sit around the yard?"

The street ran right down to the water. Reeds and willows grew along the bank, framing the expanse of blue. The white sand of the far bank gleamed in the distance.

Two flocks of geese milled around on the beach, which had been trampled by people and animals. The swan barred their way to the water.

Makhora waved her stick at him.

"Get out of the way, you layabout."

The swan waddled off unhurriedly, moving his glossy black feet slowly. He was beautiful, with shiny white feathers, a creamy head and neck and a black bump on his nose.

"Move, move! Are you afraid of ruffling your feathers?" Makhora chased him away.

The swan spread his wings and took off noisily, making a ringing sound in the air. He flew a short distance away and settled on the water, fluffing his strong wings.

Now the geese perked up and entered the water. Makhora sat on some clean stones and, not taking her eyes off the big beautiful bird, said to it:

"You may be healthy, but you're no smarter than my gander. Do the geese annoy you? Look how much water there is—plenty for everyone. But if you're going to be insolent, someone's bound to shoot you. Someone will. So you'd better get smart, don't chase the geese. Live and let live, and then we'll enjoy looking at you a lot more."

The bird swam nearby and seemed to be listening to what Makhora said. The water rippled, washing ashore the gray foam and yellow pollen from the willow catkins. The air was filled with the hum of bees and sweet odors.

Makhora scolded and reproached the cob, but in her heart she felt an intuitive respect for him and envied his consort, whose peace he guarded.

It was natural to envy such a strong family, even if only a bird's. Makhora's consort—Andrei Matveyevich—was already ten years under the earth. And without him . . . oh, how bitter life had been!

2

The family arrived toward evening on Saturday, as promised. The first ones came on the bus: Polina, son-in-law Vasily, and their daughter, Tanechka. Makhora had just greeted and kissed them when they heard a car horn on the street outside.

"The chief has arrived," said Polina. "Let's go meet them."

It was indeed Ivan and his family. He worked in the neighboring district as chief agronomist. They opened the gates and Makhora's house seemed to come alive, to ring with voices. Ivan brought his wife Galina and daughter Olechka, the same age as Tanechka. The two granddaughters were all dressed up, just like dolls, with bows in their hair. Chubby little Andryusha clattered about, chasing the kitten. Makhora wished her younger daughter were here, with her husband and Makhora's older grandsons, but they lived far away.

It was their custom, after coming in from the road, to sit down to either lunch or dinner—in this case, to eat homemade chicken noodle soup. Makhora had made a big potful, enough for everybody. They drank her home brew and made a racket, sharing news. They hadn't seen each other for a long time.

Ivan and Vasily talked about going fishing. They were trying to decide whether to fish with nets in the lake or try for carp in the ponds. Their wives spoke about going along. It was crayfish that tempted them. And as for the children . . .

Makhora sat listening, and finally said:

"But I thought you came to help me with the work."

"What's the problem?" said Ivan. "What needs doing?"

"I'm snowed under with work! The attic wall is settling. Maybe the cement has crumbled. And take a look at the floor in the pigsty. I just don't have the strength to level it properly. The pig is so stubborn that he knocks everything loose. It needs to be done right."

"And now," Polina interrupted, "you'll read us a lesson about all the things that need to be done." She spoke humorously, but firmly. "We came here for a rest. To go fishing and cook chowder."

Ivan looked at his mother.

"It's true, we were getting ready to go fishing. Is it so urgent?"

"Well no, but . . ." Makhora pursed her lips.

"She wants to put us all in harness." Polina laughed again.

"Go to hell, you little filly! As if I wanted to harness you!" Makhora was furious. "Lessons, indeed! You've gotten too soft with your 'lessons.' Why am I working here? Why am I knocking myself out? All I need are two goats and five hens—that's enough for me. But look how much work you've piled on your mother! I tend fifteen goats for the lot of you."

"But we come, we do the mowing and tend the goats."

"You come once every summer, that's all. But I wear myself out every day. And not only the goats. What about the pig? The geese? And the cow? Who benefits? 'Sour cream, Mama,' she mimicked—'What's this, didn't you make us any butter?' 'We're out of eggs!' 'We'll take the lard!' And your mother? The storm knocked over the haystack, I could hardly put it back up. The cellar caved in." She began to cry. "Buried the potatoes, all of them. I had to crawl down there like an ant. I thought—maybe the whole cellar will collapse and this would be my grave. Only the cross would be missing."

The mother's tears sobered her children. Ivan got up, put his arms around her shoulders and made her sit down.

"Enough, Mama. Don't cry. The children are watching."

The granddaughters were indeed looking with astonishment at their grandmother.

"Children," Makhora sighed, wiping her tears. "I didn't really think I'd be buried. But it's all . . . too much for me, I'm getting old. I can barely walk. My knees are swollen. My back hurts. And I can't see well. The matchmaker gave me her eyeglasses. I'm grateful to her. They seem to fit. But after I knit for a while I feel as if I had sand in my eyes. I could scream."

The meal was ruined. Ivan and Vasily started smoking. Polina sat and sulked. Only little Andryusha noisily slurped Grandma's noodle soup. Makhora calmed down and was already regretting the outburst.

"Vanya, you should eat," she said. "You're so thin, and all you do is smoke."

Her son Ivan took after his father. He was tall, thin and stooped, with a high, domed forehead.

Ivan put out his cigarette and poured them all a drink.

"Let's have a drink, Mother. We'll drink, and then finish up your soup. Anyway, we will go fishing." He smiled. "But tomorrow morning we'll help you. All right?"

Makhora took a sip.

"Sure, go fishing . . . Our carp are famous. They say there are lots of them in the ponds."

"That's right," her son went on. "We'll try for carp. And you know what, Mother?" Here he looked toward his wife. His wife was quiet and placid, and wore glasses. "Galina and I have talked things over. It's hard for you here, and it's hard for us to look after Andryusha. Hold out here until fall, Mother, because it takes time to dispose of the animals. But in the autumn you come live with us. Galina will go back to work. And you'll battle with Andryusha. So, Mother, enough—you've coped with farm work long enough."

Her son looked across the table at her, frowned and shook his head. His mother's eyes had filled with tears again. Several times previously Ivan had suggested that she move in with him, but never seriously, always in an offhand way, and Makhora had begun to think that her daughter-in-law Galina, who looked quiet but was really high-strung—and was, moreover, a city girl— didn't want her. Her younger daughter, who lived in Kiev, had invited her, but Kiev was far away and strange. Besides, older people say: If you quarrel with your son, you'll sit behind the stove, but if you quarrel with your son-in-law, you'll sit outside the door. That's the truth, the real truth. If she moved, it would be to her son's, to her eldest. It was his responsibility to take care of the old people; that had always been the custom.

But now, when Ivan said this in front of the others, in front of his wife, Makhora knew he meant it. She knew, and it was as if a weight fell from her shoulders. That was why tears sprang to her eyes.

Silence fell again at the table. Ivan looked at his mother and almost started crying himself. How she had aged! It seemed only yesterday she was strong, had worked as an equal with his father. But now the gray head bent earthward, her arms and legs were withered, her eyes faded—years, years! It seemed only yesterday that his mother had led the singing at feasts, singing louder than anyone:

> *The sturdy horses paw the ground.*
> *With Stalin as our leader*
> *We'll overcome the foe!*

But could one imagine her singing now? She burst into tears at the slightest provocation. Ivan rose from his place and, carrying his plate, sat down next to his mother.

"Don't cry, Mama. Let's drink up and eat. Don't cry. That's the way life is. We're not so young any more, either. Don't cry. Things will be easier when you're living with us."

Makhora began obediently to eat the soup, salted with her tears.

Around the table, the conversation resumed little by little.

"You want to go back to work? At what?" Polina asked her sister-in-law. "In your field?"

Galina nodded: "The chief economist is leaving. The county officials have approved me for the job." She glanced at her husband. "The pay is good, especially with the annual bonuses."

"What salaries people get now!" observed Makhora. "When you think what we worked for! If you told people nowadays, they wouldn't believe you, they'd think you're fooling them. Three measly kopeks per workday, plus less than a pound of bread. And the workday," she explained to Galina, "wasn't one day's work. It's just a basis for calculating pay, as you very well know, and in those days it could be, for example, to spade five hundred square meters of meadowland. Or mow a whole hectare by hand. Can you imagine? But nowadays women just sit in the vegetable gardens, spend the time knitting shawls, and the farm credits them with at least three rubles."

"But what am I supposed to do with my goats?" asked Polina.

Makhora tended fifteen goats for her daughters. Ten were Polina's, the others belonged to Shurochka, the younger daughter. They combed two pounds of hair from each goat, and the extra money came in handy. But now what would happen?

"Sell them, or take them with you," answered Ivan.

"Where am I supposed to keep them? In the living room? Or pasture them on the roof? How about you taking them?" she said to her brother reproachfully.

"Judge for yourself," explained Ivan. "I already have seven. Then there are Mother's. How many do you have, Mother? Five. So that's twelve. If I add yours, people in the party committee will look me in the eye and say: You're setting up quite a farm there!"

"All right." Polina dismissed the idea with a wave of the hand. "We'll think of something." But she couldn't resist reproaching her brother: "The party committee, indeed—what about your own sister?"

"After all, he's under the eyes of the authorities." Makhora backed him up. "He's part of the administration."

"Go ahead, take his side, he's your son."

They finished eating and got ready to go fishing, leaving little Andryusha with Makhora.

"Get used to him, Mother," Ivan said. "Now it'll be the old and the young together."

"We'll clear the table and then go find the goats and the calf."

"Calf," echoed Andryusha, clinging to his grandmother's skirt.

"Splendid," Ivan said approvingly. "And we'll bring back some fish."

These were just words, promises, usually they brought only enough for the cat's breakfast. This time, however, though it took the whole night long, going back and forth to check the nets, by morning they had fifteen carp so large that Makhora was amazed.

The men handed over the fish, spread out the nets to dry and lay down to sleep, directing the women to make fish chowder.

Polina looked at the catch and exclaimed: "I thought they'd bring nothing but empty bottles. But maybe they used a silver lure. Well, the main thing is that we have fish, and"—she at once decreed—"we won't cook the chowder at home, we'll cook it on the shore by the stream."

"And flatten down the grass?" Makhora objected. "What a fool you are! Afterward I'll have trouble mowing it."

"All right, don't shout! We won't flatten all of it. Even if we did, it won't be needed, since you'll be leaving. At least we'll be enjoying our shore. Soon it will just be a memory."

Makhora heard the heartache in her daughter's words and didn't object further. Nowadays people had forgotten, but in the past, when families gathered for a celebration and feast, it was always on their own stretch of beach, at the foot of the gardens running down from the house. They had named this beach for Great-grandfather Nikolai: Kolya's Beach. The water was clear, the mossy banks were overgrown with willows.

They got an old iron kettle from the storeroom, started a fire on the shore and cooked the chowder.

The weather was warm and clear. Starlings flocked on the withered crowns of the willows, their feathers gleaming black and green in the bright sunlight. The birds lived there, in the hollows of rotting trees.

The air smelled of smoke, sweet fish chowder and young bitter herbs, and willow blossoms already fading.

They spread a tarpaulin right on the shore and began scooping out pieces of the yellow fish, which had been cooked with dill seed and spring onions; then they poured the chowder into bowls and the liquor into glasses, and began feasting.

It was a long, long time since such happy revelry, laughter and song had been heard along the shore. When Grandpa Matvei was alive they had often gathered here, less often in Father's time, and not at all since his death. But now it was just like the old Cossack celebrations—people got drunk, not on liquor—they only sipped that—it was happiness that made the head spin: the family together, all alive and well, and such a marvelous day, with the sun shining, the children laughing, the water splashing and leaves rustling overhead—their dear, dear land.

> *He strolls by the Don, the Don,*
> *The young Cossack strolls by the Don.*

Ivan hadn't forgotten the old songs. He sang them with gestures. Polina, Vasily, even Galina joined in. And Makhora's voice rang out.

> *Don't cry, my girl, don't cry,*
> *Don't cry, my girl, trust no one . . .*

They sang song after song. Suddenly a voice rang out from behind some bushes in the garden:

> *In the meadow, in the field so wide*
> *A horse from the village herd ran free . . .*

Arkhip appeared, all dressed up in a blue shirt and sporting a cap.

"I couldn't resist coming, you all sounded so good I wanted to join in!"

And from the other side, the Amochevs', came Gavrila Yakovlevich, their old neighbor, the same age as their father—they'd served together in the war.

"You sing well," he said approvingly. "It's a pleasure to hear. These days people have forgotten how to sing."

> *The Cossack rode to an alien strand,*
> *Left his village on his coal-black steed,*
> *Never to return to his ancestral home.*

The village heard the merriment on Kolya's Beach, listened and rejoiced. The songs carried far across the water of lake and river and finally died away in the reeds.

The sun was past midday. Makhora milked the cow and gave

fresh milk to the children. Andryusha fell asleep in his mother's lap. They talked quietly, so as not to disturb him.

"Maybe you should keep the house, not sell it?" Polina sighed. "We could come and cut the hay and plant potatoes."

"You couldn't come often enough," her mother said, shaking her head. "When you're here you can see what to do with the potatoes, but when you're away they'll get smothered in weeds and eaten by Colorado beetles."

"And transport." Vasily backed her up. "How would you get here?"

"Well, you work on it. You're a man. Spend less on drink," Polina answered, but then added: "No, I see that it's all settled."

And, lifting up her head, she gazed at the old willows, the garden and her parents' home, its roof visible beyond the trees.

Andryusha was twisting uncomfortably in his mother's lap, so they stretched him out on some kerchiefs and sweaters. While they were busy with the boy, they didn't notice the man walking down the path through the garden. He came out onto the beach and said:

"You look comfortable."

They looked up at him. He was a stranger, thin, with closely cropped hair. A key ring dangled from his fingers.

"You're living well, as the saying goes."

"Thanks be to God," answered Makhora. "I wish the same to you."

"Mother Makhora?" the stranger guessed.

At that they all became alarmed. Makhora had been called that in the past, when there were two mothers and five children in the one house: Makhora and her sister-in-law Ksenia. That's what they were called—Mother Makhora and Mother Ksenia. But that was long ago. Mother Ksenia was dead. The old days were forgotten. And now . . .

"I've brought greetings to you, Mother, from afar," said the man. "From Volodya. You haven't forgotten him, have you? Here's a letter." He held out an envelope. "And, as the saying goes, live in health and prosper."

Handing over the letter, the stranger turned and walked back up the path through the garden, past the house, and they soon heard the sound of a car driving off.

Makhora held the envelope in both hands, not knowing what to do with it.

"Volodya?" she repeated. "What Volodya?" And gasped: "Vovka!"

Daughter and son repeated after her: "Vovka."

"Maybe that was he?" Makhora said in confusion. "No, it couldn't have been. I would have recognized him."

"What an idea," said Polina. "After thirty years! When did you see him last?"

"Oh, why did we let him go? He could have told us everything."

Makhora hurriedly opened the envelope. Her hands shook. Ivan tried to help.

"I'll do it myself."

She managed to make out the first lines:

"Live well, Mother Makhora! I bow to you from afar. . . ." Her eyes clouded over. Makhora let her hands fall.

The letter was from Vovka, from the lost Vovka, good-for-nothing Vovka.

Long ago, when they all lived together as one family, Vovka, her sister-in-law Ksenia's son, had called her Mother too. There were five children and two mothers: Mother Ksenia and Mother Makhora.

God had evidently watched over Makhora. Together with her husband, she'd raised her children and they all grew into adulthood. But Ksenia . . . They'd lived together in harmony and it still warmed Makhora's heart to think of her. But she was unlucky: her husband did not return from the war; she had buried her daughter; and then Vovka threw his life away. He went off to trade school and dropped out of sight. Since that time he had not been seen in the village; all they knew was that he was in prison.

He got out. Completed his sentence and got out, but didn't hurry back to his home and mother. And was arrested again for some other crime or offense. Ksenia wept and wept. Maybe that's why she died. Nothing had been heard from Vovka for many years; they thought he was dead, too. Grandma Natashka had prayed for the peace of his soul.

Makhora wanted to read the letter herself, but couldn't. All she saw was: "Live well, my Mother Makhora!"—and her eyes were dazzled. Ivan had to read it to her: "You probably think that I'm long gone from this world. But I'm still alive. You, I know, will not die. You're from Kargala, of Grandpa Maksai's breed."

"That's him," Makhora sighed. All her doubts disappeared.

"That's Vovka! He remembers I'm from Kargala, and he remembers Grandpa Maksai!"

Vovka's remembering her native village touched her so that Makhora took the letter from her son, but still could make out nothing.

"Mama, let me finish reading."

"Go ahead, read it."

"You already know what my life has been. That's why I haven't written. But now I'm going to be released soon. I've decided to make a break with the past. You could die on these plank beds here in prison. I want to try to live decently, like normal folk. I want to come to stay with you. I'm all alone in the world. I have no place else to go. Write, Mother Makhora, and tell me whether I can come, whether you'll welcome me. I bow to you from afar."

"I must answer right away. Immediately," said Makhora agitatedly. "Let him come. Where else should he go?"

"Well," laughed Polina, "the house won't be empty, after all. He'll take care of it for you."

"No, no," Makhora disagreed. "He mustn't be left here alone. A man, and besides that, not used to farming. I have to steer him. Otherwise our drinkers will get to him, he'll be like a lone wolf, he'll be another one who lights pots of oil in the stove and burns the house down."

A good-for-nothing named Shalyapin lived in the village. That was how he heated his house. He put pots of oil in the stove and set fire to them. Instead of coal or wood.

"But if you're moving to Ivan's, how can you be with him? Where is he supposed to go?" asked Polina. "To Ivan's, with you?"

Makhora glanced at her son. Ivan hesitated, but before he could say anything Galina spoke, turning her eyeglasses straight at Makhora.

"Mama, there's no point in even discussing it. Think about the children."

Makhora looked over at Polina.

"Don't be a fool, Mama," said Polina. "You haven't seen him for ages. Maybe he's even murdered people."

"Who has he murdered? I don't know what you'll imagine next. People used to be sent off to prison for stealing a loaf of bread. Children's lives were ruined."

"Children!" her daughter said sarcastically. "This child is already fifty. If he didn't kill anyone, he's probably a drunkard and a thief. He could hook up with someone of his sort"—she glanced at her husband—"and the two of them might . . . No, Mother, you can't glue back what's broken off."

Makhora paid no attention to her.

"Fifty years old?" she repeated. "Why, yes." She thought a bit and began counting on her fingers. She counted up to forty-five and exclaimed: "My God!"

It seemed only yesterday that this merry, good-natured little boy, with gray eyes, had carried Ivan and Polina piggyback for hours at a time.

"Remember how he used to carry you around?" she asked, smiling. "He'd set Vanya on his back and carry him about all day, and you too."

"Carried and carried"—her daughter tried to shake her—"and in the end got carried away."

"He looked just like Ksenia. So handsome. And he used to bring you fruit drops from the market." Makhora couldn't let go of the past so easily.

"Sometimes the leader of our farm field crew would let us have a couple of oxen so we could take our home-grown squash, cabbage or sunflower seeds to the market on a Sunday. That's how people made a few kopeks in those days," she explained to the children. "There was no other way. We would sell a lamb or a pig to make a few rubles. To pay taxes and buy something or other. In the evening we'd get together, load the bullock cart with whatever two or three families could put together for sale, and we ourselves would walk to the market in the morning. Vovka was such a hard worker, even as a child. As soon as he got to the market he'd find something to do: help carry, help someone unload. People would give him a few kopeks in return. And he'd buy lollipops. This one is for Vanya, he'd say, and this one's for Polina. I used to tell him: Enjoy them yourself, son. But he'd wrap them up and carry them home. The kids will be pleased, he'd say. The kids . . . and he himself. . . . My poor child. . . ." Makhora began to weep. "What you've seen in your life . . . Lord, help him."

When Makhora had cried herself out, Ivan tried to dissuade her:

"We're not opposed, Mama. Of course he must be helped. Let him try. But think, he's a stranger. Neither I nor Polina remembers him."

"You have the memory of a silly girl."

"But thirty years have gone by!" Ivan said, exasperated. "Thirty, you understand? Still, we don't refuse. Let's give him some money. Let him set himself up somewhere. He doesn't have to come here."

"Alien soil, my son, is sown with wormwood, as the saying goes. It's the truth. He's one of us. He didn't drop off a wagon, he's one of us, our kin. He was born here, his family's graves are here. Are we going to push him away like a boat from the shore? What would people say? Or should we live with blinders? We couldn't atone for such a sin. What are you saying? Think how many of our village people were exiled, but they all came back. Including our grandfather, grandma, and Aleksei. They were sent far away, yet . . ."

"That was something else, Mama," Ivan explained. "Those were excesses. But who exiled Vovka? You remember him as a child, but what's he like now? After all those years in prison? A person could make a mistake once, even twice. But how many sentences has he served, how many years has he done? Think it over, Mama. This is a serious matter. It's a question of our lives, and yours."

"What is there to think about?" his mother sighed. "He'll come, and then it will be as God wills. I don't blame you, my children." She looked from Ivan to Polina. "You, Galya, put it correctly: to you he's a stranger. Vanya is in good with the authorities, thank goodness. And Polina's life is not an easy one." She glanced at her son-in-law, who was snoring peacefully while they talked. "I don't blame you. But Vovka will come to the village and will live with me. He's a hard worker. As a boy he was good at herding cattle. He'll be taken on as one of the livestock crew. Or in summer he can pasture the goats. He'll stand on his own feet. Maybe we can find a suitable wife for him. There are lots of women who are alone these days. If only he hasn't become addicted to vodka . . ."

"Mother, Mother . . ." Polina shook her head. "You're a child yourself. You're out of your mind. He'll drink up everything and then burn the house down with both of you in it. Some herder! Move in with Ivan and live there, and be done with it."

"Your tongue runs away with you," interrupted her mother. "He'll drink, he'll set fires? You're raving. Let him come," she added firmly, "and then it will be as God wills."

Polina and Ivan understood from their mother's tone that the matter was decided. At any rate, for now, for today. They didn't want to upset either themselves or Makhora any further. Especially since the sun was getting low in the sky and it was time to make preparations for departure.

First they said goodbye to Polina and Vasily. Ivan left right after that. His car, bouncing gently over the ruts, drove past the barn and disappeared behind a line of trees.

The day was over. A weary sun hung over the hill. Arkhip was already sitting with his wife outside their yard, getting ready to bring in their livestock.

"Have they gone?" asked Arkhip.

"They've gone."

And Shura Kleimenova, her other neighbor, from across the way, said with a sigh: "My folks didn't come. Everyone's too busy."

The day was coming to an end. Vasily Solonichev was banging away with hammer and axe in his yard. All day he'd been making a cart for the new forester. The cart was ready, shiny yellow in the evening sun.

Raisa called to Makhora from her yard:

"Have they gone?"

"They've gone."

"Well, come sit down."

Makhora refused. She didn't feel like talking, answering questions—the usual routine. Her heart was troubled.

Taking the red cherrywood stick, she walked to the lake to fetch the geese. The young gander couldn't be relied on.

Beyond the barns the evening sun gilded the wheat field, and the village cemetery, surrounded by the young winter wheat, seemed so lovely and comfortable that you wanted to look and look at it. Everyone was gathered there together: her husband and sister-in-law Ksenia, all the family—those dear people with whom she'd spent her life. They were already part of the earth, beyond all human cares, griefs and joys.

But Makhora's path was not yet at an end. She had to get the geese. Her leg hurt so much—her knee ached and burned, as if foretelling a long period of damp weather.

TRANSLATED BY SHIRLEY BENSON

WHOEVER WAS
USING THIS BED

·❧·

Raymond Carver

The call comes in the middle of the night, three in the morning, and it nearly scares us to death.

"Answer it, answer it!" my wife cries. "My God, who is it? Answer it!"

I can't find the light, but I get to the other room, where the phone is, and pick it up after the fourth ring.

"Is Bud there?" this woman says, very drunk.

"Jesus, you have the wrong number," I say, and hang up.

I turn the light on, and go into the bathroom, and that's when I hear the phone start again.

"Answer that!" my wife screams from the bedroom. "What in God's name do they want, Jack? I can't take any more."

I hurry out of the bathroom and pick up the phone.

"Bud?" the woman says. "What are you doing, Bud?"

I say, "Look here. You have a wrong number. Don't ever call this number again."

"I have to talk to Bud," she says.

I hang up, wait until it rings again, and then I take the receiver and lay it on the table beside the phone. But I hear the woman's voice say, "Bud, talk to me, please." I leave the receiver on its side on the table, turn off the light, and close the door to the room.

In the bedroom I find the lamp on and my wife, Iris, sitting against the headboard with her knees drawn up under the covers. She has a pillow behind her back, and she's more on my side than her own side. The covers are up around her shoulders. The blankets and the sheet have been pulled out from the foot of the bed. If we want to go back to sleep—I want to go back to sleep, anyway—we may have to start from scratch and do this bed over again.

"What the hell was that all about?" Iris says. "We should have unplugged the phone. I guess we forgot. Try forgetting one night to unplug the phone and see what happens. I don't believe it."

After Iris and I started living together, my former wife, or else one of my kids, used to call up when we were asleep and want to harangue us. They kept doing it even after Iris and I were married. So we started unplugging our phone before we went to bed. We unplugged the phone every night of the year, just about. It was a habit. This time I slipped up, that's all.

"Some woman wanting *Bud*," I say. I'm standing there in my pajamas, wanting to get into bed, but I can't. "She was drunk. Move over, honey. I took the phone off the hook."

"She can't call again?"

"No," I say. "Why don't you move over a little and give me some of those covers?"

She takes her pillow and puts it on the far side of the bed, against the headboard, scoots over, and then she leans back once more. She doesn't look sleepy. She looks fully awake. I get into bed and take some covers. But the covers don't feel right. I don't have any sheet; all I have is blanket. I look down and see my feet sticking out. I turn onto my side, facing her, and bring my legs up so that my feet are under the blanket. We should make up the bed again. I ought to suggest that. But I'm thinking, too, that if we kill the light now, this minute, we might be able to go right back to sleep.

"How about you turning off your light, honey?" I say, as nice as I can.

"Let's have a cigarette first," she says. "Then we'll go to sleep. Get us the cigarettes and the ashtray, why don't you? We'll have a cigarette."

"Let's go to sleep," I say. "Look at what time it is." The clock radio is right there beside the bed. Anyone can see it says three-thirty.

"Come on," Iris says. "I need a cigarette after all that."

I get out of bed for the cigarettes and ashtray. I have to go into the room where the phone is, but I don't touch the phone. I don't even want to look at the phone, but I do, of course. The receiver is still on its side on the table.

I crawl back in bed and put the ashtray on the quilt between us. I light a cigarette, give it to her, and then light one for myself.

She tries to remember the dream she was having when the phone rang. "I can just about remember it, but I can't remember exactly. Something about, about—no, I don't know what it was about now. I can't be sure. I can't remember it," she says finally. "God damn that woman and her phone call. '*Bud*,' " she says. "I'd like to punch her." She puts out her cigarette and immediately lights another, blows smoke, and lets her eyes take in the chest of drawers and the window curtains. Her hair is undone and around her shoulders. She uses the ashtray and then stares over the foot of the bed, trying to remember.

But, really, I don't care what she's dreamed. I want to go back to sleep is all. I finish my cigarette and put it out and wait for her to finish. I lie still and don't say anything.

Iris is like my former wife in that when she sleeps she sometimes has violent dreams. She thrashes around in bed during the night and wakes in the morning drenched with sweat, the nightgown sticking to her body. And, like my former wife, she wants to tell me her dreams in great detail and speculate as to what this stands for or that portends. My former wife used to kick the covers off in the night and cry out in her sleep, as if someone were laying hands on her. Once, in a particularly violent dream, she hit me on the ear with her fist. I was in a dreamless sleep, but I struck out in the dark and hit her on the forehead. Then we began yelling. We both yelled and yelled. We'd hurt each other, but we were mainly scared. We had no idea what had happened until I turned the lamp on; then we sorted it out. Afterward, we joked about it—fistfighting in our sleep. But then so much else began to happen that was far more serious we tended to forget about that night. We never mentioned it again, even when we teased each other.

Once I woke up in the night to hear Iris grinding her teeth in her sleep. It was such a peculiar thing to have going on right next to my ear that it woke me up. I gave her a little shake, and she stopped. The next morning she told me she'd had a very bad dream, but that's all she'd tell me about it. I didn't press her for details. I guess I really didn't want to know what could have been so bad that she didn't want to say. When I told her she'd been grinding her teeth in her sleep, she frowned and said she was going to have to do something about that. The next night she brought home something called a Niteguard—something she was supposed to wear in her mouth while she slept. She had to do something, she said. She couldn't afford to keep grinding her teeth; pretty soon she wouldn't have any. So she wore this protective device in her mouth for a week or so, and then she stopped wearing it. She said it was uncomfortable and, anyway, it was not very cosmetic. Who'd want to kiss a woman wearing a thing like that in her mouth, she said. She had something there, of course.

Another time I woke up because she was stroking my face and calling me Carl. I took her hand and squeezed her fingers. "What is it?" I said. "What is it, sweetheart?" But instead of answering she simply squeezed back, sighed, and then lay still again. The next morning, when I asked her what she'd dreamed the night before, she claimed not to have had any dreams.

"So who's Carl?" I said. "Who is this Carl you were talking about in your sleep?" She blushed and said she didn't know anybody named Carl and never had.

The lamp is still on and, because I don't know what else to think about, I think about that phone being off the hook. I ought to hang it up and unplug the cord. Then we have to think about sleep.

"I'll go take care of that phone," I say. "Then let's go to sleep."

Iris uses the ashtray and says, "Make sure it's unplugged this time."

I get up again and go to the other room, open the door, and turn on the light. The receiver is still on its side on the table. I bring it to my ear, expecting to hear the dial tone. But I don't hear anything, not even the tone.

On an impulse, I say something. "Hello," I say.

"Oh, Bud, it's you," the woman says.

I hang up the phone and bend over and unplug it from the wall before it can ring again. This is a new one on me. This deal is a mystery, this woman and her Bud person. I don't know how to tell Iris about this new development, because it'll just lead to more discussion and further speculation. I decide not to say anything for now. Maybe I'll say something over breakfast.

Back in the bedroom I see she is smoking another cigarette. I see, too, that it's nearly four in the morning. I'm starting to worry. When it's four o'clock it'll soon be five o'clock, and then it will be six, then six-thirty, then time to get up for work. I lie back down, close my eyes, and decide I'll count to sixty, slowly, before I say anything else about the light.

"I'm starting to remember," Iris says. "It's coming back to me. You want to hear it, Jack?"

I stop counting, open my eyes, sit up. The bedroom is filled with smoke. I light one up, too. Why not? The hell with it.

She says, "There was a party going on in my dream."

"Where was I when this was going on?" Usually, for whatever

reason, I don't figure in her dreams. It irritates me a little, but I don't let on. My feet are uncovered again. I pull them under the covers, raise myself up on my elbow, and use the ashtray. "Is this another dream that I'm not in? It's O.K., if that's the case." I pull on the cigarette, hold the smoke, let it out.

"Honey, you weren't in the dream," Iris says. "I'm sorry, but you weren't. You weren't anywhere around. I *missed* you, though. I did miss you, I'm sure of it. It was like I knew you were somewhere nearby, but you weren't there where I needed you. You know how I get into those anxiety states sometimes? If we go someplace together where there's a group of people and we get separated and I can't find you? It was a little like that. You were there, I think, but I couldn't find you."

"Go ahead and tell me about the dream," I say.

She rearranges the covers around her waist and legs and reaches for a cigarette. I hold the lighter for her. Then she goes on to describe this party where all that was being served was beer. "I don't even like beer," she says. But she drank a large quantity anyway, and just when she went to leave—to go home, she says—this little dog took hold of the hem of her dress and made her stay.

She laughs, and I laugh right along with her, even though, when I look at the clock, I see the hands are close to saying four-thirty.

There was some kind of music being played in her dream—a piano, maybe, or else it was an accordion, who knows? Dreams are that way sometimes, she says. Anyway, she vaguely remembers her former husband putting in an appearance. He might have been the one serving the beer. People were drinking beer from a keg, using plastic cups. She thought she might even have danced with him.

"Why are you telling me this?"

She says, "It was a dream, honey."

"I don't think I like it, knowing you're supposed to be here beside me all night but instead you're dreaming about strange dogs, parties, and ex-husbands. I don't like you dancing with him. What the hell is this? What if I told you I dreamed I danced the night away with Carol? Would you like it?"

"It's just a dream, right?" she says. "Don't get weird on me. I won't say any more. I see I can't. I can see it isn't a good idea." She brings her fingers to her lips slowly, the way she does sometimes when she's thinking. Her face shows how hard she's concentrating; little lines appear on her forehead. "I'm sorry that you weren't in the dream. But if I told you otherwise I'd be lying to you, right?"

I nod. I touch her arm to show her it's O.K., I don't really mind. And I don't, I guess. "What happened then, honey? Finish telling the dream," I say. "And maybe we can go to sleep then." I guess I wanted to know the next thing. The last I'd heard, she'd been dancing with Jerry. If there was more, I needed to hear it.

She plumps up the pillow behind her back and says, "That's all I can remember. I can't remember any more about it. That was when the goddam phone rang."

"Bud," I say. I can see smoke drifting in the light under the lamp, and smoke hangs in the air in the room. "Maybe we should open a window," I say.

"That's a good idea," she says. "Let some of this smoke out. It can't be any good for us."

"Hell no, it isn't," I say.

I get up again and go to the window and raise it a few inches. I can feel the cool air that comes in and from a distance I hear a truck gearing down as it starts up the grade that will take it to the pass and on over into the next state.

"I guess pretty soon we're going to be the last smokers left in America," she says. "Seriously, we should think about quitting." She says this as she puts her cigarette out and reaches for the pack next to the ashtray.

"It's open season on smokers," I say.

I get back in the bed. The covers are turned every which way, and it's five o'clock in the morning. I don't think we're going to sleep any more tonight. But so what if we don't? Is there a law on the books? Is something bad going to happen to us if we don't?

She takes some of her hair between her fingers. Then she pushes it behind her ear, looks at me, and says, "Lately I've been feeling this vein in my forehead. It *pulses* sometimes. It throbs. Do you know what I'm talking about? I don't know if you've ever had anything like that. I hate to think about it, but probably one of these days I'll have a stroke or something. Isn't that how they happen? A vein in your head bursts? That's probably what'll happen to me, eventually. My mother, my grandmother, and one of my aunts died of stroke. There's a history of stroke in my family. It can run in the family, you know. It's hereditary, just like heart disease, or being too fat, or whatever. Anyway," she says, "something's going to happen to me someday, right? So maybe that's what it'll be—a stroke. Maybe that's how I'll go. That's what it feels like it could be the beginning of. First it pulses a little, like it wants my attention, and then it starts to throb. Throb, throb, throb. It scares me silly," she says. "I want us to give up these goddam cigarettes before it's too late." She looks at what's left of her cigarette, mashes it into the ashtray, and tries to fan the smoke away.

I'm on my back, studying the ceiling, thinking that this is the kind of talk that could only take place at five in the morning. I feel I ought to say something. "I get winded easy," I say. "I found myself out of breath when I ran in there to answer the phone."

"That could have been because of anxiety," Iris says. "Who needs it, anyway! The *idea* of somebody calling at this hour! I could tear that woman limb from limb."

I pull myself up in the bed and lean back against the headboard. I put the pillow behind my back and try to get comfortable, same as Iris. "I'll tell you something I haven't told you," I say. "Once in a while my heart palpitates. It's like it goes crazy." She's watching me closely, listening for whatever it is I'm going to say next. "Sometimes it feels like it's going to jump out of my chest. I don't know what the hell causes it."

"Why didn't you tell me?" she says. She takes my hand and holds it. She squeezes my hand. "You never said anything, honey. Listen, I don't know what I'd *do* if something ever happened to you. I'd fold up. How often does it happen? That's scary, you know." She's still holding my hand. But her fingers slide to my wrist, where my pulse is. She goes on holding my wrist like this.

"I never told you because I didn't want to scare you," I say. "But it happens sometimes. It happened as recently as a week ago. I don't have to be doing anything in particular when it happens, either. I can be sitting in a chair with the paper. Or else driving the car, or pushing a grocery basket. It doesn't matter if I'm exerting myself or not. It just starts—boom, boom, boom. Like that. I'm surprised people can't hear it. It's that loud, I think. *I* can hear it, anyway, and I don't mind telling you it scares me," I say. "So if emphysema doesn't get me, or lung cancer, or maybe a stroke like what you're talking about, then it's going to be a heart attack probably."

I reach for the cigarettes. I give her one. We're through with sleep for the night. Did we sleep? For a minute, I can't remember.

"Who knows what we'll die of?" Iris says. "It could be anything. If we live long enough, maybe it'll be kidney failure, or something like that. A friend of mine at work, her father just died of kidney failure. That's what can happen to you sometimes if you're lucky enough to get really old. When your kidneys fail, the body starts filling up with uric acid then. You finally turn a whole different color before you die."

"Great. That sounds wonderful," I say. "Maybe we should get off this subject. How'd we get onto this stuff, anyway?"

She doesn't answer. She leans forward, away from her pillow, arms clasping her legs. She closes her eyes and lays her head on her knees. Then she begins to rock back and forth, slowly. It's as if she were listening to music. But there isn't any music. None that I can hear, anyway.

"You know what I'd like?" she says. She stops moving, opens her eyes, and tilts her head at me. Then she grins, so I'll know she's all right.

"What would you like, honey?" I've got my leg hooked over her leg, at the ankle.

She says, "I'd like some coffee, that's what. I could go for a nice strong cup of black coffee. We're awake, aren't we? Who's going back to sleep? Let's have some coffee."

"We drink too much coffee," I say. "All that coffee isn't good for us, either. I'm not saying we shouldn't have any, I'm just saying we drink too much of it. It's just an observation," I add. "Actually, I could drink some coffee myself."

"Good," she says.

But neither of us makes a move.

She shakes out her hair and then lights another cigarette. Smoke drifts slowly in the room. Some of it drifts toward the open window. A little rain begins to fall on the patio outside the window. The alarm comes on, and I reach over and shut it off. Then I take the pillow and put it under my head again. I lie back and stare at the ceiling some more. "What happened to that bright idea we had about a girl who could bring us our coffee in bed?" I say.

"I wish *somebody* would bring us coffee," she says. "A girl or a boy, one or the other. I could really go for some coffee right now."

She moves the ashtray to the nightstand, and I think she's going to get up. Somebody has to get up and start the coffee and put a can of frozen juice in the blender. One of us has to make a move. But what she does instead is slide down in the bed until she's sitting somewhere in the middle. The covers are all over the place. She picks at something on the quilt, and then rubs her palm across whatever it is before she looks up. "Did you see in the paper where that guy took a shotgun into an intensive-care unit and made the nurses take his father off the life-support machine? Did you read about that?" Iris says.

"I saw something about it on the news," I say. "But mostly they were talking about this nurse who unplugged six or eight people from their machines. At this point they don't know exactly how many she unplugged. She started off by unplugging her mother, and then she went on from there. It was like a spree, I guess. She said she thought she was doing everybody a favor. She said she hoped somebody'd do it for *her*, if they cared about her."

Iris decides to move on down to the foot of the bed. She positions herself so that she is facing me. Her legs are still under the covers. She puts her legs between my legs and says, "What about that quadriplegic woman on the news who says she wants to die, wants to starve herself to death? Now she's suing her doctor and the hospital because they insist on force-feeding her to keep her alive. Can you believe it? It's insane. They strap her down three times a day so they can run this tube into her throat. They feed her breakfast, lunch, and dinner that way. And they keep her plugged into this machine, too, because her lungs don't want to work on their own. It said in the paper that she's *begging* them to unplug her, or else to just let her starve to death. She's having to plead with them to let her die, but they won't listen. She said she started out wanting to die with some dignity. Now she's just mad and looking to sue everybody. Isn't that amazing? Isn't that one for the books?" she says. "I have these headaches sometimes," she says. "Maybe it has something to do with the vein. Maybe not. Maybe they're not related. But I don't tell you when my head hurts, because I don't want to worry you."

"What are you talking about?" I say. "Look at me. Iris? I have a right to know. I'm your husband, in case you've forgotten. If something's wrong with you, I should know about it."

"But what could you *do*? You'd just worry." She bumps my leg with her leg, then bumps it again. "Right? You'd tell me to take some aspirin. I know you."

I look toward the window, where it's beginning to get light. I can feel a damp breeze from the window. It's stopped raining now, but it's one of those mornings where it could begin to pour. I look at her again. "To tell you the truth, Iris, I get sharp pains in my side from time to time." But the moment I say the words

I'm sorry. She'll be concerned, and want to talk about it. We ought to be thinking of showers; we should be sitting down to breakfast.

"Which side?" she says.

"Right side."

"It could be your appendix," she says. "Something fairly simple like that."

I shrug. "Who knows? I don't know. All I know is it happens. Every so often, for just a minute or two, I feel something sharp down there. Very sharp. At first I thought it might be a pulled muscle. Which side's your gallbladder on, by the way? Is it the left or right side? Maybe it's my gallbladder. Or else maybe a gall*stone*, whatever the hell that is."

"It's not really a stone," she says. "A gallstone is like a little granule, or something like that. It's about as big as the tip of a pencil. No, wait, that might be a *kidney* stone I'm talking about. I guess I don't know anything about it." She shakes her head.

"What's the difference between kidney stone and gallstone?" I say. "Christ, we don't even know which side of the body they're on. You don't know, and I don't know. That's how much we know together. A total of nothing. But I read somewhere that you can pass a kidney stone, if that's what this is, and usually it won't kill you. Painful, yes. I don't know what they say about a gallstone."

"I like that 'usually,' " she says.

"I know," I say. "Listen, we'd better get up. It's getting really late. It's seven o'clock."

"I know," she says. "O.K." But she continues to sit there. Then she says, "My grandma had arthritis so bad toward the end she couldn't get around by herself, or even move her fingers. She had to sit in a chair and wear these mittens all day. Finally, she couldn't even hold a cup of cocoa. That's how bad her arthritis was. Then she had her stroke. And my *grandpa*," she says. "He went into a nursing home not long after Grandma died. It was either that or else somebody had to come in and be with him around the clock, and nobody could do that. Nobody had the money for twenty-four-hour-a-day care, either. So he goes into the nursing home. But he began to deteriorate fast in there. One time, after he'd been in that place for a while, my mom went to visit him and then she came home and said something. I'll never forget what she said." She looks at me as if I'm never going to forget it, either. And I'm not. "She said, 'My dad doesn't recognize me anymore. He doesn't even know who I am. My dad has become a vegetable.' That was my mom who said that."

She leans over and covers her face with her hands and begins to cry. I move down there to the foot of the bed and sit beside her. I take her hand and hold it in my lap. I put my arm around her. We're sitting together looking at the headboard and at the nightstand. The clock's there, too, and beside the clock a few magazines and a paperback. We're sitting on the part of the bed where we keep our feet when we sleep. It looks like whoever was using this bed left in a hurry. I know I won't ever look at this bed again without remembering it like this. We're into something now, but I don't know what, exactly.

"I don't want anything like that to ever happen to me," she says. "Or to you, either." She wipes her face with a corner of the blanket and takes a deep breath, which comes out as a sob. "I'm sorry. I just can't help it," she says.

"It won't happen to us. It won't," I say. "Don't worry about any of it, O.K.? We're fine, Iris, and we're going to stay fine. In any case, that time's a long time off. Hey, I love you. We love each other, don't we? That's the important thing. That's what counts. Don't worry, honey."

"I want you to promise me something," she says. She takes her hand back. She moves my arm away from her shoulder. "I want you to promise me you'll pull the plug on me, if and when it's ever necessary. If it ever comes to that, I mean. Do you hear what I'm saying? I'm serious about this, Jack. I want you to pull the plug on me if you ever have to. Will you promise?"

I don't say anything right away. What am I supposed to say? They haven't written the book on this one yet. I need a minute to think. I know it won't cost me anything to tell her I'll do whatever she wants. It's just words, right? Words are easy. But there's more to it than this; she wants an honest response from me. And I don't know what I feel about it yet. I shouldn't be hasty. I can't say something without thinking about what I'm saying, about consequences, about what she's going to feel when I say it—whatever it is I say.

I'm still thinking about it when she says, "What about you?"

"What about me what?"

"Do you want to be unplugged if it comes to that? God forbid it ever does, of course," she says. "But I should have some kind of idea, you know—some word from you now—about what you want me to do if worse comes to worst." She's looking at me closely, waiting for me to say. She wants something she can file away to use later, if and when she ever has to. Sure. O.K. Easy enough for me to say, *Unplug me, honey, if you think it's for the best.* But I need to consider this a little more. I haven't even said yet what I will or won't do for *her.* Now I have to think about me and *my* situation. I don't feel I should jump into this. This is nuts. *We're* nuts. But I realize that whatever I say now might come back to me sometime. It's important. This is a life-and-death thing we're talking about here.

She hasn't moved. She's still waiting for her answer. And I can see we're not going anywhere this morning until she has an answer. I think about it some more, and then I say what I mean. "No. Don't unplug me. I don't want to be unplugged. Leave me hooked up just as long as possible. Who's going to object? Are you going to object? Will I be offending anybody? As long as people can stand the sight of me, just so long as they don't start howling, don't unplug anything. Let me keep going, O.K.? Right to the bitter end. Invite my friends in to say goodbye. Don't do anything rash."

"Be serious," she says. "This is a very serious matter we're discussing."

"I am serious. Don't unplug me. It's as simple as that."

She nods. "O.K., then. I promise you I won't." She hugs me. She holds me tight for a minute. Then she lets me go. She looks at the clock radio and says, "Jesus, we better get moving."

So we get out of bed and start getting dressed. In some ways it's just like any other morning, except we do things faster. We drink coffee and juice and we eat English muffins. We remark on the weather, which is overcast and blustery. We don't talk anymore about plugs, or about sickness and hospitals and stuff like that. I kiss her and leave her on the front porch with her umbrella open, waiting for her ride to work. Then I hurry to my car and get in. In a minute, after I've run the motor, I wave and drive off.

But during the day, at work, I think about some of those things we talked about this morning. I can't help it. For one thing, I'm bone-tired from lack of sleep. I feel vulnerable and prey to any random, gruesome thought. Once, when nobody is around, I put my head on my desk and think I might catch a few minutes' sleep. But when I close my eyes I find myself thinking about it again. In my mind I can see a hospital bed. That's all—just a hospital bed. The bed's in a room, I guess. Then I see an oxygen tent over the bed, and beside the bed some of those screens and some big monitors—the kind they have in movies. I open my eyes and sit up in my chair and light a cigarette. I drink some coffee while I smoke the cigarette. Then I look at the time and get back to work.

At five o'clock, I'm so tired it's all I can do to drive home. It's raining, and I have to be careful driving. Very careful. There's been an accident, too. Someone has rear-ended someone else at a traffic light, but I don't think anyone has been hurt. The cars are still out in the road, and people are standing around in the rain, talking. Still, traffic moves slowly; the police have set out flares.

When I see my wife, I say, "God, what a day. I'm whipped. How are you doing?" We kiss each other. I take off my coat and hang it up. I take the drink Iris gives me. Then, because it's been on my mind, and because I want to clear the deck, so to speak, I say, "All right, if it's what you want to hear, I'll pull the plug for you. If that's what you want me to do, I'll do it. If it will make you happy, here and now, to hear me say so, I'll say it. I'll do it for you. I'll pull the plug, or have it pulled, if I ever think it's necessary. But what I said about my plug still stands. Now I don't want to have to think about this stuff ever again. I don't even want to have to *talk* about it again. I think we've said all there is to say on the subject. We've exhausted every angle. *I'm* exhausted."

Iris grins. "O.K.," she says. "At least I know now, anyway. I didn't before. Maybe I'm crazy, but I feel better somehow, if you want to know. I don't want to think about it anymore, either. But I'm glad we talked it over. I'll never bring it up again, either, and that's a promise."

She takes my drink and puts it on the table, next to the phone. She puts her arms around me and holds me and lets her head rest on my shoulder. But here's the thing. What I've just said to her, what I've been thinking about off and on all day, well, I feel as if I've crossed some kind of invisible line. I feel as if I've come to a place I never thought I'd have to come to. And I don't know how I got here. It's a strange place. It's a place where a little harmless dreaming and then some sleepy, early-morning talk has led me into considerations of death and annihilation.

The phone rings. We let go of each other, and I reach to answer it. "Hello," I say.

"Hello, there," the woman says back.

It's the same woman who called this morning, but she isn't

drunk now. At least, I don't think she is; she doesn't sound drunk. She is speaking quietly, reasonably, and she is asking me if I can put her in touch with Bud Roberts. She apologizes. She hates to trouble me, she says, but this is an urgent matter. She's sorry for any trouble she might be giving.

While she talks, I fumble with my cigarettes. I put one in my mouth and use the lighter. Then it's my turn to talk. This is what I say to her: "Bud Roberts doesn't live here. He is not at this number, and I don't expect he ever will be. I will never, never lay eyes on this man you're talking about. Please don't ever call here again. Just don't, O.K.? Do you hear me? If you're not careful, I'll wring your neck for you."

"The *gall* of that woman," Iris says.

My hands are shaking. I think my voice is doing things. But while I'm trying to tell all this to the woman, while I'm trying to make myself understood, my wife moves quickly and bends over, and that's it. The line goes dead, and I can't hear anything.

... AND IN THE DARK

.❧.

Oleg Chukhontsev

... and in the dark I bumped a door I knew—
an unfamiliar light, strange hollow sounds—
where was I? going where? I glanced around
a nearby table, making a wild guess,
jumped back—the lock went click—and there I stood,
the doorknob digging in my shoulder blade.

Noise beside me; guests seated at the table.
Up came my father, and he said to me, "Let's go.
This way, where you came in. You won't be late.
You know everybody here." And pointed to a chair.
"But wait, you're dead!" I answered him, to which
he said: "Don't say what you don't know."

He sat; I took the table in: wine bottles,
a round onion oozing from a fish in aspic,
and marrow peas shining in their fat,
and the thought then struck me: They've come to weep,
when I saw the pancakes and the honey
and the cold, jellied suckling-pigs' feet.

They sat as if they were one family,
the fathers of the same age as the sons;
I recognized them all, seeing them anew,
and shuddered, and the glass froze in my hand:
I glimpsed my mother in a corner, and she
smiled at me as if everything were true.

She was sitting in a corner, strangely young,
an iron bowl, as always, in her lap,
and smiling to herself, although the marks
beneath her eyes stood out much more than ever,

as if life posed a threat to her but she
had no desire to go back into the dark.

I said to her, "It isn't you here now"; I said
to them, "Not you but my idea of you.
Someday I'll come, and, Father, you'll return
to our world here, and, Mother, you'll come, too!"
I heard a voice: "Don't say what you can't know.
If ever you find out, you'll shake with fear."

After one for the road together, they all arose.
I wanted to stand with them, but couldn't.
I wanted and wished, but the doors flew open wide
like an elevator, flew open wide, and closed,
and then went down somewhere, or maybe up,
faster and faster, and tears welled in my eyes.

As if they'd been swept away. Every single one.
When I looked up, no one was beside me,
neither Mother nor Father, nor even a list of names.
I was alone, my own life in my hands,
with a piercing chill somewhere deep inside me—
awareness of death or the death of awareness.

I drew a line beneath what I'd been through,
dividing life in two—early and late—
and summarizing what I'd learned from each.
The first was easy and carefree,
carefree and easy, bitter and naïve:
The rest I haven't yet been through.

TRANSLATED BY F. D. REEVE

THE BLUE BOAT ON
THE ST. ANNE

·❧·

F. D. Reeve

I painted my father in as pilot
of my model plane. One day it stalled
at the top of an Immelmann, then plunged
like a kingfisher into Silver Lake.
I picked the pieces up by boat.
A flawed design? a deceptive wind?
My desire seemed the worse mistake.

His death-in-plastic lasted years
while I grew older in a dream world
where he was hero; I longed to have
his medals, his women and his smile.
Hot, inconsolable nights I dived
head-over-heels into the past
to be steered by his hands and to take on his style.

"Divorced," "remarried"—like leaves the words
floated downstream in the dark; he
in a new life was rich and loved;
my god, drowned in the summer twilight.
Falling asleep miles away,
I remembered his hat above the horizon
making the bats curve in the sky.

Life, once as bright as the sun-filled meadow
scented with camomile we used to cross
to get to where the good fishing was,
became unbridgeable winter days.
He didn't care who I was, and I
retaliated: We were dead on each other.
Memory began to flatten his face.

THE HUMAN EXPERIENCE

One autumn I recalled his mortality,
sent him a letter; he sent me
a watercolor of a boat
like one that for 40 years he had fished
for salmon from, sturdy enough
for two heavy men, their rods and gear
as far into the North Woods as they wished.

Because the soul after death departs its suffering,
like lightning arcing across the sky
from nothing to nothing along the channels
of electromagnetic nuns and cans,
his spirit wearing his hat lights up
what's left of our small future together
fishing from the blue boat on the St. Anne.

AN ATOMIC FAIRY TALE

·⚶·

Yury Kuznetsov

*The oldest son shot, a prince's daughter
brought his arrow back; the second son
shot, a general's daughter brought his arrow
back; but a frog from the swamp brought
back the arrow of the youngest son, Prince
Ivan.*
— THE TSAR'S DAUGHTER WHO WAS A FROG

Here's an old-fashioned story I heard
retold in the mode of our day:
Seems Ivan went out in the fields,
shot an arrow off any which way.

Then he followed the direction it went,
led by a star like a silver wand.
It came down near a frog in a swamp
far, far from his own native land.

He could use it to make his case:
So he wrapped the frog in his kerchief,
pierced its royal white skin with a lance,
and turned on the electric current.

It lay dying for hours in agony,
ages pulsing in every vein;
while the smile of discovery flickered
on the idiot's happy face.

TRANSLATED BY F.D. REEVE

THE DREAM

· 2 ·

C. K. Williams

How well I have repressed the dream of death I had after
    the war when I was nine in Newark.
It would be nineteen-forty-six; my older best friend tells
    me what the atom bomb will do,
consume me from within, with fire, and that night, as I
    sat, bolt awake, in agony, it did:
I felt my stomach flare and flame, the edges of my heart
    curl up and char like burning paper.
All there was was waiting for the end, all there was was
    sadness, for in that awful dark,
that roar that never ebbed, that frenzied inward fire, I
    knew that everyone I loved was dead,
I knew that consciousness itself was dead, the universe
    shucked clean of mind as I was of my innards.
All the earth around me heaved and pulsed and sobbed;
    the orient and immortal air was ash.

Translator's Note: Tbilisi, capital of Soviet Georgia, in the Caucasus, is unlike any other Soviet city. It is almost Mediterranean—or perhaps Levantine—in atmosphere: famous for wines, good food, well-dressed women, romantic men, and a love of the good life, defined especially by feasting punctuated with elaborate and exuberant toasts. It is also notorious for its extravagant, high-living, black-market millionaires—ruble millionaires, that is—who indulge their every whim (until, of course, the police catch up with them and confiscate their ill-gotten wealth in the endless warfare waged upon them by the authorities). So the writer of the frolicsome tale below wonders innocently,

WHAT DOES ANYONE NEED A CRYSTAL TOILET BOWL FOR?

·❧·

Anatoly Shavkuta

The Mona Lisa's been brought to Moscow—*everybody* is talking about it! There are jeans for sale in the arcade! People scramble for them, they push through the police cordons. The lines stretch five thousand long—for the Mona Lisa *and* for the jeans. People faint in line. As for myself, I can't figure out whether they play these games in all seriousness or not. My eyes cloud over, and when I rub them I realize something's confounding me and I can't make sense of it all. Yet you only live once in this wide world; a thousand years—why, a million years will go by, and you'll never be born again—so in spite of yourself you wonder: Have I maybe been confused about the earthly hierarchy of values? Am I missing things? Am I wrong? Especially since life springs such unbelievable surprises, things so incredible you never dreamed of them and never could! Just take *this* little episode, for instance, which couldn't be more commonplace.

My uncle, Grigory Borisovich Yerastov, lives in Tbilisi. He established residence there long ago, he's a solid citizen, he's at home there and he knows the Georgian language.

I visit him often. Uncle is versed in the ways of Georgian hospitality, he selects wines according to the season and nature of the festivities, and he delivers such lofty toasts that wings sprout on your back and your mind flies up to the heavens and hovers there above this marvelous city.

Ah, Tbilisi, Tbilisi! There's Rustaveli Avenue, and the white trunks of the plane trees, and the sumptuous view from the top of Mount Mtatsminda! It doesn't take much for a visitor inclined to the sublime to tear himself from the mundane earth and touch eternity. Ah, Tbilisi, Tbilisi! There's the yogurt seller's cry in the morning, and the hot haze of a summer midday, and the cool and fresh night air. The exultant bazaars, the stadium crazy with excitement, the frenzied traffic. . . . My uncle knew the town and loved it, and he showed it to me and told me about it.

But the last time I came I saw Grigory Borisovich dumbfounded. Before my very eyes, this man who had seen so much, who understood it all, who forgave and accepted everything—this man was struck speechless. He ran up against a fact he couldn't come to terms with or make sense of. And I'll admit I myself was amazed. Here is what happened.

I arrived that time by train, from the Black Sea coast. All night our train shook and jiggled, the floor kept slanting almost vertical at the places where the roadbed had settled, and the short, dull, scary knock of ungreased wheel hubs could be heard from beneath—as if the bearings, axles and bushings were being crushed with a crowbar and at any moment would crumble, smash to pieces, collapse, and our entire train would fall apart with them. A breeze wafted through our car. The morose, weary, and unshaven conductor went from passenger to passenger, yanking each one by the legs and asking in a loud, wheezing whisper: "Any money? Hide it. It can get stolen!" Someone sang in the middle of the night, someone else had a heated argument with a neighbor. In short, it was as casual and unpredictable as any Caucasus train.

In the morning I walked around Tbilisi. A fresh wind, redolent of spring-fed waters from the mountains, stirred the glistening leaves of the plane trees, bootblacks sat at the corners of the square, their entire appearance reminding the visitor of the European beauty of the city and the need to look well dressed in it. The crowd hurried along past the windows of large and small shops and the myriad kiosks, stands, and grillrooms that beckoned. The joys of encounter and discovery overflowed in me and stirred a storm of feelings in my soul. Here was where they sold *khashi*—a whitish, tasteless, medicinal bouillon with tripe and bones in it, seasoned with garlic and served along with a small glass of *chacha*. And here was the carbonated drink pavilion: cream soda, orange, mandarin orange, pear, and peach drinks. The syrups of the South's wonderful fruits glowed with ruby, cherry, yellow, lemon, scarlet, and orange light in long glass tubes. They're heaven for the kids and a delight for all who are thirsty. . . . Where is all this? In what long-lost place? The braziers on the streets, the fumes tickling your nostrils, the bunches of skewers with charred meat on them. . . .

Ah, Tbilisi! Tbilisi! I've come to visit you again!

No sooner had I entered and embraced my relatives than the feast began. My uncle sent his eldest son for wine, and before long a dozen tall bottles were arrayed on the table among the thickly sliced meat and cheese and mounds of fresh greens. The joy was great, so consequently there was a lot of wine—clear and biting, smelling of the vine and grape, with the slight tartness of the seeds—real Kakhetian wine, not those imported synthetic ones without taste or smell.

So many things got said, right off! There were digressions into the past and good wishes for the future. And news and compliments and exclamations. We reminisced about so many individuals and so many lives. . . . It was lofty and noble and heartfelt.

In the course of the conversation, somewhere in the middle of it, the following story emerged. It couldn't help but emerge, inasmuch as a police search was going on at that very moment downstairs, directly beneath my uncle's floor, in his neighbor's apartment.

"Who would ever have guessed?" my uncle said, genuinely upset. "He's such a quiet man, a bookkeeper, and now to have such a misfortune! Six men came there this morning and they've been counting money ever since. All six of them are probably auditors."

The conversation took another turn and the neighbor was forgotten—he wasn't that close to my uncle, who is a machinist and a different type of person. But then a woman darted into the kitchen, whispered something to my aunt, clucked and shook her head, then slipped off somewhere, probably to other apartments. My uncle told me gloomily:

"They've stopped counting. She says it can't be counted, it's too much money; they've started weighing it. They've brought in some special scales. A fine thing! What did the man have to scrimp and save and hide it for? Tell me that! So he could sit as he's doing now, clutching at his heart? Eh, my dear nephew! I've

known that neighbor for twenty years, and now it turns out I
didn't know him at all! Let's drink a toast! To sitting here, like
this, a toast to you and me, to reunions, to the pleasure of seeing
each other and knowing we'll sit at this table next year and the
year after that and every year till we die. We'll have a good time
and sing songs. Let's drink to it!"

The wine sparkled in the glass. It had a clear, clean taste. We
forgot about the search and the neighbor—to be honest, we didn't
care what was going on there and what money it was they were
counting.

"Look at the new things we have, Alexander. See, we bought
a Hungarian wall system, shelves and bookcases and all. How do
you like it?"

"I like it!"

I really did like it: It was cheerful and decorative, the way my
aunt had loaded it with all sorts of toys and photographs and
souvenirs.

"And did you see the color television?"

"Sure, I did. I suppose the hockey games look better now."

"For sure," my uncle laughed, either recalling some daring play
or feeling pleased about his new possession. And why shouldn't
he? He scrimped and saved and set aside his hard-earned money,
and now there it stands and gives him pleasure.

"And see? I framed your article. See?" It was true; in a carved,
dark-cherry frame on the wall was my first article, written many
years ago, back when I was young. It brought me so much pride
then, so many hopes and so much excitement! What an uncle, to
remember it!

But again the frantic woman appeared and gesticulated and
whispered in the kitchen, and once again my aunt reported to my
uncle:

"They've stopped trying to weigh it. Now they're measuring
it!"

"How can you measure money?"

"They stacked all the money in a pile and measured it. It came
to two cubic meters."

My uncle stared at the floor, dumbstruck, as if he were hoping
to see for himself the strange spectacle of money piled in a colorful stack, with a group of stern accounting clerks gathered
around it.

"Two cubic meters?" my uncle said in amazement. "A fine
thing!" And then he burst out: "What did he save it for? Why

didn't he spend it?" His Georgian accent suddenly became pronounced. "Tell me, are there no pleasures left in life? Wasn't there anyone he could help? Anyone to give a present to? Couldn't he have thrown a party for the whole city of Tbilisi? He could have donated the money for a kindergarten—Tbilisi doesn't have enough of them. During the war, people contributed money for airplanes and tanks."

"But the money's stolen," I objected. "He couldn't give it away."

My uncle stared uncomprehendingly at me.

"Couldn't give it away? Then what did he steal it for?" he exploded again.

"So be it, Uncle Grisha," I said in a conciliatory tone. "It's none of our business anyhow, right?"

"You're right," he agreed immediately and cast a host's eye at the depleted row of bottles. "Lyuba!" he shouted to my aunt in a happier voice. "Open the refrigerator and bring out some more wine. After all, our nephew's come! We've got to give him a proper welcome."

"Take it easy there," she scolded and brought the wine, smiling knowingly in my direction. "We have plenty of wine, and snacks, too. And when these are gone I'll bring more."

"Bring them," my uncle said. "We'll drink to our relatives."

But we weren't destined to continue our merrymaking in its pure form. A new piece of information awaited us that was even more unexpected, even fantastic.

"They're removing a crystal toilet bowl!" my aunt cried, rushing into the room in the middle of the quiet conversation that had descended upon us after the fifth or sixth glass of Kakhetian Light No. 23, which is Tbilisi's favorite wine and, by the way, the cheapest.

"What toilet bowl?" my uncle asked gloomily. "And why is it crystal?"

"They found it at the neighbor's. They're taking it as material evidence."

"It can't be," my uncle said distractedly. The fact hadn't registered with him yet, and he was already tired of the unfolding story.

"No, it's true," my aunt countered vigorously. "Vasilyevna says so. She's there as a witness. That's what they wrote down: 'One toilet bowl made of pure rock crystal, green in color.'"

"But what does he need a crystal toilet bowl for?" my uncle

yelled all of a sudden, and hit the table with his huge iron fist. The bottles shook, and one toppled into the lettuce, but my uncle paid no attention. He glared heavily at my aunt. She quailed, realizing that she had picked the wrong moment to report the upsetting news and had rather spoiled our celebration, though she hadn't meant to.

"There could be many reasons," she said, recoiling under my uncle's glare. "Maybe he felt better when he was sitting there. And so what if he did? Amethysts cure drunkenness, as far as that goes." And she added something blatantly stupid. "They say that kings had crystal toilet bowls."

My uncle hit the ceiling.

"Beat it to the kitchen! And don't come out until I call you! You understand? Damn your toilet bowls!"

My aunt, her feelings hurt, tossed her head defiantly. I rushed over to comfort her. Our conversation had broken down. No matter what we started to talk about—be it good news from relatives or my uncle's interesting job—his expression would suddenly go blank and lose its focus and out of nowhere he would mutter, as if the question had newly struck him: "What *does* a man need a crystal toilet bowl for, anyway?"

"Alexander!" he said severely and looked at me insistently. "Is it possible to make a toilet bowl out of rock crystal?"

"It's possible," I replied uncertainly, "but . . ."

"But what?"

"But why do it?"

"That's what I wonder. What for?"

My uncle sighed deeply as he refilled our glasses, and said glumly:

"It's a cinch they'll put the man away. Four kids, a nice wife . . . It's all over now. It'll be jailhouse hash for him."

The next morning, having forgotten what had happened the day before, we walked around the busy city and admired its beauty. Proudly, my uncle showed me the subway, then the new bridge over the Kura, then a high-rise hotel, as if he had built them himself.

"See? Last time you came, this wasn't here."

I shared his pleasure and felt dismay when I saw that the pace of our times had left the same imprint here as in every city: one new neighborhood looked just like the next. But still we had a good time, even though he kept stopping, laughing as if he had just remembered a funny joke, and asked: "Do you know what a man needs a crystal toilet bowl for?" Then he would look around at the city surrounding us, and the hills, and the sky above the city, as if to say that beauty isn't down there in the nether regions of this world, but here, in full view, in front of us all, in the company of other people. . . . My uncle's a good man. You bet! If you're in Tbilisi, ask anybody: "So, is Yerastov a decent guy?" They'll answer, "Sure! In Tbilisi we don't have bad ones. Don't go looking for bad ones here!"

I got a hearty and noisy sendoff. All the friends of my uncle's family were there, and they were as nice and down-to-earth as his family. They drank to my departure and to fathers and sons and to sisters and brothers. Then they poured a farewell cup and, in our style—Cossack style—we drank the stirrup cup, one for the road. We sang songs, then sped off to the airport in a taxi, and the whole lot of them waved to me as my plane lifted off the runway.

But, inside the airplane, I was amazed all over again by the passengers. Lord knows who all had boarded. There was a woman about forty in red longjohns, stuck into her boots. Another woman looked even worse: she had wide scarlet silk trousers billowing down like a Zaporozhian Cossack's, with a light blue stripe down the side like some foreign general's. There was a red-haired Mingrelian man with gold teeth big enough to make a bracelet, and a huge gold ring set with a ruby. He was a Southerner, extravagant—like some sort of rich Turk, minus the harem. Two girls wore imported jackets of waterproof cotton. Two others were almost naked; their breasts showed. It was as if there were a huge factory somewhere that was turning out idiots and foisting them on us all.

Right away I recalled that crystal toilet bowl. It had had an effect on me, too! Unlike our previous get-togethers, when there was fun at the table and a sense of contentment and an impalpable rapport, this time something irksome had forced its way into our presence, something unsettling, as if somebody unseen were there, dogging us and peering over our shoulders, with no way to hide from him or lose him. A sadness came over me. Ah, Tbilisi, Tbilisi! In vain I tried to revive my earlier pure, youthful feeling about the Caucasus. Something in me had snapped and broken. Only the mountains below, beneath the airplane, were still a pleasure to look at in all their white grandeur. As were the clouds on either side, which resembled our earth so much: copses of some sort seemed to flash by, then abysses, mountains, gorges—doesn't it seem to you sometimes that the sky mirrors the earth and imitates everything on it, from wild animals to landscapes? It's as if somebody were observing secretly and, like a small boy, modeling all he has seen on our earth, but then destroys it as soon as he has finished.

In the seat next to mine was an energetic, somewhat forward but nevertheless pleasant, sociable, talkative journalist from Moscow. His unconstrained manner probably came from his profession. But he was a decent fellow, and sincere.

"Listen!" he said, in a lively, rather pushy way, when we had barely taken off and had just unfastened our seat belts. "Have I a story to tell you! You never heard anything like it."

"Is that so?"

"Absolutely."

The airplane droned, dipped into air pockets, and shook with a slight tremble like a restless horse. What a smart machine that is! It flies along with its immobile wings outstretched, and a silent shadow follows along the ground. In the morning you start in the chill gray of Moscow in April, by noon you're immersed in the South's rampant greenery. It's as if some magician had transported you far, far away, over forests and lakes, and now you're somebody else entirely, and the world around you has changed fantastically and marvelously. Ah, how I used to love the way airplanes drone and quiver, and the air pockets, and the distances stretching out below in the bluish haze of space. The sun shining on the whole universe! Horizons within reach! The announcer's voice at the airport. The stewardesses, who are like Blok's strangers. Your thrill, your purity, your wonder . . . Where are you, my youth?

As the engines whined and announcements were made about our altitude, my talkative neighbor leaned over to me, grabbed me by the sleeve, and recounted the story of the good fortune that had befallen him a few days earlier in an adjacent Caucasian republic where he had gone before stopping off in Tbilisi on assignment.

"We're sitting around, you know, a group of us, drinking wine and talking. Having a good time! With Caucasus-style toasts! And shishkebab from a ram roasted whole, and a special old cognac.

It was great! It happened I had with me a little volume of Tsve-
tayeva's poems, kind of dark blue—maybe you know it. I had
taken it along on the trip, I really love it. For some reason I was
taking it out of my briefcase to make more room, and putting it
in my suitcase. And guess what! One of the fellows says to me,
'Sell me that book. I'll give you a hundred rubles for it.' Well, of
course, I replied that I don't sell books, I buy them for my soul,
so to speak, and so on. He didn't hear me. 'I'll give you two
hundred rubles! Three hundred!' At that point his buddy joined
in. 'Why three hundred?' he says. 'I'll give you four hundred
rubles. Five hundred . . .' Then they really got going. One says,
'Seven hundred!' The other replies, 'A thousand!' The bidding
started to give me goose bumps. It was like a roulette wheel was
being spun in front of me and I was the one with the winning
ticket. They got the price up to two thousand, then counted out
the money for me. And they took the book, of course. 'It's the
most expensive book of the year,' its owner said. 'I'm going to
show it to all my guests.' "

My companion burst out laughing in joy and disbelief. "Can
you imagine: Two thousand in cash! What a windfall! Will my
wife be happy! I'm going to buy her a fur coat. There are fake
tiger coats, you know. I like them. I'll get my daughter balloon
pants—banana pants, they call them. She's driven me crazy about
them. Those things cost three hundred rubles. Where was I supposed to get that? And for our home I'll buy a glazed earthenware
toilet bowl, a pink one. It's a dream come true! I saw one at a
friend's—it was imported, and it was the color of baked milk,
only a little yellower. As delicate as a teardrop!"

I shuddered and looked at him in amazement. His face was
frozen in a contented grin. He was picturing his dream. He could
see it plainer than real: a pink, limpid, pure toilet bowl, shot with
mother-of-pearl, like some marvelous precious stone. . . . And he
himself on that toilet, a pink horse he was riding.

Our airplane shook and bounced like a bus on a bumpy road.
Someone gasped. Up front a baby started to cry. A stewardess
hurried by. We flew into a huge gray cloud, and immediately the
sound of the engines stopped as if someone had wrapped the
plane in cotton wool. There ensued that sudden and frightening
state of flying through thick clouds when the plane seems suspended in place, when the sensation of movement disappears and
you feel you aren't getting anywhere and at any moment you

could fall out of the sky to the ground. Suddenly I had the thought, apropos of nothing: Why should a man have a crystal toilet bowl? What does he need it for when he himself isn't crystalline? And I was aghast at myself for being possessed by such an obsessive thought.

TRANSLATED BY ANN C. BIGELOW

THE KING OF JAZZ

·꒜·

Donald Barthelme

Well I'm the king of jazz now, thought Hokie Mokie to himself as he oiled the slide on his trombone. Hasn't been a 'bone man been king of jazz for many years. But now that Spicy Mac-Lammermoor, the old king, is dead, I guess I'm it. Maybe I better play a few notes out of this window here, to reassure myself.

"Wow!" said somebody standing on the sidewalk. "Did you hear that?"

"I did," said his companion.

"Can you distinguish our great homemade American jazz performers, each from the other?"

"Used to could."

"Then who was that playing?"

"Sounds like Hokie Mokie to me. Those few but perfectly selected notes have the real epiphanic glow."

"The what?"

"The real epiphanic glow, such as is obtained only by artists of the caliber of Hokie Mokie, who's from Pass Christian, Mississippi. He's the king of jazz, now that Spicy MacLammermoor is gone."

Hokie Mokie put his trombone in its trombone case and went to a gig. At the gig everyone fell back before him, bowing.

"Hi Bucky! Hi Zoot! Hi Freddie! Hi George! Hi Thad! Hi Roy! Hi Dexter! Hi Jo! Hi Willie! Hi Greens!"

"What we gonna play, Hokie? You the king of jazz now, you gotta decide."

"How 'bout 'Smoke'?"

"Wow!" everybody said. "Did you hear that? Hokie Mokie can just knock a fella out, just the way he pronounces a word. What a intonation on that boy! God Almighty!"

"I don't want to play 'Smoke,' " somebody said.

"Would you repeat that, stranger?"

"I don't want to play 'Smoke.' 'Smoke' is dull. I don't like the changes. I refuse to play 'Smoke.' "

"He refuses to play 'Smoke'! But Hokie Mokie is the king of jazz and he says 'Smoke'!"

"Man, you from outa town or something? What do you mean you refuse to play 'Smoke'? How'd you get on this gig anyhow? Who hired you?"

"I am Hideo Yamaguchi, from Tokyo, Japan."

"Oh, you're one of those Japanese cats, eh?"

"Yes, I'm the top trombone man in all of Japan."

"Well you're welcome here until we hear you play. Tell me, is the Tennessee Tea Room still the top jazz place in Tokyo?"

"No, the top jazz place in Tokyo is the Square Box now."

"That's nice. OK, now we gonna play 'Smoke' just like Hokie said. You ready, Hokie? OK, give you four for nothin'. One! Two! Three! Four!"

The two men who had been standing under Hokie's window had followed him into the club. Now they said:

"Good God!"

"Yes, that's Hokie's famous 'English sunrise' way of playing. Playing with lots of rays coming out of it, some red rays, some blue rays, some green rays, some green stemming from a violet center, some olive stemming from a tan center—"

"That young Japanese fellow is pretty good, too."

"Yes, he is pretty good. And he holds his horn in a peculiar way. That's frequently the mark of a superior player."

"Bent over like that with his head between his knees—good God, he's sensational!"

He's sensational, Hokie thought. Maybe I ought to kill him.

But at that moment somebody came in the door pushing in front of him a four-and-one-half-octave marimba. Yes, it was Fat Man Jones, and he began to play even before he was fully in the door.

"What're we playing?"

" 'Billie's Bounce.' "

"That's what I thought it was. What're we in?"

"F."

"That's what I thought we were in. Didn't you use to play with Maynard?"

"Yeah I was in that band for a while until I was in the hospital."

"What for?"

"I was tired."

"What can we add to Hokie's fantastic playing?"

"How 'bout some rain or stars?"

"Maybe that's presumptuous?"

"Ask him if he'd mind."

"You ask him, I'm scared. You don't fool around with the king of jazz. That young Japanese guy's pretty good, too."

"He's sensational."

"You think he's playing in Japanese?"

"Well I don't think it's English."

This trombone's been makin' my neck green for thirty-five years, Hokie thought. How come I got to stand up to yet another challenge, this late in life?

"Well, Hideo—"

"Yes, Mr. Mokie?"

"You did well on both 'Smoke' and 'Billie's Bounce.' You're just about as good as me, I regret to say. In fact, I've decided you're *better* than me. It's a hideous thing to contemplate, but there it is. I have only been the king of jazz for twenty-four hours, but the unforgiving logic of this art demands we bow to Truth, when we hear it."

"Maybe you're mistaken?"

"No, I got ears. I'm not mistaken. Hideo Yamaguchi is the new king of jazz."

"You want to be king emeritus?"

"No, I'm just going to fold up my horn and steal away. This gig is yours, Hideo. You can pick the next tune."

"How 'bout 'Cream'?"

"OK, you heard what Hideo said, it's 'Cream.' You ready, Hideo?"

"Hokie, you don't have to leave. You can play too. Just move a little over to the side there—"

"Thank you, Hideo, that's very gracious of you. I guess I will play a little, since I'm still here. Sotto voce, of course."

"Hideo is wonderful on 'Cream'!"

"Yes, I imagine it's his best tune."

"What's that sound coming in from the side there?"

"Which side?"

"The left."

"You mean that sound that sounds like the cutting edge of life? That sounds like polar bears crossing Arctic ice pans? That sounds like a herd of musk ox in full flight? That sounds like male walruses diving to the bottom of the sea? That sounds like fumaroles smoking on the slopes of Mount Katmai? That sounds like the wild turkey walking through the deep, soft forest? That sounds like beavers chewing trees in an Appalachian marsh? That sounds like an oyster fungus growing on an aspen trunk? That sounds like a mule deer wandering a montane of the Sierra Nevada? That sounds like prairie dogs kissing? That sounds like witch grass tumbling or a river meandering? That sounds like manatees munching seaweed at Cape Sable? That sounds like coatimundis moving in packs across the face of Arkansas? That sounds like—"

"Good God, it's Hokie! Even with a cup mute on, he's blowing Hideo right off the stand!"

"Hideo's playing on his knees now! Good God, he's reaching into his belt for a large steel sword—stop him!"

"Wow! That was the most exciting 'Cream' ever played! Is Hideo all right?"

"Yes, somebody is getting him a glass of water."

"You're my man, Hokie! That was the dadblangedest thing I ever saw!"

"You're the king of jazz once again!"

"Hokie Mokie is the most happening thing there is!"

"Yes, Mr. Hokie sir, I have to admit it, you blew me right off the stand. I see I have many years of work and study before me still."

"That's OK, son. Don't think a thing about it. It happens to the best of us. Or it almost happens to the best of us. Now I want everybody to have a good time because we're gonna play 'Flats.' 'Flats' is next."

"With your permission, sir, I will return to my hotel and pack. I am most grateful for everything I have learned here."

"That's OK, Hideo. Have a nice day. He-he. Now, 'Flats.' "

WE DON'T GET TO CHOOSE OUR CENTURY

·❧·

Alexander Kushner

We don't get to choose our century,
And we exit after entering.
Nothing on this earth is cruder
Than to beg for time or blame
The hour. No marketplace maneuver
Can achieve a birth's exchange.

Though all ages are the iron age,
Lovely gardens steam and varnished
Cloudlets sparkle. I, when five,
Should have died of scarlet fever:
Live, avoiding grief and evil;
See how long you can survive.

Looking forward to good fortune?
Hoping for a better portion
Than the Terrible's grim reign?
Leprosy and plagues in Florence
Aren't your dream? The hold's dark storage
Doesn't suit your first-class aims?

Though all ages are the iron age,
Lovely gardens steam and varnished
Cloudlets sparkle. I embrace
My age and its fated ending.
Time is an ordeal, and envying
Anyone is out of place.

I embrace it firmly, knowing
Time is flesh instead of clothing.
Deep in us its seal is set,

As if fingerprints were signals
Of an age's lines and wrinkles.
In our hands our time is read.

TRANSLATED BY PAUL GRAVES

FOR THE RECORD

·✌·

Adrienne Rich

The clouds and the stars didn't wage this war
the brooks gave no information
if the mountain spewed stones of fire into the river
it was not taking sides
the raindrop faintly swaying under the leaf
had no political opinions

and if here or there a house
filled with backed-up raw sewage
or poisoned those who lived there
with slow fumes, over years
the houses were not at war
nor did the tinned-up buildings

intend to refuse shelter
to homeless old women and roaming children
they had no policy to keep them roaming
or dying, no, the cities were not the problem
the bridges were non-partisan
the freeways burned, but not with hatred

Even the miles of barbed-wire
stretched around crouching temporary huts
designed to keep the unwanted
at a safe distance, out of sight
even the boards that had to absorb
year upon year, so many human sounds

so many depths of vomit, tears
slow-soaking blood
had not offered themselves for this

The trees didn't volunteer to be cut into boards
nor the thorns for tearing flesh
Look around at all of it

and ask whose signature
is stamped on the orders, traced
in the corner of the building plans
Ask where the illiterate, big-bellied
women were, the drunks and crazies,
the ones you fear most of all: ask where you were.

ROAD STOP IN AUGUST

·2·

Anatoly Kim

A gray army truck traveled a dirt road across the steppe in August, 196–. A soldier drove, and alongside him in the cab rode a short, dark-haired officer. Inside the closed van the soldier Ivin lay on a mattress; the soldier and the mattress flew up in the air together and jolted back onto the metal floor as the truck plunged through ruts and potholes.

The officer in the cab dozed, his cap on his knee, his head lolling against the back of the seat. He was dreaming of a woman he hardly knew. He had met her once during a visit to the town of Piatigorsk. For some reason she now appeared in his dream standing before him in a soldier's long winter underwear. He shrugged in puzzlement. Then, as if shoved from behind, he fell forward toward her, while she fended him off with a sharp elbow—and he woke.

He shook his head, rubbed his cheeks hard with both hands, tossed his hair back, and picked up the fallen cap. The truck had come to a stop. The steppe no longer swam past the window. Instead, a single telegraph pole tilted toward the sky, its round porcelain insulators shining in the sun. The driver climbed down from the cab and was stretching his back under his sweat-stained army blouse.

"Why are we stopping, Yeskin?" the officer asked in a drowsy voice.

"Time for a rest, Comrade Senior Lieutenant," the driver mumbled, kicking the front wheel.

"Well. I thought it was a flat tire." The officer opened the cab door on his side and jumped down.

The truck had pulled off by the side of the road and stopped on the flat bank of a river. To the right the road went on over a bridge. At the approach to the bridge a cobbled strip of roadway glistened in the sun like the plates of an armadillo that had burrowed into the earth.

The truck stood among high, dry grass that rose straight up

like the bristles of a hairbrush. A crushed wooden fruit crate lay in the grass. At one corner a loose slat held bent and rusted nails. Scattered about were shards of broken bottles, glinting with unbearably sharp, bright light.

High above, a dark hawk circled slowly in the silver and blue of the noonday sun. Somewhere far off, women called to one another. Grasshoppers chirred loudly and happily. A tractor growled in the distance.

The air rose from the baked soil in a solid, warm flow. Encountering the motionless cold of the sky, the current began to twist and streak in huge swells, a mighty stream, imperceptible from below but forming a breeze that swirled over the smooth brown hills on the horizon. Riding this springy stream of air, the hawk extended its wings as a swimmer his arms, and soared above the steppe.

Spreading its feathers fanlike and barely moving its wings, the hawk floated in place, carefully surveying the wormwood below, the cracks in the earth, the gopher holes and the two parallel tracks in the road, worn shiny by wheels. The hawk glided along the road. It saw gophers, rooted to the spot like gray shadows at their holes, turning their heads to look up cunningly, confident they were safe. The hawk looked away scornfully and indifferently when it met a stare from one and noted the fear instantly reflected in the gleaming button eyes. It knew that the gophers were stupid and their cunning pitiful. Sooner or later one would become self-assured, grow daring, take a risk, and be doomed.

Along the left of the road stretched a swampy meadow with clumps of green reeds. At some points the marsh came quite close to the road. Here, in a patch of blue water, two herons stood side by side, their heads turning in unison on their flexible necks. The herons watched a carrion crow with calm hostility but no fear. They were strong, large birds, with sharp beaks. The hawk, exchanging glances with them, gave two swift thrusts of its wings and flew on.

The truck remained motionless near the bridge. A man stood by the truck, his hands at his sides, and stared up at the soaring hawk. The hawk looked into the man's eyes gloomily; it saw in them something strange and incomprehensible that it found particularly unpleasant in humans: the man was smiling. The hawk wheeled sharply and flew off, once more along the road, sensing behind it the man's alien, disturbing gaze.

I was dreaming. It was a good dream. This hawk was part of it. It's like a continuation of the dream, thought Ivin as he watched the hawk disappear.

Ivin had spent many days in the cramped guardhouse cell, waiting for his fate to be decided. As the days dragged on, he became obsessed with the constant, gnawing yearning for freedom that a prisoner fastens upon singlemindedly. His unit, assigned to guard a small penal camp of particularly dangerous criminals, was stationed deep in the steppe; it was not easy to get action on his case here, and the soldier Ivin languished in the cell, endlessly awaiting the investigation and trial that never came. During the days and nights locked in the dark, barred storeroom at the end of the barracks corridor, Ivin had become used to depressing, tormenting dreams, after which the reality seemed even more dismal. But this time his dream was bright and open and somehow clearly associated with the wonderful freedom he craved.

Ivin dreamed (or, more precisely, imagined, in his half-wakeful state as he tossed and bounced on the metal floor of the van) that he rode the steppe with two companions, all of them mounted on big, glossy-coated, long-maned horses. The wind lifted and ruffled the horses' manes and whipped light ripples along the grassy steppe. Above the carefree, happy riders great eagles circled at inaccessible heights. . . .

He heard a familiar, quiet, confident voice. "Well, Ivin, how are you surviving? Did the ride shake the innards out of you?" He turned. The lieutenant was coming toward him around the back of the truck.

"Everything's fine, Comrade Senior Lieutenant," Ivin replied, with a smile. "Innards in place. The mattress helped."

"Well, well! Enjoy it while you can. When we get to the regiment you won't have a mattress. So appreciate the comforts, Ivin." (Look at him, lanky devil, he's even smiling, thought the lieutenant, as if we were taking him to a dance instead of a court-martial. Is he out of his mind? If only he were! Then they'd just cashier him, and he'd be home free.)

The lieutenant searched Ivin's face with concealed pity. He liked this tall, broad-shouldered, homely, second-year draftee from Moscow, only one year younger than the lieutenant himself. A former university student, well read and with a lively mind. The lieutenant forgave Ivin much, overlooking things for which he would have chewed out anyone else. He permitted him long phil-osophical discussions that Ivin liked to hold with some of the convicts. The lieutenant used to enjoy listening as his calm, wise soldier held forth with some self-taught prison-camp sage. He particularly liked it when Ivin squelched an adversary by quoting with a good-natured grin a crushing line from some great au-thority or other. Yet it was he, this damned Ivin, who had caused the company its worst trouble.

To hell with him, let him smile, the lieutenant thought, turning away from Ivin. He walked toward the driver, who was on his knees at the wheel, tightening a nut.

"How about it, Yeskin—shall we get going?" the lieutenant said cheerily.

Dropping the socket wrench on the ground and tossing his cap down next to it, the driver raked his dusty curls with his open hand.

"It wouldn't hurt to wash up and take a swim, Comrade Sen' Lieutenant," the soldier wheedled. He spoke with an injured air, bending his head and brushing dust from his temples. "Look at the powder on my head."

"A good idea, Yeskin!" the lieutenant agreed. "Ivin!" He turned. "How do you feel about it?"

"I?" Ivin stood tall before them, his army blouse without its belt because he was considered under arrest. He shrugged and spread his hands, palms out. His homely, pockmarked face was covered with sweat.

"Follow me," the lieutenant commanded.

But as the lieutenant walked toward the river he suddenly stopped, let the others go past, and ran back to the truck. He undid his holster, with its Makarov revolver, placed them in the cab, and locked the door. It took a moment, and he followed the soldiers.

Ivin strode along, swinging his arms, the unbelted blouse dan-gling about his hips. Alongside him the squat, brawny Yeskin kicked up the dust with his clumsy boots. The lieutenant watched Ivin. Everything about him seemed pleasing, including the casual, easy gait, the sweeping gesture with which he wiped his forehead with the sleeve of his blouse, and the way he brought his face close to Yeskin, said something with a good-natured smile and then, straightening up and leaning back, placed his hand on Yes-kin's shoulder with jocular earnestness.

No, one can't say he's out of his mind, the lieutenant thought sadly. But how then could one make sense of what he had done? And what about the written statement he gave the major? The lieutenant recalled the words of the most ridiculous explanatory statement he had ever heard in his years of service:

"At the crucial moment I could not bring myself to open fire to stop the fleeing prisoner. To do so was beyond my power. To be honest, I must warn the officers that I cannot take such action in future, either. I refuse to be responsible for an action that involves taking another's life; I find it personally impossible."

Wretched intellectual! "I refuse . . ." The lieutenant remembered the phrase as he stared at the back of Ivin's head, where the hair had grown long. They'll show you an "I refuse" that will make you forget even your mama's name!

Why, he wondered, had Ivin offered any explanation at all, when he could have remained silent as a fish? But no, he had deliberately crawled into the noose. And before whom? Before Major Ovsyannikov. Fool! You had only to take one look at the major, with his shaggy gray eyebrows and clenched jaw, and your heart sank into your boots.

The lieutenant thought of the shock Anatoly Fyodorovich, his second in command, had experienced. Poor Anatoly Fyodorovich! The lieutenant chuckled as he recalled his deputy's startled face, eyes wide, mouth hanging, when Ivin had read aloud his strange written confession in the office, in front of Major Ovsyannikov, who had flown from headquarters to look into the extraordinary incident.

Ivin removed his blouse and looked around at the lieutenant, coming down the steep bank, his boyish feet taut in dusty boots, stepping lightly. A puffy, translucent cloud glowed high above them in the sky. Scanning his commander's dark face and black brows, Ivin thought: How strangely we behave! Does the lieutenant realize this? He glanced at Yeskin, for whom nothing on earth seemed strange. Seated in the grass, Yeskin was pulling fiercely at his boots, glaring at Ivin as if he were an enemy.

We three have come to a river, Ivin thought (the lieutenant had dropped his cap on the ground, removed his shoulder belt and wound it up, placed it inside the cap, then unbuttoned the collar of his field blouse, and was pulling the blouse over his head)— we, the three riders whom I saw in my dream; we have ridden hard over the steppe under a hot sun, the wormwood whipping our legs, larks sounding a heavenly, ringing tone, eagles gliding in the sky. Now we have reached a stream, dismounted, watered our horses, and decided to take a swim.

Suppose it is all true, thought Ivin: the hot sun, the horses, the long ride. But where would the horsemen be coming from and where were they going? Who were these three under the silver-blue sky, and why did they remain together? Why didn't they ride off in different directions, each on his own? What invisible chain, stronger than iron, held them together? After all, in reality there is no iron chain, just air, the hot, resilient steppe air, round about them, yet they did not move apart one step. One and the same invisible force was drawing them in a single direction, taking him, Ivin, with them. They were taking him where he least wanted to go. Yet these two, though taking him, were by no means his enemies.

The lieutenant was first to run to the river and dive, his body lifting straight up into the air and curving to cut the water almost without a splash. Ivin dived after him, and the current swept both downstream. Yeskin, unwinding the foot bindings that he wore inside his boots, soon lost sight of them in the mirror glaze of the water at the bend in the river. Yeskin sat in the dusty grass among the cast-off boots, screwing up his eyes in the sun and smiling unthinkingly as the swimmers' voices reached him. "Ivin!" the lieutenant's cry came clearly across the water. "I'll race you to the drop-off!" "I'll give you a handicap," Ivin's voice responded, "forty meters!" "Braggart!" the lieutenant shouted, in a voice that showed he was breathing deeply.

With the vague smile still on his face, Yeskin shook his head in response to some inner thought. He picked up his blackened, sweaty foot bindings by their ends and carried them to the river. There he swung them back and forth in the water, scrubbed them lightly with sand, rinsed them, and stretched them on the grass to dry in the sun. The washing done, he straightened up and peered across the water toward the bend in the stream, but he could discern neither the lieutenant nor Ivin, only hear their loud, happy shouts.

Meantime, the swimmers had reached a sandy shallow beyond the drop-off. Resting on their knees in the low water, among waving grass, beneath which the sand drifted, they saw two young women wading inshore. They were gypsies. The men called to them. One was fully clad, carrying a bag in one hand and holding up her skirt with the other. She was apparently standing guard as the other, entirely nude, washed. When they heard the men, they squealed and splashed toward the bank. The nude clutched a heap of clothes to her chest. Bent over in embarrassment, her body seemed very white against the background of dark green reeds. The lieutenant put two fingers in his mouth and whistled.

The women began to clamber up the bank like lizards, one behind the other. The first woman reached the road, placed her bag at her feet, and was calling shrilly and waving to her nude friend, who was still struggling up the bank. The naked one, catching up with her companion on the road, dropped her armful of clothing, snatched a long skirt from the pile, hastily pulled it on, then grasped a pink blouse. Dressed, she shook her hair, turned to face the men in the water, and shouted something, waving a fist. Her companion was shaking as with laughter, doubled over and holding her stomach.

"What?" the lieutenant shouted, cupping his hands. "W-h-a-a-a-t?"

"Kiss my pot!" came the gypsies' reply, like an echo. The one who had been naked turned her back and slapped her behind.

"A sight for sore eyes," the lieutenant said. "Come on out here!" he called to them. "Come on!"

The gypsy in pink was running about furiously, bending over to retrieve the articles of clothing she had dropped.

"Little devils," the lieutenant said, laughing, "how did we ever miss them?"

"We should have come upon them from shore," Ivin sympathized. "Then we would have cut off their retreat."

"If we had only known they were here!" grieved the lieutenant. "Did you see the one wading bare?" he asked, and, without waiting for an answer, laughed softly, throwing back his head.

The gypsies were going off down the road, walking slowly and somehow mournfully, in single file. Watching their small, bent figures, Ivin felt there was nothing funny about what had happened. One could, of course, guffaw and slap one's knee, bending over with laughter—but then suddenly it would be as if an invisible blade were to gleam above one's head and the heart freeze and the carefree merriment vanish. After all, what did these gypsy women have to be cheerful about if behind them lay their endless wandering and ahead they faced a night's lodging beneath a cart and cooking over a fire of twigs somewhere behind a railroad station? And he, Ivin, what was he merry about? That very morning he had lain sprawled on the floor of the guardhouse cell, arms outflung, staring up at the long, silent shadows moving across the ceiling.

But the lieutenant laughed.

They stood on the high bank. Below them the stream rolled along, flashes of light sparkling on the surface—a flood swinging around the bend in a band of incredible blue and carrying itself off into the reeds. Beyond the reed thickets the river vanished until, off in the distance, past the wooded hillocks, a strip of blue reappeared. A large heron flew lazily above the reeds as if thoughtfully testing the hot air with the tips of its outstretched wings.

"That was fun," the lieutenant said, seating himself on the level high bank and sending a trickle of sand down the slope. "But those gypsies were nothing, compared to the time when I was still a cadet and went swimming in the nude by moonlight with three girls, all of us stark naked. That was on the Volga."

"I can imagine it," Ivin said. "Do you remember how Zina the pig tender escaped from the python?"

"Python? No, I didn't hear about it."

"Quite a story." To shake off the vague disquiet that had descended upon him, Ivin set out to recount the funny story of how the pig tender had run naked through the whole village in daylight, covering herself only with her hands crossed over her breasts. It happened one day at the height of the summer hot spell, after the hogs had been fed and Zina decided to go swimming in the canal. . . . Ivin wanted to tell the genuinely droll story as humorously as he could, and he sat down next to the lieutenant, his long legs dangling over the edge of the riverbank. But now, looking about, he seemed to become freshly aware of his surroundings. With a kind of inexorable clarity he saw the iron bridge in the distance, the heated air streaming above it, the bridge's shadow in the water, the truck's dull metal body in the sunlight, and Yeskin standing near the truck in his wide shorts, shielding his eyes with both hands to peer in their direction. Something within Ivin collapsed, and the melancholy of his recent days lay heavy in his heart. He realized that the light mood he was trying to summon up was completely unreal and forced, and he couldn't make the ridiculous village incident seem comical.

Once he used to laugh at jokes and relish a swim in the river, a smoke, the taste of food, everything one was supposed to savor, but now it had all lost its flavor, and even an ordinary smoke seemed unwanted and insipid.

"So what happened to Zina?" the lieutenant reminded him. The lieutenant scratched his narrow chest and its dark, thick hair.

"Zina read in the newspaper that a python had escaped from the Rostov zoo," Ivin began, with an effort. "So . . . That day Zina went to the canal, shed her dress and brassiere, and flopped into the water. Suddenly the python rose to the surface and appeared right in front of her."

Resting his weight on both hands in the prickly grass at the top of the bank, Ivin leaned forward, head hanging, and swung his legs. The stream of sand trickling off beneath them fell all the way down the bank, stopping only at the water line. Before Ivin there arose (it would come to him over and over again, maybe his whole life long) the memory of a running man, looking back, his face distorted with pale fear. Pale fear—that described it better than anything, better than "pitiful," "quivering," "trembling."

"Zina was ready to fall in a faint, for she was a tender and sensitive girl, even though she weighed ninety kilos. She only prepared to faint, of course, because who would save her if the python began to swallow her? In short, she leaped from the water, took one breast in each hand, and flew, bare as she was, straight to the village."

"What about the python?"

"The python didn't say a word, Comrade Senior Lieutenant, it just turned its head this way and that. Zina fled through the back yards and garden plots straight to her cottage, grabbed her party dress from its hanger, put it on backward, and ran to our barracks. I was there. Zina came flying in, hair dripping, eyes up on her forehead. "Boys, quick, get your automatics and shoot the python for me! It's in the canal!' she screamed. Tedeshvili came running. 'Zina!' he cried, 'what's wrong? Are you drunk?' 'Don't be silly,' Zina said. 'It's true, honest to God! Come quick, fellows.' At that moment, Comrade Senior Lieutenant, someone remembered reading about the python in the newspaper."

Ivin fell silent. If it really seems funny to you, you laugh, but if it hurts, you cry. It's good if you can open your mouth wide and cry out in pain as loud as you can, unashamedly.

Waiting for Ivin to go on with the story, the lieutenant turned and looked carefully at him. The lieutenant's brow was furrowed with straight, even lines. He had caught the note of painful constraint in the soldier's voice and heard it grow with each word until the story became awkward, labored and not at all comical.

"We went to the officer on duty," Ivin continued. "It was Vasilyev. Asked to borrow his weapon. He wouldn't let us have it. Then we went to the camp zone. Davletov was on duty there . . ."

Ivan spoke as one forces oneself to move in a dream in which arms and legs refuse to respond, and, as happens sometimes in such a dream, he soon found it easier to go on. The scenes arose in his mind's eye without words, as in a silent movie. He remembered the career soldier Davletov, beer belly and all, being dragged by the arms, the off-duty soldiers pulling him along on the double-quick, because he wouldn't give them his revolver. He had resolved to shoot the monster himself. So he wheezed and choked and gasped for breath, his mouth open, as they rushed him along. Ivin recalled the crowd of villagers in white cotton; they had gathered on the high bank of the canal at Zina's outcry. They set up a hubbub and milled about against the background of the clear sky, pointing and shouting. Ivin had a vivid picture of the frightened expression on Davletov's plump, glossy, smooth-shaven face as, with mouth open, one eye shut, his head leaning to one side, he squeezed the trigger, raising a fountain of splashes as the bullets struck the water.

"A boot, Comrade Senior Lieutenant," Ivin finished triumphantly, "it was an ordinary old boot." The boot had been dislodged from the bottom when the generously built Zina plumped into the canal. From a distance the boot indeed resembled some huge serpent's head; the heel hung loose, moreover, and, with its nails, it suggested a reptile's maw. At the opposite side of the canal a black, half-sunken branch curved up out of the water like the end of a serpent's tail. The bystanders' imagination completed the image of a monster, its coils concealed under water.

"Did that idiot Davletov hit the boot?" the lieutenant asked coldly. "Or did he miss, in front of the whole village?"

"Who knows, Comrade Lieutenant, maybe one of the shots scored."

"I never heard about this. He should have been given what-for for wasting his fire," the lieutenant said. "Nobody reported any of this to me."

"There was nothing to report." Ivin shrugged. "Simply a free show. I myself took Davletov's revolver, went right up to the canal like a hero, and fired, too."

"Both of you should have been punished."

"We had enough to live down without that, Comrade Senior Lieutenant. At least, the village gossips forgot about us when they started on how the dog had nipped at Zina as she hoisted herself over Romanovna's fence."

"What the devil!" the lieutenant said, recovering his high spirits. "Probably bit her hams."

"No, Zina sent the dog flying over the barn with a kick."

"Well, I'd say Zina got off easy."

The lieutenant laughed, throwing back his head in his accustomed manner. Ivin smiled, glancing at him from the side. Above the lieutenant's head a low-flying duster plane buzzed, far off on the flat horizon of the steppe. The hum of its motor was barely audible.

"Wait a minute, Ivin," the lieutenant said. "When did all this happen?"

"Let me think." Ivin stared at his knee, then nodded. Yes, it was before all *that*. . . . So—"At the beginning of July, Comrade Senior Lieutenant."

"Then I understand why I didn't know about it." The lieutenant dislodged a chunk of clay with his heel and watched it skip and break into bits as it rolled down the bank. One of the lumps struck a rock, bounced as if from a springboard, and splashed into the water. "I was in town then."

He remembered why he had gone to regimental headquarters in July on his own initiative, without being summoned: to request a transfer to the reserve. The regimental commander had refused gruffly and had given him a dressing-down. Leaving headquarters, he had wept bitterly, blundered down some narrow lane, overgrown with greenery, wandered the town aimlessly until dark, and tried to force his way into a restaurant that, it turned out, had already shut for the night.

The lieutenant loved city life. He enjoyed the crowds, the music in the park of an evening, chance acquaintanceships with women, the theater lights, the bustle of department stores—these were his natural environment, without which he could not imagine living. He had joined the military because it was a family tradition. But he had never anticipated that he, a young officer who had distinguished himself in officers' training, would be torn from the city and stuck all these years in some village in the steppe.

He was doomed to spend his youth deep in the barren prairie amid the dust, the sultry heat, the terrible boredom of the steppe. He felt endless humiliation when he made his way from the bar-

racks to his cottage on cold autumn evenings, slipping and swaying in the mud like a drunk, pulling his feet from the sucking
quagmire and, once home, hunched up in the entryway, had to
use a stiff brush to scrape the mud from his boots, then spent an
hour washing them in a barrel of cold water, rubbing them clean
with cloths and setting them out to dry, only to get up almost at
dawn next morning to start fussing with the damned boots
again—after all, one can't show up before the soldiers in mud-
stained boots.

The very appearance of the dusty village, lost in the steppe,
irritated him. He despised all those crooked fences, stunted gardens, cottages with peeling paint and shuttered windows, the
whitewashed wattle-and-daub sheds with thatch piled on their
roofs. He understood none of it and didn't want to understand,
he wanted to get away once and for all from the turkeys, the
geese, the mangy curs and the endless mud that seemed to coat
all of village life. But when he had tried to break free of this
unloved world, he had failed. The unit he led had always been
stuck in the grim palisade and the four guard towers of the penal
camp, and always would be; and he would probably be com-
manding these soldiers for all eternity.

The lieutenant imagined the staff officers at regimental headquarters going about in clean uniforms and saluting one another
smartly on the parade ground. He pictured them looking askance
at some dust-coated truck from the province parked next to headquarters, as a sergeant and a seedy soldier loaded bales of uniforms, boxes of ammunition, and a happily obtained tank for
drinking water, while somewhere in headquarters a sunburned,
perspiring officer in field uniform went from office to office, sign-
ing papers and being ingratiating to the neat, cool clerks. He
envisioned one of the staff officers running into him at the door,
puffing out his smooth-shaven cheeks, then suddenly recognizing
him: "Well, look who's here! How are things? How's everything
going?"

"Comrade Senior Lieutenant, Yeskin is waving to us," Ivin reported, rising to his feet.

"Tell him to come here," the lieutenant said. Why rush to get
going? he thought to himself with annoyance. Even if we left right
away we wouldn't get there before dark, there'll be no one at
headquarters, they'll all have gone off to their mamas, and we'll
have to wait till morning. Better to drive in the cool of night.

Yeskin arrived in response to the summons. He wore his trousers now, but was barefoot.

"Here are your orders, Private Yeskin," the lieutenant told him. "Start the truck, turn it around, and ride back to the first village you find. Buy lunch for us there. Take some money—it's in the change purse in the left pocket of my blouse."

"But when will we get on the road, Comrade Sen'-Lieutenant?" Yeskin protested. "Drive all night again? Who's going to sleep for me?"

"Objections, objections! Just carry out your orders. Is that clear?" the lieutenant said with jocular sternness (though Yeskin knew that, joking or no joking, he could get three days in the brig). "Buy some bread, sausage and as many tomatoes as you can."

Yeskin brightened. He loved sausage. "Orders received!" he said. "Anything else?"

"Away you go, Yeskin!"

As Yeskin set off, he paused in half stride, one stumpy leg behind the other, and turned his eyebrowless face to look back. "What if I find something stronger? Should I take it?"

"I'll show you something stronger!" the lieutenant threatened, with a grin.

Pleased with his joke, Yeskin laughed, kicked the grass with his bare foot, and left, one hand in his pants pocket, the other shaking a fist gaily in the air.

"Be careful, don't lose the revolver!" the lieutenant called after him. "Be sure to lock the truck."

Without his uniform, in only green swimming trunks, the lieutenant, narrow-chested and slight, with slim, muscular legs, seemed a mere youth. When he ran the length of the soccer field with the soldiers and after the game sat among the sweaty, dirt-stained men, all of them loudly discussing the play, he appeared younger than his subordinates, many of whom (the Caucasians, for example) sported impressive moustaches. Vain to the point of absurdity about his soccer-playing, he had appointed himself captain of the team and was judge, jury and executioner.

On the riverbank, stripped to his bathing trunks, his hair wet, he seemed to Ivin no senior lieutenant, just a slight youth enjoying the sun that beat down on them. Ivin had a momentary impulse to take him by the hand and pull him into the water.

Meantime, Yeskin started the truck, swung it around, backed onto the cobbled stretch of roadway, and drove off, past the beds of reeds, gently bending their fluffy broom-clusters. The truck raced across the familiar steppe and Yeskin pressed down on the pedal, enjoying the speed as he always did, while the landscape rolled swiftly past.

To the hawk, however, now a black dot in the azure sky, the steppe seemed the motionless flat bottom of a world whose top the hawk had now reached. Small earthly objects moved slowly here and there across this vast, rounded surface. The hawk saw the crawling truck and another vehicle creeping toward it along the bright, serpentine road. Far away, barely visible, a strange third machine was seemingly enveloped in a white cloud. It was an irrigation truck, spraying the fields.

When Yeskin's vehicle, dragging a huge tail of dust, sped away from the bridge, the hawk decided to cross to the other side of the river, because the truck had spoiled hunting on this bank. But at that moment a gopher, apparently taking advantage of the dust cloud, dashed to the road and started across it to reach the water. The hawk, pressing its wings tight to its sides and holding its tail straight back, darted down like an arrow. The gopher turned before it reached the water and sought to flee back across the road to its hole, but too late. Sensing that it was trapped, the gopher squealed desperately, rolled onto its back and froze in that position, mouth open. A second later it was all over. The gopher's whole body shuddered and it bit the bird's rough leg as the hawk crushed it with terrible force.

Fluttering its wings rapidly, the wing tips raising dust on both sides as they brushed the earth, the hawk lifted with an effort and flew low, first along the road, then toward the water, until it came down upon a large, flat rock at the shore. The hawk let its wings droop, kept the gopher clutched in its claws, and sat, not looking at its prey but considering whether danger threatened from the direction of the road. Concluding that humans were not in pursuit, the hawk proceeded to tear apart its prey and swallow it.

When it finished, the hawk jumped up from the rock and stepped to the water, hunching its wings above its shoulders. Trying to avoid wetting its shaggy legs, it stepped gingerly into the shallow water at the edge, drank cautiously, and then stepped back, almost sideways, to the shore, where it scrambled atop the rock again. This time it turned away scornfully from the scraps of gopher bones and sat there a long time, its gloomy eyes hooded. Suddenly, as if remembering something very important, it roused, raised its flat head with its curved, stony beak, looked about, and took off in low flight above the steppe. After leaving the bridge far behind, it began to circle upward until it rested on the rising stream of air; then, setting its outspread wings at an angle to the ground, it spiraled higher and higher into the sky.

Ivin and the lieutenant followed the shore toward the bridge. Their hair had dried and the sun burned their reddened shoulders. The lieutenant was lost in admiration of a distant white cloud, the shape of a huge fish. At its bright edge he noticed a dark dot—the circling hawk. The lieutenant turned to Ivin. He wanted to say something cheerful or simply friendly. Glancing at the soldier's face, however, he merely sighed and said nothing. Again he thought of the somber purpose of their mission to headquarters. He knew what awaited Ivin, knew too that there would be unpleasantness for himself.

Parched with the heat, Ivin walked one step behind and thought, in spite of himself, that if all people were equal—they were equal, of course—why did this youth hold power over him? Ivin stared unhappily at the triangle of the lieutenant's torso, watched the play of muscles on his back, and tried to fathom why he should be addressing this slim youth as Comrade Senior Lieutenant. Ivin's thoughts were muddled, and for an instant he felt a weary desire to disappear, to be dissolved in the fierce, untroubled, sunlit air, but he shuffled on obediently after the lieutenant. Suddenly the latter chose to go back up the river and swim with the current to the clay drop-off.

"All right, let's be frank," the lieutenant said when they had once more emerged from the water, climbed the bank, and lay side by side in the short grass, from which frisky little grasshoppers jumped. "Of course you know where we're taking you."

"I can guess," Ivin answered. The grasshoppers disappeared from view as fast as they sprang from the grass, as if dissolving instantly into thin air. Ivin heard the faintest rustling somewhere nearby but could not detect its source.

"No need to guess. I'm taking you to your court-martial." The lieutenant clapped a cupped palm on the grass, trying to catch a grasshopper.

Ivin remained silent, staring at the strange, floating mass of a hill far across the steppe. The blue hill drowned in the heat haze. One could see the air flowing in waves above the horizon like a transparent, melting substance.

"There's just one thing I can't understand. Why did you write that statement?" continued the lieutenant. "It's a document, Ivin. Sure, anyone could understand if you panicked, if you simply got cold feet. It happens to everybody. You lost your head, put it that way. You wanted to justify your conduct, so you wrote that poppycock. Right?"

"Not quite, Comrade Senior Lieutenant."

"All right, let's say I accept that." The lieutenant turned on his side to face Ivin. His flat abdomen showed streaks of purple left by the grass. "Let's say I'm wrong. What then? Well? Explain. You're smart, you must realize that you've made a bad situation worse, that what you scribbled won't do. It just makes you out more of a coward. Don't you see?"

Ivin didn't answer. The tiny rustling sounded closer, right next to his ear. Squinting, Ivin saw a blade of dry grass which the wind stirred from time to time, then other such blades. Together, they gave off this gentle rustle, the soft breathing of the steppe.

"And then you went further. This ranting about 'I can't, I won't.' What does that mean? What for? Maybe you can spell it out for me. Or do you have other reasons for your behavior?" The lieutenant scanned the soldier's face. He wanted to say: Maybe you really are a Baptist, as some claim.

"Why do you have to know?" Ivin asked softly. "So I'm guilty—go ahead and try me."

"What do you mean, 'Why do I want to know'?" The lieutenant was losing his temper. "Don't be silly! Do me a favor, just explain, for my sake."

What else could he say? That he had always liked Ivin, that he respected him in spite of himself? That at the camp library he borrowed the same books that Ivin read? Or that from childhood he had always wanted just such a friend, thoughtful, wise, widely read?

Into his memory floated the recollection of a pale, sickly boy who constantly suffered persistent head colds. The future lieutenant used to visit this boy in his big, disorderly apartment, strewn with objects and books. He recalled the excitement of coming to see this anemic friend, whom he so admired, who amazed him by how much he read, knew and remembered. But once, on their way home from school, they quarreled over something, came to blows, and he pummeled his wonder-child friend. The boy didn't cry, but twisted so pitifully on the ground under the other's knee and looked so frightened, shutting his eyes at each blow, that the future lieutenant contemptuously let him up. That was the end of their friendship.

"There's nothing to explain, Comrade Senior Lieutenant," Ivin said, his blue eyes calmly taking in the lieutenant's look. "Everything in my statement is true."

"It may be the truth, damn you, it may be God's truth," the lieutenant conceded skeptically, "but tell me, Ivin my boy, why didn't you think up some *other* truth?"

The lieutenant granted that such a person as Ivin might well become flustered and experience a sudden paralysis at a critical moment; even more, that he was just the kind of person who would hesitate and fail to act. The lieutenant was prepared to forgive him this, as now, with a belated, guilty sadness, he forgave the fear and weakness of that long-ago wonder-child friend whom it had been so shamefully easy to wallop.

Why did Ivin, brainy Ivin, ask for more trouble? No one wanted his questionable confession. It would be better for everyone and for Ivin himself if it turned out to be an ordinary case of being asleep at his post or being caught off guard or if, say, he had failed to load his automatic rifle. It could all go off more or less easily, and he personally, the officer in charge, might help Ivin get off with a mere disciplinary penalty. Ivin had always been a good soldier; his service record was clean up to that point, with nothing but good words and awards.

"Why should I concoct some other truth? This one is the real truth, it's good enough," Ivin replied calmly.

"It's obvious you just want to go to jail," the lieutenant said derisively.

"Not very much, I admit. But what is there to court-martial me for?" Ivin smiled.

"What for?" the lieutenant echoed, rising on one knee, then slowly lowering himself again onto the grass. "One: You let a prisoner, a hardened criminal, escape. Two: You then admitted you wouldn't open fire on him. Three: You went on to say you'd do the same in future. What do you expect—to be patted on the head for all that? That would be real impudence, my dear Ivin."

Weird: They're sorry for me, Ivin suddenly surmised; the lieutenant himself is sorry for me. He wishes me well. The only trouble, dear Senior Lieutenant, is that if I were to renounce the real reason, then everything that has happened would be meaningless, and I would appear to be simply a pitiful coward indeed.

"Imagine that you are standing in the guard tower, Comrade Senior Lieutenant." Ivin stretched out calmly in the grass and supported his chin on his fist. "Suddenly you see someone running across the forbidden zone. 'Stop,' you shout, 'I'll shoot!' He runs right on. You lift your rifle to your shoulder and aim, but suddenly feel you can't. You can't fire. Try to understand that, Comrade Senior Lieutenant."

Here Ivin jumped up and seated himself across from the lieutenant, face to face.

"So what?" the lieutenant responded. "What is there to understand? It's all self-evident."

As he said this, the lieutenant was surprised to observe Ivin's eyes light up with a triumphant rejoicing, growing brighter and brighter until his big, coarse features reddened with embarrassment, as if Ivin, with childish simplicity, were ashamed of his inner rejoicing.

"There's nothing to understand," Ivin said softly, head downcast, and drawing lines in the soil with his finger. "You see, I could have killed a person. I had merely to squeeze the trigger to do it. But I didn't." He raised his eyes. They were wide open.

"How can I make it clearer . . . plainer . . . I just don't know how," Ivin said, almost to himself, as if listening to something, while he looked straight into the lieutenant's eyes (and the latter, returning his look, saw before him two glowing, transparent vessels holding a mysterious thought and a great, incomprehensible, alien feeling). "Apparently there was something in me, something came out that I didn't know was there," Ivin went on.

His heart beat strongly and evenly. That was it! That was what he wanted to say!

"I couldn't kill. That was the most important thing in me. The most important. I can't. It was as if I were discovering myself," he concluded with restrained exultation.

Again, forgetting everything else for the moment, he relived the instant when he had stood in the guard tower, elbow on the gun support, and slowly, very slowly, lowered his automatic rifle. A man in dark clothing, with a shaved, round head, ran through the grape arbor, bending over and dodging behind the green vines, toward the safety of the wall of forest planting. He was clearly visible through the gaps between vines as his bent back flashed by. Ivin's eyes were fastened on him and him alone in that second that stretched into an eternity.

After the man had turned his pale face to look back for the last time before diving into the dark green of the acacias, Ivin released the safety catch, raised the rifle barrel and fired a warning shot in the air. The sound was deafening. It made the ears ring. A surprising silence followed. In that silence, when the guards responded to the warning shot and came running toward him in the broad daylight, it was as if Ivin's very soul pronounced distinctly: "I couldn't. No, I couldn't."

And after that Ivin felt peace of mind.

Ivin lived with that deep peace through all the trying days that followed. He was in no hurry to reveal himself to others as, again and again, he tested this feeling within himself, as if he wanted to be certain of its truth and strength. It was with serenity that he entered the guardhouse, answered the interrogations, and wrote his statement.

The lieutenant remained silent, seized with a presentiment that Ivin had attained some great and seemingly indisputable truth. For a long moment he contemplated, without comprehending, this brief glimpse of an alien world, with all the sensible and beautiful harmony of its elements. He experienced just such a sensation when he dived deep and opened his eyes under water: silver daylight flooded down from above and disclosed a beautiful and strange underwater world moving toward him, but one couldn't breathe here, and he wanted to get back as fast as he could to the familiar blue air.

With an effort, the lieutenant shook off the hallucination. (What madness! Was this Ivin really in his right mind?) He jumped to his feet and strode before the seated Ivin, prepared to pour fierce, overwhelming arguments on the latter's lowered head. The lieutenant's shadow followed like a gaunt, mute imp imitating him. The wide steppe around them baked under the merciless sun, yet without drying up, for life had taken hold in the hot soil. If it yielded to the numbing fire of the sun, it did so only little by little and judiciously, evaporating through the infinitesimal tubes of the stalks and the invisible air vents in the green leaves as the grass grew and sweetly ripened. When the sun finally succeeded in desiccating some blade of grass, it appeared that the blade had already ripened and its dead carpel sheltered tiny seeds, those countless parachute troops of future life.

Along the road rumbled old trucks, motors roaring, worn-out bodies rattling. The whirlwind of dust that followed in their wake carried the smells of apples, plums, and cow manure, for this was the season for hauling ripe fruit to town and cattle to slaughter. As he watched the passing trucks, the lieutenant began to gain self-confidence and the special satisfaction that *he* was right.

"Then you're a Tolstoyan, Ivin!" he exclaimed. "Or in fact a Baptist, as they say you are. I hardly expected this of you, my friend."

Ivin smiled and did not reply. He sat, hugging the knee of one bent leg, the other outstretched, and thoughtfully contemplated the toes of that foot as he wriggled them. The lieutenant, one hand on his hip, stood before him, looking down at Ivin. The wriggling toes and Ivin's incomprehensible smile annoyed the lieutenant. As he turned his gaze away he saw a motorcycle rider stop on the other side of the river near the iron bridge. To wash? or drink? the lieutenant wondered, and at the same time began to muster his arguments to put this self-assured student in his place. The important thing is not to talk myself into a corner, he thought; he's erudite, he'll trap me there.

"Here we are, philosophizing, while others plow and work so that we may sit here philosophizing," he began, looking down at Ivin. "We're soldiers. Tell me, whom do we serve? We've been given weapons to defend those who feed us. Then let's defend them! You're a soldier, Ivin, do you understand?"

"Comrade Senior Lieutenant, I know all that," Ivin replied softly. "I understand it, I don't dispute it."

"*Do* you understand? No, you don't!" the lieutenant cried. He was angry with himself because, no matter how evident the truth of what he was saying, the words sounded insensitive. "You sang this touching ballad about how you took pity on a person. Do you know what kind of person this Mishka the Addict is, on whom you took pity? That he was serving his third sentence? Do you know that his first term was for murder? That's the man you let go free, Ivin. A murderer."

The motorcyclist had dismounted, rolled up his trousers to the knees, and waded into the stream. He was a deeply sunburned fellow in a blue checked cowboy shirt, his visored cap worn backward and sunglasses on his forehead. From his shirt pocket he took a round, red object, rinsed it lightly in the water, and put it to his lips. An apple. After two or three bites he tossed it far out in the river, bent over, and began to splash his face. Bobbing in the water, the red speck of apple moved downstream with the current. The lieutenant glumly watched it float away. No, he thought, I'm doing it wrong, even though I'm one hundred percent right. The world is divided into two irreconcilable camps, and if war comes, if the enemy attacks us, surely you wouldn't take pity on the enemy?—that's how I ought to put it. But no, again it will sound too much like a political lecture.

The lieutenant realized that the dispute between them was of the heart and not the mind, that Ivin was responding to some great, blinding, false feeling, not reasoned conviction. It wasn't easy to prove that. At the same time, the lieutenant sensed that he too was possessed of his own passionate feeling, his own sense of righteousness, though he couldn't define or express it. Sullenly, he focused on the motorcyclist's sinewy calves and ankles as the cyclist emerged from the water, shook his hands dry, and wiped his face with the edge of his shirt, exposing a pale, un-tanned waist. The fellow reminded him of all those louts who loitered on the porch of the village store, seated in a row, caps pulled low on their foreheads, silently following him with their eyes as he walked past to or from the barracks. The lieutenant imagined that they watched him with ridicule, ready to pick a quarrel, and he invariably tensed, ready to pick a fight with them himself.

"It wasn't that I took pity on him," he heard Ivin say, "rather, I pitied myself."

"What? What did you say? Please repeat that." He turned to Ivin with sudden animation.

"If you believe pity was involved, Comrade Senior Lieutenant, then I pitied myself, not Mishka the Addict. I'm twenty-two years old, but I've never actually fought with anyone. My mother was a librarian and I was her only son. All my life I can remember sitting somewhere behind her and burying myself in books. And here I would be killing a man! Or at least wounding him. How could I live with myself afterwards?"

"Listen, Ivin, where did you study?"

"In the historical archives institute. You knew that."

"Yes, of course," the lieutenant broke in. "I forgot. I thought it was at an old-time school for daughters of the gentlefolk. Damn it, you've described everything perfectly. Just perfectly. You've given yourself away." And he looked at Ivin with real, not as-sumed, contempt.

The lieutenant had now found and defined for himself the emotion that was his real truth and with which he could counter Ivin's feelings. As if in confirmation, the rider across the river mounted his motorcycle, started it with a roar, and sped off.

"You're an educated person. I don't have to tell you what's what," the lieutenant went on calmly now. "But you're a humane person, too, and you can't shoot anyone. Let others do what they will, but you can't, your conscience will bother you—that's it, isn't it, Ivin?"

"No, not quite. . . ." Ivin shook his head slowly.

"Yes! That's how it is, my dear young man," the lieutenant insisted. "And here's what I'll tell you. Yes, we have to do all that. The worst things in life. You can't get away from it. Even though we too would like to sit in the quiet of a library some-where. Just remember, Ivin"—here the lieutenant squatted down and fixed his gaze on Ivin—"remember that Mishka the Addict is walking free thanks to your kindness. This beast that you re-leased is capable of a great deal, Ivin. Imagine him getting to Moscow and breaking into your mother's bedroom some dark night. . . ."

"Please don't bring my mother into this exercise of yours," Ivin said quietly. He straightened up, his big face dark and flushed.

"My goodness!" the lieutenant exclaimed softly and angrily, "just look at him! He's frightened, you see, at the mere mention of his mama! Then can you imagine, mama's boy, that if he doesn't go after your mama, it will be someone else's? Does that suit you? Someone's sister, wife, child?"

"I call this a low blow."

"I don't give a damn what you call it. You think only of yourself. You're afraid of evil and you pity yourself, Ivin. All right, don't expect thanks from those you should be defending. And you needn't think you deserve pity because you want to save your soul. Don't hope you won't have to answer for what you've done, young fellow."

Crimson, with silent suffering in his transparent-blue eyes, Ivin stared across the river and rubbed the deep furrow in his cheek with a finger. The lieutenant moved off and turned away. Excited by his own words, he wondered how he had failed previously to recognize Ivin for a consummate egotist.

Suddenly he heard:

"I never hoped for anything, Comrade Senior Lieutenant. When I asked, 'What is there to court-martial me for?' I didn't mean it. I was fooling."

Ivin rose and walked toward the lieutenant, who stood now on the riverbank, looking down at the river. Ivin lifted his hand as if to place it on the lieutenant's shoulder, but the hand was left hanging in air and then he lowered it to his side. Eyes downcast, Ivin smiled sadly at his thoughts. "He was sorry for me. Now his pity has evaporated, he has written me off, crossed me off. Well, to hell with him."

There was a buzzing in his head. It felt heavy and as if filled with hot lead, and Ivin wanted to hide from the oppressive sun, to hide somewhere in an aromatic grass hut, as he used to, and doze off on a soft bed of leaves—but that cool, dark hut under the grass roof had been left far behind in childhood, long abandoned and forgotten. The wind had long since blown away the straw, the twigs and the bed of grass. (What stood in its place now? and where had it been? Was it really on earth, in a world where peace and happiness were to be found?) The hawk, still not tired of hunting, floated overhead. There was a splash in the river below, probably a big fish jumping. Ivin turned toward the bridge and saw the truck coming.

"Yeskin is returning, Comrade Senior Lieutenant," he said.

They both set off along the bank toward the bridge, the slim, erect lieutenant leading, Ivin following.

So we're enemies, Ivin thought. He remembered the faces of his comrades in the guard service. The rosy face of his squad captain, Sergeant Pellykh, flashed before him. "Lousy ass," Pellykh muttered when he came to let Ivin out for supper. (Pellykh was on duty that evening.) Pellykh stood drawn up in his clean, tight uniform, with its row of shiny badges. "Come on out, slob. All our leaves have been canceled, all because of you." Vasilyev, Muzychka, Baliyev, Zadorozhko, Maryn, all of them turned their familiar faces toward him with a single, common expression of estrangement. They sat around the tin half-barrel planted in the center of the smoking room for a common ashtray. Sated and relaxed after supper, the "guard boys" were smoking their cheap cigarettes when Ivin was brought out. When he addressed any of them he got a mumbled answer, but no one sat next to him. That was when Ivin realized for the first time that in his comrades' eyes he had committed a crime for which he now had to bear the punishment.

Yeskin was coming from the truck with the lieutenant's purse in his hand.

Still far off, he touched his stubby fingers, held playfully wide, to his cap and shouted: "Comrade Sen'-Lieutenant, Private Yeskin reports mission accomplished."

"At ease!" the lieutenant responded gaily, advancing toward Yeskin with a pleased expression.

Stopping in front of the soldier, he suddenly grasped Yeskin's blouse and pulled it, in the process managing to pinch a fairly large lump of skin. Yeskin yipped and pushed aside the officer's hand disrespectfully as he jumped back from it. The blouse had pulled out from under Yeskin's belt.

"You've shortened your blouse!" the lieutenant said, still advancing on him. "Have you taken to wearing a baby's shirt?"

Yeskin took refuge behind the truck's radiator.

"No, Comrade Sen'-Lieutenant, don't come closer, hands off Vietnam," Yeskin cried, squinting slyly at the lieutenant and prepared to take flight around the truck if . . . The lieutenant leaned a hand on the mudguard—and then adroitly vaulted across it. Yeskin barely had time to jump out of the way.

"All right, Yeskin!" the lieutenant gaily threatened as the soldier backed away. "When we get back I'll order the master sergeant to sew a hem onto your blouse. You'll wear it down to your knees, is that clear?"

"You can't do that!" Yeskin argued, still on guard as he continued to watch the lieutenant cautiously. "It's my last year in the service, and old-timers have the right!—Where shall I put this?" Above his head he raised a fist clutching the purse. "Check out what I spent, or you'll say I stole some."

"Never mind, cut the talk and just put the purse in the pocket where you got it," the lieutenant told him, and walked to the shade of the truck. "And bring something to chew on!"

Ivin knew that the lieutenant always showed the soldiers complete and frank trust, and not because of self-complacency. The lieutenant glanced sideways at Ivin before seeking the shade. Yet Ivin knew that the trust was youthfully sincere. There was much that was still boyish and unself-conscious in the lieutenant's vanity, in his sometimes capricious imperious manner and role-playing, and the soldiers liked it.

Yeskin spread out a rainproof poncho in the shade near the wheel and set his booty on it. There was an impressive pile of tomatoes, and Yeskin had brought salt—he had snatched up a glass salt shaker from the village lunchroom—fine, free-flowing salt. The dark, smooth loaf of fresh black bread was soon broken into large lumps; but the sausage proved to be hard and dry, with a stiff casing that was hard to peel. Several green cucumbers and large, dark-skinned white onions shone on the newspaper where the sausage and tomatoes lay.

Yeskin bit off bread, then an onion, and a lump swelled in his ruddy cheek and bobbed up and down.

"Good onion, straight from the garden," he said, sighing with satisfaction, and chewed hastily as he eyed the sausage. He had wanted to try it when he was buying it in the village store, but, knowing his weakness for sausage, he had refrained out of self-conscious pride from breaking off even a small bit of the tempting end projecting from the paper wrapping.

"Swiped the onions, did you?" the lieutenant guessed, and bit into a small tomato. In one second the tomato was squeezed flat and its gleaming skin was shriveled. After sucking out the liquid, the lieutenant salted the damp crimson wound in its side and popped the whole in his mouth.

"Why pinch them, just go and pull up as many as you want," Yeskin responded, unoffended, and carefully took the smallest of sausage slices. "There's a whole onion field, and next to it those—what do you call them?—Bulgarian peppers."

"Choose what you wish, but I go for the tomatoes. I love them," the lieutenant said, picking the biggest and juiciest from the heap.

"They're good," Yeskin agreed. "As for me, I love sausage, ho-ho!" he said, unable to keep his secret.

"Go right ahead," the lieutenant invited him, with a pleased expression. "Why don't you dive in, Ivin?"

"I'm doing fine, Comrade Senior Lieutenant." Ivin nodded his thanks, and bit into a fragrant mouthful of bread and onion.

"Yeskin! Are you swallowing sausage casing?" The lieutenant stared at him. "Watch out, you'll be sick."

"Never mind, it's healthy."

"Healthy? You're crazy." The lieutenant poked Yeskin in the side with a cucumber. Yeskin drew his stomach in as if it had jumped back inside his body. He moved away from the lieutenant.

Heavyset, ruddy-faced, with stubby arms and legs covered with blond fuzz, and with a similarly pale blond head of curly hair, the seated Yeskin seemed much heavier and bigger than the tall, broad-shouldered Ivin. Yeskin had almost no neck, and his heavy head turned with his body.

"I'm ticklish. I can't stand to be tickled," he explained, tearing apart a big, ugly tomato. Juice and seeds spattered on his arm and trickled down to his elbow. Raising his arm, Yeskin licked the juice, then wiped his fingers on his thigh and reached for the salt.

All three sat in their shorts, looking carefree and very young.

"I can wrestle anyone, but I'm afraid of tickling," Yeskin declared. "Can't stand it! But wrestling, I'll take on anybody. Tedeshvili always boasts, but I wrestled him. I beat him, too. Ask Ivin if you don't believe me."

"Yes, he did," Ivin confirmed.

"Really? Tedeshvili himself?" the lieutenant said in surprise.

"Sure," Yeskin answered with a satisfied air as he sniffed the soft inside of the bread. "What's Tedeshvili? He tries to trip you, but nobody can get me by tripping me, and I took him underarm. Good bread, soft! It was still hot when I got it at the store."

"You ought to have seen Tedeshvili. He almost started a fight," the smiling Ivin added in praise of Yeskin. "He couldn't believe it and wanted to do it over."

"So what happened?"

"What happened?" Yeskin echoed. "If you want to try again, you'll get it again. My pleasure! Try a hundred times, if you want to. No-o-o!" he said with conviction, holding up a piece of sausage. "Nobody can put me down. I'm very solidly built and my arms are very strong."

"What a braggart you are, Yeskin!" The lieutenant stared at him in amazement, shook his head, then looked around for something to wipe his hands on. "What do you think you are now, world champion?" He tore a corner off the newspaper, wiped his lips, then wiped his fingers thoroughly. "No modesty at all. What do you think, Ivin?"

"He may be quite right." Ivin smiled. "Thanks for the grub."

He took a tomato, moved aside and lay down, but his head was in the sun and he wanted to doze on the grass. He was sated, but there were still many tomatoes, all so fresh and enticing that he could not resist, reached into the pile and took another. The tomato was pleasantly smooth, soft and warm. It seemed almost to breathe gently and felt alive in his hand.

Yeskin began to swear that when he had served in another unit he had pinned down a first-category wrestler, but the lieutenant refused to believe him. Behind the lieutenant the coarse, thick rubber tire stood motionless, with its worn treads. Stalactites of caked gray mud clung to the underside of the mudguard. The brown iron bridge and the strip of road paved with smooth, glazed cobbles were visible in the gap between the wheels. Above the bridge shone a blue patch of sky with a small, fluffy cloud. Across this bright expanse some invisible sower scattered now a handful of sparrows, now a single dove, now darting black swallows.

Ivin mentally calculated the length of the shadow covering his leg, comparing this distance with the progress of a small brown ant running erratically along the dirty rubber tire, and tried to estimate how long it would take the ant to cross this distance and emerge into the sunlight. Diverted by the calculation, he ceased to listen to the others' conversation and he finished the tomato, hearing only the sound of their voices. He drifted into that limbo in which it seems life is possible without either happiness or unhappiness; at such times both vanish into oblivion and, though you rack your brains, you want only to stretch out on the ground and yield to sleep, sweet sleep.

"Hey, Ivin! Did you fall asleep?" The lieutenant's voice roused him. "Let's go for another swim."

"No, Comrade Senior Lieutenant, I'll go back to the truck and take a nap." Ivin rose from the grass.

He regretted that he had been stirred from his blessed, peaceful rest on the warm ground. Now it would always be like that, he thought. He would never have freedom or rest. He felt a momentary bitterness.

"As you wish. Forward, Yeskin!" commanded the lieutenant, and slapped the latter on his bare shoulder.

They left.

Ivin opened the back door of the truck and climbed in, bending his head. Trusting him, the lieutenant didn't consider it necessary to lock the back, and on the road Ivin enjoyed relative freedom. If he tired of lying on the mattress he could open the back door and sit on the tailgate with legs dangling, watching the road unroll.

To the right of the door was a short bench as a seat for a guard, and across from it, on the left, a narrow cell which could hold a single person, seated. The cell door had a grille at eye level. The remainder of the truck body was a large area for twelve persons, barred by a wire grating with a door in the center. Ivin opened the door in the grating, climbed within and stretched out on the mattress, head toward the door. Reaching over to the guard's bench, he retrieved a book and opened it.

The portrait on the page showed a young poet with hair wavy

as fleece and with ordinary eyes, ears, nose, forehead; yet all these features added up to an extraordinary look. Its impact could not be broken down into the individual features and analyzed part by part, but everything in it was genuinely humane.

> Your face, aglow, appears before me,
> Wondrous in the silent night,
> My soul enchanted by the spell
> Of old songs conjured by that sight . . .

Moved by the poetry, he thought: How could anyone live without clarity, purity, the happiness that passed all understanding? *That truth* existed in spite of everything, that truth found "in the silent night" and requiring no proof. Man must know such purity and happiness even at risk of his own ruin. If a person never knew them he was an unfortunate wretch, an impoverished soul, and then at last, when his body was lowered into the earth, his transparent, disembodied spirit would forever haunt the world above ground where he had lived, stand like a phantom where he fell, under all the rains that might come, stand in the noisy square if a city should be erected there, and, holding out his hand, ask the generations rushing by why he had ever lived on earth and died.

Yet the truth that poets proclaimed had its own harsh side. It completely denied the world that Ivin and his companions inhabited. It denied this very truck, its iron grating, its smell of herring, the grime left by human grief on the wooden benches; it denied the lieutenant, Yeskin, the whole company of Ivin's fellow-soldiers, his comrades-in-arms; denied the automatic rifles, the revolvers, the army soup, the coarse and stinking foot bindings, the guards' sheepskin coats, the guard dogs, the thieves, robbers and murderers incarcerated in the zone, the barracks jokes, the drills, the regiment's free-and-easy Masha, girlfriend of all the soldiers, perhaps even the dusty road along which they had jolted these many hours, even the rusty iron bridge over the river and the hawk in the sky. That truth required this denial; it was based upon it.

Ivin realized now how much this denial embraced. He understood the lieutenant's contemptuous anger. Ivin remembered the raw, cold autumn when a convict escaped from the construction zone. A pursuit squad was sent out to catch him, checkpoints were set up on the roads. Ivin remembered the misery that the soldiers experienced, tramping the frozen November earth; he remembered the unhappy, grim, exhausted look of these soldiers, essentially still youngsters from Kirghizia, Georgia, Vladimir Province, Moscow. . . .

And still Ivin knew that if he had to do it again, he could not do otherwise.

It seemed to Ivin now that he could never explain to anyone why he cast judgment upon no one, including himself. Let those judge who would come to live without evil, crime, murder, war, to whom all these would be alien. But would they come to live thus?

> *You tread your path more slowly,*
> *Blue ribbon that runs on ahead;*
> *Two stars, unmoving, high above you*
> *Cast silver light upon your head.*

As he read on, the poetry erased his doubts; above Ivin's upturned face as he stared at the metal ceiling of the van glowed the poet's image, holding the liberating clarity he hungered for.

Lying on his back, looking at the dark, rusty metal ceiling and waiting for his fellow travelers, he recalled a recent guard-duty incident. The convicts were building a barn for a state farm in the construction zone, thirty kilometers from the prison camp. The convict work crew arrived in two trucks that morning, but when they lined up to return in the evening the farm sent only one truck; the second had broken down on the way. All of them had to squeeze into the one vehicle. They stacked the automatic rifles in the cab, let down the tailgate, and the soldiers and the captain of the guard piled into the body of the van with the prisoners, all of them standing squeezed together, clinging tightly to one another. It was a terrifying but cheerful ride. Thieves, rapists, murderers and the young guards; all of them were crammed together, gasped together, roared with laughter together, and cursed and swore gaily as the truck rolled slowly through the dense, oncoming dark of the steppe, wheels lurching through potholes. They all arrived safely, but the captain of the squad, Sergeant Pellykh, got a dressing-down from the commander, Ivin recalled.

The lieutenant and Yeskin swam almost to the reed beds. Yeskin swam with rapid motion and wasted effort, whirling his arms and lifting half out of the water, so that he soon tired and came to shore. He noticed small, dark holes in the clay soil where the water lapped. Exploring one of these holes with groping hand, he grasped a crayfish and shouted to the lieutenant, who came rushing up. The large crayfish was bluish with white specks. Yeskin tossed it far up on shore. They plumbed many other holes but found no more crayfish. The sun singed their backs and shoulders, and Yeskin soon wearied of the futile occupation and dived back into the deep water, making big waves. For a while the lieutenant continued searching, alone, casting a glance now and then at Yeskin, frisking in the water; then himself thrashed through the shallows into the deep, leaving a falling fountain of splashes and a trail of foam.

The crayfish on shore was forgotten. Yeskin, his mouth taking in now gulps of air, now warm and muddy water, struggled back toward the shallows with the lieutenant in hot pursuit, reaching for his pale blond crown and ducking him mercilessly. Yeskin roared, swore, and begged for mercy in a show of pretended fright, but he really was afraid of drowning. It was far to shore and he was tiring rapidly. As soon as he set foot on the bottom, however, he promptly forgot his fear and began to splash the swimming lieutenant fiercely as the latter came up behind. The lieutenant dived and disappeared under water, and Yeskin, laughing loudly and somewhat foolishly by himself, strode hastily to shore, looking back and swinging his outspread arms from side to side. The lieutenant's head lifted from the surface, small, with dark wet hair plastered to his skull; he spat, jumped to his feet, and raced after Yeskin. Soon, finding a stretch of clean white sand, they lay shoulder to shoulder. Time stood still, drifting smoothly in place like the hawk in the sky among the ghostly mirages of the heat haze, an eternal and seemingly unmoving time permeated by the trilling of grasshoppers unseen in the dry grass. For the dying crayfish in this grass, time became a tall, impenetrable and sticky shroud, in which the crayfish thrashed vainly, sharply and convulsively, bending and unbending its spiny back.

After a while the lieutenant and Yeskin moved on, until they found a sandy bar where green reeds crested. From here the truck looked small as a matchbox. Yeskin addressed the lieutenant anxiously:

"Comrade Sen'-Lieutenant, what about Ivin? Maybe we ought to be on guard. He might run away."

"Nonsense." The lieutenant ignored Yeskin's alarmed concern.

He was looking down, as they walked through the wide, mirror-like overflow of the river, searching for any stray fish among the reeds. They had already spotted two bream, but only at a distance. The two fish danced before them and disappeared into the depths.

"Just think, Yeskin, where can he go?" the lieutenant reasoned. "And why? He's no fool."

"But still!" Yeskin persisted, "but still!" He passed close to the lieutenant and also looked down into the transparent water. It hardly came up to his knees. "Suppose he really turns out to be a Baptist, Comrade Sen'-Lieutenant?"

"Ridiculous." The lieutenant did not even look around at Yeskin.

"You laugh. You don't believe it, but I think that's the truth," Yeskin admitted with great conviction. "He let Mishka the Addict go because they had an agreement."

"I tell you it's drivel!" the lieutenant cried, straightening up. He stopped, and looked darkly and sternly at Yeskin.

"But what if the convicts themselves believe it?" objected Yeskin, who also stopped and lifted his head.

"Don't spend your time listening to jailbirds' chatter! Get it?" The lieutenant's voice came sharp and severe over the quiet surface of the river. "And don't blab it around yourself if you don't want to find yourself in a foolish position. Think carefully, whose word do you trust?"

"I don't believe it, Comrade Sen'-Lieutenant, I just . . ." Yeskin tried to justify himself. "If there's talk, there must be something to it. All that talk can't be for nothing."

"What surprises me most is, what does it matter to you?" the lieutenant asked insinuatingly, frowning. "Why are you upset about it? Do you want him to be accused of conniving with convicts, in addition to everything else?"

"What would I need that for?" Yeskin muttered crossly. "I don't care even if they don't court-martial him. I don't give a damn about him."

"Then why do you malign him?"

"I don't malign him. I just . . . Well, why didn't he shoot?" Yeskin cried, voicing what bothered him. "You know yourself . . . Ivin always started up discussions with them, he coddled them."

"You're lying, Yeskin! And why are you lying, if you please?" the lieutenant asked sarcastically. "Ivin always was a good soldier, and if he lost his head, well, who hasn't, at one time or another? Who can say what you would have done in his place?"

"I?" Yeskin, who had been energetically swishing the grass in the water with his heel, stopped. "I would have . . . I'd . . . You can rest easy about me! I'd have shot him dead on the spot." And Yeskin turned his broad, bulging chest to the lieutenant and placed hands on hips.

"Don't be so sure. I know all about such boastfulness," the lieutenant interrupted. "You're a great one for shooting off your mouth. I don't want to hear you blabbing about things you know nothing about, do you understand?" he warned. "Especially at regimental headquarters."

This was not the first time he had heard rumors of connivance between Ivin and the escaped convict. Some of the officers in the commission that had come with Major Ovsyannikov had also voiced such a presumption. If it were to be confirmed, it would be the worse not only for Ivin. "Associating with prisoners" was a serious charge; moreover, the fact might come to light that the lieutenant had himself furthered undesirable contact. . . . The reason he had chosen to conduct Ivin to headquarters himself was that on the way he could cautiously check out whether there was any possibility the rumors of connivance might be true. But after talking with Ivin the lieutenant had dismissed all such doubts. Something in Ivin's eyes made the lieutenant trust him completely. He did not try to make out what it was in those eyes that made it so, he simply set his mind at rest and dismissed all secret apprehensions. There had been no connivance, there couldn't be.

Now the lieutenant almost regretted that he had come himself, instead of sending his deputy, Anatoly Fyodorovich. No matter what else happened at headquarters, the lieutenant would be in hot water, he'd have to accept some blame. He'd have to face the regimental commander, whose gruffness the lieutenant still remembered. The commander would haul him over the coals again, while lucky Anatoly Fyodorovich would be imperturbably napping in the office, too lazy even to turn out for the posting of the guard, handing over that duty to the master sergeant. And in the evening, picking up his newspaper-wrapped bundle of dirty shirts (Galya would wash them!), he would trot the whole length of the village to his beloved postmistress.

———

There was a sudden big splash right next to them, followed by a stir in the reeds. The lieutenant jumped involuntarily, but immediately collected himself. He caught a glimpse of a huge Sazan carp, and his heart leaped. Its side was copper-colored, and it rubbed its dark, thick back on the reed stalks like a hog rubbing on a fence, shook its caudal fin, fanned its gills, and looked calmly at the lieutenant. For the first time the lieutenant was seeing such eyes in a fish, the eyes of one free in its own element. The eyes held an intelligent expression.

"Yeskin! Come here, damn it!" the lieutenant cried, waving his arms, and rushed toward the carp.

The fish shuddered, slapped the water with its tail, raised its dorsal fin, and swam off through the reeds in a spray of bubbles. Its heavy body parted the reeds, their crests bowing before it as if they were sentient beings. The lieutenant sprang after the carp like a goat, bucking up out of the water at each step; fell twice, scratched chest and knee, but could not reach the immense fish. The carp was seized with the fury of a powerful, confident beast that has been disturbed. Its copper scales flashed in rows, its tightly stuffed sides rocked, it raged, but its unerring instinct told it to avoid the foe and put forth all its strength to escape through the reeds.

Breathing hard, the lieutenant realized the futility of pursuit and watched the fish swim off.

Yeskin came running heavily, enveloped to the waist in a cascade of splashes as his feet smacked the water.

"Where? What?" he wheezed.

"It's gone," the lieutenant barely managed to say. "What a carp . . . Yeskin! It must have weighed at least fifteen kilos."

"Shit!" Yeskin groaned, grasping his head with both hands.

"We should have taken the pistol," the lieutenant said, sick at heart, and held his hand up with the fingers curled as if around the butt.

"Who could have foreseen it, Comrade Sen'-Lieutenant?" Yeskin tried to comfort him. "Maybe I should run and get it?"

"No, damn it. A fish like that doesn't turn up twice in a lifetime." The lieutenant now despaired entirely of finding the carp. Suddenly he froze, as if at a frightening new thought. Then, in an entirely different tone, cautious and cold-blooded, he asked:

"Listen, Yeskin, did you lock the cab?"

"Of course. Here are the keys," Yeskin answered, and pulled

at the elastic band of his shorts to turn up the inner pocket, where the keys jangled.

"Everything's all right, then." The lieutenant regained his calm. "Let's go back, young fellow. Soon time to be on the road. And we couldn't catch that damned fish without a net."

"A net would be no good here. Too shallow," Yeskin objected. "You'd need a shotgun."

"That's a good idea," the lieutenant said, to praise Yeskin. "Well, let's go, let's go." He was hurrying, with a lingering vague sense of alarm at the thought that he had left the loaded revolver in the truck with Ivin. Could Ivin have gone off his rocker, with all that had happened? he wondered. He might somehow get into the cab and put a bullet in his forehead—and with his officer's revolver, no less.

But when they climbed the knoll he saw the bridge in the distance, the truck, and Ivin's lonely figure not far off. Ivin wore his uniform, as if ready to resume the journey, and stood on the bank, looking at the river. The lieutenant's qualms vanished, as if they had never existed. Again he felt pity for this soldier. He was prepared to help him, heart and soul—but how? Much depended on the way Ivin answered the interrogation at headquarters.

"Well, Yeskin?" the lieutenant cried derisively, turning to the soldier. "Look, your 'Baptist' is standing there and hasn't run off anywhere."

"I see," Yeskin responded reluctantly. He was trying carefully to keep to the soft dust and avoid stepping on the prickly grass and lumps of hard clay.

Walking behind the lieutenant, he sighed loudly, regretting that he had been a fool not to take leave in the spring, when he was offered it. He had wanted to postpone his leave to the autumn, when the harvest of cucumbers and tomatoes would be in. That was a mistake. All leaves were canceled until this case of the convict's escape was settled. It would be a long time, and meanwhile you might commit some infringement yourself and lose the leave entirely.

Yeskin envisioned himself arriving in his home village outside the town of Borovsk in Kaluga Province. He would hitch a ride on a truck going in that direction and get off at the first cottage on the edge of the village. He'd jump down, straighten his tunic, and walk on along the village street, carrying his suitcase. Evening would be coming on, the cows not yet in the barns, the old women dozing on the benches or gathered on someone's porch, gossiping about their dreams, their gardens, and their pickling. The young girls would be washing their feet in the yards after the day's work. Everything as usual, the normal life of the village running on, and here he'd come: "Greetings, old folks! Greetings, girls!" "Who's that? Not Kolya! Yes, it's Kolya, Kolya Yeskin!" "Why is he on foot?" "Probably took the footpath from Sovyaki!" "My, he's red! A real red devil. The way his face has fattened, you'd hardly recognize him!" "Hurry up, you'll make your mother happy, she isn't expecting you, and Alka doesn't know you're coming. What a pleasure it will be for her!" and so on.

"What a stupid ass!" he thought, watching Ivin slowly walking along the bank of the river. "A real ass. You made trouble for everyone, including yourself. Read some books or other, spoiled yourself, did dirt to others. That bandit Mishka the Addict wouldn't have tried to escape if anyone else had been on guard duty. Knew just who would let him get away. Those convicts are smart bastards, they study the guards before they try anything. Smart and dangerous guys!" Yeskin shook his head thoughtfully.

When they came up to him, Ivin asked, with a smile:

"What were you up to out there? Catching a fish?"

"Not a chance of catching it," the lieutenant said regretfully, and then, to Yeskin: "Open up the cab, lively now!"

"Right away. I'm hopping to it," Yeskin grumbled.

He swept his boots and clothing from the driver's seat and tossed them on the dry grass. With a gloomy air he pulled on his tight trousers. He sat down to put on his boots and watched the lieutenant, who was dressing quickly and easily. The lieutenant straightened his blouse under its belt, took a comb from his breast pocket, and ran it through his hair, head to one side. Yeskin tugged one boot on, then the other, grunted, rose, and stamped his feet.

"Well, what now? To horse?" he asked glumly, looking to the lieutenant for orders.

"Let's go," the lieutenant answered briefly, and went toward the cab.

"Start it up, Yeskin." He slapped Yeskin on the back and placed his long arm around Ivin's shoulder.

"Ouch!" screamed Yeskin, making a face. "Stop it! I'm all sunburnt. It hurts!" Looking as if the whole wide world was one big pain, he hobbled to the cab.

Ivin turned to go around to the back of the truck. Suddenly he was seized with a merciless vision that was to remain with him obsessively forever after. There arose before him, as from the dust of ashes, the image of the big, pockmarked, loutish face of Mishka the Addict, gnarled, cruel and wooden, his loose-lipped mouth glittering with steel teeth—Mishka the thief, murderer, rapist, who had killed God knows how many souls.

TRANSLATED BY LEO GRULIOW

THE HALFWAY DINER

· ⚘ ·

John Sayles

Some of the other girls can read on the way but I get sick. I need somebody to talk to, it don't matter who so much, just someone to shoot the breeze with, pass time. *Si no puedes platicar, no puedes vivir*, says my mother, and though I don't agree that the silence would kill me, twelve hours is a long stretch. So when Goldilocks climbs on all big-eyed and pale and almost sits herself in Renee's seat by the window I take pity and put her wise.

"You can't sit in that seat," I say.

Her face falls like she's a kid on the playground about to get whupped. "Pardon?" she says. *Pardon.*

"That's Renee's seat," I tell her. "She's got a thing about it. Something about the light."

"Oh. Sorry." She looks at the other empty seats like they're all booby-trapped. Lucky for her I got a soft heart and a mouth that needs exercise.

"You can sit here if you want."

She just about pees with relief and sits by me. She's not packing any magazines or books which is good cause like I said, I get sick. If the person next to me reads I get nosy and then I get sick plus a stiff neck.

"My name's Pam," she says.

"It would be. I'm Lourdes." We shake hands. I remember the first time I made the ride, four years ago, I was sure somebody was gonna cut me with a razor or something. I figured they'd all of them be women who'd done time themselves, a bunch of big tough mamas with tattoos on their arms who'd snarl out stuff like "Whatsit to you, sister?" Well, we're not exactly the Girl Scout Jamboree, but mostly people are pretty nice to each other, unless something happens like with Lee and Delphine.

"New meat?" I ask her.

"Pardon?"

"Is your guy new meat up there?" I ask. "Is this his first time inside?"

She nods and hangs her head like it's the disgrace of the century. Like we're not all on this bus for the same reason.

"You hear from him yet?"

"I got a letter. He says he doesn't know how he can stand it."

Now this is good. It's when they start to get comfortable up there you got to worry. We had this girl on the bus, her guy made parole first time up, only the minute he gets home he starts to mope. Can't sleep nights, can't concentrate, mutters to himself all the time, won't take an interest in anything on the outside. She lives with this a while, then one night they have a fight and really get down and he confesses how he had this kid in his cell, this little *mariquita*, and they got to doing it, you know, like some of the guys up there will do, only this guy fell in *love*. These things happen. And now he's *jealous*, see, cause his kid is still inside with all these *men*, right, and damn if a week later he doesn't go break his parole about a dozen different ways so he gets sent back up. She had to give up on him. To her it's a big tragedy, which is understandable, but I suppose from another point of view it's kind of romantic, like *Love Story*, only instead of Ali MacGraw you got a sweetboy doing a nickel for armed robbery.

"What's your guy in for?" I ask.

Pam looks at her feet. "Auto theft."

"Not *that*. I mean how much *time*."

"The lawyer says he'll have to do at least a year and a half."

"You don't go around asking what a guy's rap is in here," I tell her. "That's like *per*sonal, you know? But the length of sentence—hey, everybody counts the days."

"Oh."

"A year and a half is small change," I tell her. "He'll do that with his eyes closed."

The other girls start coming in then. Renee comes to her seat and sets up her equipment. She sells makeup, Renee, and her main hobby is wearing it. She's got this stand that hooks onto the back of the seat in front of her, with all these drawers and compartments and mirrors and stuff and an empty shopping bag for all the tissues she goes through during the trip. I made the mistake of sitting next to her once and she bent my ear about lip gloss for three hours straight, all the way to the Halfway Diner. You wouldn't think there'd be that much to say about it. Then after lunch she went into her sales pitch and I surrendered and bought some eye goop just so I wouldn't have to hear her say "our darker-complected customers" one more time. I mean it's all relative, right, and I'd rather be my shade than all pasty-faced like Renee, look like she's never been touched by the sun. She's seen forty in the rearview mirror though she does her best to hide it, and the big secret that everybody knows is that it's not her husband she goes to visit but her *son*, doing adult time. She just calls him "my Bobby."

Mrs. Tucker settles in front with her knitting, looking a little tired. Her guy is like the Birdman of Alcatraz or something, he's been in since back when they wore stripes like in the Jimmy Cagney movies, and she's been coming up faithfully every weekend for thirty, forty years, something incredible like that. He killed a cop way back when, is what Yayo says the word on the yard is. She always sits by Gus, the driver, and they have these long lazy Mr. and Mrs. conversations while she knits and he drives. Not that there's anything going on between them off the bus, but you figure over the years she's spent more time with Gus than with her husband. He spaces out sometimes, Gus, the road is so straight and long, and she'll bring him back with a poke from one of her needles.

The ones we call the sisters go and sit in the back, talking nonstop. Actually they're married to brothers who are up for the same deal but they look alike and are stuck together like glue so we call them the sisters. They speak one of those Indio dialects from up in the mountains down south, so I can't pick out much of what they say. What my mother would call *mojadas*. Like she come over on the *Mayflower*.

Dolores comes in, who is a sad case.

"I'm gonna tell him this trip," she says. "I'm really gonna do it."

"Attagirl."

"No, I really am. It'll break his heart but I got to."

"It's the only thing to do, Dolores."

She has this boyfriend inside, Dolores, only last year she met some nice square Joe and got married. She didn't tell him about her guy inside and so far hasn't told her guy inside about the Joe. She figures he waits all week breathless for her visit, which maybe is true and maybe is flattering herself, and if she gives him the heave-ho he'll fall apart and kidnap the warden or something. Personally I think she likes to collect guilt, like some people collect stamps or coins or dead butterflies or whatever.

"I just feel so *guilty*," she says and moves on down across from the sisters.

We got pretty much all kinds on the bus, black girls, white girls, Chicanas like me who were born here and new fish from just across the border, a couple of Indian women from some tribe down the coast, even one Chinese girl, whose old man is supposed to be a very big cheese in gambling. She wears clothes I would kill for, this girl, only of course they wouldn't look good on me. Most of your best clothes are designed for the flat-chested type, which is why the fashion pages are full of Orientals and anorexics like Renee.

This Pam is another one, the kind that looks good in a man's T-shirt, looks good in almost anything she throws on. I decide to be nice to her anyway.

"You gonna eat all that?"

She's got this big plastic sack of food under her feet, wrapped sandwiches and fruit and what looks like a pie.

"Me? Oh—no, I figure, you know—the food inside—"

"They don't let you bring food in."

Her face drops again. "No?"

"Only cigarettes. One carton a month."

"He doesn't smoke."

"That's not the point. Cigarettes are like money inside. Your guy wants anything, wants anything done, he'll have to pay in smokes."

"What would he want to have done?"

I figure I should spare her most of the possibilities, so I just shrug. "Whatever. We get to the Halfway you get some change, load up on Camels from the machine. He'll thank you for it."

She looks down at the sack of goodies. She sure isn't going to eat it herself, not if she worked at it for a month. I can picture her dinner plate alone at home, full of the kind of stuff my Chuy feeds his gerbil. A celery cruncher.

"You want some of this?" she says, staring into the sack.

"No thanks, honey," I tell her. "I'm saving myself for the Half-way Diner."

Later on I was struck by how it had already happened, the dice had already been thrown, only they didn't know it. So they took the whole trip up sitting together and talking and palling around unaware that they weren't friends anymore.

Lee and Delphine are as close as the sisters only nobody would ever mistake them for relatives, Lee being blonde and Delphine being one of our darker-complected customers. Lee is natural blonde, unlike certain cosmetics saleswomen I could mention, with light blue eyes and a build that borders on the chunky although she would die to hear me say it. Del is thin and sort of elegant and black like you don't see too much outside of those documentaries on TV where people stick wooden spears in lions. *Negro como el fondo de la noche,* my mother would say, and on Del it looks great. The only feature they share is a similar nose, Del because she was born that way and Lee because of a field-hockey accident.

Maybe it was because they're both nurses or maybe just because they have complementary personalities, but somehow they found each other on the bus and since before I started riding they've been tight as ticks. You get the feeling they look forward to the long drive to catch up on each other's lives. They don't socialize off the bus, almost nobody does, but how many friends spend twelve hours a week together? Some of the black girls are friendly with some of the white girls, and us Chicanas can either spread around or sit together and talk home-talk, but black and white as tight as Lee and Del is pretty rare. Inside, well, inside you stay with your own, that's the beginning and the end of it. But inside is a world I don't even like to think about.

They plunk down across from us, Del lugging all these magazines—*Cosmo, People, Vogue, Essence*—that they sort of read and sort of make fun of, and Lee right away starts in on the food. Lee is obsessed with food the way a lot of borderline-chunky girls are, she can talk forever about what she didn't eat that day. She sits and gets a load of the sack at Pam's feet.

"That isn't food, is it?" she asks.

"Yeah," Pam apologizes. "I didn't know."

"Let's see it."

Obediently Pam starts shuffling through her sack, holding things up for a little show-and-tell. "I got this, and this," she says, "and this, I thought, maybe, they wouldn't have—I didn't know."

It's all stuff you buy at the bus station—sandwiches that taste like the cellophane they're wrapped in, filled with that already-been-chewed kind of egg and chicken and tuna salad, stale pies stuffed with mealy applesauce, spotted fruit out of a machine. From all reports the food is better in the joint.

"How old are you, honey?" I ask.

"Nineteen."

"You ever cook at home?" Lee asks.

Pam shrugs. "Not much. Mostly I eat—you know, like salads. Maybe some fish sticks."

Del laughs. "I tried that fish-sticks routine once when Richard was home," she says. "He ask me, 'What is this?' That's their code for 'I don't like the look of it.' It could be something *basic*, right, like a fried egg starin up at em, they still say, 'What's this?' So I say, 'It's fish, baby.' He says, 'If it's fish, which end is the *head* and which is the *tail*?' When I tell him it taste the same either way he says he doesn't eat nothin with square edges like that, on account of inside they always be cookin everything in these big cake pans and serve it up in squares—square egg, square potato, square macaroni. That and things served out in ice-cream scoops. Unless it really *is* ice cream Richard don't want no *scoops* on his plate."

"Lonnie's got this thing about chicken bones," Lee says, "bones of any kind, but especially chicken ones. Can't stand to look at em while he's eating."

"Kind of rules out the Colonel, doesn't it?"

"Naw," she says. "He *loves* fried chicken. We come back with one of them buckets, you know, with the biscuits and all, and I got to go perform surgery in the kitchen before we can eat. He keeps callin in—'It ready yet, hon? It ready yet? I'm starvin here.' I'll tell you, they'd of had those little McNugget things back before he went up our marriage woulda been in a lot better shape."

They're off to the races then, Lee and Del, yakking away, and they sort of close up into a society of two. Blondie is sitting there with her tuna-mash sandwiches in her lap, waiting for orders, so I stow everything in the sack and kick it deep under the seat.

"We get to the Halfway," I tell her, "we can dump it."

Sometimes I wonder about Gus. The highway is so straight, cutting up through the Valley with the ground so flat and mostly dried up, like all its effort goes into those little square patches of artichokes or whatever you come past and after that it just got no more green in it. What can he be thinking about, all these miles, all these trips, up and down, year after year? He don't need to think to do his *yups* and *uh-huhs* at Mrs. Tucker, for that you can go on automatic pilot like I do with my Blanca when she goes into one of her stories about the tangled who-likes-who in her class. It's a real soap opera. *Dallas* for fifth-graders, but not what you need to concentrate on over breakfast. I wonder if Gus counts the days like we do, if there's a retirement date in his head, a release from the bus. Except to Mrs. Tucker he doesn't say but three things. When we first leave he says, "Headin out, ladies, take your seats." When we walk into the Halfway he always says, "Make it simple, ladies, we got a clock to watch." And when we're about to start the last leg, after dinner, he says, "Sweet dreams, ladies, we're bringin it home." Those same three things, every single trip. Like Mrs. Tucker with her blue sweater, always blue. Sometimes when I can't sleep and things are hard and awful and I can't see how they'll ever get better I'll lie awake and invent all these morbid thoughts, sort of torture myself with ideas, and I always start thinking that it's really the same exact sweater, that she goes home and pulls it apart stitch by stitch and starts from scratch again next trip. Not cause she wants to but cause she has to, it's her part of the punishment for what her husband done.

Other times I figure she just likes the color blue.

For the first hour or so Renee does her face. Even with good road and a fairly new bus this takes a steady hand, but she is an artist. Then she discovers Pam behind her, a new victim for her line of cosmetics, and starts into her pitch, opening with something tactful like, "You always let your hair go like that?" I'm dying for Pam to say, "Yeah, whatsit to you, sister?" but she is who she is and pretty soon Renee's got her believing it's at least a misdemeanor to leave the house without eye-liner on. I've heard all this too many times so I put my head back and close my eyes and aim my radar past it over to Lee and Del.

They talk about their patients like they were family. They talk about their family like they were patients. Both are RNs, they work at different hospitals but both on the ward. Lee has got kids and she talks about them, Del doesn't but wants some and she talks about that. They talk about how Del can eat twice as much as Lee but Del stays thin and Lee gets chunky. They talk about their guys, too, but usually not till we get pretty close to the facility.

"My Jimmy," Lee says, "is now convinced he's the man of the house. This is a five-year-old squirt, he acts like he's the Papa Bear."

"He remembers his father?"

"He likes to think he does, but he doesn't. His favorite saying these days is 'Why should I?' "

"Uh-oh."

"At least he doesn't go around saying he's an orphan like his sister. I introduce her, 'This is my daughter, Julie,' right, she says, 'Hi, I'm a orphan.' Cute."

"I used to do that," says Delphine. "Evertime my daddy spanked me that's what I'd spread round the neighborhood."

"So Julie says she's an orphan and Jimmy says his father works for the state."

Del laughs. "That's true enough."

"And he picks up all this stuff in the neighborhood. God, I want to get out of there. Lonnie makes parole this rotation I'm gonna get him home and get his head straight and get us moved outa there."

"Like to the country or something?"

"Just anywheres it isn't so mean and he's not near his asshole so-called buddies."

"Yeah—"

"And I want—oh, I don't know, it sounds kinda stupid, really—"

"What?" Del says.

"I want a *dish*washer."

Del laughs again. Lee is embarrassed.

"You know what I mean—"

"Yeah, I know—"

"I want something in my life I just get it started and then it takes care of itself."

"I hear you *talk*in—"

"The other night Jimmy—now I know some of this is from those damn He-Man cartoons and all, but some of it is not having a father, I swear—he's in their room doing his prayers. He does this thing, the nuns told him praying is just talking to God, that's the new breed of nuns, right, so you'll go by their room and you'll hear Jimmy still up, having like these one-sided telephone conversations. 'Uh-huh, yeah, sure, I will, no problem, I'll try, uh-huh, uh-huh,' and he thinks he's talking with *God*, see, like a kid does with an imaginary friend. Or maybe he really *is* talking to God, how would I know? Anyhow, the other night I peek in and he's doing one of these numbers only now he's got that tough-guy look I hate so much pasted on his face like all the other little punks in the neighborhood and he's quiet for a long time, listening, and then he kind of sneers and says—'Why should I?' "

We all sort of pretend the food is better at the Halfway than it really is. Not that it's bad—it's okay, but nothing to write home about. Elvira, who runs the place, won't use a microwave, which makes me happy. I'm convinced there's vibes in those things that get into the food and ten years from now there'll be a national scandal. Whenever I have something from a microwave I get bad dreams, I swear it, so if something comes out a little lukewarm from her kitchen I don't complain.

The thing is, Elvira really seems to look forward to seeing us, looks forward to all the noise and hustle a busload of hungry women carry into the place, no matter what it is that brung them together. I imagine pulling into someplace different, with the name of the facility rolled up into the little destination window at the front of the bus, us flocking in and the waitresses panicking, the cooks ready to mutiny, the other customers sure we're pickpockets, prostitutes, baby-snatchers—no way José. So maybe the food here tastes better cause it comes through Elvira, all the square edges rounded off.

She's a big woman, Elvira, and if the country about here had a face it would look like hers. Kind of dry and cracked and worn, but friendly. She says she called the Halfway the Halfway because everyplace on earth is halfway between somewhere and somewhere else. I don't think being halfway between the city and the facility was what she had in mind, though.

When we bust in and spill out around the room there's only one other customer, a skinny old lizard in a Tecate cap and a T-shirt, never once looking up from his grilled-cheese sandwich.

"Make it simple, ladies," Gus says. "We got a clock to watch."

At the Halfway it's pretty hard to make it anything but simple. When they gave out the kits at Diner Central, Elvira went for bare essentials. She's got the fly-strip hanging by the door with a dozen little boogers stuck to it, got the cornflakes pyramided on a shelf, the specials hand-printed on paper plates stuck on the wall behind the counter, the morning's Danishes crusting over under their plastic hood, the lemon and chocolate cream pies with huge bouffants of meringue behind sliding glass, a cigarette machine, a phone booth, and a machine that tells your exact weight for a quarter which Lee feeds both coming in and going out.

"Have your orders ready, girls!" Elvira calls as we settle at the counter and in the booths, pretty much filling the place. "I want to hear numbers."

Elvira starts at one end of the counter and her girl Cheryl does the booths. Cheryl always seems like she's about to come apart, sighing a lot, scratching things out, breaking her pencil points. A nervous kid. What there is to be nervous about way out there in the middle of nowhere I couldn't tell you, but she manages. I'm sitting at the counter with Mrs. Tucker on one side, Pam on the other, then Lee and Del. Lee and Del get talking about their honeymoons while Pam goes off to pump the cigarette machine.

"So anyhow," says Lee, "he figures we'll go down to Mexico, that old bit about how your money travels further down there? I don't know how *far* it goes, but after that honeymoon I know how *fast*. He was just trying to be sweet, really, he figured he was gonna show me this wonderful time, cause he's been there and I haven't and he knows what to order and I don't and he knows where to go and all that, only he *doesn't*, you know, he just *thinks* he does. Which is the whole thing with Lonnie—he dreams things up and pretty soon he believes they're *true*, right, so he's more surprised than anybody when the shit hits the fan."

"Sounds familiar," says Del.

"So he's heard of this place—jeez, it's so long ago—Santa Maria de la Playa, something like that—" Lee looks to me for help. "You must know it, Lourdes. It's on the coast—"

"Lots of coast down there."

"There's like these mountains, and the ocean—"

"Sorry," I tell her. "I've never been to Mexico."

Delphine can't feature this. "You're shittin me," she says. "*You?*"

"You ever been to Africa?"

Del cracks up, which is one of the things I like about her. She's not oversensitive about that stuff. Usually.

"Anyway," says Lee, "he says to me, 'Baby, we're talkin Paradise here, we're talkin Honeymoon *Heaven*. I got this deal—"

"They *always* got a deal," says Del.

Elvira comes by then with her pad, working fast but friendly all the time. "Hey, girls," she says, "how's it going? Mrs. Tucker?"

"Just the water," Mrs. Tucker says. "I'm not really hungry."

She doesn't look too good, Mrs. Tucker, kind of drawn around the eyes. Elvira shakes her head.

"Not good to skip lunch, Mrs. Tucker. You got a long ride ahead."

"Just the water, thank you."

Lee and Del get the same thing every week. "Let's see, we got a Number Three and a Number Five, mayo on the side," Elvira says. "Ice tea or lemonade?"

They both go for the lemonade and then Pam comes back dropping packs of Camels all over.

"How bout you, hon?"

"Um, could I see a menu?" More cigarettes tumble from her arms. I see that Pam is one of those people who is accident-prone for life, and that her marrying a car thief is no coincidence. A catastrophe waiting to happen, this girl. Elvira jerks a thumb to the wall. Pam sees the paper plates. "Oh um—what are you having?"

"Number Three," says Lee.

"Number Five," says Delphine.

"Oh. I'll have a Number Four, please. And a club soda?"

"You know what a Number Four *is*, hon?"

"No, but I'll eat it."

Elvira thinks this is a scream but writes it down without laughing. "Four and a club," she says and moves on.

"So he's got this deal," says Del, getting back to the story.

"Right. He's got this deal where he brings these tapes down to San Miguel de los Nachos, whatever it was, and this guy who runs a brand-new resort down there is gonna give us the royal-carpet treatment in exchange—"

"Like cassette tapes?"

"Fresh from the K mart. Why they can't go to their own stores and buy these things I don't know—what's the story down there, Lourdes?"

"It's a mystery to me," I say.

"Anyhow, we got thousands of the things we're bringing through without paying duty, a junior version of the scam he finally went up for, only I don't know because they're under the back seat and he keeps laying this Honeymoon Heaven jazz on me."

"With Richard his deals always have to do with clothes," says Del. "Man come in and say, 'Sugar, what size dress you wear?' and my stomach just hits the *floor*."

"And he brings the wrong size, right?"

"Ever damn time." Del shakes her head. "We took our honeymoon in Jamaica, back when we was livin high. Girl, you never saw nobody with more fluff in her head than me back then."

"You were young."

"Young ain't no excuse for *stupid*. I had one of those posters in my head—soft sand, violins playing, rum and Coke on ice and

I was the girl in the white bikini. I thought it was gonna be like
that *always.*" Del gets kind of distant then, thinking back. She
smiles. "Richard gets outa there, gets his health back, we gonna
party, girl. That's one thing the man knows how to do is party."

"Yeah, Lonnie too. They both get clear we should all get together sometime, do the town."

As soon as it's out Lee knows different. There's a silence then,
both of them just smiling, uncomfortable. Guys inside, black and
white, aren't likely to even know who each other is, much less
get together outside and make friendly. It does that to you, inside.
Yayo is the same, always on about *los gachos gavachos* this and
los pinches negros that, it's a sickness you pick up there. Or maybe
you already got it when you go in and the joint makes it worse.
Lee finally breaks the silence.

"I bet you look great in a white bikini," she says.

Del laughs. "That's the *last* time I been to any *beach,* girl."

Cheryl shows with the food and Mrs. Tucker excuses herself
to go to the ladies'. Lee has the diet plate, a scoop of cottage
cheese with a cherry on top, Del has a BLT with mayo on the
side, and Pam has the Number Four, which at the Halfway is a
Monte Cristo—ham and cheese battered in egg, deep fried, and
then rolled in confectioner's sugar. She turns it around and around
on her plate, studying it like it fell from Mars.

"I think maybe I'll ask him this visit," says Del. "About the
kids."

"You'd be a good mother," says Lee.

"You think so?"

"Sure."

"Richard with a baby in his lap . . ." Del grimaces at the
thought. "Sometimes I think it's just what he needs—responsibility, family roots, that whole bit, settle him down. Then I think
how maybe he'll just feel more *pres*sure, you know? And when
he starts feelin pressure is when he starts messin up." Del lets the
thought sit for a minute and then gives herself a little slap on the
cheek as if to clear it away. "Just got to get him healthy first.
Plenty of time for the rest." She turns to Pam. "So how's that
Number Four?"

"It's different," says Pam. She's still working on her first bite,
scared to swallow.

"You can't finish it," says Lee, "I might take a bite."

Del digs her in the ribs. "Girl, don't you even *look* at that

Number Four. Thing is just *evil* with carbohydrates. I don't wanta be hearing you bellyache about how you got no willpower all the way home."

"I got willpower," Lee says. "I'm a goddamn tower of strength. It's just my *ap*petite is stronger—"

"Naw—"

"My appetite is like God*zil*la, Del, you seen it at work, layin waste to everything in its path—"

"Hah-*haaah!*"

"But I'm gonna whup it—"

"That's what I like to hear."

"Kick its butt—"

"Tell it, baby—"

"I'm losin twenty pounds—"

"Go for it!"

"An I'm quittin smoking too—"

"You can do it, Lee—"

"And when that man makes parole he's gonna buy me a dishwasher!"

"Get *down!*"

They're both of them giggling then, but Lee is mostly serious. "You know," she says, "as much as I want him out, sometimes it feels weird that it might really happen. You get used to being on your own, get your own way of doing things—"

"I hear you talkin—"

"The trouble is, it ain't so bad that I'm gonna leave him but it ain't so good I'm dying to stay."

There's hardly a one of us on the bus hasn't said the exact same thing at one time or another. Del looks around the room.

"So here we all are," she says, "at the Halfway Diner."

Back on the road Pam gets quiet so I count dead rabbits for a while, and then occupy the time imagining disasters that could be happening with the kids at Graciela's. You'd be surprised at how entertaining this can be. By the time we pass the fruit stand Chuy has left the burners going on the gas stove and Luz, my baby, is being chewed by a rabid Doberman. It's only twenty minutes to the facility after the fruit stand and you can hear the bus get quieter, everybody but Dolores. She's still muttering her good-bye speech like a rosary. The visits do remind me of confession—you go into a little booth, you face each other through a window, you feel weird afterward. I think about the things I don't want to forget to tell Yayo. Then I see myself in Renee's mirror and hit on her for some blush.

The first we know of it is when the guard at security calls Lee and Del's names and they're taken off in opposite directions. That sets everybody buzzing. Pam is real nervous, this being her first visit, and I think she is a little afraid of who her guy is going to be all of a sudden. I tell her not to ask too much of it, one visit. I can't remember me and Yayo just sitting and taking a whole hour that many times *before* he went up. Add to that the glass and the little speaker boxes and people around with rifles, and you have definitely entered Weird City. We always talk home-talk cause all the guards are Anglos and it's fun for Yayo to badmouth them under their noses.

"Big blowout last night in the mess," he says to me. "*Anglos contra los negros*. One guy got cut pretty bad."

I get a sick feeling in the pit of my stomach. The night Yayo got busted I had the same feeling but couldn't think of anything to keep him in the house. "Black or white?" I ask.

"A black dude got stabbed," he says. "This guy Richard. He was a musician outside."

"And the guy who cut him?" I say, although I already know without asking.

"This guy Lonnie, was real close to parole. Got him up in solitary now. *Totalmente jodido*."

It was just something that kind of blew up and got out of control. Somebody needs to feel like he's big dick by ranking somebody else in front of the others and when you got black and white inside that's a fight, maybe a riot, and this time when the dust clears there's Lee's guy with his shank stuck in Del's guy. You don't ask it to make a lot of sense. I tell Yayo how the kids are doing and how they miss him a lot but I feel this weight pulling down on me, knowing about Lee and Del, I feel like nothing's any use and we're wasting our time squawking at each other over these microphones. We're out of rhythm, it's a long hour.

"I think about you all the time," he says as the guard steps in and I step out.

"Me too," I say.

It isn't true. Whole days go by when I hardly give him a thought, and when I do it's more an idea of him than really him in the flesh. Sometimes I feel guilty about this, but what the hell. Things weren't always so great when we were together. So maybe it's like the food at the Halfway, better to look forward to than to have.

Then I see how small he looks going back inside between the guards and I love him so much that I start to shake.

The bus is one big whisper when I get back on. The ones who have heard about Lee and Del are filling in the ones who haven't. Lee gets in first, pale and stiff, and sits by me. If I touched her with my finger she'd explode. Pam steps in then, looking shaky, and I can tell she's disappointed to see I'm already by someone. When Del gets on everybody clams up. She walks in with her head up, trying not to cry. If it had been somebody else cut her guy, somebody not connected with any of us on the bus, we'd all be around bucking her up and Lee would be first in line. As it is a couple of the black girls say something but she just zombies past them and sits in the very back next to Pam.

It's always quieter on the way home. We got things that were said to chew over, mistakes to regret, the prospect of another week alone to face. But after Del comes in it's like a morgue. Mrs. Tucker doesn't even knit, just stares out at the Valley going by kind of blank-eyed and sleepy. Only Pam, still in the dark about what went down inside, starts to talk. It's so quiet I can hear her all the way from the rear.

"I never thought about how they'd have those guns," she says, just opening up out of the blue to Del. "I never saw one up close, only in the movies or TV. They're *real*, you know? They look so heavy and like if they shot it would just take you *apart*—"

"White girl," says Del, interrupting, "I don't want to be hearin bout none of your problems."

After that all you hear is the gears shifting now and then. I feel sick, worse than when I try to read. Lee hardly blinks beside me, the muscles in her jaw working as she grinds something out in her head. It's hard to breathe.

I look around and see that the white girls are almost all up front but for Pam who doesn't know and the black girls are all in the back, with us Chicanas on the borderline between as usual. Everybody is just stewing in her own thoughts. Even the sisters have nothing to say to each other. A busload of losers slogging down the highway. If there's life in hell this is what the field trips are like. It starts to get dark. In front of me, while there is still a tiny bit of daylight, Renee stares at her naked face in her mirror and sighs.

Elvira and Cheryl look tired when we get to the Halfway. Ketchup bottles are turned on their heads on the counter but nothing is sliding down. Gus picks up on the mood and doesn't tell us how we got a clock to watch when he comes in.

Pam sits by me with Dolores and Mrs. Tucker on the other side. Dolores sits shaking her head. "Next time," she keeps saying. "I'll tell him next time." Lee shuts herself in the phone booth and Del sits at the far end of the counter.

Pam whispers to me, "What's up?"

"Big fight in the mess last night," I tell her. "Lee's guy cut Delphine's."

"My God. Is he okay?"

"He's alive if that's what you mean. I've heard Del say how he's got this blood problem, some old drug thing, so this ain't gonna help any."

Pam looks at the booth. "Lee must feel awful."

"Her guy just wrecked his parole but good," I say. "She's gettin it with both barrels."

Elvira comes by taking orders. "Rough trip, from the look of you all. Get your appetite back, Mrs. Tucker?"

"Yes, I have," she says. Her voice sounds like it's coming from the next room. "I'm very, very hungry."

"I didn't tell him," Dolores confesses to no one in particular. "I didn't have the heart."

We order and Elvira goes back in the kitchen. We know there is a cook named Phil but we have never seen him.

I ask Pam how her guy is making out. She makes a face, thinking. I can see her in high school, Pam, blonde and popular, and her guy, a good-looking charmer up to monkey business. An Anglo version of Yayo, full of promises that turn into excuses.

"He's okay, I guess. He says he's going to do his own time, whatever that means."

I got to laugh. "They all say that, honey, but not many manage. It means like mind your own business, stay out of complications."

"Oh."

Delphine is looking bullets over at Lee in the phone booth, who must be calling either her kids or her lawyer.

"Maybe that's how you got to be to survive in there," I say.

"Hell, maybe out here, too. Personally I think it bites." Mrs. Tucker puts her head down into her arms and closes her eyes. It's been a long day. "The thing is," I say to Pam, "we're all of us doing time."

Lee comes out of the booth and goes to the opposite end of the counter from Del. It makes me think of me and Graciela. We used to be real jealous, her and me, sniff each other like dogs whenever we met, on account of her being Yayo's first wife. Not that I stole him or anything, they were bust long before I made the scene, but still you got to wonder what's he see in this bitch that I don't have? A natural human reaction. Anyhow, she's in the neighborhood and she's got a daughter by him who's ahead of my Chuy at the same school and I see her around but it's very icy. Then Yayo gets sent up and one day I'm stuck for a baby-sitter on visiting day. I don't know what possesses me, but desperation being the mother of a whole lot of stuff I ask Graciela. She says why not. When I get back it's late and I'm wasted and we get talking and I don't know why but we really hit it off. She's got a different perspective on Yayo of course, talks about him like he's her little boy gone astray which maybe in some ways he is, and we never get into sex stuff about him. But he isn't the only thing we got in common. Yayo, of course, thinks that's all we do, sit and gang up on him verbally, and he's not too crazy about the idea. We started shopping together and sometimes her girl comes over to play or we'll dump the kids with my mother and go out and it's fun, sort of like high school where you hung around not necessarily looking for boys. We go to the mall, whatever. There's times I would've gone right under without her, I mean I'd be *gonzo* today. I look at Lee and Del, sitting tight and mean inside themselves, and I think that's me and Graciela in reverse. And I wonder what happens to us when Yayo gets out.

"Mrs. Tucker, can you hear me? Mrs. Tucker?"

It's Gus who notices that Mrs. Tucker doesn't look right. He's shaking her and calling her name, and her eyes are still open but all fuzzy, the life gone out of them. The sisters are chattering something about cold water and Cheryl drops a plate of something and Pam keeps yelling, "Where's the poster? Find the poster!" Later she tells me she meant the anti-choking poster they're supposed to have up in restaurants, which Elvira kind of hides behind the weight-telling machine cause she says it puts people off their feed. Mrs. Tucker isn't choking, of course, but Pam doesn't know this at the time and is sure we got to look at this poster before we do anything wrong. Me, even with all the disasters I've imagined for the kids and all the rescues I've dreamed about performing, I've never dealt with this particular glassy-eyed-older-lady type of thing so I'm no help. Gus is holding Mrs. Tucker's face in his hands, her body gone limp, when Lee and Del step in.

"Move back!" says Lee. "Give her room to breathe."

"You got a pulse?" says Del.

"Not much. It's fluttering around."

"Get an ambulance here," says Del to Elvira and Elvira sends Cheryl running to the back.

"Any tags on her?"

They look around Mrs. Tucker's neck but don't find anything.

"Anybody ever hear her talk about a medical problem?" asks Del to the rest of us, while she holds Mrs. Tucker's lids up and looks deep into her eyes.

We rack our brains but come up empty, except for Gus. Gus looks a worse color than Mrs. Tucker does, sweat running down his face from the excitement. "She said the doctor told her to watch her intake," he says. "Whatever that means."

"She didn't eat lunch," says Elvira. "You should never skip lunch."

Lee and Del look at each other. "She got sugar, maybe?"

"Or something like it."

"Some orange juice," says Lee to Elvira and she runs off. Mrs. Tucker is kind of gray now, and her head keeps flopping if they don't hold it up.

"Usually she talks my ear off," says Gus. "Today she was like depressed or something."

Elvira comes back out. "I brung the fresh-squoze from the fridge," she says. "More vitamins."

Del takes it and feeds a little to Mrs. Tucker, tipping her head back to get it in. We're all of us circled around watching, opening our mouths in sympathy like when you're trying to get the baby to spoon-feed. Some dribbles out and some stays down.

"Just a little," says Lee. "It could be the opposite."

Mrs. Tucker takes another sip and smiles dreamily. "I like juice," she says.

"Here, take a little more."

"That's good," she says in this tiny, little-girl voice. "Juice is good."

By the time the ambulance comes we have her lying down in one of the booths covered by the lap blanket the sisters bring, her head pillowed on a couple of bags full of hamburger rolls. Her eyes have come clear and eventually she rejoins the living, looking up at all of us staring down around her and giving a little smile.

"Everybody's here," she says in that strange, far-off voice. "Everybody's here at the Halfway Diner."

The ambulance guys take some advice from Lee and Del and then drive her away. Just keep her overnight for observation is all. "See?" Elvira keeps saying. "You don't never want to skip your lunch." Then she bags up dinners for those who want them cause we have to get back on the road.

Nobody says anything, but when we get aboard nobody will take a seat. Everybody just stands around in the aisle talking about Mrs. Tucker and waiting for Lee and Del to come in and make their move. Waiting and hoping, I guess.

Lee comes in and sits in the middle. Pam moves like she's gonna sit next to her but I grab her arm. Delphine comes in, looks around kind of casual, and then like it's just a coincidence she sits by Lee. The rest of us settle in real quick then, pretending it's business as usual but listening real hard.

We're right behind them, me and Pam. They're not talking, not looking at each other, just sitting there side by side. Being nurses together might've cracked the ice but it didn't break it all the way through. We're parked right beneath the Halfway Diner sign and the neon makes this sound, this high-pitched buzzing that's like something about to explode.

"Sweet dreams, ladies," says Gus when he climbs into his seat. "We're bringin it home."

It's dark as pitch and it's quiet, but nobody is having sweet dreams. We're all listening. I don't really know how to explain this, and like I said, we're not exactly the League of Women Voters on that bus but there's a spirit, a way we root for each other, and somehow we feel that the way it comes out between Lee and Delphine will be a judgment on us all. Nothing spoken, just a feeling between us.

Fifty miles go past and my stomach is starting to worry. Then, when Del finally speaks, her voice is so quiet I can hardly hear one seat away.

"So," she says. "San Luis Abysmal."

"Huh?" says Lee.

"Mexico," says Delphine, still real quiet. "You were telling me about your honeymoon down in San Luis Abysmal."

"Yeah," says Lee. "San Something-or-other—"

"And he says he speaks the language—"

You can feel this sigh like go through the whole bus. Most can't hear the words but just that they're talking. You can pick up the tone.

"Right," says Lee. "Only he learned his Spanish at Taco Bell. He's got this *deal*, right—"

"*Finalmente*," one of the sisters whispers behind me.

"*¡Qué bueno!*" the other whispers. "*Todavía son amigas.*"

". . . so we get to the so-called resort and he cuts open the back seat and all these *cassettes* fall out, which I know nothing about—"

"Course not—"

"Only on account of the heat they've like *liqu*efied, right—"

"*Naw*—"

"And this guy who runs the resort is roped off but so are we cause this so-called brand-new resort is so brand-new it's not *built* yet—"

"Don't *say* it, girl—"

"It's just a con*struc*tion site—"

"Hah-*haaah*! "

The bus kicks into a higher gear and out of nowhere Gus is whistling up front. He's never done this before, not once, probably because he had Mrs. Tucker talking with him, but he's real good, like somebody on a record. What he's whistling is like the theme song to some big romantic movie, I forget which, real high and pretty and I close my eyes and get that nice feeling like just before you fall to sleep and you know everything is under control and your body just relaxes. I feel good knowing there's hours before we got to get off, feel like as long as we stay on the bus, rocking gentle through the night, we're okay, we're safe. The others are talking soft around me now, Gus is whistling high and pretty, and there's Del and Lee, voices in the dark.

"There's a beach," says Lee, "only they haven't brought in the *sand* yet and everywhere you go these little fleas are hoppin around and my ankles get bit and swole up like a balloon—"

"I been there, girl," says Del. "I hear you talkin—"

"Honeymoon Heaven, he says to me—"

Del laughs, softly. "Honeymoon *Heaven*."

ON THE SUBWAY

·ζ·

Sharon Olds

The boy and I face each other.
His feet are huge, in black sneakers
laced with white in a complex pattern like a
set of intentional scars. We are stuck on
opposite sides of the car, a couple of
molecules stuck in a rod of light
rapidly moving through darkness. He has the
casual cold look of a mugger,
alert under hooded lids. He is wearing
red, like the inside of the body
exposed. I am wearing dark fur, the
whole skin of an animal taken and
used. I look at his raw face,
he looks at my fur coat, and I don't
know if I am in his power—
he could take my coat so easily, my
briefcase, my life—
or if he is in my power, the way I am
living off his life, eating the steak
he does not eat, as if I am taking
the food from his mouth. And he is black
and I am white, and without meaning or
trying to I must profit from his darkness,
the way he absorbs the murderous beams of the
nation's heart, as black cotton
absorbs the heat of the sun and holds it. There is
no way to know how easy this
white skin makes my life, this
life he could take so easily and
break across his knee like a stick the way his

own back is being broken, the
rod of his soul that at birth was dark and
fluid and rich as the heart of a seedling
ready to thrust up into any available light.

SATURDAY EVENING

·❧·

Yunna Moritz

On wet roofs—sunset glow
Furiously crimson
Like looking from inside out
At your own blood
I am rushing to you, friends
On a far edge of Moscow
No taxis on Saturday
I take the tram
Then the bus, then the metro
Then an ancient jalopy

In my satchel are good fruit soda
And a dozen meat patties
Medicine—for the old folks
For the kids—paint and glue
And a multitude of bags
With farm produce.
I'm a prodigal, a spendthrift,
And I do love ham.

I will tell you a story
And compose for you a song
In it, say what you will,
There'll be a sort of surprise

Like looking from inside out
At your own life.

TRANSLATED BY THOMAS P. WHITNEY

THE ABORTION

.ᘐ.

Alice Walker

They had discussed it, but not deeply, whether they wanted the
baby she was now carrying. "I don't *know* if I want it," she said,
eyes filling with tears. She cried at anything now and was often
nauseous. That pregnant women cried easily and were nauseous
seemed banal to her, and she resented banality.

"Well, think about it," he said, with his smooth reassuring
voice (but with an edge of impatience she now felt) that used to
soothe her.

It was all she *did* think about, all she, apparently, *could*; that
he could dream otherwise enraged her. But she always lost when
they argued. Her temper would flare up, he would become instantly reasonable, mature, responsible if not responsive, precisely, to her mood, and she would swallow down her tears and
hate herself. It was because she believed him "good." The best
human being she had ever met.

"It isn't as if we don't already have a child," she said in a calmer
tone, carelessly wiping at the tear that slid from one eye.

"We have a perfect child," he said with relish. "Thank the good
Lord!"

Had she ever dreamed she'd marry someone humble enough
to go around thanking the good Lord? She had not.

Now they left the bedroom, where she had been lying down
on their massive king-size bed with the forbidding ridge in the
middle, and went down the hall—hung with bright prints—to
the cheerful, clean kitchen. He put water on for tea in a bright
yellow pot.

She wanted him to want the baby so much he would try to
save its life. On the other hand, she did not permit such pre-
sumptuousness. As he praised the child they already had, a
daughter of sunny disposition and winning smile, Imani sensed
subterfuge and hardened her heart.

"What am I talking about?" she said, as if she'd been talking
about it. "Another child would kill me. I can't imagine life with

two children. Having a child is a good experience to have had, like graduate school. But if you've had one, you've had the experience and that's enough."

He placed the tea before her and rested a heavy hand on her hair. She felt the heat and pressure of his hand as she touched the cup and felt the odor and steam rise up from it. Her throat contracted.

"I can't drink that," she said through gritted teeth. "Take it away."

There were days of this.

Clarice, their daughter, was barely two years old. A miscarriage brought on by grief (Imani had lost her fervidly environmentalist mother to lung cancer shortly after Clarice's birth; the asbestos ceiling in the classroom where she taught first-graders had leaked for 40 years) separated Clarice's birth from the new pregnancy. Imani felt her body had been assaulted by these events and was, in fact, considerably weakened and was also, in any case, chronically anemic and run-down. Still, if she had wanted the baby more than she did not want it, she would not have planned to abort it.

They lived in a small town in the South. Her husband, Clarence, was—among other things—legal advisor and defender of the new black mayor of the town. The mayor was much in their lives because of the difficulties being the first black mayor of a small town assured, and because, next to the major leaders of black struggles in the South, Clarence respected and admired him most.

Imani reserved absolute judgment, but she did point out that Mayor Carswell would never look at her directly when she made a comment or posed a question, even sitting at her own dinner table, and would instead talk to Clarence as if she were not there. He assumed that as a woman she would not be interested in or even understand politics. (He would comment occasionally on her cooking or her clothes. He noticed when she cut her hair.) But Imani understood, for example, why she fed the mouth that did not speak to her; because for the present she must believe in Mayor Carswell, even as he could not believe in her. Even understanding this, however, she found dinners with Carswell hard to swallow.

But Clarence was dedicated to the mayor and believed his success would ultimately mean security and advancement for them all.

On the morning she left to have the abortion, the mayor and Clarence were to have a working lunch, and they drove to the airport deep in conversation about municipal funds, racist cops and the facilities for teaching at the chaotic, newly integrated schools. Clarence had time for the briefest kiss and hug at the airport ramp.

"Take care of yourself," he whispered lovingly, as she walked away. He was needed, while she was gone, to draft the city's new charter. She had agreed this was important; the mayor was already being called incompetent by local businessmen and the chamber of commerce, and one inferred from television that no black person alive knew what a city charter was.

"Take care of myself." *Yes,* she thought. *I see that is what I have to do.* But she thought this self-pityingly, which invalidated it. She had expected *him* to take care of her, and she blamed him for not doing so now.

Well, she was a fraud, anyway. She had known after a year of marriage that it bored her. "The Experience of Having a Child" was to distract her from this fact. Still, she expected him to "take care of her." She was lucky he didn't pack up and leave. But he seemed to know, as she did, that if anyone packed and left, it would be her. Precisely *because* she was a fraud and because in the end he would settle for fraud and she could not.

On the plane to New York her teeth ached and she vomited bile—bitter, yellowish stuff she hadn't even been aware her body produced. She resented and appreciated the crisp help of the stewardess who asked if she needed anything, then stood chatting with the cigarette-smoking white man next to her, whose fat hairy wrist, like a large worm, was all Imani could bear to see out of the corner of her eye.

Her first abortion, when she was still in college, she frequently remembered as wonderful, bearing as it had all the marks of a supreme coming of age and a seizing of the direction of her own life, as well as a comprehension of existence that never left her: that life—what one saw about one and called Life—was not a facade. There was nothing behind it which used "Life" as its manifestation. Life was itself. Period. At the time, and afterward, and even now, this seemed a marvelous thing to know.

The abortionist had been a delightful Italian doctor on the Upper East Side in New York, and before he put her under he told her about his own daughter, who was just her age and a junior at Vassar. He babbled on and on until she was out, but not before Imani had thought how her thousand dollars, for which she would be in debt for years, would go to keep his daughter there.

When she woke up it was all over. She lay on a brown naugahyde sofa in the doctor's outer office. And she heard, over her somewhere in the air, the sound of a woman's voice. It was a Saturday, no nurses in attendance, and she presumed it was the doctor's wife. She was pulled gently to her feet by this voice and encouraged to walk.

"And when you leave, be sure to walk as if nothing is wrong," the voice said.

Imani did not feel any pain. This surprised her. *Perhaps he didn't do anything*, she thought. *Perhaps he took my thousand dollars and put me to sleep with two dollars' worth of ether. Perhaps this is a racket.*

But he was so kind, and he was smiling benignly, almost fatherly, at her (and Imani realized how desperately she needed this "fatherly" look, this "fatherly" smile). "Thank you," she murmured sincerely: she was thanking him for her life.

Some of Italy was still in his voice. "It's nothing, nothing," he said. "A nice, pretty girl like you, in school like my own daughter, you didn't need this trouble."

"He's nice," she said to herself, walking to the subway on her way back to school. She lay down gingerly across a vacant seat and passed out.

She hemorrhaged steadily for six weeks and was not well again for a year.

But this was seven years later. An abortion law now made it possible to make an appointment at a clinic, and for $75 a safe, quick, painless abortion was yours.

Imani had once lived in New York, in the Village, not five blocks from where the abortion clinic was. It was also near the Margaret Sanger clinic, where she had received her very first diaphragm, with utter gratitude and amazement that someone apparently understood and actually cared about young women as alone and ignorant as she. In fact, as she walked up the block with its modern office buildings side by side with older, more elegant brownstones, she felt how close she was still to that earlier self. Still not in control of her sensuality, and only through violence and with money (for the flight and for the operation itself) in control of her body.

She found that abortion had entered the age of the assembly line. Grateful for the lack of distinction between herself and the other women—all colors, ages, states of misery or nervousness —she was less happy to notice, once the doctor started to insert the catheter, that the anesthesia she had been given was insufficient. But assembly lines don't stop because the product on them has a complaint. Her doctor whistled and assured her she was all right and carried the procedure through to the horrific end. Imani fainted some seconds before that.

They laid her out in a peaceful room full of cheerful colors. Primary colors: yellow, red, blue. When she revived she had the feeling of being in a nursery. She had a pressing need to urinate.

A nurse—kindly, white-haired and with firm hands—helped her to the john. Imani saw herself in the mirror over the sink and was alarmed. She was literally gray, as if all her blood had leaked out.

"Don't worry about how you look," said the nurse. "Rest a bit here and take it easy when you get back home. You'll be fine in a week or so."

She could not imagine being fine again. Somewhere her child —she never dodged into the language of "fetuses" and "amorphous growths"—was being flushed down a sewer. Gone all her or his chances to see the sunlight, savor a fig.

"Well," she said to this child, "it was you or me, kiddo, and I chose me."

There were people who thought she had no right to choose herself, but Imani knew better than to think of those people now.

It was a bright, hot Saturday when she returned.

Clarence and Clarice picked her up at the airport. They had brought flowers from Imani's garden, and Clarice presented them with a stouthearted hug. Once in her mother's lap she rested content all the way home, sucking her thumb, stroking her nose with the forefinger of the same hand and kneading a corner of her blanket with the three fingers that were left.

"How did it go?" asked Clarence.

"It went," said Imani.

There was no way to explain abortion to a man. She thought castration might be an apt analogy, but most men, perhaps all, would insist this could not possibly be true.

"The anesthesia failed," she said. "I thought I would never faint in time to keep from screaming and leaping right off the table."

Clarence paled. He hated the thought of pain, any kind of violence. He could not endure it; it made him physically ill. This was one of the reasons he was a pacifist, another reason she admired him.

She knew he wanted her to stop talking. But she continued in a flat, deliberate voice.

"All the blood seemed to run out of me. The tendons in my legs felt cut. I was gray."

He reached for her hand. Held it. Squeezed.

"But," she said, "at least I know what I don't want. And I intend never to go through any of this again."

They were in the living room of their peaceful, quiet and colorful house. Imani was in her rocker, Clarice dozing on her lap. Clarence sank to the floor and held both of them in his arms. She felt he was asking for nurturance when she needed it herself. She felt the two of them, Clarence and Clarice, clinging to her, using her. And that the only way she could claim herself, feel herself distinct from them, was by doing something painful, self-defining but self-destructive.

She suffered his arms and his head against her knees as long as she could.

"Have a vasectomy," she said, "or stay in the guest room. Nothing is going to touch me anymore that isn't harmless."

He smoothed her thick hair with his hand. "We'll talk about it," he said, as if that was not what they were doing. "We'll see. Don't worry. We'll take care of things."

She had forgotten that the third Sunday in June, the following day, was the fifth memorial observance for Holly Monroe, who had been shot down on her way home from her high school graduation ceremony five years before. Imani *always* went to these memorials. She liked the reassurance that her people had long memories and that those people who fell in struggle or innocence were not forgotten. She was, of course, too weak to go. She was dizzy and still losing blood. The white lawgivers attempted to get around assassination—which Imani considered extreme abortion—by saying the victim provoked it (there had been some difficulty saying this about Holly Monroe, but they had tried), but they were antiabortionist to a man. Imani thought of all this as she resolutely showered and washed her hair.

Clarence had installed central air conditioning their second year in the house. Imani had at first objected. "I want to smell the trees, the flowers, the natural air!" she had cried. But the first summer of 110-degree heat had cured her of giving a damn about any of that. Now she wanted to be cool. As much as she loved trees, on a hot day she would have sawed through a forest to get to an air conditioner.

In fairness to him, he asked her if she thought she was well enough to go. But even to be asked annoyed her. She was not one to let her own troubles prevent her from showing proper respect and remembrance toward the dead, although she understood perfectly well that once dead, the dead do not exist. So respect, remembrance, was for herself, and today herself needed rest. There was something mad about her refusal to rest, and she felt it as she tottered about getting Clarice dressed. But she did not stop. She ran a bath, plopped the child in it, scrubbed her plump body while on her knees, arms straining over the tub awkwardly in a way that made her stomach hurt—but not yet her uterus—dried her hair, lifted her out and dried the rest of her on the kitchen table.

"You are going to remember as long as you live what kind of people they are," she said to the child, who, gurgling and cooing, looked into her mother's stern face with lighthearted fixation.

"You are going to hear the music," Imani said. "The music they've tried to kill. The music they try to steal." She felt feverish and was aware she was muttering. She didn't care.

"They think they can kill a continent—people, trees, buffalo —and then fly off to the moon and just forget about it. But you and me, we're going to remember the people, the trees and the fucking buffalo. Goddammit."

"Buffwoe," said the child, hitting at her mother's face with a spoon.

She placed the baby on a blanket in the living room and turned to see her husband's eyes, full of pity, on her. She wore pert green velvet slippers and a lovely sea-green robe. Her body was bent within it. A reluctant tear formed beneath his gaze.

"Sometimes I look at you and I wonder, *What is this man doing in my house?*"

This had started as a joke between them. Her aim had been

never to marry, but to take in lovers who could be sent home at dawn, freeing her to work and ramble.

"I'm here because you love me" was the traditional answer. But Clarence faltered, meeting her eyes, and Imani turned away.

It was a hundred degrees by ten o'clock. By eleven, when the memorial service began, it would be ten degrees hotter. Imani staggered from the heat. When she sat in the car she had to clench her teeth against the dizziness until the motor prodded the air conditioning to envelop them in coolness. A dull ache started in her uterus.

The church was not, of course, air-conditioned. It was authentic Primitive Baptist in every sense.

Like the four previous memorials, this one was designed by Holly Monroe's classmates: All twenty-five of whom—fat and thin—managed to look like the dead girl. Imani had never seen Holly Monroe, though there were always photographs of her dominating the pulpit of this church where she had been baptized and where she had sung in the choir—and to Imani, every black girl of a certain vulnerable age *was* Holly Monroe. And an even deeper truth was that Holly Monroe was herself. Herself shot down, aborted on the eve of becoming herself.

She was prepared to cry and to do so with abandon. But she did not. She clenched her teeth against the steadily increasing pain and her tears were instantly blotted by the heat.

Mayor Carswell had been waiting for Clarence in the vestibule of the church, mopping his plumply jowled face with a voluminous handkerchief and holding court among half a dozen young men and women who listened to him with awe. Imani exchanged greetings with the mayor, he ritualistically kissed her on the cheek, and kissed Clarice on the cheek, but his rather heat-glazed eye was already fastened on her husband. The two men huddled in a corner away from the awed young group. Away from Imani and Clarice, who passed hesitantly, waiting to be joined or to be called back, into the church.

There was a quarter hour's worth of music.

"Holly Monroe was five feet, three inches tall and weighed one hundred and eleven pounds," her best friend said, not reading from notes but talking to each person in the audience. "She was a stubborn, loyal Aries, the best kind of friend to have. She had

black kinky hair that she experimented with a lot. She was exactly
the color of this oak church pew in the summer; in the winter
she was the color [pointing up] of this heart-pine ceiling. She
loved green. She did not like lavender because she said she also
didn't like pink. She had brown eyes and wore glasses, except
when she was meeting someone for the first time. She had a sort
of rounded nose. She had beautiful large teeth, but her lips were
always chapped, so she didn't smile as much as she might have
if she'd ever gotten used to carrying chapstick. She had elegant
feet.

"Her favorite church song was 'Leaning on the Everlasting
Arms.' Her favorite other kind of song was 'I Can't Help
Myself—I Love You and Nobody Else.' She was often late for
choir rehearsal though she loved to sing. She made the dress she
wore to her graduation in Home Ec. She *hated* Home Ec . . ."

Imani was aware that the sound of low, murmurous voices had
been the background for this statement all along. Everything was
quiet around her; even Clarice sat up straight, absorbed by the
simple friendliness of the young woman's voice. All of Holly
Monroe's classmates and friends in the choir wore vivid green.
Imani imagined Clarice entranced by the brilliant, swaying color
as by a field of swaying corn.

Lifting the child, her uterus burning and perspiration already
a stream down her back, Imani tiptoed to the door. Clarence and
the mayor were still deep in conversation. She heard "Board meeting . . . aldermen . . . city council . . ." She beckoned to Clarence.

"Your voices are carrying!" she hissed.

She meant: *How dare you not come inside?*

They did not. Clarence raised his head, looked at her and
shrugged his shoulders helplessly. Then, turning, with the ab-
stracted air of priests, the two men moved slowly toward the
outer door and into the churchyard, coming to stand some distance from the church beneath a large oak tree. There they remained throughout the service.

Two years later, Clarence was furious with her: What is the matter
with you, he asked. You never want me to touch you. You told
me to sleep in the guest room and I did. You told me to have a
vasectomy I didn't want and I *did*. (Here, there was a sob of
hatred for her somewhere in the anger, the humiliation: he
thought of himself as a eunuch and blamed her.)

She was not merely frigid, she was remote.

She had been amazed after they left the church that the anger she had felt watching Clarence and the mayor turn away from the Holly Monroe memorial did not prevent her accepting a ride home with him. A month later it did not prevent her smiling on him fondly. Did not prevent a trip to Bermuda, a few blissful days of very good sex on a deserted beach screened by trees. Did not prevent her listening to his mother's stories of Clarence's youth as though she would treasure them forever.

And yet. From that moment in the heat at the church door, she had uncoupled herself from him, in a separation that made him, except occasionally, little more than a stranger.

And he had not felt it, had not known.

"What have I done?" he asked, all the tenderness in his voice breaking over her. She smiled a nervous smile at him, which he interpreted as derision—so far apart had they drifted.

They had discussed the episode at the church many times. Mayor Carswell—whom they never saw anymore—was now a model mayor, with wide biracial support in his campaign for the legislature. Neither could easily recall him, though television frequently brought him into the house.

"It was so important that I help the mayor!" said Clarence. "He was our *first!*"

Imani understood this perfectly well, but it sounded humorous to her. When she smiled, he was offended.

She had known the moment she left the marriage, the exact second. But apparently that moment had left no perceptible mark.

They argued, she smiled, they scowled, blamed and cried—as she packed.

Each of them almost recalled out loud that about this time of this year their aborted child would have been a troublesome, "terrible" two-year-old, a great burden on its mother, whose health was by now excellent; each wanted to think aloud that the marriage would have deteriorated anyway, because of that.

THANK YOU, MUSIC

·❦·

Vladimir Sokolov

Thank you, music, whatever betides,
for not abandoning me someplace,
for not covering your face,
for never running off to hide.

Thank you, music, whatever betides,
for being a marvel that's unique,
for being a soul and not a freak,
for never choosing sides.

Thank you, music, whatever betides,
for not letting smarties fake what's true;
and thanks that no one in the whole wide
world knows what to do with you.

TRANSLATED BY F. D. REEVE

·2·

Georgy Semyonov

"We've nothing but warriors in our family," the young woman said, looking up saucily. "My grandfather's an officer, my father's an officer, and so's my brother. All three! Thank goodness my husband's not. But he's so completely civilian he's the direct opposite of all the other men in my family. They can't understand him and don't like him, because he's like he is. He's an artist.

"You can't imagine how wonderful oil paints smell, especially outdoors, on a hot summer day, in a clearing in the woods, with flowers all around. He'll open up his paintbox, and the smell suddenly strikes you. I can't even describe the feeling. There are wildflowers all around, and bees buzzing, and there he is, squeezing the paints out of the tubes and onto his palette. You can't compare any other odor to the smell of those paints. There's nothing as exciting as that smell. Our room at home is permeated with it. He's been promised a studio, but so far—you know how hard it is . . . He's a landscape painter," she said and smiled wrily. "He paints things like aspens, or little streams meandering through alder groves. He loves alder trees. They're so inconspicuous, but he loves them and says, just imagine, that it's a challenge to get the shading right, so's it won't look muddy, so's the colors will all be true. Well, need I say what that brings in? Whoever made money painting alders? If not for my salary, we'd never make ends meet," she said in the same surprised and happy voice and laughed. "He's been promised a one-man show for ages, but nothing's ever come of it.

"You know, he's a very talented and sensitive artist. I'm good at determining such things. Honest, I'm never mistaken. He understands it all, too. But still and all, it's a shame when things never turn out as you want them to. I guess it's a lack of intellect." She laughed again. "I mean, you could never call him stupid, but in the sense I mean, he lacks intellect. As he says, that's an instrument given to man to help him achieve material wealth. That's the sense I meant it in. It comes from the Latin: 'to choose between.' For instance, between a lambskin coat and a car. I think they probably cost about the same now. They're both status symbols.

"My husband says that one's soul is the true essence of any person. It's not only his essence but, one may say, his divine essence. Understand? One's intellect can be honed to a fine point, to be adapted in the best possible way to achieve all the bounties of life, to take all that can be taken from it. But my husband says that the soul has other needs. He's a philosopher. I mean, if the intellect acquires, the soul distributes all that is best in a person, all his best qualities: kindness, love, sympathy, compassion—all a person has. His soul distributes it all to others. Common sense would say he stands to lose all he has in this way. But actually, he acquires all the wealth of the world. Understand? It's difficult to understand, but it's so. I came to understand this once, and ever since I've known that there's not a happier person in the world than my husband. That's the kind of philosopher he is. And he'll never change."

Maria Khutorkova sized me up, as though trying to decide what I was capable of. She did it with such a trusting smile and as frankly as only women can who have grown up in the society of men, or, rather, those in whose families all the men are warriors.

When she spoke of her husband, one could not but envy the man who ought to have been happy, if for nothing else than because he was loved by such a charming woman, one who possessed the rare quality of being able to be frankly happy in the presence of others with her strange and mysterious joy, a joy that filled her heart to overflowing and one which she seemed ready to share with one and all.

However, she did not forget to poke fun at her husband and his failings, and her own as well, charming everyone by her sincerity and intelligence, which seemed to displease her and which she tried to hide behind her laughing gray eyes, just as she tried to demean and ridicule the frank story of her life.

We met by chance at a conference. We were all very interested and pleased to be going to the conference, to be held in the capital of one of the Central Asian republics. We were leaving behind the cold and snow of the north at a time when very few of us had expected to find ourselves in a bright, sunny clime in December, when even a suit jacket felt too heavy. We found it difficult to comprehend that we had been transported into Eden, where roses were in bloom in flowerbeds along the city streets, where the heavy streams of the fountains shot up into the blue sky in white foaming plumes, where bees buzzed in the marketplace rows that were piled high with melons, dusky grapes, apples, pears, and all sorts of sun-dried fruit, to say nothing of the bright rows of flowers or the dark-green piles of shiny watermelons set out on the dirty pavement. One half of a cracked watermelon had become an undulating mass of brown-black bees. They scared off prospective buyers, whom the vendor tried to soothe by saying that the bees were drunk on watermelon and were incapable of stinging anyone.

We were all in the same state of drunkenness. We felt that we loved each other and everyone else who walked the streets of this warm city. We felt ecstatic for having outwitted nature herself, and each rejoiced in his own way, never ceasing to wonder, and yet knowing that we would never get enough of drinking this weird December in, the likes of which none of us had ever experienced, nor would we ever be likely to experience again. This thought was constantly at the backs of our minds. It made us feel sad at the fleeting nature of the life we had outwitted and at the transience of all things.

This nervous excitement, the pairing of two incompatibles— joy and sadness—influenced our relationships. We felt that we could not live without each other, that we should be unable to endure the burden of these startling impressions by ourselves.

A bus took us from the airport to a strange barracks-like house in the suburbs. We would never have guessed what the building had been intended for originally if not for the following. The U-shaped building was set at the edge of a large apple orchard. Huge plane trees rose high into the sky above the house. The boughs still bore their dry rusty-brown leaves. The heavy trunks seemed like granite pillars that supported the fragile light-blue plastered walls. The roof and the ground about were covered with a layer of curled brown leaves which rustled underfoot, breaking the watchful silence. It seemed as though someone lived down there among the piled-up leaves, as though that someone were crawling around or scurrying away before we took notice of him. Whenever an invisible stream of air wafted over the ground, or whenever another leaf fell from a plane tree, the earth would respond with a rustle. However, we often caught sight of the mice that actually did live in the orchard, now bare and gnarled, under the roots of the lead-gray trees, and we heard them rustling in the leaves.

We were quartered regally: each was given a room furnished

with three cots, one table, two chairs and a wardrobe. The bare walls had been sloppily painted the same cold light-blue hue as the outside of the house.

When I decided to see if the ceiling light worked, I found, to my utter surprise, that there was no switch. Looking through the screened window, I could see the sunny day outside, but inside the room was gloomy, as though the ceiling were hung with gray cobwebs. I found two little holes of a painted-over wall socket near the window, but there was no light switch in the room.

It was impossible. Could they have hung up a ceiling light and forgotten the switch? Incredible. But what was the answer to the riddle?

Our host, who had met us at the airport, list in hand, and who had then settled us in the strange house which now smelled of tangy sauce and fried meatballs, had vanished, having shaken our hands warmly and promised to call for us in a bus at nine sharp the next morning. Whom could I complain to? And what was the use of three beds if I couldn't even turn on the light?

"What the hell!" I muttered as I opened the door and went out into the corridor. "Where the hell's the light switch?"

The door opposite opened. There was light in the room! I caught sight of the woman who had been sitting opposite me in the bus, staring out of the window with the same look of wonder that she now bestowed on me, as though I, too, were another sight of Central Asia.

"How'd you manage it?" I said, indicating the ceiling light in her room. "I don't even have a wall switch."

She extended her hand and flicked the switch outside her door. The light in her room went out. She flicked it again, and the light went on. "This is a children's summer camp. When it's time for 'lights out,' the counselor walks down the hall, turning the lights off in all the rooms. Understand? So's the kids go to sleep. It doesn't really matter, does it?" she added and looked at me with such a friendly smile that I readily agreed with her.

The dining hall in which we had our meals was downstairs. It was a very convenient arrangement. Our living as a group in a children's summer camp, within easy reach of the city, drew us together, as though we had for a time become children ourselves, with one significant distinction: there was no counselor to walk down the hall, switching off the lights.

Actually, none of us felt like sleeping at night. We would get together in the evenings, laugh and joke, and drink wine, now in one room, now in another, sitting in rows on the bare, squeaky spring beds, making merry till midnight, then drinking green tea in the women's rooms in this "loony house," as we had named the building. At night we walked in the stillness of the dead orchard, listening to the water gurgling in the irrigation ditch and finally dispersing to our rooms in the small hours. The one great inconvenience of our living here was the choice we had of either getting undressed in the dark or darting out into the hall to switch off the light. But this, too, was a source of merriment.

"Do you know," Maria said, scraping her feet along through the rustling leaves, "I practically made my husband marry me. He's a very shy man. 'Be sure to come, Slavik,' " she said, mimicking a telephone conversation she must've had long ago. Her voice took on a singsong, plaintive quality. " 'What d'you mean, you can't come? You've got to. I won't take no for an answer. I'll be expecting you. Hear me? I'm expecting you.' " She laughed as she concluded the little skit and then continued, "I'd hang up, and he'd come over, feeling so embarrassed he'd be all on edge. He thought I was making fun of him, and he didn't want to be made a fool of. If I took his arm, he'd look at me as though I were about to bite him. If you want to know, I kissed him first. He'd never have gotten up the courage to kiss me."

She took my arm when we reached the far end of the dark orchard. It seemed that if a mouse's eyes were to glitter now, they would somehow dispel the velvety blackness that made us feel as though we were blind. She was afraid of the dark and pressed close to me. But, strangely, I understood, I sensed that it was only fear that made her press close to my arm and not at all that which I unwittingly imagined as I felt her breast and thigh brush against me.

The sky was studded with stars, huge and bright, small and tiny, swirled together in the sweep of the Milky Way to form a swath across the sky. But most amazing of all, we could clearly discern those stars that were closest to us, those that were farther away, and those that were shining down from unfathomed space. The sky had never seemed so three-dimensional to me. How strange that the bright glitter of the stars did not reach the earth, which seemed plunged in soot. We felt our way along the path, with only the hard ground underfoot to tell us we had not wandered from it.

Maria was afraid of the silence and spoke loudly and rapidly:

"You've such a muscular arm. My husband's are so thin his sleeves seem to flap. But you know, strange as it may seem, he's very strong." She was speaking excitedly, and I detected an anxious note in her voice. "He's the sinewy kind, and they're always strong. Even though they sometimes look like weaklings. D'you know, he can cover forty kilometers on foot in a single day, pick a basketful of mushrooms on the way, lug it ten kilometers back to the station and then, when he finally gets home, he'll sit down to sort and clean the mushrooms. You can't imagine how much that full basket weighs. I could never even lift it."

I mumbled something about having to lose some weight and so on, and she agreed.

"Yes, perhaps," she said with feeling, "but I'm not one to judge. You know!" she exclaimed and then suddenly fell silent, as though at a loss for words. The only sound was that of the rustling leaves she was purposely scuffing up, so as not to hear the scampering mouse-sounds that frightened her.

"No, I don't know. I don't know a thing. All I know is that I've never seen a night like this before, especially in December, and I'll never see another like it."

"What I wanted to say was that I understand it all now. I think I do, though maybe I'm just imagining it. But I suddenly feel that I know why Asia is known for its ancient philosophers and star-gazers. If I'd been born here, under a sky that's never clouded, or hardly ever clouded, I think I'd have been a very different kind of person. I think I'd have looked upon others differently and formed different opinions of them. D'you think we'll ever come to the end of this orchard?" she said with a twinkle in her voice as she suddenly stopped short. "We've come so far. Can you see anything? I can't. Maybe the orchard's someplace far behind by now?"

By the time we returned, the door was locked. We had to knock long and hard until we finally awakened the cross old woman caretaker. We felt guilty and did not even try to make any excuses, but waited in silence as she grumbled and unlocked the door. Maria slipped by her into the dark corridor, averting her face from the old woman, and was immediately swallowed up by the creaking stuffiness of the house.

Everything in the bone-dry building squeaked and creaked: the doors, beds, chairs, tables, window frames and wardrobes, but nothing could match the shattering sound of the corridor floorboards. It seemed that each board had been laid down in such a way as to produce the loudest possible sound, so that anyone who dared pass at an untimely hour would be discovered by the caretaker. This time Maria and I were the culprits. I was surprised to see how childishly frightened she was at the sight of the bent old woman in the white smock who opened the door to us.

"You know," Maria said in an undertone, and I discerned the awe in her voice as we headed back to the house and the distant light of the sole lamppost, "my husband's grandfather is still alive. He's ninety-four years old, but his mind's as clear as ever. And he gets about, and even comes to visit us sometimes, to play with his great-granddaughters. He has four: our three girls and my sister-in-law's girl. My youngest is terribly scared of him. He doesn't like to wear his dentures. He keeps chewing his gums all the time, and his face keeps crinkling up like a sponge. His chin rises up to his nose, and his nose keeps bobbing up and down. We think we have a big family, but Grandpa sniffs and says that's nothing, that he was one of ten children. He says that his neighbor only had five, and his father used to say that with only five mouths to feed, their neighbor was in clover. Grandpa always gets angry if we complain. I don't mean really complaining, it's just that we're concerned.

"Now you take our room, for instance. It's an old house, and there's no hot water or bath, but the room is huge. It's forty-six square meters. There are two windows, and there's the balcony door besides. It doesn't sound bad, with over nine meters per person, which is the sanitary norm. And that means we've no hope of ever being put in line for an apartment. And we'll never have the money for a condominium. But there are windows and doors on every wall, which makes it very hard to place the furniture conveniently. Then again, my husband has so many paintings and frames. There are paintings on every wall. There are paintings on the wardrobe and behind the wardrobe, and even under the couch. Then there's his easel and paintboxes and brushes. I've ended up sharing our tremendous couch with my daughters, and my husband sleeps on a folding cot in the middle of the room. It's a weird life." Maria laughed uncertainly, as though mistrusting her own words.

The lamppost, which seemed to exist in the night of its own accord and not for us, picked out the trees in the darkness, charting their branches vaguely, and the bumpy, leaf-covered path that seemed darkly pitted with bottomless holes. Maria drew away from me. She was no longer afraid, though she still scuffed up the leaves at every step.

"Here I am, chattering away," she said with a guilty smile, "and you haven't even said a word in all this time. I guess it's because I'm nervous. I put my name down on the speakers' list. I don't know whether I'll be given a chance to speak or not, but I'm awfully scared. I don't have any experience at all in public speaking. It's awful!

"My husband talked me into coming here. He said it would do me good to get away from the house for a while, and that I could tell him all about Central Asia when I got back. He's right. I'd never have had a chance to come here on my own. If only he were here now!" Maria exclaimed and laughed. "The colors are so brilliant. There's so much light! Have you noticed that the leaves have no smell at all? It's so dry here they just crinkle up and rustle. There's no smell of moisture in the air. Isn't it strange? It's not at all like our autumn. If only he—he'd be overwhelmed. You know, I'm sorry for him. I mean, it's a shame that I'm here, and he, an artist, is back home, taking care of the girls, preparing their meals, putting them to bed. D'you know what I mean? It's not fair. It's stupid. And such a shame. I must say, the girls are not wild or cranky. The eldest is nine. She's very independent, and she'll be a big help to him now, but he has to take the younger ones to kindergarten every day, and he has such difficulty getting up early in the morning.

"Our mornings always start the same way: my eldest girl gets up first, dresses and turns on the small lamp. I can hear her in my sleep. Then my middle daughter wakes up. She takes after her father and likes to sleep late. She also gets washed and dressed, and then the two of them begin to waken their dolls. They talk to them, and dress them, and feed them, though they've had no breakfast yet and are hungry. That's why I always wake up with a smile and get up so easily in the morning. But my husband's a sleepyhead. I start each morning with a set of awful exercises. They're torture. You said you have to lose weight, but do you know you can exercise in bed? I do all kind of stretching exercises while I'm still in bed. They're so vigorous, I break out in a sweat. When my youngest daughter wakes up, she watches me for a while and then begins swinging her legs up and down, too."

Maria laughed infectiously, and the sound of her laughter, the only living sound in this still and fascinating December night, was like a nightingale's trill. The night was so warm that neither of us was at all chilled, though all we had on were sweaters.

Her face seemed strangely beautiful in the dim light of the lamppost. This strong young woman, the mother of three children, had a vague aura of shimmering, inexplicable beauty about her. It was in her movements, her voice, the curves of her body, her gait, her trustful glance and even in the early wrinkles, which were not a sign of grief but seemed like the trace of a vanished smile, like shadows cast by the leaves of a tree on a hot day, that little network of wrinkles at the corners of her eyes which made her face look good-natured and laughing even when it was sad or in repose.

The old woman's practiced ear evidently told her that we had gone to our different rooms. I lay there in the darkness, on a creaking bed that was too short for me, and the knowledge that I could not stretch out my hand and turn on the light was depressing. As insomnia claimed me, I thanked my lucky stars that never again would I have to experience that terrible, unjust time called childhood which, for some reason or other, is believed to be the happiest time of one's life. The awakened child in me raged and ranted against the bent old woman and the darkness that were watching over me. The cross old hag could hear my every sigh, and it would be imprinted on her mind. I cursed the villain who had invented those outside switches and tried to calm my nerves by telling myself that this was just temporary and, like my childhood, would soon end.

I tried to think of the following day and the conference, but a blunt force kept returning me to my foolish situation, to my walk across the dark orchard and my patient silence, which had apparently been conducive to frankness and which now embarrassed me, as if, like the cross old woman, I had been eavesdropping, as if I had glimpsed a bit of Maria's life through a keyhole. My imagination conjured up a scene in which Maria lay with her arms spread wide amidst her sleeping daughters. I could see the happy maternal smile on her face as she awakened to the chirping of her little girls at play and tried to imagine the movements of her lithe body.

I could not understand myself.

I could not wait for morning, when I would once again see this woman who could not help speaking with such sincere awe of her husband, as though that mediocre artist were a first-class painter, and every mortal being had to know the story of his life.

In my mind's eye I could once again hear her surprised and taunting voice:

"Here I am chattering away. I guess it's because I'm nervous. I'm nearly positive I won't get to speak. I'm too far down on the list, and there's just one day left. Actually, only half a day, till noon. There'll just be the concluding remarks by the principal speaker in the afternoon, and that's it. There simply won't be time for me. But you know what's so strange? On the one hand, I'm glad I won't have to speak, but on the other, I feel disappointed. Isn't that just human nature?"

"D'you believe in God?" she suddenly asked as we approached the gurgling irrigation ditch. The light cast by the lamppost fell in a yellow beam on the slick oily-black water, picking out patches of undulating quicksilver and tinting them bronze, the whole gleaming dull at our feet. There was a rustling in the grass. Something plopped into the water with a splash. It was probably a water rat.

Maria gasped and clutched my hand. "What's that?" she said, having forgotten all about God. "What d'you think it was?" Black spots glided across the flickering bronze of the water. It seemed as though the rats were bathing, diving and reappearing, their little black muzzles cutting through the surface, sending circles out across the water.

"You know, my husband has two strange paintings," Maria said when we had come to the cool bench that was sunk into the ground under one of the stone-like trunks and sat down. "One of them is of a three-ruble bill stuck onto a blade of sedge. The sedge is a gray-brown, as it is in autumn, and you can see a bit of gray water among the leaves. The bill is crisp and new, and green, and just slightly creased. It's a strange painting. The bill looks like it's a photograph of a real three-ruble bill. The second painting is of some cloudy, soapy water. All you can see are two cupped hands in the cloudy water and some huge pike perch swimming towards them. Understand?

"They seem so weird, but he swears both paintings are taken from life. He was out rabbit-hunting with his friends one day when he was a boy. When they came upon a clump of bushes in the middle of a field, he headed for it. There was a little marshy ground there among the bushes. There weren't any rabbits, but he flushed a double-snipe out of the bushes. My husband said the season for snipe had ended and that they'd all long since flown South. This one was probably wounded or sick and so had remained. My husband fired and missed. The snipe flew over the sedge and disappeared in the bushes. He followed and flushed it out again, and fired, and missed again. This was repeated about six times, but never once did the snipe fly away. When my husband finally went over to where the bird had landed to flush it out again, he saw it was gone, though he'd noted the exact spot where it had landed. All of a sudden he saw that three-ruble bill." Maria's soft voice took on a note of surprise. "When he picked it up, he saw that it was brand new. It wasn't even wet, though it was drizzling. It was lying there on the sharp sedge blades as if someone had just laid it down. He put the money in his pocket and was so happy at his find that he forgot all about the snipe. It was as though it had never existed. Don't you see how weird it was? Naturally, none of his friends believed him when he told them about it. But I believed him. He's incapable of lying.

"The second incident was even stranger. My husband was fishing from a rowboat on a big lake, but hadn't caught anything worth mentioning. It was a murky day, and the fish had stopped biting. He rowed back to the shore, got out a cake of toilet soap and leaned over the side to wash his hands. All of a sudden, there were the pike perch. They were huge and bronze, and prickly, and their bellies were snow-white. First one swam up from the bottom like it was drunk and began gulping the soapy water. It swam right up to my husband's hand and began rubbing against it like a cat, first on one side, then on the other. It even turned upside down, so that its pointed spur stuck up out of the water. Can you imagine that? My husband was astounded. He picked one fish out of the water and dumped it into the boat. Meanwhile, another was swimming right into his hands. He caught six of them in all like that, but then he let them go, because he got scared. He thought the fish might be sick or something. You never can tell.

"When he got home, the first thing I noticed was that he'd lost a lot of weight. His eyes were sunken. He seemed crazy. When he told me what had happened, I couldn't really believe him. 'What d'you think I am, crazy?' he shouted. And I began to believe him. He told his friends about it, every last detail. Naturally, they didn't believe him, either. But he tried to prove it so persistently that it was impossible not to believe him. He even described the incident in a letter he sent to an ichthyological institute, but he never got a reply. Nobody would believe him. Nobody except me. Now, just a short while ago, people finally began to believe him, but this was in connection with something else entirely. If you want my opinion, it's all very mysterious.

"I can't understand it. You know, everything's topsy-turvy. We're even sorry we told anybody about it, because now they keep after us to tell them all about it. They want to know all the details, and they're astounded. And you know what's so strange? They believe us! Though I must tell you those two incidents, I mean the fishes and the three-ruble bill, can be easily explained. They're not half as strange as the amazing story I'll tell you now. But nobody believes those two incidents ever occurred. They don't believe things that can very well be true and real. You take the incident of the fishes, for example. Nobody who ever heard about it could help smiling. I'm sure you've washed your hands in the shallows near a riverbank at one time or another in your life. D'you remember how many small fry used to come streaking towards the soapy trails of water? Perhaps at some period of their lives, at some special hour, in some specific kind of weather, the big fishes might also come swimming up, drawn by the scent of the perfumed toilet soap? Why should this be so improbable?" Maria laughed nervously. She looked at me keenly, to see whether I believed her or not, and whether or not I was listening to what she was saying with a condescending smile or with genuine interest.

"That's just it!" she said, having apparently become convinced that I agreed with her and was sincere.

"You know, I'm beginning to think that people are usually mistaken about their own mental capacity: the more improbable a story or an event, the more acceptable it seems to be. Then again, if you tell them of some amazing thing, some little wonder that's occurred in your everyday life and that can only be viewed with awe, why, they think it's impossible, a play of fancy, some foolishness, or the result of being high-strung. Why is this so?

"My eldest girl started talking at an early age. One day, when she was looking out the window, she noticed the lampposts on the street and said: 'What do people have down there?' Imagine putting it that way: What do people have down there? As though she were one of the gods, a genius, no less, a being who casts

light instead of a shadow. I remember telling her that what people
had down there was a great miracle called electricity. But now
we're spoiled. Nothing short of a galactic wonder can stir our
imaginations.

"It's all so strange and unpleasant," she said and smiled shyly
to conceal the uneasiness she felt. It obviously irked her, as a
mother would be irked by a rambunctious child. "But of course,
if you reason along the '2F' system—d'you know it?" she said
and added with unexpected and deliberate coarseness: 'A finger
up your nose and your feet on the table!—then, naturally, everything can be viewed with doubt. For example, if I were to suddenly
have a terrible urge to become religious, I'd be unable to do so.
You know why? Because the concept of God does not have the
slightest hint of a smile or a game. Understand?

"All my conjectures are also built on the '2F' system. But
still— The very idea is inhuman. My husband's not religious, but
he's a Utopian by nature. He believes in the miracle of healing
through art and the imagination. Understand?" Maria repeated,
and her trilling laughter could again be heard above the dark
water. "I told you he lacks intellect. He's become rather strange
of late. Say, he'll be painting for a while. Then he'll have something
to eat and he'll go out and stand stock-still on the balcony for
an hour or two, gazing off into space. I'll say, 'Come on, let's go
for a walk.' And he'll snap: 'I'm tired. Don't I even have a right
to relax?'

"I've even begun to worry about him. His play of fancy's to
blame for it all. He's too serious, too—I don't even know how
to put it. Everything in his life is superlative. Yes, that's the word
I want: superlative. Actually, though, it's not as simple as all that.

"One night, after I'd fallen asleep, I suddenly heard strange
creatures conversing in the room, or just outside the door. At any
rate, it was someplace close by. I could understand their language,
though I couldn't grasp what they were. This is what I overheard:
'Don't worry, we won't wake anyone up. We'll just pass through
the wall.' Then the other one—there were two of them—agreed
and said that's what they'd do. I felt so anxious. On the one hand,
I seemed to be asleep, yet I realized this was not a dream at all,
but something quite different. I knew there were outsiders in the
room with us, but I couldn't wake up or move an arm or a leg,
or call for help. I don't know how long I remained in this state.
All of a sudden I saw that the light was on and my husband was

leaning over me, looking at me with a mingled expression of fear and guilt, as though he were about to beg my forgiveness for something.

" 'What is it?' I said, and he replied: 'You know, I don't know whether I dreamed it all or not, but I was just talking to somebody. Somebody was just here in the room.' And he handed me a sheet of paper, saying: 'Here. Here's the formula.' And he had this sheepish grin on his face. I nearly died of fright," Maria whispered, and I sensed that she had recounted the tale before, this story of the little night visitors who gave off electricity so that a constant crackling sound accompanied them.

She spoke in such a mysterious tone of voice that I felt she was determined to scare me with a story in which one element alone was truly mysterious.

Her husband had written down a senseless formula of a type of energy unknown to man, but which the mysterious visitors had given him. Having no knowledge at all of modern physics and never having studied the subject, he had managed to commit to paper a number of symbols used by nuclear physicists. The symbols seemed to have been drawn by the unpracticed hand of an artist, rather than written, as though they had been copied out in haste and from memory. Here was the riddle: This man, who, as Maria had laughingly said, was short on intellect, had indeed never had any brushes with science after the age of fourteen, when he had transferred to an applied arts school, from which he had gone on to a fine arts institute where science was never even mentioned.

Maria succeeded, for a mystical chill crept into my heart and spurred my imagination. Needless to say, our surroundings played no small part in this: the gurgling black water of the irrigation ditch reflecting the yellow light of the lamppost; the plane tree above us like some petrified sentinel, with leaves falling now and then in the dead silence, their rustling startling us anew each time. This rustling was born somewhere high up among the stars, in the cosmic nebulae, and gained force as each curled leaf fell earthward, hitting against the branches or other dying leaves until it finally settled with a little crunch onto the dry leaves on the ground. A shiver ran down my spine at each little crunch, though I knew it was only a dry leaf falling, and not the mysterious creatures from outer space Maria was speaking about. She, too, seemed to be experiencing something akin to this, for she smiled, glanced at me quizzically and continued her story in an undertone, her voice echoing the excitement she felt.

If someone were watching us, he might've decided that Maria was either saying she loved me or else rebuking me, for she spoke so sincerely and her tone of voice was so intimate. Her surprised and frightened eyes were so close to my face as she seemed to be silently saying: "Do you believe me? Do you understand?" And so close to despair at the very thought that I did not believe her and did not understand.

However, I nodded as I listened. I could not control my trembling limbs. This trembling was not caused by her eerie tale. No, she was simply standing too close to me, this other—heavenly being, as she seemed to me, who had visited me on this warm and starry Asiatic night in December. I don't know what was more unbelievable: her story or our combined efforts to understand the incomprehensible, something neither of us could approach in the familiar way. We both sensed this and were perhaps instinctively searching for a roundabout way: she by speaking of her husband, and I by listening attentively. In this strange way we tried to approach each other.

"You know, it really is strange," she continued in the same mysterious and passionate tone. "He never liked physics and never studied the subject, not even enough to know the symbols. And he certainly had never written them down before. Why, he didn't even know they existed! Understand? No doubt about it."

Her pliant voice dropped to a near-whisper, yet I could hear her distinctly, for her face was very close to mine. "Honestly, I haven't made up a word of this. We both had the same dream, and the result was that strange formula. I really regret that it happened to us." Her cold fingers touched my hand as a sign of complete confidence. "The reason I'm telling you this is to rid myself of this feeling of banal mystery.

"I keep waiting for someone to laugh at my story, but nobody does. In fact, some have even suggested that I show the formula to a mathematician or physicist. They think it must've been some other civilization trying to establish contact with my husband." Maria laughed again as she looked up at the stars with mock entreaty. "Lord, how gullible some people are. Even if they were trying to establish contact, they came knocking at the wrong door. But my silly fool is certain of it, and now he keeps going out to the balcony whenever he takes a break. He really has a bee in his bonnet. Try to imagine a grown-up man standing out there on the balcony, staring up at the stars. It's a joke. In fact, it's so funny that I've begun to wonder whether it didn't really happen after all.

"It's most unpleasant when so many people tell you it's so. Actually, it's not so much what they say as that they themselves believe it all. You find yourself caught up in this general hypnotic trance and also begin to believe in the impossible. I don't even know whether, if somebody ever comes along who will doubt all this, whether I won't begin trying to convince him. It's bigger than I am, because I can't explain it: how could we both have had the same dream? And where did he get those symbols from? It makes me uneasy, but there's nothing I can do about it. That's what's so awful.

"There are so many simple wonders all around us, so much joy in life, like this December night, and the two of us here together, complete strangers, actually, and this black water. Isn't it all a wonder? And you know what's so terrible? It's when a person gets used to all this and stops noticing anything. You know, I have to keep telling myself that our everyday life—even our breathing, our ability to see—is also one of the greatest of wonders!

"Before, I simply used to live. I was simply happy. I simply had my children, admiring each of my little girls as the greatest of wonders. But now, oh horrors! My head is aswirl with unknown civilizations and strange formulae.

"And something's happening to my husband. I keep telling myself that our lives are also a joy, that life is passing so quickly, and is so vulnerable, it should be idolized, and that we must cherish every moment of it. I know, someone might say, but what about the struggle? After all, that's life's chief manifestation. Right! I'm all for life's contradictions, I'm all for the struggle, not merely for idolizing and cherishing all things indiscriminately.

"But isn't man himself contradictory? Take two such basics as instinct and conscience. Man is contradictory by nature, and the battle between instinct and conscience rages within him constantly. Isn't this struggle enough? Maybe it isn't. I understand. But that's not what I really mean. I mean life itself, this everyday wonder. Understand?

"But actually, that's not what I mean at all. I'm talking too much," Maria said and smiled sadly. "What if I suddenly have to get up and speak tomorrow?"

I also smiled as I tried to contain my trembling and found myself thinking of the struggle she had just spoken of, for it was raging in my soul, too, and I did not know which would conquer: instinct or conscience.

Circumstances conquered: the old hag with the flour-white ears, the creaking floorboards and the outside light switches, the every-day wonders dear Maria had spoken of.

After the conference closed, Maria, who was not given the floor after all, took a night flight to Moscow. She said she was in a hurry to get back home to her family. She apparently missed them very much and was probably feeling guilty, for none of them, and especially her husband, had had a chance to see, and now, unless the occasion arose, would probably never see, Central Asia in December.

I stayed on till the following morning, unable to turn down the invitation to the banquet that was being held for us all, including Maria, who had disdained the bountiful repast in favor of what I considered to be the dubious joy of rejoining her husband and children before any of the other conference participants rejoined their families. She had taken flight so that she might look on with tender tears as her three little girls sank their teeth into the fragrant melon slices and wiped the pear juice running down their wet chins. And then, stretching out on the huge couch with them, she would tell them a wondrous tale for a bedtime story, a tale of the earthly wonders she had glimpsed in the middle of a frosty, snowbound winter.

She had taken flight to get back to her household chores as quickly as possible: to washing clothes, washing dishes and pre-paring meals. To once again each morning on her way to work pulling her youngest daughter along on her little sled. To holding her middle daughter's little hand, for she took after her daddy and was still half-asleep as they walked towards the kindergarten. And then to rush off to work, hurrying so as not to be late, squeezing into the jam-packed Metro car. Finally, when she was settled at her desk, to spend the day thinking, calculating, drawing, making notations, arguing, protesting, acquiescing and feeling upset and disturbed as she continued, day in, day out, minute after minute, to proceed with her main task in life.

Didn't she want to spend at least one day feeling recklessly carefree? Just one evening, one night, one morning. Wasn't that a lot?

I could neither understand nor condone her flight. In fact, I took it as an insult. The indignant, self-confident male in me was fuming, for a pretty woman had preferred a stupid dauber to me. My only consolation was a vague feeling I had that she had taken flight on account of me. She was afraid of what a remote December night in a land which winter had bypassed might hold, a night which had never occurred and now would never occur.

I sat by the window, looking through the rusty screen at the coffee-colored puppy playing in the yard by the kitchen. He was playing in the rustling leaves, now stiffening as he listened to their whispering, now pouncing awkwardly onto a pile. The layer of fallen leaves was so high that the puppy sank into the cracking, rustling heap up to his head and floppy ears. His coat blended with the leaves, making him look like a little wild animal. He was enjoying himself immensely, now stretching out, squirming along on his belly, jumping up with all four paws in the air, shaking himself, suddenly stiffening and then pouncing on the rustling sounds again. At last, tiring of the game, he stretched out and fell asleep, disappearing completely, as though he had never existed, so that the thrush that flew down to the kitchen door did not even notice him.

Maria and I had parted hastily before the banquet. She shook my hand warmly, looked embarrassed and then, for some reason or other, thanked me in a voice heavy with suppressed emotion.

"Thank you. For everything." she said, making me feel uneasy, for I had never expected this strange gratitude. "You know, I'm leaving now. I'm sure it'll be a wonderful banquet, but it's not for me. I'm in a hurry now. I want to get to the bazaar before it closes and buy some fruit. No, no, I don't need any help. You'll only be in my way. I don't want to offend you, I'm just being frank." And she walked off with a guilty smile and then looked back at me tenderly.

I glimpsed her eyes behind someone's back. They were bright even though they seemed a bit sad. She raised her hand and waggled her fingers uncertainly, sending me a last farewell.

As I waited for the bus which was to take us to the banquet, I sat in my dim room, looking out at the golden hues of evening.

Maria was now airborne. Her plane, a tiny silver cross flashing white in the rays of the setting sun, sent the muffled roar of its jets down to the unknown lands over which it flew. Perhaps someone standing there below heard the sound and looked up absently, mindless of the people who were sitting in the seats of the huge plane and certainly knowing nothing of Maria, who was now inside that tiny metal speck in the sky.

I was the only one who knew it. Perhaps she was now looking out through the round window and thinking of me, a tiny dust mote in the purple twilight. Only she knew or could know now of me, an infinitesimal speck on the ground below.

We both seemed to have dematerialized, as regarded each other. We had ceased existing in the habitual dimensions in which we had but recently related to each other.

I could not understand why this had happened, I thought with enmity of the man standing silently on his balcony, knowing full well that today a beautiful woman, one as life-sized as himself, would return home to relieve him of all his cares and let him once again feel that he was the happiest man in the world, a man who despised intellect, that base instrument of profit and material gain, both of which he had relinquished to his solicitous wife.

I was perhaps unjust in my evaluation of a man I did not know, although Maria had told me so much about him. However, I now imagined him to be an irritable grumbler, always on the verge of snapping at everyone, a man who picked fights, a bilious failure, a dreamer and idler whom it was impossible to love.

I hated this lucky man, towards whom a tiny, live dust mote was now speeding, that wonder of wonders, a woman who encompassed such powers of love and such goodness and to whom all the civilizations of the universe would be unable to add even the tiniest bit if they were to suddenly establish contact with us. What formula, what other kind of energy, did this man want?

I could still see the dear woman's face and trusting eyes which seemed forever to be saying: "Do you believe me? Do you understand?"

Perhaps it was the leaves rustling outside my window, or perhaps, in my misery, I imagined the sound of the surf, and women's voices heard through its pounding and resembling the cries of seagulls.

"He's a philosopher, you know. I just have to accept it."

TRANSLATED BY FAINA SOLASKO

THE MAGICIAN'S WIFE

·✲·

Mary Gordon

Unlike most of her friends, Mrs. Hastings did not think of herself first as the mother of her children. She was proudest of being Mr. Hastings' wife. So that in their old age it grieved her to see her husband known in the town as the father of her son, Frederick, the architect, who was not half the man his father was, for beauty, for surprises. Frederick had put up buildings, had had his picture taken with mayors outside city halls, with the governor outside office buildings. She ought to have been proud of Frederick, and of course she was, really, and he was very good to them; they would not be half so well off without him. She valued her son as she valued the food she had cooked, the meals she had produced, very much the same since the day of her marriage.

Her husband had added to his salary by being a magician. Not that he hadn't provided perfectly well for them; still, it was something else that life would have been meaner without, the money he had made on magic. How had it first started? That was one of the arguments she had with his mother. His mother said he had always been that way, putting on magic shows in the barn as a boy. But she knew it hadn't started that way; she remembered the way it had. It was on their honeymoon. They saw a vaudeville show in Chicago, and there was a magician, the amazing Mr. Kazmiro, whose specialty was making birds appear. That night on the way to the hotel, Mrs. Hastings could see her husband brooding over something. When he brooded his eyes would go dull, the color of pebbles, and she could see him rolling the idea from one side of his brain to another as you would roll a candy ball from one side of your mouth to the other if you had a sore tooth. In the morning (it shocked her, how handsome he was in his pajamas) he said, "May, let's go shopping." They went down to the area behind the theater where the shops sold odd things: white makeup in flat little tins, wigs for clowns or prima donnas, gizmos comedians used. It was in one of those stores that he bought his first trick; she remembered it was something with balls and hoops and wooden goblets with false bottoms. She never looked too closely at his tricks—not then, not ever. It had shocked her how much the trick cost, ten dollars, but she had said nothing. It was her honeymoon. She never said anything about the expense except to ask what it was about these things that cost so much money. Her husband said it was a highly skilled business, that each of his tricks was the work of craftsmen. But that was how he got started, she remembered, on the fourth day of their honeymoon. No matter what his mother said, it had nothing to do with his life before he got married, his magic.

Once he had performed for the Roosevelts. It was 1935 and one of the Roosevelt grandchildren was recovering from measles. The boy was crotchety and there was nothing you could do to please him, one of the servants had said, one who had seen Mr. Hastings entertaining at the County Fair in Rhinebeck. It was a wicked night, she remembered. It thundered and flashed lightning so that the lights flickered on and off. When the telephone rang, they thought it was a joke, some lady calling to ask if Mr. Hastings would care to come over to Hyde Park and do a small performance for a sick child. Her husband and children had thought it was a joke, for one minute. Of course her husband would be called to entertain the President, of course the car, the big black car driven by a man in a uniform, would come for him. She remembered how her husband had talked to the chauffeur, as if he had been brought up to order servants about. She remembered what her husband had said, not looking at the man in the uniform, but not looking at his feet either, looking straight ahead of him. She remembered he had said, "Do you mind if I bring my wife?" and the chauffeur had said, "As you wish, sir," and opened the door. That was the gallantry of him, so that she would get to meet Franklin Roosevelt, and Eleanor, who was as plain as she looked in her pictures and had a voice that was an embarrassment; but she was, as Mrs. Hastings said to the people whom she told about it, "very gracious to us, and a real lady."

All the vivid moments of her life had been marked by her husband's magic. Not only the Roosevelts—although how would she ever have met the Roosevelts if she had not married Mr. Hastings?—but the moments that heightened the color of everyone's ordinary life. There was a show for each of her birthdays and anniversaries, for each important day of each child's life. On one occasion Frederick had sulked and said, "It's my party and everyone's paying attention to *him*." And she had told him he should thank his lucky stars not to have a father like everyone else's, dull as dishwater, and that any other boy would give his eyeteeth to have a father who could do magic. And Frederick said—where did he get those eyes, those dull, brown, good boy's eyes, they weren't hers, or his father's—Frederick said, "Not if they really knew about it."

Frederick was not nearly so handsome as his father, particularly when his father was doing magic. Mrs. Hastings remembered the look of him when he was all dressed up, with his hair slicked back and his mustache. He looked distinguished, like William Powell. She knew all the women in the town envied her her husband, for his good looks and his beautiful manners and his exciting ways. Once Mrs. Daly, the milkman's wife, said, "It must be hard on you, him spending all his spare time practicing in the basement." It was well known that Mr. and Mrs. Daly had had separate bedrooms since the birth of their last child. Mrs. Hastings wanted to tell Mrs. Daly about the trick her husband had played on her in bed one night, pulling a pearl from the bodice of her nightgown, putting it in his mouth and bringing out a flower. But that was exactly the kind of detail Mrs. Daly wanted, which Mrs. Hastings had no intention of giving her. So she turned to Mrs. Daly and said in her high-falutin' voice—her husband said, "Okay, Duchess," when she used it on him—"He always shows me everything while he's working on it," which was partly true, although he would never show her anything until he was sure it worked. But it was true enough for someone like Mrs. Daly, who slept in a single bed near the window, true enough to knock her off her high horse.

How could she be lonely up in the kitchen with the knowledge of him below her doing things over and over with scarves and boxes and cards and ribbons. She could imagine the man she loved, alone, away where she could not see him, practicing over and over the tricks that would astound not only her but every person they knew. Why would she prefer conversations at the kitchen table about money or food or what who wore when? She thought it a great and a kingly mercy that he kept his job as a machinist, which he hated, instead of quitting to work full time as a magician, which he sometimes talked about. When he talked about it, a little flame of fear would go up in her, as if someone had lit a match behind one of her ribs. But she would say, "Do whatever you want. I have faith." What she liked really, though, was that during the day he went to his job, like anyone else's husband, but he spent his nights doing magic. He would come up the stairs every night in triumph, and every night he wanted her because, he said, she was the best little wife a man ever had; and every night she wanted him because she could not believe her good fortune, since she was, compared with her husband, she knew, quite ordinary.

And the years had passed as they do for everyone, only for her it was different. Her years were marked not only by the birth and aging and ceremonies of children, but by the growth of her husband's art. After 1946, for example, he gave up the egg and rope tricks and moved into scarves and coins. His retirement was nothing that he feared. He did not go around like other men, taking a week to do a chore that could have been done in an hour. Nor did she go around like other women, saying, "I can't get him out of my hair; he doesn't know what to do with himself." She loved being the wife of a retired husband as she had never loved being the mother of young children. She loved hearing him take long steps from one end of the basement to the other, loved the times she could hear him standing still, could hear, she thought, his concentration coming up to her through the ceiling, could see it seeping through the floorboards like waves of visible heat. She would never, never interrupt him, but she always knew when it was the last second of his work and she would hear his step on the stairway, would hear him say, "Got any beer?" And she would say, "I've had it waiting." It was the happiest time of her life, the years of his early retirement.

But then his eyes began to go. At first it was rather beautiful, the way his eyes misted over. It was like, she said to herself, a lake the first thing in the morning. He wore thicker glasses with a pink tint which the doctors said were more restful. They would have made any other man look foolish, but not her husband, with his fine, strong head, his way of holding his shoulders. Even at his age his looks were something other women envied her for. She could see the envy in the way they'd look at her as she walked with him in the evening.

She began to notice how queerly he held things, the funny angle at which he held the newspaper. Now she would hear him in the basement, snorting with frustration, using words that she imagined he used only on the job, not words for her or the house. And worst of all, she could hear him drop things; sometimes she would hear things break. She would pretend to be sewing or reading when he came looking for the broom or the dustpan.

The doctors said nothing would reverse the process, so, as time passed, there were more and more things he couldn't do. But the miracle of it was that the losses did not enrage him as, she knew, they would have enraged her. He simply accepted the loss of each new activity as he would have accepted the end of a meal. Finally one night he said to her, "Listen, old girl, you're my only audience now. I'm blind as a bat, and one thing nobody needs is a half-blind magician."

Did she like it better that he did his tricks only for her now, in the living room? Or had she liked it better sitting in the audience, watching the wonder of the people around at what he could produce from the most surprising places. On the whole she thought she liked it better watching the stupefaction, the envy. But it was in her nature, that preference. She had not as nice a nature as his. It was his nature to take her hand and say, after he had done a trick she had seen five hundred times, perhaps, and was not tired of, "I only make magic for *you* now." Making his almost total blindness into a kind of gift for her, a perfect glass he had blown and polished.

On the whole she blamed Frederick for what happened on the Fourth of July, although she knew the idea had come from the grandchildren. Sometimes her husband would take them down to the basement with him to show them some of the equipment. Sometimes he would do tricks for them, the simpler ones that he had done almost from the beginning and knew so well that he didn't have to see to do them. She understood the children's enchantment with him and his magic; he was a perfect grandfather, indulgent, full of secret skills. Of course she understood their pride—there was no one like him. But she didn't understand Frederick's going along with their damn fool idea. His great virtue had always been his good sense. Why did he put his father up to it, without even asking her?

It was tied up with the grandchildren and the way they were so proud. They wanted their friends to see that their grandfather was a magician, so they egged him on to give a show at the Fourth of July Town Fair. Finally Frederick got behind them.

At first she thought it would be all right because of the look on her husband's face when he talked about it, because she knew what gave him that look: the prospect of once again astonishing strangers. Nothing could make up for the loss of it, and it was something she could not give him. Sitting in that living room, honored as she was by the privacy of this intimate performance for her only, no matter how much she loved him, she had seen it all before.

And so she had to tell him what a good thing it was, how proud she would be, what a miracle he was in the lives of his grandchildren. At first she thought he would do only old tricks, and she felt safe. The audience would love him for his looks and because he was Frederick's father. She pressed his suit herself, weeks before; she pressed it several times just for practice. She looked through all her dresses to find the one that would most honor him. Finally she decided on her plainest dress, a black cotton with short sleeves. It was an old woman's dress but, being without ornament, the dress of an old woman who knows herself to be in a position of privilege. She would braid a silver ribbon into her long hair.

As the weeks went on, all ease was drained from her, a slow leak, stealing warmth, making the center of her chest feel full of cold air as if she had just walked into a cave. It was not the old tricks, the ones he almost didn't need eyes for, that he was doing. He was trying to do the newer, more complicated ones. She knew because of the household things he asked for: ribbon now instead of string, scarves instead of cotton handkerchiefs. When he showed her the act, as he always did before the performance, she saw him fumble, saw him drop things that he did not see so that the trick could not possibly go right. But she saw, too, that sometimes he was unaware that he had not done the trick properly. Sometimes the card was not the right card, the scarf the wrong color. All the life in her body collected in one solid disk at the center of her throat when she saw him foolish like that, an old man. But she would not tell him. It was not something that she could do, to say to him: Your best life is entirely behind you—you are an old man. She could not even suggest that he do the simpler things. It was not in her; it had never been in her, and she understood what he was doing. He was risking foolishness to get from his audience the greatest possible astonishment, the greatest novelty of love.

She could not sleep the night before, looking at his sweet white body, the white hairs on the chest that still had the width and the toughness of the young man she had married. She poured boiling water over her finger so she had to go to the fair with her hand in a bandage. That annoyed Frederick, who said, "Today of all days, Mother."

Frederick was looking very foolish. He was wearing red, white and blue striped pants and a straw boater which, with his thinning hair, his failure of a mustache, was a grave tactical error. His father came down wearing his white suit, blue shirt, red bow tie and provided, by his neat, hale presence, all the festivity Frederick had worked so hard to embody.

They had set up a stage on the lawn of the courthouse. First some of the women in the Methodist choir sang show tunes. Then the bank president's daughter, dressed like Uncle Sam, did her baton routine, then somebody played an accordion. Then Frederick got up onstage. All his business friends whistled and stamped and made rude noises. She was embarrassed at the attention he was bringing to himself.

"Now I don't want to be accused of nepotism," he said. (It must have been some joke, some business joke; all the men laughed rudely as she imagined men laughed at dirty jokes.) "But when you have a talent in the family, why hide it under a bushel? My father, Mr. Albert Hastings, is a magician *extraordinaire*. He had the distinction of performing before Franklin Delano Roosevelt. And as I've always said, what's good enough for the Roosevelts is good enough for us."

The men guffawed again. Frederick stretched out one of his arms. "Ladies and gentlemen, the amazing Hastings."

Albert had been backstage all the time. She was glad he had not been with her to sense her fear, perhaps to absorb it. A woman behind her tapped her on the shoulder and said, "You must be very proud." Mrs. Hastings put her finger to her lips. Her husband had begun speaking.

It was the same patter he had used for years, but there was a new element in it that disturbed her: gratitude. He kept telling the audience how good it was to allow him to perform. *Allow* him? He would never have spoken like that, like a plain girl who has finally been asked to dance, ten years ago, five even. She hoped he would not go on like that. But she could see that the audience loved it, loved him for being an old man. But was that the kind of love he wanted? It was not what she thought he was after.

One of the grandchildren was onstage helping him. He made some joke about it, hoping that no one would doubt the honesty of his assistant. For the first trick the child picked three cards. It was a simple trick and over quickly. The audience applauded inordinately, she thought, for it was a simple trick and he used it first, she knew, simply to warm them up.

The second trick was the magic bag. It appeared tiny, but out of it he pulled an egg, an orange, grapes, and finally a small bottle of champagne. "I keep telling my wife to take it to the supermarket, but she won't listen," he said, gesturing at her in the first row of the audience. She got the thrill she always had when he acknowledged her from the stage. She began, for the first time, to relax.

The next trick was the one in which he threaded ribbons through large wooden cards. He asked his grandson to hold the ribbons. It was important that they be held very tightly. She could see her husband struggling to see the holes in the cards through which the ribbon had to be threaded. She could see that he had missed one of the holes, so when he pulled the ribbon, nothing happened. It was supposed to slip out without disturbing the cards. But he pulled the strings and nothing moved. He looked at the audience; he gave it an old man's look. "Ladies and gentlemen, I apologize," he said.

Then they applauded. They covered him with applause. How she hated them for that. She could feel their embarrassment and that complicity that ties an audience together, in love or hatred, in relation to the person so far, so terribly far away on the stage. But it was not love or hate they felt; it was embarrassment for the old man, and she could feel their yearning that it might be all over soon. To hide it, they applauded wildly. She sat perfectly still.

If only the next trick would go well! But it was the scarf trick, the one he had flubbed in the living room. She felt as though she could not breathe. She thought she was going to be sick. She should have told him that it had not worked. She should not have been a coward. Now he would be a fool to strangers. To Frederick's business friends.

"Ladies and gentlemen, I have a magic box, a magic cleaning box. I keep trying to get my wife to use it, but she's a very stubborn woman."

She knew what was supposed to happen. You put a colored scarf in one side of the box and pulled a white one out of the other side. But in the living room he had pulled out the same colored scarf that he had put in. But she had not told him. And he had not seen the difference.

He did the same thing now. At least it was over quickly. He held up the colored scarf, the scarf he thought was white, and twirled it around his head and bowed to the audience. He did not know that the trick had not worked. The audience was confused. There was a terrible beat of silence before they understood what had happened. Then Frederick started the applause. The audience gave Mr. Hastings a standing ovation. Then he disappeared backstage with a strange, old man's shuffle she had not seen him use before.

Frederick got up on the stage again. He was saying something about refreshments, something about gratitude to the women who had provided them. She was shaking with rage in her seat. How could he go on like that, after the humiliation his father had endured? And it was his responsibility. How could he go on talking to the audience, about games, about prizes when that audience had witnessed his father's degradation? Why wasn't he with his father, to comfort him, to cover his exposure, when it had been his fault, when it was Frederick, through thickheadedness, or perhaps malice, who had caused his father's failure in this garish public light?

"Let me get you some supper," said Frederick, offering his mother his arm. He was nodding to other people, even as he spoke to his mother.

She turned to her son in fury.

"Why did you allow him to do this?"

"Do what?"

"This performance. This failure."

"He got a big kick out of it. He's a good sport," said Frederick.

"Everyone saw him fail," said Mrs. Hastings through closed teeth.

"It's all right, Mother. He thinks he did fine."

"It was a humiliation."

He shook his head and looked at her but with no real interest. He walked slightly ahead of her, too fast for her; she could see him searching the crowd for anyone else to talk to. He looked over his shoulder at her with the impatience of a young girl.

"Shall I fix you a plate?" he asked.

"You'll do nothing for me after what you've done to your father."

He stopped walking and waited for her to catch up.

"You know, Mother, Father is twice the person you are," he said, not looking at her. "Three times."

She stood beside him. For the first time in his life, Mrs. Hastings looked at her son with something like love. For the first time, she felt the pride of their connection. She took his arm.

THE HOSPITAL
CHRISTMAS TREE

·ᘓ·

Bella Akhmadulina

They have set a Christmas tree up in a hospital ward.
It clearly feels out of place in a cloister of suffering.
The moon over Leningrad comes to my window ledge
but does not stay long—many windows, much waiting.

The moon moves on to a spry, independent old woman;
outside you can hear the susurrous sound of her trying
to hide from her neighbors and from her own shallow sleep
her breaking the norm—the blunder of illegal crying.

All the patients are worse; still, it is Christmas Eve.
Tomorrow some will get news; some, gifts; some, calls.
Life and death remain neighbors: the stretcher is always loaded;
through the long night the elevator squeaks as it falls.

Rejoice eternally, Virgin! You bore The Child at night.
There is no other reason for hope, but that matters so much,
is so huge, so eternally endless, that it
consoles the unknown, underground anchorite.

Even here in the ward where the tree makes some people cry
(did not want it; a nurse, in fact, ordered it brought)
the listening heart beats, and you hear people say,
"Hey, look! The Star of Bethlehem's in the sky!"

The only sure facts are the cattle's lament in the shed,
the Wise Men's haste, the inexperienced mother's elbow
marking The Child with a miraculous spot on His brow.
All the rest is absurd, an age-old but fugitive lie.

The Hospital Christmas Tree

What matters more or brings more joy to sick flesh
wasted by work and by war than so simple a scene?
But they reproach you for drinking or some other fault
and stuff your brain with the bones of a system picked clean.

I watched the day begin breaking some time past nine;
it was a drop, a black light shining absurdly
onto the window. People dreamt that they heard
a little toy bell-ringer ringing the bell on the tree.

The day as it dawned was weak, not much of a sight.
The light was paler than pink, pastel, not harsh,
the way an amethyst shimmers on a young girl's neck.
All looked down, once they had seen the sad, humble cross.

And when they arose, reluctantly opening their eyes,
a trolley flew by through the snowstorm, gold trim inside it.
They crowded the window like children: "Hey, look at that car!
Like a perch that's gotten away, all speckled with fire!"

They sat down to breakfast; they argued, got tired, lay down.
The view from the window was such that Leningrad's secrets
and splendors brought tears to my eyes, filled me with love.
"Isn't there something you want?" "No, there's nothing."

I have long been accused of making up frivolous things.
Frivolity maker, I look at those here around me:
O Mother of God, have mercy! And beg your Son, too.
On the day of His birth, pray and weep for us each.

TRANSLATED BY F. D. REEVE

TRUCKSTOP

·2·

Garrison Keillor

It has been a quiet week in Lake Wobegon. Florian and Myrtle Krebsbach left for Minneapolis on Tuesday, a long haul for them. They're no spring chickens, and it was cold and raining, and he hates to drive anyway. His eyesight is poor and his '66 Chev only has 47,000 miles on her, just like new, and he's proud of it. But Myrtle had to go down for a checkup. She can't get one from Dr. DeHaven or the doctors in Saint Cloud because she's had checkups from them recently and they say she is all right. She is pretty sure she might have cancer. She reads "Questions and Answers on Cancer" in the paper and has seen symptoms there that sound familiar, so when she found a lump on the back of her head last week and noticed blood on her toothbrush, she called a clinic in Minneapolis, made an appointment, and off they went. He put on his good carcoat and a clean Pioneer Seed Corn cap, Myrtle wore a red dress so she would be safe in Minneapolis traffic. He got on Interstate 94 in Avon and headed south at forty miles an hour, hugging the right side, her clutching her purse, peering out of her thick glasses, semis blasting past them, both of them upset and scared, her about brain tumors, him about semis. Normally she narrates a car trip, reading billboards, pointing out interesting sights, but not now. When they got beyond the range of the "Rise 'N Shine" show, just as Bea and Bob were coming to the "Swap 'N Shop" feature, a show they've heard every morning for thirty years, they felt awful, and Florian said, "If it was up to me, I'd just as soon turn around and go home."

It was the wrong thing to say, with her in the mood she was in, and she was expecting him to say it and had worked up a speech in her mind in case he did. "Well, of course. I'm sure you would rather turn around. You don't care. You don't care one tiny bit, and you never have, so I'm not surprised that you don't now. You don't care if I live or die. You'd probably just as soon I died right now. That'd make you happy, wouldn't it? You'd just clap your hands if I died. Then you'd be free of me, wouldn't you—then you'd be free to go off and do your dirty business, wouldn't you."

Florian, with his '66 Chev with 47,003 miles on it, wouldn't strike most people as a candidate for playboyhood, but it made sense to her—forty-eight years of marriage and she had finally figured him out, the rascal. She wept. She blew her nose.

He said, "I would too care if you died."

She said, "Oh yeah, how much? You tell me."

Florian isn't good at theoretical questions. After a couple minutes she said, "Well, I guess that answers *my* question. The answer is, you don't care a bit."

It was his idea to stop at the truckstop, he thought coffee would calm him down, and they sat and drank a couple cups apiece, and then the pie looked good so they had some, banana cream and lemon meringue, and more coffee. They sat by the window, not a word between them, watching the rain fall on the gas pumps. They stood up and went and got in the car, then he decided to use the men's room. While he was gone, she went to the ladies' room. And while she was gone, he got in behind the wheel, started up, checked the side mirror, and headed out on the freeway. Who knows how this sort of thing happens, he just didn't notice, his mind was on other things, and Florian is a man who thinks slowly so he won't have to go back and think it over again. He was still thinking about how much he'd miss her if she was gone, how awful he'd feel, how empty the house would be with him lying alone in bed at night, and all those times when you want to turn to someone and say, "You won't believe what happened to me," or "Did you read this story in the newspaper about the elk in Oregon?" or "Boy, Johnny Carson is looking old, ain't he? And Ed too," and she wouldn't be there for him to point this out to —and he turned to tell her how much he'd miss her and she wasn't there. The seat was empty. You could have knocked him over with a stick.

He took his foot off the gas and coasted to a stop. He hadn't noticed her crawl into the backseat, but he looked and she wasn't there. She hadn't jumped—he would've noticed that. (Wouldn't he?) It couldn't've been angels taking her away. He thought of the truckstop. He was a good ways from there, he knew that. He must've gone twenty miles. Then, when he made a U-turn, he noticed he wasn't on the freeway anymore. There was no median strip. He was on a Highway 14, whatever that was.

He drove a few miles and came to a town named Bolivia. He never knew there was a Bolivia, Minnesota, but there it was. Went into a Pure Oil station, an old man was reading a Donald Duck comic book. Florian asked, "How far to the Interstate?" He didn't look up from his comic. A pickup came in, the bell dinged, the old man kept reading. Florian went down the street into a cafe, Yaklich's Cafe, and asked the woman where the Interstate was. She said, "Oh, that's nowheres around here." "Well, it must be," he said, "I was just on it. I just came from there."

"Oh," she says, "that's a good ten miles from here."

"Which way?"

"East, I think."

"Which way's east?"

"What way you come in?"

"That way!"

"That way is northeast. You want to go that way and then a little southeast when you get to the Y in the road. Then keep to your left. It's about two miles the other side of that old barn with Red Man on the side. Red Man Chewing Tobacco. On your left. You'll see it."

There was a funny look about her: her eyes bulged, and her lips were purplish. Her directions weren't good either. He drove that way and never saw the barn, so he turned around and came back and looked for the barn on the right side, but no barn, so he headed back to Bolivia, but Bolivia wasn't there anymore. It was getting on toward noon.

It was four o'clock before he ever found the truckstop. He had a long time to think up something to tell Myrtle, but he still had no idea what to say. But she wasn't there anyway. The waitress said, "You mean the lady in the blue coat?" Florian didn't remember what color Myrtle's coat was. He wasn't sure exactly how to describe her except as *real mad*, probably. "*Ja*, that's the lady in the blue coat," she said. "Oh, she left here hours ago. Her son come to get her."

Florian sat and had a cup of coffee and a piece of apple pie. "Can you tell me the quickest way to get to Lake Wobegon from here?" he asked. "Lake what?" she said. "I never heard of it. It can't be around here."

But it was, not too far away, and once he got off the freeway he found his way straight home, although it was dark by then. He stopped at the Sidetrack for a quick bump. He felt he owed it to himself after all he'd been through and what with what he was about to go through. "Where's the old lady?" asked Wally. "Home, waiting for me," he said.

He headed south and saw his house, and kept going. Carl's pickup was in the driveway and he couldn't see facing the both of them. He parked on the crossroad and sat, just beyond Roger Hedlund's farm, where he could watch his house. It was dark, except a light was on in the kitchen and one in the bathroom. Roger's house was lit up. What if Roger should see him and come out to investigate? Out here in the country, a parked car stands out more than a little bit, you might as well be towing a searchlight behind you. It's considered unusual for a man to sit in his car in the evening on a crossroad an eighth of a mile from his own house, just sit there. If Roger came out, Florian thought he'd explain that he was listening to the radio and it was a Lutheran show so the old lady wouldn't have it in the house—Roger was Lutheran, he'd like that.

He ducked down as a car came slowly past, its headlights on high beam. The preacher on the radio might be Lutheran, he didn't know. It sure wasn't the Rosary. The man was talking about sinners who had wandered away from the path, and it seemed to Florian to fit the situation. "Broad is the road that leadeth to destruction, and narrow is the path of righteousness"—that seemed to be true too, from what he knew of freeways. The preacher mentioned forgiveness, but Florian wasn't sure about that. He wondered what this preacher would do if *he* had forgotten his wife at a truckstop and gotten lost; the preacher knew a lot about forgiveness theoretically but what would he do in Florian's situation? A woman sang, "Softly and tenderly Jesus is calling, calling for you and for me. See by the portals he's waiting and watching. Calling, O sinner come home."

> Come home, come home—
> Ye who are weary come home.

Florian felt weary. Seventy-two is old to get yourself in such a ridiculous situation. He waited as long as he could for Carl to leave, and then the coffee inside him reached the point of no return and he started up the engine. Taking a leak in another man's field: he drew the line at that. He turned on his headlights, and right when he did he saw Carl's headlights far away light up and the beams swung around across the yard and Carl headed back toward town.

Florian coasted up his driveway with the headlights out. He still did not have a speech ready. He was afraid. He also had to pee. Outside, on the porch, he smelled supper: breaded fish fillets. He was surprised that the door was unlocked—they never have locked it but he thought she might if she thought he was coming.

He hung up his coat in the mud room and looked around the corner. She was at the stove, her back to him, stirring something in a pan. He cleared his throat. She turned. She said, "Oh thank God." She dropped the spoon on the floor and ran to him on her old legs and said, "Oh Daddy, I was so scared. Oh Daddy, don't ever leave me again. I'm sorry I said what I did. I didn't mean it. I didn't mean to make you so angry at me. Don't leave me again like that."

Tears came to his eyes. To be so welcome—in his own home. He was about to tell her that he hadn't left her, he'd forgotten her; then she said, "I love you, Daddy. You know that."

He was going to tell her, but he didn't. It occurred to him that leaving her on account of passionate anger might be better than forgetting her because of being just plain dumb. There wasn't time to think this through clearly. He squeezed her and whispered, "I'm sorry. I was wrong. I promise you that I'll never do a dumb thing like that again."

She felt good at supper and put on the radio; she turned it up when she heard "The Saint Cloud Waltz." *Sometimes I dream of a mansion afar but there's no place so lovely as right where we are, here on a planet that's almost a star, we dance to the Saint Cloud Waltz.* That night he lay awake, incredulous. That she thought he was capable of running away, like a John Barrymore or something. Seventy-two years old, married forty-eight years, and she thought that maybe it hadn't worked out and he might fly the coop like people do in songs? Amazing woman. He got up at six o'clock, made scrambled eggs and sausage and toast, and felt like a new guy. She felt better too. The lump on her head felt like all the other lumps and there was no blood on her toothbrush. She said, "I wonder if I hadn't ought to call down there about that appointment." "Oh," he said, "I think by now they must know you're all right."

HILLS

·❧·

Vasily Belov

He was awakened by a vague aching agitation. He looked at the bright, solid patch of sunshine at the end of the wooden shed and tried to penetrate to the origin of this indefinite and in some way pleasant inner ache. Perhaps a dream?—But all memories of nocturnal fantasy had gone and he was left baffled.

The sun beat in through the chinks as well. Swallows darted through the window, pressed their tails to the rafters, twittered and flew out again. The air was full of the scent of grass and drying dew. From the river came the shouts of children bathing, and on the field a horse-drawn mower rattled.

Nobody was at home. His mother, obedient to old habit, would probably have gone off with the sighs and groans of age to the mowing, and his wife took the two children every morning to a pool some distance off to splash about and sunbathe.

He recalled the previous day's meeting with an old friend, a contemporary from the village, and realized the cause of that nagging depression.

Yesterday he had not paid attention to how much older this contemporary looked—elderly, in fact, though the man was actually even a little younger than himself. But during the night, that feeling had come to him of years irretrievably gone.

Up to that time he had thought of himself as young, but now, while sleeping, his unconscious had told him that he had already changed the second half of his life into the small coinage of everyday use. H'm—one way of putting it.

The village was empty. Just as in his childhood, swallows and swifts flew over the roofs in the blue sky, poles stood ready by the gates for haystacks to be built round them, and the morning sun warmed the soft dust on the road.

He went out into the green field vibrant with grasshoppers, his gaze slowly passing over the village and its surroundings, last seen so many years ago. He was conscious of a strange feeling of being part of it all, a feeling both sad and glad, and marveled at himself.

Where had he come from and what was the meaning of it all? Where were the first beginnings of his own life—say, four hundred years ago? Where were all his forebears, how was it they had gone? Could they really have gone into nothingness and only he and his two sons remained? Queer. Incomprehensible.

He came to a steep green mound embraced by a horseshoe-shaped lake. The cupola of a church floated in the sky amidst a few clouds—floated with them but could not float away. Bees hummed softly over the willows. Down below, the lake shimmered and rippled in the sun and wind, and its blueness darkened, ruffled in its endless changing. But up here on the mound all was quiet and green. Heat poured down from the sky, distorting the forest horizon with its wavy vertical currents. A new fence was out of accord with the old grey crosses, scanty and tipped drunkenly askew by time, as was the archway of the new pinewood gate soaring into the sky with the cupola.

He wandered for a long time about the mound seeking graves and not finding them, pushing through the strong young docks. His aunt's grave was some distance outside the fence, he knew it by the stone. But where did Grandma lie? He remembered that her grave had been by a willow, but he could not find it and in the end sat down on a comparatively recent mound. Yes, not much use looking for his four great-grandmothers if even Grandma's grave had disappeared. And somewhere there should be a second grandmother, his father's mother. But where was she? Not a sign of her grave, everything had sunk and leveled, overgrown with grass and docks.

For the first time he was struck by a clear, scorching tooth-clenching thought: it had never entered his head before that here, in his home village, only women were buried in the graveyard. He remembered—in his own family not a man had been buried on that mound. They had been born here on this soil, but not one had returned to it, as though shy of entering the community of women in it. Generation after generation they went away, exchanging rakes for guns and haymaking shirts for army tunics. They went off as though going to the fair, as soon as they'd built a house and begotten sons. And so the great-grandmothers and grandmothers lay here, lonely even in death.

He lighted a cigarette. The picture on the box reminded him that one of his forebears had been killed in Bulgaria fighting the Turks. Grandma had told him about it. And with bitter irony he thought of the injustice of women's lot—even in this, Great-grandfather had been fortunate. Perhaps a monument stood on his grave erected by the Bulgarians to the heroes of Shipka. But Great-grandmother's grave was lost.

Grandfather, too, had not done so badly, it must be pleasant to lie in a Manchurian hill that is described in story and song, and to this day descendants gather round canvases depicting battle scenes while plaintive waltzes about the Manchurian hills come over the radio. But Grandma's grave has disappeared, there is neither cross nor stone to be seen.

He stubbed out his cigarette but at once lit another. What the—? He was forgetting his own father, damn it. Grandfather and Great-grandfather—all right, but nowhere in the world was there such a magnificent, impressive monument as the one on Mamaev Kurgan. The previous summer he had been in Volgograd and he remembered how he had spent the whole day wandering about Mamaev Kurgan. This hill which had taken his father into its bosom was great and sorrowful, the mighty sculpture which crowned it cast a massive shadow over the town. Work was not yet complete on the Hall of Fame, but he, the son of a sergeant who had been killed on the Volga, could see his name on the granite wall.

They had gone, to rest under monuments on famous hills. Grandfathers and great-grandfathers had gone, and his father had gone. And not one had returned home to that green mound embraced by the horseshoe lake where their wives and mothers lay. And nobody brought flowers here, nobody came to visit these women, to comfort them in their loneliness which did not end even beneath the ground.

He sat there under a willow on the quiet, green, sultrily warm mound and thought about it.

Perhaps his turn, too, would come? To follow the path of his male forebears to alien hills?

TRANSLATED BY EVE MANNING

THE LONG BOAT

·⚘·

Stanley Kunitz

When his boat snapped loose
from its moorings, under
the screaking of the gulls,
he tried at first to wave
to his dear ones on shore,
but in the rolling fog
they had already lost their faces.
Too tired even to choose
between jumping and calling,
somehow he felt absolved and free
of his burdens, those mottoes
stamped on his name-tag:
conscience, ambition, and all
that caring.
He was content to lie down
with the family ghosts
in the slop of his cradle,
buffeted by the storm,
endlessly drifting.
Peace! Peace!
To be rocked by the Infinite!
As if it didn't matter
which way was home;
as if he didn't know
he loved the earth so much
he wanted to stay forever.

AT FORD'S THEATER

·2·

Andrei Voznesensky

With an actress here this afternoon
I've come to test the microphone:
An empty stage, a simple light,
where Abraham Lincoln was shot one night.

What spirits are there lurking here?
What echo somehow pierces through?
It's not the fault of the engineer—
it's the ghost of Lincoln, I am sure.

In Russian Lincoln speaks to me—
or it's his ghost that so speaks out.
Mr. Belltower he might be
with that deep voice and that great height.

I'm the first Russian to appear
upon this famous haunted stage
for Lincoln and Whitman to recite
my poems in a quavering voice.

Art is a church that's built on blood;
in blood alone has it verity.
Let's leave these flowers, for in truth
they belong to Lincoln, not to me.

TRANSLATED BY WILLIAM JAY SMITH AND
INNA BOGACHINSKAYA PERLIN

BIOGRAPHIES

William Styron. Born in 1925 in Newport News, Virginia. Received B.A. from Duke University in 1947. Served in the Marine Corps during World War II. Received the American Academy of Arts and Letters Prix de Rome in 1952 for *Lie Down in Darkness*, the Pulitzer Prize in 1968 for *The Confessions of Nat Turner*, and the American Book Award in 1980 for *Sophie's Choice*. Served as editor of *Paris Review* and *Best Short Stories*.

Daniil Granin. Born in 1919 in Volyn, Kursk Province, the son of a forester. Graduated in 1940 from Electromechanical Department of Leningrad Polytechnical Institute. Lives in Leningrad. Among his works are the novels *The Seekers* (1954), *Into the Storm* (1962), *Book of the Siege* (1979, with A. Adamovich), *The Painting* (1980), *Bison* (1987). His collected works, in four volumes, were published in 1978–80 by the Leningrad division of Khudozhestvennaya Literatura publishers. Awarded USSR State Prize in 1978 for the novella *Klavdia Vilor*.

Wendell Berry. Lives and farms in Kentucky, where he was born in 1934. Received his B.A. and M.A. from the University of Kentucky in 1956 and 1957 and held a Wallace Stegner Writing Fellowship at Stanford University 1958–59. Taught at the University of Kentucky 1964–1977. Published numerous volumes of poetry, along with novels and collections of essays, including *Unsettling of America: Culture and Agriculture* (1977) and *Home Economics* (1987).

Yevgeny Yevtushenko. Born in 1933 in Zima, Irkutsk oblast. Lives in Moscow. Studied 1951–54 in the Gorky Literary Institute. Poems include "Zima Station" (1956), "Bratsk Hydroelectric Station" (1965), "Beneath the Skin of the Statue of Liberty, Kazan University" (1970), *Tokyo Snow* (1975), and "Mama and the Neutron Bomb" (1982), for which he received the Soviet State Prize in 1984. Poetry collections include *Scouts of the Future* (1952), *The White Snows Are Coming* (1969), *Intimate Lyrics* (1973), *Two Pair of Skis* (1982), etc. Prose works include *Berry Places* (1981), *Fuku* (1987), and a screenplay, *I Am Cuba*. Translates American poets such as James Dickey.

Biographies

Valentin Rasputin. Born in 1937 in Ust-Ude, Irkutsk oblast, where he currently resides. Graduated from the Historical and Philological Department of Irkutsk University in 1959. Published works include *Money for Marya* (1967), *The Final Stage* (1970), and *Farewell to Matyora* (1976). Winner of the 1977 Soviet State Prize for the story "Mark You This" and the 1987 Soviet State Prize for the story "Fire."

Joyce Johnson. Born in New York City, where she lives with her son. Author of two novels, *Come and Join the Dance* and *Bad Connections*, and of a memoir, *Minor Characters*, that won the 1983 National Book Critics Award.

Tatyana Tolstaya. Born in 1951 in Leningrad and lives in Moscow. Graduated from the Philology Department of Leningrad University, 1974. Her stories have appeared in *Neva* and *Novy Mir*. Her book of stories, *On the Golden Roof They Sat*, was published in 1987 by *Molodaya Gvardiya* (Young Guard).

Charles Baxter. Born in 1947 and teaches at Wayne State University in Detroit. His books include two volumes of short stories, *Harmony of the World* and *Through the Safety Net*, and the novel *First Light*. The story published here, "Gryphon," was adapted for public television in 1988.

Ruslan Kireyev. Born in 1941 in Kokanda, Fergana oblast, Uzbekistan, and graduated from the Gorky Literary Institute in 1967. Currently resides in Moscow. Was a sheet-metal worker and motor-pool dispatcher in the Crimea. Published collections of satirical poems, *God's Mistakes* (1962) and *Robinson's Feat* (1971), as well as articles and humorous stories. Best known for his stories "Lerka," "Filya" and "Ludmilla Vladimirovna" (1968) and the novel *Continuation* (1973).

Robert Penn Warren. Born in Kentucky in 1905. Received a B.A. from Vanderbilt University in 1925; M.A., University of California at Berkeley, 1927; Yale University 1927–28; B. Litt. Oxford University, 1930. Author of numerous novels, books of criticism and poetry, including *All the King's Men* (1949) and *New and Selected Poems* (1985). Awards include: Pulitzer Prize for *All the King's Men* and *Promises* (1958) and *Now and Then* (1979). Poet Laureate of the United States, 1986.

Bel Kaufman. Born in Berlin, Germany, and raised in Russia. Came to the United States at age twelve. Received a B.A. from Hunter College and an M.A. from Columbia University. Taught in the New York City school system for twenty years. Published *Up the Down Staircase* (1965) and *Love, Etc.* (1978). Contributor to *Esquire, Saturday Review, To-*

day's Education, McCall's, The New York Times, and other publications. Was named to Hall of Fame by the National Bestsellers Institute in 1966 for *Up the Down Staircase.* Winner of the National Education Association/P.E.N. short story contest in 1983 for "Sunday in the Park."

Bulat Okudzhava. Born in 1924 in Moscow, where he now lives. Volunteered for the front in 1942. Graduated from Tbilisi University in 1950, became a teacher, and published his first collection of poetry, *Lyrics,* in 1956. Known as an author and songwriter/performer. Published a series of historical novels, including *Journey of Dilettantes* (1979), *An Assignation with Bonaparte* (1985), and *A Taste of Liberty* (Ardis, Ann Arbor, 1987), translated into English by Leo Gruliow.

Joyce Carol Oates. Born in Lockport, N.Y., completed her B.A. at Syracuse University in 1960, and was awarded an M.A. by the University of Wisconsin in 1961. Her second novel, *A Garden of Earthly Delights,* won the Rosenthal Foundation Award of the National Institute of Arts and Letters in 1968. Her fourth novel, *them,* won the National Book Award in 1970. Her most recent works include *Raven's Wing* (a collection of stories), *On Boxing* (essays), and *You Must Remember This* (a novel). She was the 1986 recipient of the O. Henry Award for Continuing Achievement in the art of the short story. She currently teaches at Princeton University.

Yevgeny Vinokurov. Born in 1925 in Bryansk and currently lives in Moscow. Graduated from the Gorky Literary Institute in 1951. Poetry collections include: *Poem of Duty* (1951), *Sky Blue* (1956), *The Human Face* (1960), *Characters* (1965), *Metaphors* (1972), *Living* (1982), etc. Received Soviet State Prize in 1987 for *Living and Hypostasis.* Collection of essays in three volumes was published by Khudozhestvennaya Literatura in 1983–84. Literary criticism includes: *Poetry of Thought* (1966) and *Still in Force: On the Classical and Modern* (1979).

John Updike. Born in 1932 in Shillington, Pennsylvania. Author of novels, poetry, and short stories. Visited the U.S.S.R. as part of the cultural exchange program of the U.S. Department of State in 1964. Received a Guggenheim Fellowship for poetry in 1964; a National Book Award in 1963 for *The Centaur,* the O. Henry Award for fiction, and many other honors. His books include the novels *Rabbit Run* (1959) and *Couples* (1968) and a collection of short stories, *Trust Me* (1986).

Arnold Kashtanov (Epstein). Born in 1938 in Volgograd and now lives in Moscow. Graduated from the Moscow Automechanical Institute in 1961. Member of the Soviet Writers Union since 1975. His published works include two novels, *Factory Region* (1973) and *Peddlers,* as well as stories, "My Rain" (1982), "Petr and Liza" (1985), "An Epidemic of Happiness" (1986), and screenplays.

Henry Taylor. Born in Loudoun County, Virginia. Received a B.A. from the University of Virginia and an M.A. in creative writing from Hollins College. Taught at various universities, including the University of Utah and American University in Washington, D.C. Has published literary criticism as well as poetry. His books include *The Horse Show at Midnight* (1966), *Breakings* (1971), and *An Afternoon of Pocket Billiards* (1975). Winner of the Witter Bynner Foundation Poetry Prize from the American Academy and Institute of Arts and Letters in 1984 and the Pulitzer Prize for poetry in 1986.

Robert Rozhdestvensky. Born in 1932 in Kosikha village in the Troitsky region of Altai krai. Now lives in Moscow. Studied at the Petrozavodsky University and graduated from the Gorky Literary Institute in 1956. His published works include *Flags of Spring* (1955) and *Collected Writings in Three Volumes* (1985). Has written the texts for songs, "Letter to the Thirtieth Century," "Peace," "Unopened Islands," "The Vast Sky" and others. For his book of poems *Voices of the City*, and the poem "Two Hundred Twenty Steps," he was awarded the 1979 Soviet State Prize.

Mary Ward Brown. Born in 1917 in Brown, Alabama. Received her B.A. from Judson College in Marion, Alabama. Her stories have appeared in *Prairie Schooner, McCall's,* and *Best American Short Stories.* Her collection of stories, *Tongues of Flame,* was published in 1986. Winner of the Ernest Hemingway Foundation Award and the Lawrence Foundation Prize in 1980.

Boris Yekimov. Born in 1938 in Igarka and now lives in Volgograd. In 1957 he finished general high school. Member of the Soviet Writers Union since 1976. His published stories include "The Girl in the Red Jacket" (1974), "A Christmas Tree for Mother" (1984), "The Last Hut" (1980), "The Officer's Wife" (1978), "Kolyushino Townhouse" (1984), "A Night of Recovery" (1986).

Raymond Carver. Born in 1938 in Clatskanie, Oregon. Received B.A. from California State University, Humboldt. Taught at various colleges and universities, including University of California at Santa Cruz and Berkeley, State University of New York at Syracuse, the University of Iowa, and the University of Texas at El Paso. Has received numerous awards and prizes, including a National Endowment for the Arts Discovery Award for Poetry in 1970 and a Guggenheim Fellowship in 1977–78. Has published novels, books of poetry, and short stories.

Biographies

Oleg Chukhontsev. Born in 1938 in Pavlovsk district near Moscow, where he currently resides. Graduated from the Philology Department of the Moscow Regional Pedagogical Institute in 1962. A member of the editorial board of the literary monthly *Novy Mir*. Has published two books of poems, *From Three Notebooks* (1976) and *The Dormer Window* (1976). Translator of Verlaine, Keats, Goethe, Whitman, Robert Penn Warren and others.

F(rank) D(olier) Reeve. Born in Philadelphia in 1928. Received a Ph.D. from Columbia University. Poet, novelist, and critic, currently residing in Vermont. Published three books of verse, *In the Silent Stones, The Blue Cat*, and *Nightway*. His translations include the two-volume *Anthology of Russian Plays*. He has received a Ford Fellowship, American Council of Learned Societies/USSR Academy of Sciences Grant, PEN Syndicated Fiction Awards, and an Award in Literature from the American Academy of the National Institute of Arts and Letters.

Yury Kuznetsov. Born in 1941 in Leningradskaya village, Krasnodar krai, and lives in Moscow. Graduated from the Gorky Literary Institute in 1970. Poetry collections include *Awe* (1966), *Inside Me and Around Us Is Distance* (1974), *The World of Light Is Just Around the Next Corner* (1976), *Russian Knot* (1983), *Neither Early nor Late* (1985), *The Soul Is Reliable to Unknown Lengths* (1986).

C(harles) K(enneth) Williams. Born in Newark, N.J., in 1936. Received a B.A. from the University of Pennsylvania in 1959. Author of numerous volumes of poetry, including *A Day for Anne Frank* (1968), *Lies* (1969), *I Am the Bitter Name* (1972) and *With Ignorance* (1977). Recipient of the Guggenheim Fellowship and contributing editor to *American Poetry Review*.

Anatoly Shavkuta. Born in 1937 in Stravropol krai and now lives in Moscow. Graduated from the Grodno Petroleum Institute and became a member of the Soviet Writers Union in 1961. Winner of the 1981 Ostrovsky Prize. Published stories include "Such Different People" (1975), "A Blizzard in Ryazan" (1978), "Stories of an Old Master" (1983), "Sorry for Beauty" (1986), "Grafoy and Others" (1986).

Donald Barthelme. Born in 1931 in Philadelphia, Pennsylvania. Author of short stories and novels, including *Come Back, Dr. Caligari* (1964), *Snow White* (1967), *City Life* (1970) and *Paradise* (1986). Recipient of numerous awards, including the Guggenheim Fellowship (1966), the National Book Award for Children's Literature for *The Slightly Irregular Fire Engine or The Hithering Thithering Djinn* (1972), and the PEN/Faulkner Award for Fiction for *Sixty Stories* (1982).

Alexander Kushner. Born in 1936 in Leningrad, where he still resides. Graduate of the Herzen Pedagogical Institute. Author of eight books of verse: *First Impressions* (1962), *The Night Watch* (1966), *Signs* (1969), *Letter* (1974), *The Tauride Park* (1984), *Daydreams* (1986), and the recent collection *Poems* (1986). Also writes children's verse, works of criticism, and translations.

Adrienne Rich. Born in Baltimore, Md., in 1929. Received a B.A. from Radcliffe College in 1951. Author of numerous books of criticism and poetry, including *A Change of World* (1952), *The Diamond Cutters and Other Poems* (1955), *Leaflets: Poems of 1962–1965* (1972), *Diving into the Wreck* (1973), *Dreams of a Common Language* (1978) and many more. Recipient of the Yale Series of Younger Poets prize for *A Change of World*, Guggenheim Fellowships in 1952 and 1961, National Institute of Arts and Letters Award, the National Book Award for *Diving into the Wreck* and many more.

Anatoly Kim. Born in 1939 in Sergievka in the Tyul-Kubassk region of Kazakhstan and now lives in Moscow. Graduated from the Gorky Literary Institute in 1971. Member of the Writers Union since 1978. Awarded the Badge of Honor. Published works include *Blue Island* (1976), *Jade Belt* (1981) and *Weedpickers* (1983).

John Sayles. Born in 1950 in Schenectady, New York. Received a B.A. from Williams College in 1972. First published story, "I-80 Nebraska," received the O. Henry Short Story Award in 1976. Published *The Pride of the Bimbos* (1975), *Union Dues* (1977) and *The Anarchists' Convention* (1979). Screenwriter and director for numerous films, including *The Return of the Secausus Seven* (1980), *Lianna* (1983), *Baby, It's You* (1983), *The Brother from Another Planet* (1984) and *Eight Men Out* (1988).

Sharon Olds. Born in 1942 in San Francisco. Received a B.A. from Stanford University in 1964 and a Ph.D. from Columbia University in 1972. Books include *Satan Says* (1980), *The Dead and the Living* (1984), *The Gold Cell* (1987) and the forthcoming *World War*. She received a Guggenheim Fellowship in 1980, an NEA Fellowship Grant in 1981, the National Book Critics Award and the Lamont Award in 1984.

Yunna Moritz. Born in 1937 in Kiev. Lives in Moscow. Graduated in 1961 from the Gorky Literary Institute. Poetry collections include: *Conversations About Happiness* (1957), *Cape of Good Hope* (1961), *The Vine* (1970), *In the World of the Living* (1977), *Blue Flame* (1985), *Selection* (1982), and others. Writes children's verse and translates American poets such as Theodore Roethke, Randell Jarrell, etc.

Alice Walker. Born in 1944 in Eatonton, Georgia. Received a B.A. from Sarah Lawrence College in 1965. Her published works include *Revolutionary Petunias and Other Poems* (1973), *In Love and Trouble: Stories of Black Women* (1973), *You Can't Keep a Good Woman Down* (1981) and *The Color Purple* (1982). She has received numerous awards and grants, including a Guggenheim Fellowship and the Pulitzer Prize and National Book Award for *The Color Purple*, which was subsequently made into a popular motion picture.

Vladimir Sokolov. Born in 1928 in Likhoslavl, Kalinin oblast, and lives in Moscow. Graduated in 1952 from the Gorky Literary Institute. Poetry collections include: *Morning on the Road* (1953), *On the Sunny Side* (1961), *September Snow* (1968), *Thank You, Music* (1978), *The Subject* (1980), *Selected Works in Two Volumes* (1981), *New Times* (1986) and *Poems* (1987). Received the Soviet State Prize in 1983.

Georgy Semyonov. Born in 1931 in Moscow, where he still lives. Former sculptor. Graduated from the Higher Industrial College (Stroganova) in 1949 and the Gorky Literary Institute in 1960. In print since 1961. Published collections of stories include *Forty-four Nights* (1964), *At Night After It Rained* (1969), *Street Lights* (1975), *City Landscape* (1985) and *The Smell of Burning Gunpowder* (1985). Awarded the 1981 RSFSR State Prize for his book of stories *Blue Smoke.*

Mary Gordon. Born in 1949 in Long Island, N.Y. Received a B.A. from Barnard College and an M.A. from Syracuse University. Taught at various colleges, including Amherst College in Massachusetts. Published *Final Payments* (1978) and *The Company of Women* (1981). Her stories regularly appear in magazines such as *Redbook, The Atlantic,* and *Harper's.*

Bella Akhmadulina. Born in 1937 in Moscow, where she still lives. Graduated from the Gorky Literary Institute in 1960. Poetry collections include: *String* (1962), *Music Lessons* (1969), *Lines of Poetry* (1975), *The Garden* (1987). Translator and author of essays on Pushkin and Lermontov. Honorary member of the American Academy of Arts and Letters (1977).

Garrison Keillor. Born in Anoka, Minnesota, in 1942. Author of best-selling books of short stories, *Happy to Be Here* (1982), *Lake Wobegon Days* (1985) and *Leaving Home* (1987). Radio announcer and storyteller for "Prairie Home Companion."

Vasily Belov. Born in 1932 in Vologda oblast to a peasant family and currently lives in Vologda. Graduated from the Gorky Institute in 1964.

His first book was a collection of poems, *My Wooded Village* (1961). His works include the story "That's How Things Are" (1966), *Carpenter's Stories* (1968) and the novel *The Eve* (1972–76). Winner of the 1981 Soviet State Prize for his short stories.

Stanley Kunitz. Born in 1905 in Worcester, Massachusetts, and now lives in New York City. Received a B.A. and M.A. from Harvard University in 1926 and 1927. Critic, poet and translator. His books of poetry include *Intellectual Things* (1930), *Passport to the War: A Selection of Poems* (1944), *The Wellfleet Whale and Companion Poems* (1983) and *Next-to-Last Things: New Poems and Essays* (1985). His translations include *The Poems of Akhmatova* (1973) and Andrei Voznesensky's *Story Under Full Sail* (1974). The winner of numerous awards, including the Pulitzer Prize for poetry in 1959.

Andrei Voznesensky. Born in 1933 in Moscow, where he still lives. Graduated from the Moscow Institute of Architecture in 1957. Published works include *Antiworlds* (1964), *A Violoncello Oakleaf* (1976), and *Collected Writings in Three Volumes* (1983). For his book, *Master of Stained-Glass Windows*, he received the 1987 Soviet State Prize. Translator of American poets such as Robert Lowell.

"Capital Punishment," © 1987 by Joyce Carol Oates. Published in *The Southern Review*, 1987. Used with permission of the author.

"I Know Life Well," © by Yevgeny Vinokurov. Trans. © 1989 by F. D. Reeve.

"Still of Some Use," from *Trust Me* by John Updike. © 1987 by John Updike. Reprinted by permission of Random House, Inc.

"Hypnosis," © by Arnold Kashtanov. Trans. © 1989 by Leo Gruliow. From *Znamya* (Banner) magazine, 1987, no. 4.

"Master of None," © 1987 by Henry Taylor. First appeared in *Poetry*, October–November 1987. © 1987 by the American Poetry Association. Reprinted by permission of the editor of *Poetry*.

"Song of the Years," © by Robert Rozhdestvensky. Trans. © 1989 by F. D. Reeve. From *Song of the Years*, in *Return*, Petrozavodsk. Karelia Publishers, 1972.

"The Cure," from *Tongues of Flame* by Mary Ward Brown. © 1986 by Mary Ward Brown. Reprinted by permission of the publisher, E. P. Dutton, a division of N.A.L. Penguin, Inc.

"A Greeting from Afar," © 1987 by Boris Yekimov. Published in *Novy Mir*, No. 3, April 1987. Trans. © 1989 by Shirley Benson.

"Whoever Was Using This Bed," © 1986, 1988 by Raymond Carver. From *Where I'm Calling From: New and Selected Stories*, by Raymond Carver, Atlantic Monthly Press, 1988. First appeared in *The New Yorker*, 1986. Used by permission of the author.

". . . And in the Dark," © 1983 by Oleg Chukhontsev, *Slukhovoe okno* (*The Dormer Window*), Sovetsky Pisatel Publishers, Moscow. Trans. © 1988 by F. D. Reeve.

"The Blue Boat on the St. Anne," reprinted from *The Sewanee Review* (Winter 1989). © 1989 by F. D. Reeve. Used with permission of the author.

"An Atomic Fairy Tale," © by Yury Kuznetsov. From *Inside Me and Around Is Distance*, Sovremennik Publishers, Moscow. 1974.

"The Dream," from *Flesh and Blood*, © 1987 by C. K. Williams. Used with permission of Farrar, Straus, and Giroux, Inc.

"What Does Anyone Need a Crystal Toilet Bowl For?" © by Anatoly Shavkuta. Trans. © 1989 by Ann C. Bigelow.

"The King of Jazz," Reprinted from *Great Days* by Donald Barthelme,

A   NOTE   ON   THE   TYPE

*The text of this book was set in Sabon, a type face
designed by Jan Tschichold (1902–1974), the well-known
German typographer. Based loosely on the original designs
of Claude Garamond (c. 1480–1561), Sabon is unique in
that it was explicitly designed for hot-metal composition on
both the Monotype and Linotype machines as well as for
film setting. Designed in Frankfurt, Sabon was named for
the famous Lyon punchcutter Jaques Sabon, who is
thought to have brought some of Garamond's matrices
to Frankfurt.*

*Composed by
Crane Typesetting Service, Inc.
Barnstabie, Massachusetts*

*Printed and bound by Fairfield Graphics
Fairfield, Pennsylvania*

Designed by Val Astor